CELESTIAL VELOCITY

ROGUE JUSTICE | BOOK ONE

MARY ASHE

Celestial Velocity

This is a work of fiction. Names, places, and incidents are products of the author's very active imagination. Any resemblance to people and things outside of the Rogue Justice world is entirely coincidental.

Ebook ISBN: 979-8-9882484-0-8

Paperback ISBN: 979-8-9882484-1-5

Cover design byMiblart.com

First published in 2023 by Merry Spinster Studios, LLC

www.maryashe.com

For the phoenix who burns to ash before she rises

1

BEA

Space pirates could suck giant, hairy troll balls. Bea kicked her bound feet at the one who had her slung over his shoulder, hoping to nail him in the junk with her grav boots. She missed. Unfortunately. He grunted and readjusted his hold, pinning her legs against his chest as the cargo lift glided to a halt on the lower level of the *Intrepid*, where the pirate ship had attached. Once they got her and the crew aboard, it was game over.

She wouldn't make it easy on them, but with her hands bound behind her, she didn't have a whole lot of options. She wriggled and banged her head against her captor's back. It hurt more than she expected, her head meeting a solid mass of muscle. She gave a muffled yelp when he smacked her lightly on the ass.

"Settle down or I'm going to drop you, and you might get hurt," the pirate said, his voice a low growl. The doors whooshed open, and he stepped out, his crew and their prisoners following them.

Bea fumed. That was it. He was dead. This asshole thought he could spank her without her permission? Absolutely not. She did not consent. Normally, she was a very peaceable person, but by the holy tits of Saint Agnes, she'd make him pay for laying a hand on her.

After he and his motley crew had hacked their way on board the *Intrepid* and rounded up its small crew, her captor had introduced himself as Quin Sidron, captain of the *Laughing Dragon*. As soon as he said that, the *Intrepid's* crew stopped resisting.

But not Bea. She didn't know who he was and, honestly, couldn't give two flying fucks. They could fall into the nearest sun for all she cared. Lately, she'd had enough of running and hiding, enough of people pushing her around and trying to do her harm. So, instead of going peacefully like her crewmates, she fought them with all her might.

And look where it got her. She shifted her jaw, trying to dislodge the rectangle of tape Quin had slapped over her mouth after she'd told him and his crew where to go, doing her best to verbally rip the skin off their faces and feed it to them. Now, here she was, gagged, bound, and slung over this cretin's shoulder like a sack of potatoes. The indignity of it. If her sister heard about this, Bea would never live it down. She banged her head against the pirate captain's back in frustration.

"Stop it," he growled again, adjusting his grip across her thighs, his arm a steel band. "You're making it very difficult to rescue you. I've already told you we're not here to harm you or your crewmates. But you are coming with us, Beatrix Farsirus."

She frowned, unsure she'd heard him correctly over the cadence of grav boots as they tromped down the corridor. Rescue? A likely story. And how did he know her real name? She'd been on the run under a fake identity for close to a year. Were they here to haul her back to jail? Last time she'd been behind bars, she'd wound up with a shank in her side, nearly killed. She couldn't let them take her back. She had things to do like clear her name of the false charges of murder and arson laid against her.

While it was nice to hope they weren't here for the usual maiming and killing, she trusted nothing they said. Pirates were going to pirate, after all. Trust them at your peril. Despite Captain Sidron's odd claim of rescue, most likely they were here for the cargo the *Intrepid* was hauling. But then why didn't they just take it and leave? That's what usually happened. It was the quickest and most economical way for pirates to make a buck. Taking captives or hostages could bring in additional credits, but it was extremely risky for a variety of reasons, including running afoul of the Starguard, the overzealous guardians of the space between inhabited worlds.

However, these pirates had gathered up the entire crew. Surely, they weren't going to space everyone and take the ship? The pirate claimed no harm, but a hot flash of worry coursed down her spine anyway. She shifted, her captor's broad shoulder digging uncomfortably into her stomach.

They made slow progress along the corridor, the *Intrepid's* crew dragging their feet. From her upside down position, she saw they were headed towards the t-junction that would lead them either to the hold or to the escape pods. Her heart pounded harder. She had to get free before they took her off the ship. Her sister, Dai, taught her to do everything in her power to get away before her captor took her to a secondary location. Bea's busy brain worked through and discarded a variety of escape plans, each more daring and ridiculous than the last.

At the same time, her brain was furiously trying to parse the captain's claim of rescue. It was a weird thing for him to say, unless he was just trying to calm her down so she'd be a more docile captive. But he knew her real name. How? Only her sister knew where she was. She'd joined the *Intrepid* crew under the false identity her sister had set her up with after breaking her out of jail. With only a verbal reference from a Colony 86-b mechanic, Captain Bessa had hired her on to replace his engineer. To him, she was Mala, a temporary member of his crew, working in exchange for passage to the planet Badin. Once there, she'd deliver the data dot she carried in exchange for information she hoped would help her clear her name.

So who or what was he supposedly rescuing her from? Of course, she couldn't ask him to explain because of the damned gag.

At least she'd had time to send a coded message to her sister before the pirates had pried her out of her tiny cabin. Now retired from whatever shady shit she'd done as an agent of the Melorian government, Dai would find a way to help her. Somehow. If worse came to worst, she'd make sure these pirates paid dearly for laying a finger on Bea. And her sister would take care of and protect Bea's daughter, Essalin.

Dai would be proud of her little sister, though. Bea hadn't gone easily, putting up the best, loudest fight possible, letting out all the pain, anger, and frustration she'd kept bottled up since she'd been forced into running for her life. Though, in retrospect, trying to take on an invading group of strong, well-trained men probably hadn't been the smartest move, considering the end result of that resistance.

She kicked at the pirate captain again, wishing she had a better angle so she could nail him in the balls. So much more satisfying than a puny kick to his stomach. He cursed and gave her a little bounce against his painfully broad shoulder, knocking the breath out of her. *Dear gods, please don't let me throw up, choke, and die upside down like this*, she thought.

He dropped his voice so low she barely heard it. "Stop squirming, you nitwit. I swear on my mother's life, we're trying to help you here. I promise I'll explain everything once you're safely aboard my ship. So trust me and settle down."

There it was again: the claim that he was here to help her. But with nothing to back up that claim, how could she possibly believe him when all evidence pointed to the contrary? Was this some new kind of gaslighting where the dashing pirate captain made out like he was the good guy? Well, she certainly wasn't stupid enough to fall for his brand of bullshit. She might not be half as smart as her daughter or nearly as talented with a knife as her sister, but she knew when someone was screwing with her.

Closing her eyes and taking slow, deep breaths to calm her

nerves, she tuned out the captain, the clunk of boots along the passageway, and the whining complaints of Captain Bessa. It would be okay. She needed to stay calm, focused, and wait for her opportunity. She traced a finger over the small, hard bump near the base of her thumb, a flap of nu-skin disguising the data dot she was bringing to an information broker named Ghost in Badin. In exchange, Ghost promised her information about what happened the night her workshop burned to the ground, killing her ex-lover, Arden deVan, and destroying her notes as well as the prototypes of her new propulsion system. She hoped whatever intel Ghost had would give her some insight into what happened and why Arden was in her workshop that night without her. When the police charged her with arson and Arden's murder, she was stunned; when someone tried to kill her in jail, she ran.

If this Ghost had the information they'd promised, she might be able to clear her name and return to her life. But only if she could get to Badin before Ghost's deadline. She grimaced, the tape pulling at the corners of her mouth. All these worries were making her head hurt. Or maybe all the blood rushing to her head was making her delirious. On the plus side, at least she had a nice view of the pirate captain's perfectly formed ass encased in soft black leather pants to distract her.

Back on Colony 86-b, Bea had messaged Dai to tell her about Ghost's offer. Her sister sent back, *I don't think you should go. Too dangerous. You could be walking into a trap. But knowing you, you've already evaluated all the angles and possibilities and decided to chance it anyway. Please be careful and be prepared. If and when it goes sideways, let me know where to point my weapon.*

Of course Dai would think it was a trap, given that her job for decades was doing sneaky spy shit for the Melorian government's clandestine branch, aka The Unit. Still, she could always count on her big sister to have her back, one of the very few people in the galaxy who did.

But these damned pirates were putting a giant crimp in her plans. Or were they there to prevent her from finding out the truth of what happened to Arden and her prototypes? How had they found out where she was? Had they tracked her to the colony and then onto the *Intrepid*? How? She'd been so careful... but obviously not careful enough. Shit. She had to escape and get to Badin. Though futile, she bucked against the man holding her captive again. He grunted and tightened his grip on her thighs.

"Told you we should have brought the hover cage, Captain," a pirate called from his position behind the small group of *Intrepid* crew members.

Bea raised her head and glared in his general direction, her vision partially obscured by the black curls that had come loose from their braid. Instead of finding the joker, she made eye contact with a massive tree of a man with pale, freckled skin, a heavy beard, and a shock of red hair walking a step behind the captain. Looking somewhat embarrassed by his crewmate, he gave her a half-smile and shrugged, as if apologizing for the whole mess.

"Navi, you numbskull. We decided no cages after the last time, remember?" She heard a thunk but couldn't see anyone beyond the ginger mountain man.

"Oh, yeah," Navi said, laughter in his voice. "Took me forever to clean up the mess, too. You know, if we do ever decide to go back to cages, I'm not getting stuck with that job again. Rafiel can do it."

"In your dreams, pretty boy," a deep voice rumbled in response. "You're the noob. The scut work is on you."

"Shut it, all of you. No cages. No need to threaten them. They're behaving," the red-headed pirate said, a growl punctuating his words.

"Sure, Ivan. Except the one Cap's got slung over his shoulder." Navi snickered.

When she got out of this predicament, she was going to kick Navi's ass. No, she'd kick all of their asses. Not that she was good at much beyond basic self defense, but she'd find a way to make their lives miserable. They didn't know what they were in for. She strained against her bonds, but the sturdy fabric flexicuffs had no give to them. How long was this damned corridor anyway? She needed to be on her feet and unbound to fight or flee or to even just let the blood go back where it was supposed to be.

Quin chuckled, the deep vibration of it rumbling up through her body. "Hey, if this one had acted like a lady instead of a wild hellion, she wouldn't have to be tied up, and I wouldn't have to carry her. But here we are."

A shudder jolted the ship, making everyone stumble. The ship's lighting switched to a dull red as the emergency system blared forth an earsplitting klaxon of warning.

The unexpected motion unbalanced Quin, who stumbled to the side but twisted Bea away from the wall, taking the brunt of the impact with a pained grunt. Bea winced at the sound his head made when it connected with the hard plasticine of the ship's inner wall. Widening his stance against a second jolt, he set Bea on her feet, leaning her against the wall like a cord of wood. "Behave," he warned, rubbing his head where he'd smacked it.

She rolled her eyes. She was bound, hand and foot. Where did he think she was going to go? To be fair, she would hop away if she had even a slim chance in the three hells of escaping. As that was an impossibility at the moment, she took the time upright to appreciate her blood returning to its regular flow pattern. She fiddled with the smooth band of the ring her daughter had given her for her birthday last year and considered her options.

To the left, the ship's escape pods were barely ten feet away. If they took the ladder in front of them down the lowest level, they'd wind up in her domain, the guts of the ship. Going right would take them to the cargo hold, back to where the pirates breached the *Intrepid*. At least they were smart pirates. If she were ever to turn to a life of crime amongst the stars, that's how she would have done it, too. Attaching to the hold was the least damaging way of getting on board just about any ship without an invitation. It was also usually the best way to directly access the ship's systems, through a difficult-to-reach outer control panel. Every other way in — vents, emergency air locks — required a hard breach, ripping into the ship itself and endangering those inside. But, if you had no regard for human life, that was the fastest way aboard. Just sucker on, set a seal, and breach. Easy, if you didn't mind a body count.

When the rear guard herded the crew left, a pirate with close-cropped dark brown hair and twisting, colorful tattoos covering his brown arms took position to the right.

"Cormac," Quin said, pressing a nearly invisible circle flush to his skin behind his ear. He shook his head. "Damn thing isn't working again. Piece of crap comm."

"I've got him." Stepping up next to Quin, Ivan double tapped his thumb and middle finger together and held out his hand. The blue holo of a man flickered to life above his palm.

"Cormac. Report," Quin said, eyebrows drawn together in a frown as his eyes shifted from holo Cormac to scan the surrounding area and back again. "And can you get that fucking alarm turned off? It's giving me a headache."

"Gimmie a sec," Cormac said, his voice crackling over the connection.

Bea noted the pirates' constant vigilance and the redundancy systems for when things went FUBAR. It was something she'd also observed with Dai, her team, and in others who'd served in some branch of service. Interesting. Something to remember when she told Dai about them. Quin and his team moved as a unit, like they were trained and had worked together for a while. There was a quiet competence to their actions. Even the hijacking of the ship had been smooth, with minimal violence and zero casualties. Planned and precise. She silently cursed. That would definitely make escaping more challenging.

Now that she was right-side up and had a moment, Bea contemplated her captor. If he weren't kidnapping her, she might be inclined to admit how hot he was. She absolutely would have flirted with him at a bar. But since he was pirate scum, she would do her level best to ignore those arms corded with muscle, the chocolatey brown hair pulled back in a low tail, the squared-off jaw, the skin tanned like he'd been basking in the sun, those thick thighs encased in black leather... *dammit, Bea. Do not picture him naked*, she scolded herself. She felt a pulse of lust flow through her body and cursed again. Great time for her libido to raise its head after an extended downtime.

The klaxon cut off. In the quiet, Bea heard loud banging and strange hisses echoing down the corridor. Sounds like that meant trouble on board a ship.

"Another ship has latched onto the *Intrepid*, captain, and they're coming in through the hull." A pause and then Cormac cursed. "It's the *Dog's Day*, those gods-damned pirates."

Bea snorted, and Quin flicked a glance her way, his dark eyes narrowing. She shrugged. Pirates in glass houses shouldn't throw stones. But the last thing she needed right now was more damn pirates. In fact, it would be great if they turned on each other, leaving the *Intrepid* crew alone so she could do what she came out here to do: get to Badin, pick up the promised intel, get the false charges dropped, and get back to work. A simple, straightforward plan, if she did say so herself. If only she could execute it by Ghost's deadline.

"Fuck." The intensity of Quin's voice underscored the seriousness of their situation. "Looks like we weren't as ahead of the game as I'd hoped."

"Cap, they're suckered onto the *Intrepid*'s side like a leech and, by my calculations, it won't take them long to cut through the hull. Also, it doesn't look like they're taking any precautions to protect anyone inside," Cormac said, his blue image flickering over Ivan's hand as the ship shuddered again.

At that bit of news, the *Intrepid*'s small crew muttered and shifted their feet. "Well, do something about it, pirate," Captain Bessa demanded. He was a short, pasty white man with a perpetually pinched expression whose default was complaint mode. After an initial burst of pleasantness when he'd offered her a job and a way off Colony 86-b, Bessa had reverted to his true self once they'd lifted off from the colony, and she couldn't change her mind. Bea had done her level best to avoid interaction with the disagreeable man unless absolutely necessary. "Doesn't your ship have weapons? Shoot them or something."

Victor, the *Intrepid*'s pilot, rolled his eyes. When he saw Bea looking his way, he gave her a wink. It made her feel a little better, like maybe they'd all get out of this situation with minimal damage. If they did, she'd buy the first round at the closest pub.

The pirates ignored Bessa, which made his face turn red. He didn't like being ignored, but there was nothing he could do about it.

"What about airlocks? We lock down the hallways, and buy us some time," Ivan said, his entire body tense as he braced for action.

"Would work if they weren't cutting their way in so close to your current location," Cormac replied. He exchanged his image for a diagram of the ship. The big red dot of the other ship was too close to the little green dots representing those on board the *Intrepid*. "Once they're through, that entire area will depressurize. You're screwed if you're still there."

Quin eyed his crew and that of the *Intrepid*. "We need to move. Get those people into escape pods before the hull's cracked, and life support destabilizes. We do not want the *Dog's Day* crew to get their hands on any of these people, no matter who they are or what they've done. There are very few who deserve to wind up in the hands of Amaryllis and her pirates."

Bea took a hopeful hop towards the *Intrepid*'s crew and the escape pods. She didn't want to be separated from them. They were known. Quin and his crew were unknown. Those on the *Intrepid* had helped her out, offering her a lift and a job when she'd needed to get off Colony 86-b quickly. Bessa'd told her the *Intrepid* rarely took on new crew members, but their engineer had disappeared, and they needed a new one before they could depart. Bea fit the bill and, according to Bessa, he was generous enough to make allowances for her. No one wanted to travel into the black of space without someone to fix their ship if something went catastrophically wrong, after all. On the other hand, Quin was a pirate, one who'd done nothing but manhandle and bark orders at her all while claiming he was rescuing her, which she didn't trust or believe, not for a hot minute. Bessa and his crew were definitely the preferable choice.

"Oh, no. Not you," Quin said, stepping in her path and turning her to face him. "You're coming with us." When he pulled a blade from his boot, she reared back, bumping into the wall behind her. "Calm down, Daisy. I've already told you we're not here to hurt you," he said, his voice gentle as he bent to slice through the zip-tie around her ankles. He left her hands bound as he took her arm again, leading her in the opposite direction of the *Intrepid*'s crew, towards the hold and his ship.

She struggled against his grip, still determined to follow the rest of her people. Victor and several other crew members tried to come for her, lunging towards Quin and Bea, but were stopped by the big blasters and burly pirates who shoved them into the escape pods lining the wall of the ship and sealed the doors behind them. Before the crew members even attempted to get out, Ivan hit release on the pods, sending them hurtling away from the ship and towards the surface of Cinzia, the closest planet. Orbiting close to the system's star, the scraggly planet was mostly desert and rock. Not an ideal place to wind up, but better than being stuck with these pirates.

As the last pod detached and fell away from the *Intrepid*, Bea made a small sound of distress behind her gag. She gave one more half-hearted attempt to tug her arm free as Quin hauled her down the hall to the hold, though she knew it was a losing proposition. Still, she just couldn't give in. Her nature wouldn't allow it.

Quin ignored her struggles. It was as if he were made of the heaviest element in the galaxy for all the good her resistance was doing. Finally, he ground to a halt, a muscle jumping in his jaw. Scrubbing a free hand over his eyes, he said, "Look, my job is to rescue you and you alone and get you to safety. This," he gestured around him, "is not safe."

Bea argued with him through her gag, trying to tell him in muffled mumbles that this was all a mistake, that she had places she absolutely had to be and couldn't he just let her go.

"Look," he said, taking her arm again to keep them moving quickly despite her continued resistance, "You're the reason we're here. Your shipmates will be safe — since they're currently suckered onto this ship, *Dog's Day* doesn't have any way to grab the pods. They won't shoot them because their captain doesn't work that way, and those pods headed to an inhabited planet. They'll be fine, and you'll be safe with us. Trust me."

Bea snorted. As if. Trust had to be earned. If anything, Pirate Captain Quin had a negative balance in her books. She'd trust him when pigs grew wings and flew.

The rest of his crew caught up to them. "Even if their hard breach doesn't depressurize the corridor we're currently standing in, there aren't enough of us to hold them off if they come in with a full assault," Navi said, all joking wiped from his face as he ran a hand through his close-cropped red hair. "Not if we want to avoid large amounts of bloodshed."

Quin gave a sharp nod. "I'm aware. We just need to get on board the *Dragon*, and we're golden. They won't be able to disengage from the *Intrepid* quickly enough to form a response, so once we're aboard, Amaryllis will have lost any hope of picking up this bounty."

"Wait. Bounty?" Bea tried to ask as she struggled against his grip, mostly on principle now. She needed to know more about what was going on. It was all moving too fast for her.

"Cap, we've gotta move," Ivan said, his eyes on the corridor behind them. A red-hot glow appeared on a far wall in a messy oval shape. "We've got less than a minute before they breach."

Bea's adrenaline spiked, and digging her heels in, she dragged Quin to a stop.

"Fuck." Quin glared at her. "We need to go. I'm sorry for the rough treatment, but we have no time for your meltdown." In one smooth motion, he bent and tossed her back over his shoulder and took off.

She closed her eyes as she bounced along and again another prayer to the Mother that she wouldn't puke. That wouldn't be fun at all.

The hold's large double doors swished opened. "Rafe, get those sealed behind us," Quin said, as he hustled them across the cavernous hold, skirting around stacks of large boxes strapped to the floor.

"On it," came the quick reply.

Bea worked furiously at removing the gag from her mouth, pushing with her tongue at the sticky side and rubbing her face against her upper arm. To keep her mind off her discomfort, she considered what her sister would do in this predicament. Well, first, Dai would never have allowed herself to get trussed up like a moonsday hen and thrown over the broad and muscled shoulders of a freaking space pirate. Dai would already have come up with a workable plan to save the *Intrepid* and its crew before knocking both pirate ships out of the sky.

But she wasn't Dai. Give her a busted engine to fix, and she'd be all over it. Or teenage hormones to navigate, though thank the gods that her daughter was past that particular stage of life and off at university. That, too, she could handle. But physically fighting back, going toe-to-toe with someone and winning? It had never been her thing. That didn't mean she wouldn't fight like the three hells were threatening to devour her, right up to the end.

Bea swallowed the bile that threatened to choke her. Dammit. When she finally got herself out of this mess, she was going to have Dai teach her everything she knew about self defense and combat. Honestly, she should have paid better attention during those lessons all those years ago. Anger at her predicament surged through her entire body, and she rubbed her face against Quin's muscled back, using the friction of his shirt to pull the sticky gag away, freeing her mouth.

Not having the courtesy to sound the least bit out of breath as he sprinted across the wide space, he chuckled. "Don't worry. Like I said, you're safe with us. Even if you weren't the one we were sent here to get, I wouldn't leave you for Amaryllis's crew. They're not nice people. Not like us." He stopped next to the airlock.

This asshole. He must have thought she was burying her face in his back because she was scared. Nope. She bucked against him, throwing her torso farther down his back until she was in the perfect position. Then she bit him hard, directly on his tight, leather-covered ass.

With a yelp, he jumped, his hips bowing forward as he tried to escape her teeth. "Shit. She bit me!" He slid her off his shoulder and shoved her at Navi.

From his position at the control panel, Ivan snorted. "That's what you get for threatening her."

She glared at Quin and would have cursed him out, but her throat and mouth were too dry to form words.

"Put that gag back on before she bites me again and make sure it stays on this time. That fucking hurt." Quin rubbed his ass and frowned at her. Behind him, the airlock chirped and hissed its way through the first decompression cycle.

"Good," Bea croaked, giving him a bright, feral smile and tossing her head.

"Poor baby. You want someone to rub it for you?" Navi said, a wide grin spreading across his face. "Though, to be clear, I'm not volunteering for that duty."

"Sorry. Captain's orders," Ivan said to her, gently reattaching the gag, keeping it loose so she'd be able to remove it with little effort. "Do we really need to gag her?"

"Can't have her biting the captain again, as much as he deserves it," Navi said with another irritating cackle. "Look, lady, I fully support your right to bite whomever's ass you want. I'll even volunteer mine. But let's wait until we're out of danger, okay?"

Shooting a glare at Navi, she mentally added him to her list of People Who Needed Their Asses Bitten. But as she was bound and in the grasp of another overly muscled pirate, there wasn't much she could do about it. Yet. But the wheels turned in her head. It wasn't over. She couldn't let it be. Ever since the workshop fire and Arden's death, her life had spun out of her control, and when she finally had a chance to take back some of that control, to actually do something to clear her name? Pirates. She wasn't about to let the opportunity slip through her fingers because of some pirate who claimed he was saving her.

Quin let out a heavy sigh. "Leave her alone, Navi. She's had a rough go of it and, honestly, I don't blame her for her actions. My fault for presenting such a tempting target and putting her in a position to take advantage of that," he said, still rubbing his backside.

She felt a surge of pride at his wince. She'd really sunk her teeth into him. Hopefully, he'd have a big bruise to remember her by after she escaped.

Rafiel jogged over to join them. "Hold doors are sealed, but I don't know how long it'll last. I didn't have the materials for more than a shit patch job."

Quin gave a brisk nod. "Just needed to slow them down." The airlock hissed open. "Looks like they're going to be too late."

Navi handed her back into Quin's iron grip as they left the *Intrepid*. Since Bea didn't want to die or be captured by another set of pirates, she resigned herself to being their captive. Temporarily. But as soon as they let their guard down, they'd better watch out.

2

QUIN

Quin let out a quiet sigh of relief when Bea allowed him to guide her through the airlock and across the short bridge connecting the two ships, rather than fighting against him. He understood where she was coming from — if he were in her position, he'd fight with every ounce of strength he had, too — but the Knight had called in a favor for them to do this job. That favor alone was well worth a bite on the ass. He resisted the urge to rub where the hellion's teeth had sunk in.

Not trusting Bea's sudden acceptance of her captivity, he made certain his team was between her and the temporary airlock, cutting off any last-ditch effort at escape. A quiet beeping and then a whir signaled the *Laughing Dragon*'s airlock finishing its decompression cycle.

And then they were on board his ship, Rafiel sealing the airlock behind them.

Loosening his grip on Bea's arm, Quin snapped out orders. "Ivan, get up to the bridge and help Cormac. Rafiel, get us uncoupled from that ship. We need to be on our way before they realize they missed us. Navi, you're with me. Cormac, report."

"You cut it pretty close there, Cap. The *Dog's Day* crew is now on board the *Intrepid*. I give them maybe ten minutes to do a full sweep before they realize their quarry's gotten away," Cormac said over the ship's comms, his voice echoing through the corridors.

Quin touched the patch behind his ear. Nothing. His internal team comms were still silent. Amaryllis must have a new signal jammer to play with. That or the cheap shit Cormac had been so excited to get a deal on had crapped out on him. After this job, they'd be out from under the Knight's thumb and would have the time and funds to upgrade the rest of their equipment. Not that he wasn't grateful to his cousin for his support and aid in their time of need but, after years of following orders in the Starguard, Quin and his crew craved their autonomy and freedom of choice.

"I sure hope this is worth all this trouble." Ivan's voice was a low grumble.

Ivan, ever the worrywart. "You know how I hate owing people favors, especially family," Quin said. But Ivan wasn't wrong. This was supposed to be a simple grab-and-go but, with *Dog's Day* on the scene, it amplified the stakes. He couldn't risk this rescue going wrong. He'd have to appeal to Amaryllis's better nature to get them off his back. Not that she had one. "I'm taking her to holding." Quin wrapped his fingers around Bea's upper arm and got them moving while his crew split off to do their thing. Navi fell in behind her.

As they made their way through the ship, Quin tried to ignore the visual daggers Bea was stabbing him with until he finally sighed. "I realize you don't believe me, but we weren't going to hurt you back there on the *Intrepid*. Just playing the role of big, bad space pirates so that Captain Bessa wouldn't get suspicious when we snatched you from him." He shot her a look. "There's a bounty on your head, and Bessa took the contract. Someone wants you in their hands, and they're willing to pay handsomely for it."

Navi piped up. "They'd prefer alive, if that makes you feel any better."

Bea's eyes widened and her nostrils flared as she sucked in a deep breath.

She had no idea the danger she'd been in and considering how much she struggled, still didn't believe him despite his reassurances that they were there to help. He sighed again. His own damn fault. He shouldn't have tied her up. He shouldn't have thrown her over his shoulder. And he most definitely shouldn't have smacked her ass. But it was such a nice ass, round and soft. He wouldn't mind doing it again, under different circumstances and with her full consent, of course. Not that she was going to let him within a hundred meters of her once this job was over. Alas. "Look, without us, you'd be on your way to whoever set that bounty, blissfully unaware of the danger you were in. Hells, the *Dog's Day* crew might have gotten to you before we did, and then you'd be in the hands of real pirates. If you truly understood the danger, you'd be thanking us for saving you. In fact, we're getting a payment worth more than a full hold of cargo for helping you out."

She rolled her eyes and gave a half-hearted tug at his grip on her arm.

"Chance like that comes along once in a blue moon." Navi stepped forward to unlock the holding area. The door swished open.

He grunted in agreement. "The Knight is stingy when it comes to cashing in the favors people owe him. Prefers to hoard them, keeping people under his thumb."

She shrugged, unimpressed.

To be honest, he didn't really understand why the Knight had gotten involved in the first place. The thin file the Knight had on her showed a relatively normal life. Then a bump: just over a year ago, her ex-lover, Arden deVan, died in a fire that also destroyed her workshop. Local constabulary ruled the fire to be arson and deVan's death to be murder. With shaky evidence and little motive, they charged Bea with both and promptly threw her in prison. Within two days of being behind bars, she'd been shanked by a fellow detainee, almost killed while eating breakfast. Somehow, she'd escaped from the medi-bay and had been on the run ever since.

Quin had no idea why the Knight wanted her protected or even how his cousin had tracked her down. The man had his ways. But, as long as this wiped the slate clean for him and his crew, he wasn't going to ask too many questions.

No matter who she was or what she'd done, their job was to grab her from Bessa and protect her, ideally bringing her back to the Knight. That was it. A supposedly straightforward job.

He should have known better. The Knight wouldn't cash in the last favor Quin's team owed on a simple snatch-and-grab. Sneaky bastard, his cousin. Of course there was more to this entire story, information the Knight possessed and hadn't included in the file. The man did love to hoard both favors and information.

They came to a halt before the door of a holding cell, and she struggled again. "Relax," Quin said. Did she think he was going to chain her up and torture her or something?

Navi sighed as he shifted to unfasten the flexicuffs holding her arms behind her back. "You really going to do this, Quin? Despite what she thinks, she's not our prisoner."

"It's for her own good," Quin said, stepping close to her to remove the gag. But he let his guard down, and she kneed him right in the balls.

Stars exploded in front of his eyes as Quin dropped to the floor with a loud groan. Motherfucker, that hurt. It had been a long time since he'd experienced this particular level of pain. He concentrated on taking deep breaths and not puking as he used the walls of his ship to get back on his feet.

She growled at him, straining against the careful bear hug Navi had her in to prevent any further damage.

"Damn, woman. I realize you don't believe it, but we are actually trying to help you here," Navi said as they watched Quin try to catch his breath from her blow to his pride.

Even though it cost him, his vision graying slightly around the edges as he did it, he straightened to his full height so he could look down at her. Unclenching his jaw, he ground out, "You don't want me to untie you? Fine. Do it yourself." He ran a finger over the biometric lock and the door to a stark white cell slid open. "In you go." He took her from Navi, hauled her across the cell's threshold, and pushed her into the room.

She spun to confront him, her honey-brown eyes wide and wild, the tail of her long braid flaring out over her shoulder as the door slid closed, locking her inside.

QUIN'S BALLS ACHED. His ass, too. He eased around the command deck of the ship and wished he could say fuck it, go to his quarters, and soak in a tub of ice. Sadly, as baths were untenable on most ships except for those ridiculous R-Class super yachts no respectable pirate, er... privateer would be caught dead flying unless he'd stolen it and taken it on a joy ride before stripping it for parts, he popped a pain reliever. He was getting too old for this shit. Maybe it was time to think about slowing down, rather than running all over the galaxy and getting beat up or beating others up. Once they delivered the hellion into the Knight's hands, maybe he'd find a place on the lake near where he grew up, take a year or so off and learn how to fish or crochet or some calm shit like that. Or not. Either way, he needed a break.

Chasing the fast-acting painkiller with a long drink of water, Quin tossed the empty pouch into the recycler. "Cormac, let's see what *Dog's Day* is up to. Put outside visuals on the front screen."

Cormac, who'd been keeping a close eye on their competition, flicked the visuals from his screen to the full-sized panoramic viewer that took up the top half of the deck's forward wall. "No move to disengage, but I figure it won't be too much longer.

Intrepid isn't that big of a ship. And no attempt at communication yet."

"Probably absconding with the cargo we had to leave behind." Disappointment at the loss of income colored Navi's words. He wasn't wrong. That loss stung financially.

Quin sank into his chair, trying not to wince. While the *Laughing Dragon* had some pretty sweet upgrades, unfortunately, it did not include extra padding for the seats. Next time they docked at a port, he'd be sure to install more comfortable chairs.

"Got you good, did she?" Ivan's tone lacked any sympathy for Quin's suffering as he ran the *Dragon* through a weapons check.

"He deserved it." Navi settled into his seat at the station behind his brother. "Shouldn't have manhandled her like that. And then he didn't even let me take off her flexicuffs."

Ivan tutted.

Quin let out a heavy sigh and readjusted his aching balls, the chair creaking under his weight. Those pain relievers needed to work faster, dammit. He rotated his chair so he could see his crew on the command deck. "I know. You're right. But she wasn't budging, and the options were limited."

Pausing in his work, Ivan crossed his arms and stared at Quin. Somehow, his perpetual frown was even frownier than usual. Quin could feel the disapproval rolling off his second in command.

He rolled his eyes. "Fine. Besides that, I wasn't expecting her to be such a handful, and my temper got the better of me." To be honest, he'd expected no resistance from the lady. Digitally, she read as more brains than brawn, a middle-aged mom and engineer rather than someone who fought like a she-wolf when cornered and who had the aim of an expert marksperson when it came to a man's delicate bits. Who knew?

"Looks like I missed all the fun," Cormac said, his fingers flying over the touchscreens facing him. As their eyes and ears, Cormac stayed on board during missions so, according to him, he always 'missed all the fun'. Quin shook his head. The man had eyes and ears on the team every mission and never missed a thing. The only thing he missed out on was the danger.

"Doubtful she'll ever pay you back enough for smacking her ass. Like, ever." Navi snickered, but kept his eyes focused on plotting the hops they needed to take to travel safely home.

Ivan grunted in agreement. "Bad enough you slung her over your shoulder like a sack of potatoes, but then you had to compound it with that spank. What happened to consent and bodily autonomy, Cap? You're going to need to apologize for your actions."

"If I was her, I'd make him beg," Cormac added.

They weren't going to let this go, were they? Quin allowed himself a moment to grind his teeth before relenting. "Fine, yes. I've already said I handled the situation poorly, and I'll apologize to her at some point. Just not until my balls stop aching, okay?" He leaned back in his chair, his legs sprawled out, and slung an arm over his eyes. "Rescuing someone isn't usually this hard."

"Guess it is when the person you're rescuing doesn't know she's in danger." Ivan smoothed his thick red beard. "The whole thing would have been easier if we could have quietly taken out the captain, then spoken to the woman like I suggested, rather than acting like pirates and taking over the entire ship. I don't like pretending to be something I'm not."

"Privateer, pirate. You're talking semantics here, Ivan." Cormac didn't take his eyes off the screens. A clank sounded and the *Laughing Dragon* gave a small jolt. "We're fully separated from the *Intrepid*, Cap."

"Also, we don't kill people willy-nilly anymore, remember? We agreed on that last year after...you know." Navi gestured, rolling a hand in the air.

"Whatever." Ivan returned to his weapons panel. "Some people just need killing."

Quin grunted. The man wasn't wrong. "My plan was the least bloody way to get the job done. Because there's a bounty on Beatrix Farsiris's head, by convincing the *Intrepid*'s crew that fearsome space pirates now have the woman in their grasp, we've effectively removed her from the playing field. That's the idea anyway. Our job — one Rhain actually called in this last favor for, remember — was very specific: get the lady off the *Intrepid* and keep her safe until we get to Gyan Station, where we get to hand her off to the Knight and his Shields. How we did it was up to us."

But she wasn't safe yet. The *Dog's Day* crew joining the hunt had jacked up a perfectly good plan. As much as he didn't want them on their tail, he also didn't want them taking out the escape pods for the fun of it. Dammit. Being a moral pirate, er, privateer was hard.

"Cormac, the *Intrepid*'s pods okay?" The last thing he wanted was innocent blood on his hands because of a bad call. But he hadn't wanted them on his ship or incapacitated and vulnerable to attack on theirs, so the escape pods were the best option. They were better off on Cinzia than in Amaryllis's grasp.

"Safe and secure and headed planetside."

"Good." He gave a sharp nod before spinning to face the forward screens. "Navi, get us to a safe distance away from the *Intrepid* and be ready to make a quick escape. Let's deal with the *Dog's Day* and make sure they aren't going to do anything stupid."

They'd had several run-ins with the *Dog's Day* crew recently, though nothing overtly violent. Usually, one of them backed off before weapons were discharged or too much blood was spilled. Well, except that one time in Laran, when they'd gotten into an all-out brawl in that little dive bar. If Ivan hadn't overreacted to their captain's teasing and taken the first shot, they wouldn't have had to use most of their score to keep everyone out of jail and the bar owner from laying charges.

"They're disengaging from the *Intrepid*, Cap." Cormac stood, his holo keyboard shifting with him to float at waist-height. He did some fast typing and swiping before tossing a colorful 3D image of the *Dog's Day* into the open space between their arc of stations. Everyone swiveled to look as Cormac enlarged the holo of the other ship. "Looks like they've added some new hardware since the last time we ran up against them." He pointed out the two new ports along the once-sleek sides of the other ship.

"Fuck." Ivan growled. "What kind of job did they pull to afford those beauties?"

"I see them." Rail guns. Those would poke some sizeable holes in the *Laughing Dragon*, and if those pirates turned them on the pods, there would be nothing left but tiny bits of scrap metal. "Ivan, prep tube one, but keep it cold and hold off getting a lock on the *Dog's Day*. We don't want to start anything unless they start shooting at us or the pods. If they do, we'll have to take them out."

"On it." Ivan swiveled back to his panel.

"Captain, you sure about that?" Navi asked. "If we fire on them, no matter the reason, that'll put us in the shit with the Cabal. Getting on their wrong side won't help us. Those mother-fuckers hold serious grudges."

"Yeah, and it's Lore's niece who captains the *Dog's Day*," Cormac said. "Also, I'm 99 percent sure the Shields recently signed a treaty with the Cabal. The Knight would not be pleased if we blew up *Dog's Day* and fucked that deal up. We might even wind up owing him more favors than what we started with."

Quin pushed out of his seat to pace, the edges of the holo blurring as he walked through it. At least the painkillers finally kicked in. One thing was going right. "That fucking cousin of mine. May the fiery gods swallow him whole. I can't keep track of Rhain and his constant political maneuvering. If he ever left his precious lair on Gyan Station, he might realize how hard he makes things sometimes."

His cousin was brilliant and loved his games of strategy like his sister, the laird and matriarch of their clan. Secrets and games made Quin's brain itch. Quin took after his father, who preferred to take things head on and damn the consequences. Secrets had a way of fucking things up.

Quin continued to curse his cousin as Cormac waved a hand

to dismiss the holo and slid back into his seat. Stopping in front of the screens, Quin rubbed his forehead. As much as he wanted to keep the ledger of favors he owed the Knight clear, he also wasn't about to let innocent people or even a weasel like Captain Bessa get killed because of some political maneuvering he had no interest in. He'd done his level best to leave his dark and blood-soaked days in his past, where they belonged. "Open a channel to the *Dog's Day*, Cormac."

"Really? Can't we blow them out of the sky and be done with it?" Ivan asked plaintively.

Quin pinched the bridge of his nose.

Moments later, a woman with skin the shade of hammered copper, lightning streaks of verdigris climbing her neck, and a pile of multicolored braids twisted into a crown on her head appeared on screen. "Quin. Fancy seeing you here. Guess you're after the same prize as we are." She looked past him, taking in everyone on deck. At the sight of one in particular, her dark gold eyes widened and her full, purple-stained lips parted in a carnivorous smile filled with promises. "Ivan." She purred his name. "So good to see you again."

Ivan turned the same color as his shock of red hair while also pretending not to drink in her image. The rest of the crew pretended to be busy at their stations, though Quin knew they were all storing their interaction away for fodder to use against Ivan.

"Amaryllis, stop tormenting the man." Quin honestly wished the two of them would just bang it out and be done with it. Every time they ran up against one another, Amaryllis teased and tormented while Ivan blushed, threatened, and harrumphed. When the two of them were in the same space, violence exploded and blood spilled, as per the Laran dive bar. Way too much repressed sexual tension between them. As entertaining as it was to see his first mate and weapons master lose his infamously cool head, their flirting was driving him insane.

She returned her bright gaze to him. "But he makes it so easy."

Ivan grunted and turned his attention to the small screen before him.

"He does. But he's not the reason we're calling," Quin said.

"Didn't think so." She folded her arms over her chest and cocked her head, waiting for him to spit it out.

Aware he could be making a mistake, he said, "Don't fire on the escape pods. They don't have what you're looking for."

Her smile grew, her sharp teeth gleaming white. "Oh, Quin. You're taking all the fun out of our hunt with that squishy little heart of yours. This is why I'll always be a better pirate than you." She paused, pursing her lips. "So, if we break off, what are you going to do to make it up to us?"

"Not blow you out of the sky, for one." Ivan pushed out of his seat and mirrored her folded arms. "Back off, Rilly."

"Oh, Ivan. Anything for you." She blew him a kiss, bending forward so Ivan could get a peek down her loose white shirt.

Cormac rolled his eyes while Navi snickered quietly at his brother's predicament.

Quin didn't think it was possible for Ivan to get any redder, but he went ahead and proved that theory wrong. He tried not to laugh at Ivan's obvious distress. Doing his best to ignore Amaryllis's display of her ample assets, he cleared his throat and said, "Look, once we're done with this job, I'd be happy to provide the two of you with a room on Badin so you can work through your issues, as long as you back off now."

She straightened and patted her hair, her eyes glinting with laughter. "Since you asked so nicely, fine. No blowing the pods out of the sky, no matter how much fun it would be to watch them explode." She raised a perfectly arched eyebrow. "But that means you have our prize onboard the *Laughing Dragon*. Why don't you turn her over, and we won't have to scrap."

"This bounty isn't worth it, Amaryllis."

"It's enough coin to keep us flying for at least another couple of months, Quin."

It was a surprisingly large bounty for someone like Bea. Quin tamped down his curiosity. He'd have time to work out the puzzle that was Beatrix Farsiris on their way home. For now, he needed to deal with the situation at hand. "But is it enough coin to put you in the path of the Knight and his Shields? I understand there is a new treaty between the Shields and your Cabal, right?"

"The Cabal isn't mine," she said absently, her brows drawn together as she absorbed the rest of what he shared. "You're working for the Knight on this one?"

He nodded. "The Knight called in a favor from us to grab her and keep her safe." For this job, Rhain had personally contacted Quin to take it on. Again, Quin wondered why this particular woman was so important to Rhain. Whatever the reason, he and his crew had accepted the job. Much like the mythical dragons from which his clan claimed to be descended, Rhain liked to hoard the favors owed him just as much as he loved to collect information of all kinds. It gave him power over those who owed him, so Quin knew that striking this last one from his crew's tab had to hurt his cousin. Yet another reason to do it. Tormenting family was always fun.

"Well, fuck. Hold on." She paused the transmission. When she came back on, she tipped her chin at him. "Fine. But don't expect us to be so generous next time we go up after the same prize. We're out of here. Bye, Ivan." She waggled her fingers at him. "Can't wait to see you on Badin."

Glowering, Ivan closed the link. "You shouldn't have told her all that. You gave her far too much information that she will turn around and sell to her aunt."

"Hey, just trying to be economical here. It was the fastest way to get her to back off, even if she winds up selling the info. Did you really want to get into a tussle with her?"

"I don't think that's the kind of tussle he wants to have with her," Navi said.

Ivan growled. "Navi, I swear by the three hells, I will kick your ass straight out of the airlock if you don't shut up."

"Gentlemen, how 'bout we finish this job first, huh?" Quin

scrubbed a hand over his jaw. "Cormac, confirm receipt of the package with our client. Navi, did you get those jumps locked in yet? I want to get this hellion off my ship as soon as possible." He should check on Bea but, as his balls still ached from his last encounter with her despite the painkillers, he really didn't want to yet. "Let me know when Amaryllis has left the area so we can jump away. I'll be in my quarters." They needed to stay close, in case Amaryllis changed her mind about using her new rail guns on escape pods.

"You're not freeing the woman? Or at least checking on her?" Ivan asked.

Quin felt a pang of guilt, but shook it off. He had nothing to feel guilty about. He was helping her, after all. She just hadn't accepted what he'd told her.

"What, you worried about her, Ivan?" Navi's eyes glinted with mischief. "What a soft heart and hard head my brother has."

"For the last time, don't make me come over there, Navi." Ivan shook a fist at him, then turned back to Quin. "I mean, what if she's hungry or has to...you know." His cheeks which had faded to their usual pale shade, flushed pink again.

"Take a piss, Ivan? Is that what you're trying to say? Fuck, even ladies pee, man. It's a natural bodily function. Anyway, there's a drain in there. She just needs to aim a little." Navi propped his feet up on the corner of his station. "Course plotted, Cap. Waiting on an all-clear from home base and your go-ahead."

"Acknowledged. And leave your brother alone, Navi. Our Ivan is a sensitive soul. He doesn't want to picture a flower as delicate as the one we have trussed up in our holding cell taking a piss." Quin grinned.

Ivan frowned harder, switching his glare from Navi to Quin. "Don't you start now, Cap. I'm worried about the lady."

Damn Ivan for being his conscience. "Look, Rafiel is in the cargo bay. I'll have him check on her and bring her some food. Will that ease your mind, Ivan?" He pushed out of his chair and headed to the door. "Comm me when home base responds. And be ready to leave on my word."

"Got it." Navi spun to face his screen.

Ivan glowered at him as Quin left the bridge. He swore he heard Ivan mutter "chicken" under his breath as the door swished closed behind him. Maybe he was being chicken, but his delicate bits were happier for it.

3

BEA

Bea heard the snick of a lock engaging and the clomp of footsteps as her captors walked away, leaving her alone in a prison cell. Okay, so kneeing the captain in the balls wasn't the smartest move, but it sure had been satisfying to see him writhing on the floor. She hoped she hadn't damaged him permanently. That would be a real shame. Women around the galaxy would weep.

Gods, what a predicament, she thought as she worked to free her left hand from the cuffs. At least Navi had loosened it a little before her temper got the better of her. Releasing her hands, she let out a hiss of pain, her muscles protesting being in one position for so long, and then ripped off the gag, dropping it to the floor and stomping on it.

Why, oh why, had she half-assed the self-defense lessons that Dai had tried to teach her? Oh, right. Because she'd been confident in her belief that nothing bad or dangerous would ever happen to her — her sister was the one who sought out trouble, not her. So sheltered and naïve. And so very wrong, Bea thought with a groan. At least some of her sister's lessons had stuck.

Like the one where she absolutely had to have a weapon or something sharp hidden on her person at all times. Dai's instructions on the matter were clear: always hide something small but useful, preferably in a place that wouldn't be found during a pat-down or body scan. Bea had several items of her own design hidden on her person, things that most people wouldn't look at twice. She just hadn't had the chance to use them before now.

Bending down, she pressed the second eyelet on her right boot. The hilt of a small bone knife, undetectable by scanners, popped out of the heel. She pulled it out and slid the blade under the soft, sturdy fabric of the right cuff, shivering as the cool of the blade brushed against her skin. With a quick flick of her wrist, it split open and fell to the floor. Smiling, she tucked the blade back into its hidden compartment.

Gods, but she was stiff. Even with the advances in medicine, getting older was no joke. Given that she was no longer in her 30s, her body was telling her exactly how unhappy it was at its recent treatment. "Blame that damned pirate," she muttered at her aching muscles as she rubbed a kink out of her neck and massaged her bruised torso. She worked her shoulders through a series of stretches and twisted against the wall to crack her back, moaning at the sweet relief as the stiffness eased slightly. What she wouldn't give for a nice massage or a pain powder right about now.

Standing in the middle of the small room, she took a moment to breathe and assess her circumstances. A bunk, firmly attached to the wall. No toilet, but there was a drain. She wrinkled her nose. Gross, but whatever. She'd make do. No worse than peeing outside. And a small metal spigot. She stumbled over, pressing her palm against the flat blue square above it. A thin stream of water flowed from its mouth, making a gentle splattering sound as it hit the edge of the floor drain and disappeared. Bea stuck her head under it and drank deeply. Finally, she sat on the bunk, bit her lip, inhaled a shaky breath, and allowed herself to relax enough to cry.

Wiping her eyes and nose on the hem of her shirt once the well-earned crying jag had run its course, she lay back on the hard mattress, absently twisting her ring around her finger. She was so out of her depth. She'd been out of her depth since Dai had broken her out of the prison medi-ward, handed her a false ident card, and told her to disappear for a while. What she wanted was to hug her daughter, fix a cup of tea, and tinker with her propulsion design, not fight pirates, run for her life, or meet with shady contacts in dark bars. How had she gotten here?

For a moment, she could still taste the ashes that swirled around the place where her workshop once stood, the smell of smoke and the suppressants they'd used to extinguish the fire permeating the air. A decade of work — her physical notes, the scaled-down prototypes of her interstellar propulsion system, the whiteboard covered with various configurations of the power structure of the system — gone. She'd still been in shock a week later when, upon finding a tooth in the ashes and identifying it as her ex-lover's, investigators appeared on her doorstep to charge her with arson and Arden deVan's murder. Despite a lack of physical evidence and a shaky motive, she'd gone quietly, protesting only enough that they allowed her to send a message to her sister before locking her up until the trial.

Getting shanked with a sharpened piece of plasticine while eating a disgusting breakfast of reconstituted eggs and almost dying in the jail's medi-ward finally snapped her out of her shock. She traced a finger over the jagged scar on her side. If the shank had gone in an inch lower, she would most likely be dead. At least that's what her sister told her after they made it past the last guard station. Someone had tried to kill her.

She shifted to her side, tucking her hands under her cheek as her brain chewed on the questions that plagued her since this whole nightmare began. What had Arden been doing at her workshop that night? Was he the one who set the fire? On purpose? And if not him, who? Did Arden have a partner in whatever scheme he'd been involved in? Was that partner the one who murdered him or someone else, or did something else happen? And why?

The investigators were right about one thing: the fire was arson. There was no other explanation. She was safety-conscious and had gone overboard with her security systems and built-in redundancies, yet not one of those systems functioned that night. Someone disabled them. Someone wanted her propulsion system destroyed. Someone wanted her removed from the playing field. Permanently.

Current interstellar propulsion systems relied heavily on a very specific formula of power pellets that included a rare mineral for their reactors. Besides deteriorating quickly, the pellets were also exorbitantly expensive, and one massive monopoly, Vanid Shipping, controlled their production and distribution. Her system used a new form of fusion that, if she could just figure out the last pieces of the puzzle, wouldn't require as much power to run and could use other, less expensive sources of power. Dai called her system a game-changing disrupter that would have far-reaching repercussions on space travel and the industry as a whole. Bea had laughed her off, telling her it was just a project she'd been experimenting with, one she still hadn't gotten to work. But Dai had been right and, until the night of the fire, Bea hadn't really understood the dangers involved in what she was doing, only the possible benefits.

A rattling at the door jolted her out of her deep thoughts as someone on the other side slid a covered tray through a slot at the bottom of the door. "Captain thought you might be hungry, ma'am," a deep voice said.

She rolled off her cot and ran to the door. "Let me out of here," she said, banging a fist against the clean, white surface.

There was a pause and a shuffle of feet. The man cleared his throat. "I'm sorry, but I can't do that. Captain's orders."

"Thought he said you were here to rescue me, not lock me up like a prisoner," she said, anger straining her voice.

"You'll have to take that up with the captain. But I'll pass along your request to be released."

She smacked the flat of her hand against the door as she heard him move away. Gods damned pirates. They were ruining every-thing. Ignoring the food tray, Bea counted steps as she paced, hoping to calm her brain, but she kept returning to the growing list of questions she didn't have satisfactory answers to. She was tired of obsessing about that night. She was tired of the instability and constant hum of fear she felt every day she was on the run. And there were only so many ways to distract herself in a stripped-down cell when her brain refused to shut up.

What she couldn't figure out was how Arden fit into any of it. The investigators believed she had motive to kill him because they had a very public argument about money three days prior to the fire. But, as mad as she'd been, she'd only kicked him to the curb, ending their relationship. Murder had never crossed her mind. Dismemberment or a painfully embarrassing injury, sure. But murder? Definitely not.

She thought she knew the man. After all, they'd been seeing each other for nearly a year. For the majority of their relationship, she'd enjoyed his company, though she didn't love him. He made her feel special, cherished even. He was fun to be around, always dragging her out to new restaurants and music fests. He'd passed the daughter crucible, earning Essy's thumbs up when she came home over a school holiday. When he'd asked what she was working on, Bea shared some basic details about her system and her hopes for it, but nothing specific. No one but her sister knew all the details. They'd floated comfortably along as a pair. Or so she thought.

Until she'd noticed credits disappearing from one of her accounts and traced it back to Arden. They'd had a massive argument and broken up. He'd packed up his things that night and left. She hadn't seen or talked to him since. And then his tooth turned up in the ashes of her workshop, and her comfortable little world imploded.

Had she missed the red flags? According to her sister, she didn't always have the best instincts, believing the best of people until they betrayed her. So, had Arden betrayed her or just in the wrong place at the wrong time? But why had he even been at her workshop? She shook her head, at a loss for answers.

In the months she'd been on the run, she'd hopped a dozen ships and worked odd jobs. The job before the *Intrepid*, she worked on the air filtration systems of the new habitat on Colony 86-b. While she didn't love looking over her shoulder for the slate gray uniforms of the Starguard or eyeing her fellow humans wondering if she could trust them, she enjoyed the challenge of working on a variety of machines and engines. She'd focused on her project for so long, it felt good to tinker again.

And then, two standard weeks ago, among the tri-weekly data drop to her personal account, was a message:

Beatrix Farsirus, aka Mala Jones, I have information about your workshop fire and Arden deVan. I'm willing to share that information if you'll do something for me. Meet my intermediary, Clyde, at The Red Door Pub in three standard days. He'll be wearing a purple hat. Come alone and make sure you aren't followed.

–Ghost

Through coded channels, she'd forwarded the message to her sister, not sure she'd get a response before the meet. Two standard days later, Dai responded:

Haven't heard of any information brokers named Ghost, but I've been out of the game a while. Will check around. In the meantime, why not see what they've got? Please be careful. Go armed. Let me know what happens.

She'd been curious and desperate enough to grasp at anything that might help her clear her name and get some answers, and buoyed by her sister's response, she decided to go. But she wasn't foolish—she'd learn what this Ghost wanted her to do for them before she made a final decision, no matter how tempting the promise of information was.

The Red Door was the shadiest of the three bars on the colony. Bea took Dai's instructions to heart and hid weapons all over herself. But no one messed with her. One of the odder things about hitting middle age was the way she could become invisible with minimal effort. Slightly looser clothes, rounded shoulders, and minimal eye contact and boom, no one gave her a second look. Even her contact had overlooked her at first, jumping when Bea slid into his booth.

"Who are you?" Bea asked the man across from her.

"Clyde," he said, tugging on his purple hat. He was barely old enough for the peach fuzz on his upper lip to be called a mustache. "Mala? I'm supposed to see your ID to verify."

Bea nodded, tapping her middle finger against her thumb and pulling up her fake ID to show him.

He leaned forward to verify that she was who she said she was and took a casual glance around the semi-crowded bar before sliding his hand across the table. "Here. Take this."

She placed her hand over his. When he pulled his hand away, he left behind a small envelope. Resisting the impulse to open it, she slipped it into her coat pocket.

"Instructions are inside." He shifted to the edge of the bench seat.

"Wait," she said. "Who is your contact? How did they get this information? What is it they want me to do?"

"I'm just the messenger." Clyde shrugged. "Sorry, can't help you. Got this job from an anonymous source. Envelope and instructions just showed up at my door one day. Said to come here, meet you, give you the sealed envelope. That's it. I know nothing else, I swear."

She opened her mouth to ask more questions, but he shook his head and walked away, resettling his cap to shield his face.

Back in her tiny bunk that she rented by the week, she opened the envelope, shaking out a drive and small card with a data dot attached. The card read, "Warning: Do not access the information on this data dot or bad things will happen. But the drive is for you." She cocked her head. Bad things, huh? Curious.

Setting the card aside, she slid the drive into her tablet. It contained two files. The first file, labeled "Just a taste", showed a large deposit to the lead investigator after his investigation into the fire. Someone paid him off, though the document didn't specify who. The other file contained instructions: she was to deliver the data dot to the person sitting in the last booth at the Lazy Pelican Diner on Badin, three standard weeks from the day she received it. In exchange, Ghost would provide her with all the information they had on the circumstances of the fire. It seemed too good to be true.

But with that one tidbit of information, Ghost had whet Bea's appetite for more. If that info on the lead investigator was true, it confirmed that her arrest was a set-up and made her even more determined to find the answers to her multitude of questions. What kind of information would Ghost provide when Bea delivered whatever was on the data dot to them? Bea didn't trust this Ghost person, but she also didn't have many other options. She was going to do it.

Though she knew a response from Dai wouldn't arrive before Bea hopped a ship to Badin, she still wrote to her sister, letting her know the plan and her destination. Anyway, she knew what her sister would say — that it was obviously a trap of some kind. Still, it was worth the risk. She just needed to be smart about it. She sighed. Something to work on.

"So now, I'm on a quest filled with travel to faraway places, with danger around every corner. Oh, and we can't forget the pirates," Bea muttered to the ceiling as she rolled on her back and threw an arm over her eyes. She rubbed a finger over the bump of nu-skin she'd bonded over the data dot. "And of course I have to take on the quest even if involves doing sketchy things like this courier job because you don't turn down a quest that might lead to the truth and help prove that I absolutely did not commit the crimes they accused me of."

She smacked a hand against the hard plasticine of the cot and cursed. She just wanted to have control of her life again, for it to return to some sense of normality. As her anger faded and her adrenaline crashed, the events of the day — of the past months, to be honest — caught up to her. Bea felt as if her body was weighted down by chains *Maybe a little nap will help,* Bea thought as she pulled the scratchy blanket up to her chin. *I'll wake refreshed and ready to conquer the universe.* She let out a low groan. Or at least, figure a way to get out of this room, get away from these damnable pirates, and get to Badin before Ghost's deadline.

4

QUIN

He'd just finished cleaning up the kitchen area after his meal when the ship jolted and the power flickered. He tapped his wrist comm and contacted the command deck. "Report," he barked.

Navi said, "Unclear. Looks like we're dead in the water. Don't know why or what happened. The drive system shut down. Could be that Rafe didn't replace the power pellet..."

"In-fucking-correct," Rafe said. "Full charge on the reactor and a new pellet when we left home base, and I double-checked it two days ago, when we got a bead on the *Intrepid*. Don't make me come up there and kick your ass, Navi."

"Why is everyone always threatening to kick my ass?" Navi asked, sounding hurt.

"Stop arguing, figure out what the problem is, and fix it. We're sitting ducks out here," Quin said. Though the pods were safely out of reach, *Dog's Day* was still lurking around the area, and they'd take full advantage of the situation, threat of the Knight or not. And, for fuck's sake, could his crew possibly get shit done without bitching? He'd knock some heads together if they didn't stop bickering. When they got back home, they all needed to take a little downtime and blow off some steam. "I'm going to go check on our guest. The ship better be up and running by the time I'm done dealing with the hellion."

"Make sure you bring her some breakfast," Ivan said. "She's bound to be hungry by now."

"Rafiel brought her dinner," he grumbled. "She's not starving." The scolding tone of Ivan's rebuke got Quin's back up. Of course, he made sure they fed her. He wasn't a complete monster. After all, they were rescuing her, not kidnapping her. Though, if his mother or sisters ever got wind of how he'd treated this woman, he was the one who'd get his ass kicked. He'd just dumped her in the brig at first because that's what he did with all the hotheads he worked with. A little me-time allowed them to cool off and consider their actions. Never hurt anyone.

Still muttering under his breath about mother hens, Quin pulled out some MREs stacked in the cabinet for when they went out on missions. The meals-ready-to-eat probably weren't food she was used to, but they were both nutritious and filling, which would tide her over until they got the ship fixed and headed home.

The lights in the corridor flickered and died before switching over to blue-tinged emergency lighting, and Quin swore. Systems were falling faster than they should. If those chuckleheads didn't stop dicking around and get the power restored, they were going to be in some deep shit. Emergency power wasn't meant to last forever and, if systems continued to shut down, the gravity sys would go next. While everyone on the team was all perfectly capable of doing repairs and moving around in microgravity, it made life that much more difficult. For one, repairs would take longer, especially if they needed to be in suits. The Mother forbid life support systems crashed, too. He hoped they weren't cascading into a catastrophic failure because then they'd be joining the *Intrepid*'s crew on Cinzia's surface. And Amaryllis would laugh her ass off at them.

Quin let out a frustrated sigh. "Get us power, team. Give me five to check in with the Farsirus woman and let her know we'll be underway shortly. Rafiel, I'll meet you in engineering." With the *Dragon* out of commission, this wasn't the ideal time to check in with their guest, but Ivan was right. He'd put off setting the record straight long enough. Whether or not she believed him, he'd be on guard against any sudden moves on her part. He didn't think his rod and tackle could take another round with her knee.

"Copy that. We're on it, Cap," Cormac said.

After tucking the water pouches and MREs into his pockets, Quin slid down a ladder to mid-level, which housed their two holding cells and froze, his senses tingling. Something was off. Unsnapping the holster of his blaster, he moved forward quickly on cat's feet. Had someone snuck on board while they were attached to the *Intrepid*? Maybe a crew member they'd missed? At a juncture, he paused, listening. This area of the ship was eerily silent without the reassuring hum of the ship's engines in the background. He took a quick glance down the corridor to his right, then moved down to the cell door and slapped a palm against the bio reader. It didn't open. No power.

"Ms. Farsirus, don't worry. We'll have power restored and be on our way shortly," he said, rapping his knuckles against the door. It shifted under his hand. He frowned and pushed at it, manually sliding it back to reveal an empty room. All that remained of the hellion was an empty food tray and her cuffs and gag, the discarded black bindings stark against the room's bare, white floor.

"Fuck." Quin entered the room and picked up the cuffs, one sliced cleanly open. Now how had she managed that? He was going to have to talk to Navi about how to do a proper pat-down. The man had obviously missed something. But Quin had been the one carrying her, and he hadn't noticed anything sharp on her person either. Instead, he'd been doing his best not to notice how soft her curves were or how good she smelled.

He tossed the ruined cuffs on the bed and walked over to the faucet, bending down to inspect the floor near the drain. Damp but no puddle. She couldn't have been out of the room for long, sometime after Rafe delivered her dinner and spoke with her. By the door, there was a small pile of thin metal splinters and a neat little hole in the wall exposing the door's control panel. Dismantled. Quin crouched and picked up a piece of the metal, nearly slicing open his finger on it. How in the three hells had she managed that?

Dropping the razor-sharp metal splinter, he stood and cursed. He'd underestimated her. Again. He activated the crew's personal comms, not wanting to use the ship-wide system and alert their escapee that they were onto her. "Woman's gone. Be on the lookout." Eyeing the damage, he had the creeping suspicion that Bea might have something to do with the issues his ship was currently experiencing. He clenched his jaw, the muscle jumping in his cheek.

"Well, shit," Navi said. "We need to find her."

"You think, Navi? You think we might need to find her?" And Navi wondered why people were always threatening to kick his ass. If Navi was standing next to him, he might very well do it, just to let off some frustration. "Navi and Ivan, sweep the ship. Rafiel and Cormac, get the damn ship back online. We're fucked if we have to stay in one place for too long."

"On it, boss," Ivan said. "I got a message off to home base before power completely carked it so, if we don't get engines back soon, at least someone knows where we are."

"Does this mean we're going to wind up owing the Knight another favor if he has to send someone to rescue us?" Navi asked.

"Oh, hells no. We are not going in debt to that man again," Cormac said. "It was his crappy intelligence on the Farsirus woman that led to this. If anything, this job is worth double what we're getting for it."

Quin stepped back into the corridor and scanned in both directions. If she was behind the system failures that brought the *Laughing Dragon* to a halt, he was going to be pissed. She'd surprised the hells out of him so far — he was starting to believe that she would have been completely fine on her own against both the *Intrepid*'s captain and Amaryllis's crew. Whoever took up the bounty on her was taking their lives into their own hands.

"I wouldn't tell the Knight he gave us crappy intelligence to his face but, yeah. Not having all the information on this job has made it much more difficult than it should have been." Unless his cousin was tormenting with him, something the Knight enjoyed doing. Either way, he wasn't about to let Rhain add another tally to their column in his books, not when they were almost free and clear.

"If I was her," Ivan drawled, humor coloring his words, "I might find a way to fuck up the drive system. I mean, if I happened to know enough about things like that to do some damage, being an engineer and all. And then, I'd find a way off this ship and away from the pirates I believe kidnapped me and are holding me for ransom or hoping to sell me or whatever terrible thing my imagination has conjured up."

"Are you a mind reader now, Ivan?" Navi asked.

Ivan grunted.

"I didn't see her along the way but I'm almost to engineering," Rafiel said. "There wasn't an alert, but I'll detour to check that all the escape pods are still there."

Quin expelled a frustrated sigh. "I'll take the pods, Rafe. You focus on getting us back online. I'm almost done with my sweep of this level. And just a reminder, we did not kidnap her," he said through clenched teeth as he moved down the corridor.

"Yes, but does she believe that?" Ivan asked, not cutting Quin a break. "She obviously doesn't trust you and still thinks we're pirates, the bad guys. Honestly, we've done very little to prove otherwise. In fact, I imagine someone's actions cemented it in her brain, especially considering you didn't bother trying to actually explain things to her once we off the *Intrepid* and out of immediate danger. Just locked her in a cell and had Rafiel slide food under her door."

"Hey!" Rafiel said. "That's what I was supposed to do, no?"

Quin cursed. He finished sweeping mid-level, checking every possible hiding space with no joy. "She knows."

"Oh, yes. I remember: you informed her of your heroic rescue while you had her slung over your shoulder like a cut of meat. And, of course, you didn't explain anything, so she had to take it at face value."

He was going to kill Ivan. First, find the woman. Second, get the ship powered back up and on the move. Third, kill Ivan. If he still had the time, he'd kick Navi's ass. His to-do list was growing. "Ivan, unless you have something useful to contribute to the conversation or to getting this ship functional, shut the fuck up."

"Yeah, Ivan. Even though you're right about everything you said, you heard what the captain said," Navi said.

"Navi, I swear to our Mother of Dragons..."

Quin tuned out the two of them as they devolved into their pattern of constant bickering. "Rafiel, report." Silence. He tried again. "Rafe?"

When Rafiel didn't respond, Quin double-timed it down to engineering, skidding around the corner to see the man groaning on the floor.

Rafiel blinked blearily up at Quin. "She nailed me good, Cap. Don't know what happened. Just walked in and bam, it all went dark." From his prone position, he raised a hand to the back of his head and came away with blood. "Ow."

But it was more than just Rafiel's injuries. Engineering didn't look so hot either. In fact, it looked like someone had set rabid tree rats loose in the place, with panels popped open and wires strewn across the floor. The reactor was dark. It would to take a solid chunk of time and energy to undo the damage. He cursed again. "Cormac, we need you in engineering. Rafe's got a head wound, and he's going to need help to the medi-bay. Plus, that woman that Ivan is so concerned about completely jacked the engine and drained the reactor."

"Shit. Okay. On my way."

Crouching, Quin helped Rafael into a sitting position,

leaning him against the broad leg of a worktable. "You okay until Cormac gets here, Rafe?"

Rafiel started a nod but let out a groan instead, pain darkening his brown eyes. "She rang my bell, that's for certain, but I'm not gonna die from a bump to the head." He squinted at Quin. "She is pissed and hella determined. I stepped into engineering, and she apologized even as she clocked me with my own wrench. Man, you should have heard the obscenities coming out of her mouth as she messed things up. I might have been in and out of consciousness, but what I heard, it was impressive. Even learned a couple of new ones that I can't wait to try out on you guys."

"Told you." Ivan's voice was smug. "Next up, escape from the ship."

Quin closed his eyes for a minute, gathering himself. Not that he would admit it out loud, but Ivan was right. They wouldn't be in this mess if he'd taken the time to explain who they were and why they'd boarded the *Intrepid* and hadn't just tossed her in a cell. This particular misunderstanding was his fault, and he was confident enough to admit it. He fucked up and now his crew was in danger, dead in the water in an area known for pirates and not just the quasi-reasonable ones like Amaryllis and her *Dog's Day* crew.

Cormac barreled around the corner and skidded to a halt, his eyes widening as he took in the scene. "Holy fire. That is one seriously pissed off lady. How did she manage all this?"

Rafiel put a hand on Quin's knee, shaking him out of his guilt spiral. "Hey. We'll be fine. We're big boys and can take care of ourselves and the ship."

"Yeah." Cormac helped Rafiel to his feet. "You go find her and fix this mess before she does any more damage."

Quin put a hand on Rafe's shoulder and looked into his eyes. He was pale but his pupils were even. Although Bea rang his bell, he should be okay. "Fine. You all get this ship back underway. I'll find our destructive Ms. Farsirus." Following Ivan's prescience, Quin took off for the escape pods.

5

BEA

"Hurry, hurry, hurry," Bea chanted to herself. But her fingers were shaking, her body telling her to go find a dark hole to hide in. She'd hit that man. Hit him hard enough to send him crashing to the floor. To be fair, he'd come around the corner as she was disabling the reactor and scared the crap out of her. Without thinking, she'd grabbed the big wrench right there on the table and walloped him upside the head as he approached her.

Thank the gods she hadn't killed him. Some violence in the name of escape? That she could handle. But violence that led to serious injury or death? She really didn't want that on her conscience. She soothed herself with the belief that any damage she'd done to him could be fixed with a quick trip to the ship's doc-in-the-box. Even though this was an older F-model starship, it was a Vanid design, so it should have a fully equipped medi-bay. *He'll be fine*, she reassured herself.

Working quickly, she loosened some connections and dumped wires on the ground, making it seem like she'd completely drained the reactor and destroyed the power pellet. The destruction looked worse than it was, but could be repaired rather easily, if you knew your system. She didn't want to kill them after all, just distract them and gain enough time to get away. Then, following the universal "go this way to get out" glyphs on the walls, she booked it for the escape pods.

She was taking a chance using the pods. Several chances, in fact. One, that they didn't have an expert-level engineer on their crew, so it would take them a decent amount of time to get themselves back online, and they wouldn't be able to follow her immediately. Two, that those other pirates, the ones that Quin claimed to be worse than them, wouldn't be nearby to pluck her from her escape pod like a ripe piece of fruit as soon as she was away from this ship. Three, that they were still close enough to Cinzia that the pod would head there rather than leave her floating in the depths of space, hoping for a rescue from someone not a pirate.

Though she wasn't sure, she guessed she'd been aboard less than a full standard day and during that time, she hadn't felt the ship power up its propulsion system for a quick hop or the tingle of a charge for a long jump. That meant, depending on which direction they were traveling and how fast they were moving at sub-light, they should still be near enough to Cinzia or maybe even approaching Badin — though the way her luck was running, it definitely wouldn't be the planet she desperately needed to get to as soon as possible. Oh, no. That would mean things were going right for once.

She had to hope that, if she wasn't close enough to a planet, the pod's emergency beacon would bring actual helpful help and not more pirates. Maybe help in the form of a passing cruise ship on the way to Badin? Because she could really use a massage and a stiff drink after this particular adventure. She snorted out a laugh at herself. Hey, a girl could dream. Even a tiny crotch-rocket of a mining ship from Cinzia would be more welcome than this damned pirate ship filled with giant, handsome lying liars.

She came to an abrupt halt at a dead end, despite having followed the glyphs. Shit. Typical pirates, changing things around, so it was harder to find your way around an unfamiliar ship. At least this ship wasn't one of the bigger ones, like a cargo hauler or cruiser. She took a meditative breath, trying to calm her racing heart so she could think straight. Okay, so the pods weren't here, which meant they'd most likely be at mid-level, closer to the center of the ship and still easily accessible in case of an emergency. She cursed. The cell they'd had her in was closer to the pods than engineering.

At the top of the ladder, she paused to check the area. Blue backup lighting still bathed the corridors, but there was no alarm and she didn't hear anyone nearby. Hopefully, they were all too busy trying to fix the problems she'd left them to focus on her. Hurrying down an outer corridor towards a line of four oval doors, she skidded to a halt in front of the first pod. Putting her thumb on the scanner to verify her sentient life form status, she danced with impatience as the door slid open to reveal a rounded interior with two jump seats and a simple terminal next to the door. With a swipe of her hand, she powered it up. "Computer, launch pod."

"Unable to detect life-threatening emergency onboard the ship," the computer said in its non-gendered monotone. "Please state emergency."

"Emergency verified. I'm very much having an emergency. I need to get off this ship now. Override protocols and let's go."

"Unable to comply."

"Oh, you motherfucker," Bea said, pounding on the terminal. These cheap-assed computers that couldn't deviate from a short, prescribed script sucked. Right now, she needed to get off this ship. She'd had enough of this leg of her adventure, thank you very much.

She took another deep breath. *Calm down, Bea. You can do this*, she thought. Usually, developers left themselves at least one back door so they could do fun things like override protocols, even if they weren't the captain or part of its recognized crew.

A couple of years ago, Izumi, one of her sister's retired spy friends, taught her a simple saying which supposedly gave the user a five-second override, a back door that worked for a majority of these types of basic systems. She just had to remember it. Shit. She was running out of time, and her brain was empty of everything but the overwhelming urge to flee. "Panic is not helpful," she told herself, taking a deep breath and closing her eyes to remember. "We were installing a new, uncooperative engine in the *Mordaith*... I was irritated because the engine wouldn't pair with the ship... Izumi said there was always a back door, an override code..." She wiggled her fingers over the small keypad as she dug deep into her memory. "Seven to free the four once more. 7-2-3-4-7-2-3-4." She opened her eyes, sketched a minor rune of luck in the air, then typed it in. "Emergency verified. Computer, launch pod," she said, holding her breath.

A pause. Then, "Order accepted."

"Thank you, Izumi. I owe you a drink next time I see you. So there, you damned machine," she said, resting her hand above the terminal and bowing her head as the inner door slid shut. Freedom beckoned.

She yelped as a hand clamped down over her wrist, and the tall form of her captor muscled his way into the pod with her, the door snapping shut behind him. "Absolutely not," Quin said through clenched teeth, his large fingers warm against her skin. "You're not going anywhere."

"Let me go, pirate," she said, planting her feet and pulling hard against his grip. She might not be able to overpower him completely, but she most definitely could stand her ground and resist until the doors sealed and the pod launched. Sure, then she'd be trapped in a small space with the damned man, and no escape route, but she'd leave that for Future Bea to worry about.

"I told you," he said through gritted teeth as he held her wrist in one hand and tried to pry open the door with the other, "I'm trying to help you. Stop resisting."

"Like I trust that," Bea said. He might be gorgeous, with those dark eyes and the shadow of a beard shading his square jaw.

He might claim that he was trying to help her, but he'd done nothing but manhandle her since they met. Granted, he'd never actually hurt her. Even now, his grip was gentle but uncompromising. But still. "Actions speak louder than words and you have done nothing to make me think you're anything more than a shitty pirate with bad intentions."

As they struggled, the door sealed itself with a soft hiss. Quin let go of her wrist and put some genuine effort into physically prying open the door, his muscles flexing under his midnight blue technical shirt. When that didn't work, he banged a fist against it. "Open up, you piece of shit. This is the captain speaking."

"Unable to comply," the computer intoned. "Emergency declared. Launching in twenty, nineteen, eighteen..."

He cursed and repeated his command with the same response. "What did you do?" he said, whirling on her, his hands on his hips as he loomed over her.

Though he had several inches on her own five-foot ten-inch frame, his looming wasn't nearly as effective as he thought. The thought that it wasn't right that a bad guy was so good looking flitted through her traitorous brain again. With eyes the color of her favorite forest and light tan skin, he had broad shoulders and muscles for days — she was positive he had at least a six-pack under that tight shirt of his. Those eyes promised all kinds of bad things in the best possible way, though they sparked with the promise of retribution at the moment. A muscle in Quin's jaw jumped as he ground his teeth at her, but she didn't look away. Instead, she set her own jaw and glared back at him. If looks could kill, they'd both be ashes on the ground.

"You'd better strap in, Captain, because we're going for a ride." Bea said as she broke eye contact to slide into one of the two jump seats, clicking into the five-point harness.

Quin growled at her and mashed at buttons on the terminal, as if that would change anything. "Computer, end countdown. This is Captain Quin Sidron, code alpha-four-nine-seven-xi ordering an immediate shutdown of pod launch," he barked.

"Unable to comply."

"Fuck." He pressed at a spot behind his ear to activate the team comm. "Ivan, Navi, Cormac, respond." He waited a second, then tried again.

Bea watched his face darken in real time. She didn't think she'd ever actually seen someone's head look like it was about to explode. Both fascinating and scary.

He shot her a glare as he smacked at the terminal. "Command, this is Quin."

"Go ahead, Cap," someone on the command bridge responded.

"I'm on board escape pod number one with the Farsirus woman, and the doors are sealed tight. My internal comms have crapped out again, and the computer on this bloody thing isn't responding to my orders or command code. You've got to shut it down on your end." He continued to enter random sequences into the terminal, as if that would do anything. But she wasn't about to say anything and draw more of his ire.

"No joy on this end, Cap. But we'll keep trying." The voice echoed through the small space. Navi, she thought, remembering his snarky, teasing tones.

Quin spun to glare at her and she braced for potential violence, but he made no such moves. Instead, he gritted out, "What did you do? Shut it down immediately."

The computer continued its measured countdown.

From the security of her seat, Bea merely smiled at him as the seconds ticked away. There was absolutely nothing he could do about their imminent departure, and she enjoyed the feeling of having outsmarted this man. "Captain. You need to get strapped in before this pod launches or you're going to get hurt," she said in a calm voice.

With a growl of frustration, he slid into a seat and yanked at his harness. "Navi. We've got about ten seconds before this thing launches. Get it shut down asap!"

"It's not responding on our end, Cap. She got in some back-door, and it locked us out," Navi said. "Looks like you're going for a ride."

"Just do your job and protect the asset," a voice that reminded her of a growly bear said.

"Yeah, what Ivan said. And don't lose your temper. Remember, our job is to protect her, not strangle her because she outsmarted us," Navi said.

Quin glowered at her, but Bea refused to be intimidated, folding her arms and lifting her chin. She was in the right here. Any sane person would do whatever possible to get away from their kidnappers, especially sneaky ones who tried to convince them that they were being "saved" for their own good. As if. She watched him struggle with an uncooperative harness. He'd better hurry up and get strapped in the rest of the way, or he'd get hurt when the pod disengaged from the ship.

"Don't worry," Navi said. "We'll be back up soon, Cap."

The computer continued its countdown in a calm voice. "Six... five..."

"This is Rafiel. I'm patched up and on my way back to engineering." When Rafiel's voice came over the intercom, Bea felt a rush of relief. She must not have done too much damage if he was already up and on his feet. "Cormac's down there, working on figuring out what she did to our reactor. We've got a few of the systems back online already."

Shit. They were faster than she'd expected.

Quin grunted, pulling at the straps. He had his arm and torso through the left side of it, but the right half of the harness remained retracted instead of gliding out smoothly.

"Seriously, captain. You need to brace yourself so you don't get hurt," Bea squinched up her face as she watched him struggle, unable to help unless she wanted to be in the same predicament. The last thing she needed was to be burdened with an injured man as she made her getaway.

"Ivan's got a fix on you, so wherever you land, we'll head in your direction as soon as humanly possible." Navi's voice sounded confident, but it didn't wipe the look of doom from Quin's face.

However, landing sounded good to Bea. That meant that they were indeed close enough to some planet — Cinzia, she guessed — that the pod would automatically head there, rather than drifting out into space. There was at least a spark of hope that she would get herself out of this mess in one piece.

The computer finished its countdown. "... one. Pod launching."

Bea grabbed onto the arms of her seat and braced herself. Though he did his best to hold on, because he'd gotten only partially strapped in, the initial shove of propulsion flung Quin to one side, his head hitting the metal frame of the terminal with a loud crack. Bea shuddered. His body went limp and then weightless, floating half out of his seat as the initial push eased.

"Dammit." As much as she didn't trust him, Bea wasn't about to let him float there like that. He'd only break his neck when they hit atmo, and then where would she be? Stuck on an unfamiliar planet with a dead guy, that's where.

"Captain, we've got another problem," Ivan of the growly bear voice said.

She ignored him, focusing on her own problem, namely the unconscious captain. She unclasped her harness and, lightly pushing off her seat, floated over to him before engaging her grav boots and connecting to the metal flooring. With a gentle tug, she slid out the right side of the harness and slipped the straps around his torso, tightening them down so he wouldn't be jostled too badly when they hit the planet's atmosphere. Once she got him buckled in, she checked the bump on his head where a nice-sized goose egg was developing. A head injury wasn't ideal in microgravity, but hopefully, they wouldn't be on the float for long. She slapped a quick-fix patch from the first aid kit on his bump and called it good enough for now. His breathing was steady, and the patch should take care of the swelling and pain at the site, though he'd still have a headache when he woke up.

But what did she know? She had zero medical training, and blood made her stomach turn. They were lucky that he hadn't gashed open his head on that corner because then there would be both blood and puke free-floating in the pod and that wasn't something she wanted to experience.

"Captain, respond." Ivan's voice got more growly. "Are you okay?"

"Don't tell me that woman killed you, Cap," Navi said.

Bea rolled her eyes. May as well let them know what was going on. "Your captain is alive, just unconscious," she answered.

"Damn, girl." Navi whistled. "Just joking up here."

"Wasn't me. His harness wouldn't latch, and he was knocked unconscious when the pod shot away from your ship." She wedged herself into the small space between Quin's seat and the console so she could do a pat-down on him. Ooh, water. She cracked open one of the water pouches she found, squeezing out every last drop before tucking the flat, empty container back in his pocket so it wouldn't float through the cabin.

"Is he alright?" Ivan asked.

"I patched him up the best I could." She cast an eye over the unconscious man next to her. "I don't think it's life-threatening, but he might benefit from some time in a medi-tube just to be sure." That would keep them focused on getting their captain the medical attention he needed, while she got as far away from them as possible.

She continued her pat-down. He won't be needing this, she thought as she unstrapped the holster holding his blaster from around his thigh, which she couldn't help but notice was as thick and as well-muscled as the rest of him.

She eyed him as she strapped the confiscated blaster to her thigh. Quin Sidron was an almost uncomfortably good looking man. He looked to be somewhere in his 40s, close to her age, with a light sprinkle of gray at his temples. Even the stubble along his cheeks and along his square jaw had a little salt in the pepper. Laugh lines radiated from the corners of his eyes, fringed by the longest eyelashes she'd ever seen on a man. How was that even fair?

Ivan's voice came over the pod's comm, making her jump and pulling her from her inappropriate thoughts about an unconscious man. "Ms. Farsirus, we've run into some logistical problems, and it's going to be a while before we can get to where you are. So, please tell me he will survive if he doesn't get immediate medical attention."

Logistical problems? Like the ones she caused? But what she'd done was repairable. "What kind of logistical problems?"

The comm remained silent.

"I won't share more information about your captain until you give me details." She wouldn't give up any advantage she might have without good reason.

Navi responded, "The other pirates, you know the ones cutting into the *Intrepid* as we left? Well, seems they were pissed about losing their prize and fired on us..."

"Even though originally their captain agreed to back off," Ivan growled. "Damn that woman. Knew she wouldn't keep her word."

Bea's eyebrows shot up at his tone.

"And we fired back with a warning shot and, well, somehow the *Intrepid* got blown up during our exchange..."

"No doubt because Rilly lost her temper," Ivan said.

"... which attracted the attention of the Starguard. Because we do our best to avoid any entanglements with them and didn't want to be caught at the scene of the crime, we had to remove ourselves from the area."

"So, you ran," Bea said, wincing at the *Intrepid*'s destruction. She'd liked that ship. She'd put time into it and had just gotten the engines purring again after the hack job their last engineer did on them.

"Absolutely we did. Have you met those Starguard assholes?" Navi asked. "I swear they've gotten even worse since our team left.

Good thing Cormac and Rafe figured out how to give us enough juice for a quick hop."

"Enough, Navi," Ivan said, probably worried Navi was giving out too much information.

Unfortunately, yes, she had encountered members of the Starguard, and it had been less than pleasant. And she didn't blame Quin's crew for taking off. The bonus being it got them out of her hair for the time being. "Did either of them notice our escape pod?" she asked, holding her breath. If yes, she was screwed. If the 'Guard got a hold of her, they'd put her back in jail and this time, she didn't think she'd survive. If those other pirates got their hands on her, they'd turn her over to goddess-knew-who for the bounty, which might be worse.

"Don't think so," Navi said. "Last we saw of them, they were chasing down *Dog's Day*, giving us enough time to limp away."

Forcing herself to take deep breaths to calm her pounding heart, she finished her inexpert pat-down. She confiscated several knives while doing her best to ignore the warm sparks that lit up along her spine as she touched him. She needed to remain as professional and distant as possible. Accosting an unconscious man right here in the escape pod was where she drew the line, especially with his crew just a comm away. But having to run her hands over his body to check for more weapons, well, that was just good sense.

She cleared her throat. "In my non-medical opinion, Quin will be fine. His head has a good-sized knot on it, but his pupils are even so that's good. Right?"

"Thank you, Ms. Farsirus," Ivan said. "Your pod will land on Cinzia within the next few hours. I realize you don't believe that we were on board the *Intrepid* to aid you, even though I can promise you that we were, and that you still plan to run from us. So I must ask a favor of you. Please make sure our captain is out of harm's way before you leave him."

She saw no harm in promising that. After all, she didn't want the man dead, just far away from her. "I'll do my best."

"That is all we can ask," Ivan said. "Safe journey."

"You, too," she said, before reaching over to the terminal and turning off the open comm. Then she checked Quin again, brushing back his hair from his temple to check the patch she'd placed over his injury. Swollen but not bleeding. She could feel the heat of his body as she leaned in close to check his pupils again and a thrum of attraction slid through her veins.

"Fuck," she whispered, pushing away from him. "What are you doing, Bea? This isn't you."

It wasn't. She'd never been sexually adventurous or even that into it, to be honest. With Arden and the lovers before him, she was what her friends called "plain vanilla". Of course, she tried not to compare herself to anyone, and especially not Dai, who enjoyed a buffet rather than settling for a single meal. But there was something about this man that made her want to do all kinds of dark and delicious things with him, things she'd never even considered with her other partners. It had to be because he was the villain in this piece, right? In her stories and vids, she'd always preferred the bad boys and naughty villains. But this was real life, and there was nothing romantic about getting involved with a dangerous, scruffy pirate. And this man was a prime example of the toxic males she'd done her level best to avoid her entire life, though she hadn't been very successful on that front.

Later, when she told Dai this story, her sister would probably tease her for not taking the opportunity to jump his bones when he was awake, telling her how adventures and dangerous men added spice to the bedroom. Sure, he was pretty when he was unconscious, but when he was awake, he was rude and liked to manhandle her. A torrid affair with a scruffy space pirate was just a wild daydream straight out of one of her novels anyway. If anything ever happened between them — not that she'd ever actually do anything with a pirate, not even one as ridiculously hot as Quin Sidron — he would be awake, and he would enjoy every minute of it. And so would she. Instead, she'd do the sensible thing. She tied his ass up so that when he did finally regain consciousness, he couldn't easily escape his seat and strangle her.

She snagged one of the MREs he had in his pocket and settled into the jump seat next to his, turning slightly so she could keep an eye on him. The food wasn't great and kept trying to float away from her, but it was sustenance and filled her growling stomach.

Since she didn't trust Ivan or the rest of Quin's crew, she asked, "Computer, any sign that the ship we just left is coming after us?"

"Unknown."

"How long before we reach the planet?"

"Unknown."

"You don't know much, do you?" Bea rolled her head on her neck, trying to loosen some of the tension held there, and let out a wide yawn.

"Request not recognized."

"Of course not," she muttered. "Computer, how long until we reach safety?"

"Unknown. Distress signal active."

Bea groaned. Now that she knew more pirates and the Starguard were in the area, she'd be better off with no signal. Unfortunately, she had no idea how to turn it off. Izumi had stressed that particular back door worked only once. Hopefully, they'd make planetfall before the signal brought trouble to their door, and she'd have enough time to get far enough away that anyone looking wouldn't find her. She had to hope that she got lucky, though good luck hadn't been on her side for a while now. Bad luck? Now that followed her around like a lost puppy.

Nothing to be done about it now, she thought, yawning so hard her jaw popped. She hadn't slept well on that hard cot. Hard to feel rested when your brain treated you to anxiety dreams filled with mazes, tangles of wires, and things chasing you. For now, she was relatively safe, even if there was a giant pirate strapped in not five feet away. Had she secured him well enough? What would he do if he got himself loose? If he did get free, she didn't think that he'd actually kill her, considering he kept trying to convince her that he was there to help.

One hand on her confiscated blaster, she settled in to keep watch, counting time until they landed and she could make a break for it.

6

QUIN

Quin swam to consciousness, surrounded by what sounded like...motorcycles? Keeping his eyes closed and breathing deep and easy, he tried to get a read on the situation without alerting whomever was nearby that he was conscious. The low grumble of the engines and the crunch of tires over a loosely packed surface had him envisioning the two-wheeled land machines his grandfather had on his farm. But United Body of Planets outlawed combustion motors on most settled planets because of their consumption of fossil fuels and pollution of the environment. There were better and less environmentally damaging ways to move these days.

Last thing he remembered was trying to get that blasted woman out of the escape pod, the computer ignoring his commands, and the harness malfunctioning. He'd been meaning to dock the *Laughing Dragon* to fix all the little shit that was on the verge of catastrophic failure, but there never seemed to be enough time. Guess now he was paying for not making the *Dragon*'s overall functionality a priority. But he wasn't on his ship anymore. So where was he? And where was the woman? If he'd lost her, not only would the Knight be pissed, but he'd never let Quin live it down.

The air tasted of dust, hot and metallic. The surface he was sweating all over was exceptionally hard and provided no shock absorption as they bounced along what might be the worst road ever constructed. Which he guessed meant they'd landed on Cinzia. Based on the amount of sweat finding its way down his ass crack, they were probably somewhere in the Movit desert region, a glorious sand pit filled with rocks, biting insects, snakes, and a variety of other things that could kill you. Good times.

Someone sneezed, loud and high pitched, and let out a string of muttered words lost beneath the rumbling of the surrounding machines. At least he wasn't suffering alone. He recognized that voice.

He cracked open an eye, taking in a dim, boxy space pierced by thin shafts of light from holes punched at random intervals in the roof and sides. In a shadowed corner, he made out the shape of a single fellow passenger. He shifted and felt the weight of the cuffs binding his wrists together. A heavy chain ran from his wrists to an O-ring welded to the metal wall.

"Quin." Out of the gloom, the current bane of his existence leaned forward, a shaft of light illuminating her face. She looked a little banged up, coated in a layer of reddish dirt, and irritated. So, not much the worse for wear since the last time he'd seen her. The sense of relief that swept through him shocked the hells out of him. "Oh, thank the Mother. You're awake," the hellion said.

The box hit a particularly large bump on the poor excuse for a road they were traveling along, and a massive headache bloomed behind his eyes, wringing a groan out of him. He struggled up into a sitting position and stretched his legs out in front of him, the scrape of his chains against the metal flooring loud in the small space. "Bea." It came out as a croak. He swallowed hard, cleared his dry, scratchy throat and tried again, raising his voice over the rumble of the machines. "Are you okay? Where are we? What happened? Last thing I remember, you were trying to launch my escape pod."

She snorted, swiping a sleeve over her forehead, smearing the dirt and sweat. "I did launch your damn pod, for all the good it did me." She waved a hand at their accommodations. "Same situation, different prison. Why couldn't you just let me go?"

Still a little fuzzy, he touched his fingers to where his head hurt the most, wincing as his fingers grazed over a large bump covered by what felt like a quick-fix patch. "What..."

"Don't touch that," she snapped, sliding closer. He lowered his hand. "You cracked your head on the pod's terminal during takeoff and knocked yourself out. I got you patched up okay, but I couldn't grab the first aid kit before trolls snatched us so we don't have any extras. Or any pain meds."

Well, at least the injury explained his head feeling like it was about to split open. He closed his eyes as they hit another hole and willed the pain away. It didn't work. Clearing his throat, he opened his eyes again. "Trolls?" Wonderful. This situation just kept getting better and better. Injured, chained in a box with a woman who didn't trust him or even like him, plus trolls. If they actually made it out of here alive, he was going to renegotiate for hazard pay.

"Yep. Crash-landed on this godsforsaken pile of rocks and almost immediately, these giant, hairy trolls on massive motorcycles surrounded us. No doubt you hear them out there." She jerked a thumb over her shoulder. "They must have intercepted the pod's distress signal because those bastards were on us as soon as the pod landed. Out of the frying pan and into the fire." She cursed under her breath, something about giant hairy troll balls.

He grunted. Not at all good. He'd heard that parts of Cinzia had a troll problem but didn't realize it had escalated to them ransacking escape pods. Most trolls, if they couldn't eat or sell something, they usually left it alone. He wondered which category these particular trolls placed him and Bea into: eat or sell.

Bea scooted closer and waggled a finger at him. "How 'bout instead of grunting at me when I say, 'we're prisoners of biker trolls', you say something reassuring like 'Hey, Bea. It'll be alright. We'll come up with a plan to get out of this mess.' I mean, you're a pirate. Don't you have some kind of bond with these cretins, something reciprocal 'like don't attack us and we won't attack you' in case of situations like this?"

"First, technically my crew and I are not pirates. We're privateers. Mercenaries, if you prefer. We take paid jobs and don't randomly attack and pillage the shipping lanes, for a start."

She rolled her eyes and folded her arms over her chest.

He tried not to notice how that movement pressed her breasts together, a valley of delight made visible by the deep scoop of her form-fitting black shirt. Honestly, he could be such a gentleman sometimes. But he doubted she'd appreciate him pointing it out. "Second, you do realize it's your fault we're in this situation to begin with. If you'd only listened to me, we'd be sitting on my ship in these big, comfy chairs with cold drinks in our hands toasting a successful rescue mission rather than stuffed in a box on our way to stars knows where."

She glowered at him.

He frowned back. "Wait. How are you unchained, and I'm trussed up like a moonsday hen?"

"Good gods. That's what you're focused on?" She threw her hands up in the air. "Those knocks must have really scrambled your brains. You're no good to me if you're not thinking straight. Let me look." She leaned forward and immediately started poking at the knot on his head.

"Ow," he said, jerking back from her painful fingers. "I thought you said not to touch it."

She grabbed his chin and pulled him back towards her, leaning close to look into his eyes. "Don't be such a baby. It only hurts so much because when we landed, you hit your head in the same place again."

He tried to evade her probing. She held him in place with fingers of steel.

"Good. It's only a tiny bump, and both of your pupils are the same size. You'll survive."

He grunted. "Your bedside manner is appalling."

"Not a doctor."

Trying not to wince at her not-so-tender ministrations, he took a moment to truly look at her. She'd re-braided her black hair, though several waves had found their way out of the plait and curled around her round face. Her honey-brown eyes narrowed as she assessed his injuries, nibbling on the corner of her plump, dark red bottom lip. Briefly, he wondered how hard she would hit him if he closed the few inches between them and stole a kiss. Probably hard enough to knock him into next cycle. It might be worth it, but as he'd already taken two bumps to the head, he resisted the temptation. Still, he took a moment to imagine how she would taste. Sweet with a sharp kick, he guessed, his eyes lingering on her lips.

As if she knew what he was thinking, she pushed on his bump again. Hard.

"Ow." He pulled back. "You never answered my question. Why are your hands free?"

"Because I didn't want to be bound yet again." She glanced at the pile of metal in the box's corner and rolled her eyes. "Those chains are heavy, and they hurt my wrists. They had to go."

So she had some way to pick the locks, probably the same things she'd used to escape the me-time room. Guess the trolls are as bad as Navi at doing pat-downs. But her tools could come in handy. He offered his bound hands to her. "My turn."

With a shake of her head, she retreated to the opposite side of their mobile prison.

Did she not understand their predicament? "Once we stop, we need to make a break for it, and I won't be any help to either of us like this." He rattled his chains at her. "I'm good, but I'm not that good."

"Not going to happen. I don't trust you any farther than I can throw you and, judging by your muscle mass, that wouldn't be very far." She folded her arms over her chest. "Also, you try anything and those trolls won't hesitate to kill you. Not that I care because I don't like you but I promised Ivan I'd do my best to get you out of harm's way before ditching you."

He threw his most charming grin in her direction, one that had served him extremely well in the past. "Come on, now, Daisy. Don't be like that. Didn't you just say that we're in this together?"

She was unfazed by his attempt to convince her via a charm offensive. Or maybe she couldn't see him in the gloom because she said, "No. No, we're not. I've changed my mind. You're as bad as these trolls, thinking that you can tie me up, throw me in a box and sell me to the highest bidder." She sniffed. "I got away from you on my own; I can get away from these rock heads by myself, too."

"Yeah, about that. Remember when I told you I was rescuing you?"

"Oh, you mean when you had me tied up and slung over your shoulder and then had the nerve to smack me on my ass? Like I believe a handsy space pirate. Classic toxic male behavior. No, thank you."

"I'm being truthful. We were hired to rescue you off the *Intrepid*." Yeah, he really should have listened to Ivan. Trying to convince her that he actually was on her side after he'd done just about everything wrong was going to take more than words. But he had to try. Especially since he didn't want to be fighting both her and the trolls at the same time. The trolls he could take. Her, he wasn't so sure about. He hadn't done well so far.

"You mean you were there to save me from Captain Bessa and his crew?" she asked, cocking her head to the side. "The crew that was scheduled to deliver a shipment to that colony long before I knew I needed a ride? The colony no one but my sister knew I was on? Those guys?"

Quin opened his mouth and closed it again. Well, shit. She had a point. "Well, when you put it that way, I can understand why you don't think you were in any danger. But our client was quite specific: our job was to rescue you from a dangerous situation, and they directed us to the *Intrepid*."

Eyes narrowed, she shot questions at him. "Who hired you anyway? And who told you I was in danger? And how did they know where I would be? You mentioned something about a knight..." she paused, expecting him to fill in the blanks.

"You know, really good questions," he said, scratching his chin, the day-old growth rasping under his fingers. He didn't want to get into it about the Knight unless he absolutely had to. Bringing favors owed and family connections into the conversation at this point would only complicate things.

She braced herself as the box took an especially hard bounce that rattled his bones. "You don't know or you won't answer? Seems like you should know who's hiring you, especially when it involves a kidnapping."

"Well, now, Daisy, here's the thing about being a pirate," he said, affecting an exaggerated drawl. "We don't ask many questions, as long as we get paid. The cargo from that ship was the first half of our payment and, with the safe delivery of you, we'll get the second half of that payment." Granted, they didn't get that cargo because they had to sacrifice it to the Dog's Day crew, but easy come, easy go. Anyway, this particular job wasn't about the money, it was about debt erasure. Owing the Knight favors meant they were beholden to him. Autonomy was the ultimate goal. He and his team had enough of taking orders in the Starguard. Now, they wanted full control of their own lives and the jobs they took.

"Thought you weren't a pirate." She sniffed and shifted her legs. "And how generous of your mysterious boss to offer up the *Intrepid*'s cargo as part of your payment."

"It was, wasn't it?"

They slowed down then jerked to a halt. The steady rumble of the motorcycles grew louder, filling the air with growls before the engines cut off. He heard movement and the sound of rocks rubbing together. Troll language, one of the few languages his universal translator didn't recognize. He understood only a few of words but not enough to comprehend what they were saying. The voices drew close.

"Sounds like we reached our destination," he said. "Quick, put your cuffs back on and play like you're still tied up." When she looked at him aghast, he said, "You got out of them once. You'll get out again. Now put them on and pretend so they don't realize you can pick locks."

"You mean you're not going to suggest rushing them when they open the door again?" she asked sarcastically, though she followed his directions and loosely secured the cuffs over her wrists.

"That would be foolhardy and probably get me killed," he said, using the wall as leverage to stand. His vision wavered, then steadied. Definitely a concussion.

"I don't see a problem with that." She moved next to him. She was tall, only a few inches shorter than his height of 6'2", with a sturdy build that reminded him of the warrior women in his family. There was a hint of fear in her eyes, but she squared her shoulders against it and raised her chin, daring him to mention it.

Keeping up the banter to distract both, he said, "Of course you don't. But I'm not ready to risk life and limb only to get knocked into a wall and smashed by a giant troll."

He stepped in front of her as the door swung open. One of their captors shoved a torch toward them, temporarily blinding him with light. A troll dressed in leather chaps and a red cut waved them forward with the barrel of a blaster that looked ridiculously small in his massive hands. "Move," he barked, flicking the gun in a hurry up gesture.

"That's my gun," Bea whispered as they shuffled to the door.

"You mean my gun," he said, recognizing the weapon that normally rested in a holster on his thigh. The torch-bearing troll unlocked Quin from the wall.

"Shut it," another massive troll said, slamming a hand against the side of their prison, shaking the entire vehicle.

Why couldn't it have been the smaller variety of trolls who'd found them? These were mountain trolls, said to be as big as the mountains from which they originated. While these weren't quite that large, the smallest of this batch, hovering over by the motor-cycles parked in a row, was still over seven feet tall and built like the box they used to transport their prisoners. With mottled, pebble-textured skin the color of the surrounding dark gray rocks, they sported black hair tufting from their heads and shoulders. Several of them had formed their hair into tall spikes, while others let it grow long, flowing down their backs like a mane.

After another grunt from the gun-toting troll, they stepped down from the back of the box, Bea stumbling a little as she landed. Quin moved forward to help her, but a troll with green spikes of hair covering his head and arms snarled at him.

"Just trying to help the lady," he said.

"Don't."

They'd driven into a massive cave. The entrance itself had to be fifty feet wide and at least twenty feet high. Stalactites dripped from the ceiling, and a cool breeze circulated through the open space. To the left, a long row of motorcycles were parked in front of several square metal vehicles, like the one that had transported them. A group of ten bikers stood near the dusty machines, talking loudly and slapping each others' backs.

The trolls herded Quin and Bea to the right, through one of three archways carved into the back of the cave, and down a winding tunnel that split about thirty feet in. He couldn't quite see where the path to the left lead but, when he paused to get a better look, Green Spikes shoved him forward. "Move."

Green Spikes unlocked a thick door with a small bar-lined window. Beyond it was a dark prison. A few spluttering torches jammed into sconces illuminated the tool marks on the walls and ceiling where they'd tunneled into the space. Cages with metal bars driven into the stone floor and stretching all the way to the ceiling lined both sides of the tunnel.

Quin wondered if they'd driven the spikes in with their own hands. He wouldn't put it past them. Mountain troll skin was supposedly as hard as rocks, though he'd never tried to stab one to verify.

Green Spikes pulled a second set of keys from his belt and unlocked the first cell to the right. The door swung open with a foreboding creak, and he gestured for them to get in, punctuated by another jab and grunt from Gun-Stealing troll.

They stepped inside, and Green Spikes said, "Hands."

They presented their wrists, and Green Spikes removed their cuffs before stepping back and slamming the heavy iron door in their faces with a sneer, the snick of the lock echoing off the damp stone walls. The trolls and their bright torches left, closing the door to the dungeon shut behind them and leaving Quin and Bea trapped in the cold, dank cell. The shuffling of feet and a few coughs from the gloom of the other cells told him they weren't the only prisoners of the trolls.

Her voice shaky, Bea cursed. "Well, this is just great. What is it with people wanting to put me in a cage lately?" She kicked a bar on their cell and threw a glare in his direction.

If they were going to survive this, he needed Bea on his side. Barring that, at least not openly combative. To get there, he knew what he needed to do. It was as if there was a teeny Ivan sitting on his shoulder, whispering in his ear. He didn't say it often but when he was wrong, he admitted it.

He took a deep breath and said, "I apologize for mishandling your rescue. But if you had come with us peacefully instead of fighting, I wouldn't have had to carry you or put you in our holding cell."

She froze at his words and slowly turned towards him, her eyes bright with anger. "What did you say?"

Was this what a rabbit felt like when a large jungle cat stalked it? "I apologized."

"And?" Her voice was dangerously low.

His mind frantically replayed what he'd said to her and where he'd gone wrong. "And explained why I had to do it?"

"That is not an apology, pirate." She put her hands on her hips. "Adding the word 'but' to what started out as a decent apology automatically negates it."

His eyes followed her hands and, for a split second, he admired how they emphasized her curves before his brain reminded him that she was pissed and if she caught him checking her out or doing anything other than listening to her with his full attention, she might very well slit his throat in his sleep.

Luckily, she hadn't noticed his wandering gaze. She continued, "With the addition of that 'but', you shift the blame to me for a perfectly logical response to armed men forcefully boarding our ship, invading my space, and demanding I leave with them. Don't you dare blame me for your choices."

He opened his mouth to respond. Whatever small progress they'd made in the box, he'd just shattered with his words. He needed to fix it. He wanted to fix it. He had to explain so she understood.

But she held up a finger and shot it at him. "No. No more explanations. All I want to hear is 'I'm sorry. It won't happen again.'"

After that scathingly delivered lesson, he did the only logical thing and said, "I'm sorry. It won't happen again, Buttercup." And then he shut his mouth.

Her shoulders relaxed, and she nodded. "Thank you." She rubbed at her wrists where the cuffs had left red marks, chafing her delicate skin. "You know my name is not Buttercup or Daisy. Are you just trying to be clever with all the flower names because my name is Bea?"

"I don't have to try, Daisy. Clever is as clever does." He winced internally as his grandmother's favorite expression popped out of his mouth. But then he laughed at himself. Hey, if you couldn't amuse yourself by teasing the person you're locked in a cell with, then when could you?

She gave him a look of pure disgust and pointed to a dimly lit corner with a large rock that both time and multiple asses had worn smooth. "I'm going to go sit there and pretend you never tried to 'rescue' me. Why don't you use that clever brain of yours and figure a way out of here, huh?"

An impossible task, Quin thought, leaning back against the front bars of the cage and propping up one leg. But then, he always had a fondness for impossibilities.

7

BEA

"Mala, is that you?" a voice called out from the gloom. Coming alert, Quin gave her a look and shifted from his spot in the shadows.

Bea left her uncomfortable rock seat and wrapped her hands around the cell bars, the chill of the iron making her shiver. Squinting into the dark, she called, "Hello? Who's out there?"

"Shh! Not so loud or they'll hear you," the voice responded in a loud whisper. A stubby white hand waved from a cell down the line, then a face pressed up against the bars. "It's me. Captain Bessa." In the spluttering torchlight, she saw that he'd fared poorly since the *Intrepid*. One eye was almost swollen shut, and drips of blood stained the front of his white shirt. He was missing his jacket, and his pants, normally a light tan and pressed within an inch of their life, now sported a ripped knee and dark smears of an indeterminate origin. Bessa tilted his head to look at her with his one good eye. "How did you get here? The last I saw of you, you were over the shoulder of some ugly pirate captain while the rest of his crew jettisoned us off our own ship."

"Hey, now." Quin moved to stand beside Bea. "I'm right here. No need to say rude things about me."

Bea rolled her eyes, something she'd done more since meeting

Quin than ever in her life. Okay, so that wasn't quite true — her daughter's teenage years still held the title — but it was as if he'd made it his life's purpose to get under her skin. Maybe the trolls would sell him off soon. If karma was kind, he'd wind up thrown into a deep pit and have to wrestle giant slugs for the entertainment of the masses. She'd bring popcorn, though it was a toss-up as to if she'd root for him or the slugs.

"It's a long story." Exhaustion pulled at her, weighing her body down and dulling her senses when she needed to remain sharp. She leaned her forehead against the cold bars and took a deep breath. Too many months on the run, of trying to figure out what happened and why, of putting on a positive front while giving her daughter only the bare details of the troubles that had befallen her and reassuring Essy it would all work out, of trying to convince her sister not to do anything risky or dramatic to clear her name was taking its toll. She'd started to think that her life might never return to normal when Ghost contacted her, giving her a kernel of hope. And then came the pirates and surprise trolls to fuck it up. She was so over it all.

Breathe in. Count to five. Breathe out. Do it again until you're more peaceful and centered. Bea heard her therapist's calm voice in her head and, closing her eyes, took several beats to do just that.

It helped, but she still felt the exhaustion right down to her bones. Too much stress and too many situations over which she had zero control. It wasn't good for her blood pressure and at this very moment, she just wanted to get out of this cell, curl up in a comfortable bed under a fluffy blanket, and forget about everything. But she wouldn't. She couldn't. Not yet. She deserved answers. She deserved to have her life back, to have a chance to hug her daughter again, and to find justice.

She took one more deep breath, opened her eyes. Okay. One problem at a time. "So, what do these trolls want with us, anyway?" she asked. "I'm assuming it's nothing good."

"Sell us, kill us, eat us," someone in the cage across from theirs recited in a melodic, childish voice. "Captives come and captives go. Once you leave through that door, you never come back."

Bea peered into the darkness, trying to see who was there, but they remained tucked away in their cell's inky shadows.

Quin crossed his arms. He was close enough that, if she wanted, she could lean over and rest her head against his shoulder. She wondered if he'd let her. She could really use a hug right about now, even if it was from a scruffy pirate. "Wonderful," he said. "Getting eaten by biker trolls was just what I planned to do today."

She groaned. "Could you maybe leave off the sarcasm, at least until we get out of here? It's tiring." Except it wasn't. Arguing with Quin was strangely energizing and made her bold in ways she hadn't been in quite a while. Granted, she still didn't trust him, wasn't sure if she entirely liked him, and wanted to see him in that slug-wrestling pit, but bantering with him was better than a double shot of caffeine.

It would certainly make things easier if she could put her trust in him at least a little. After all, he hadn't really done anything to harm her physically. Embarrass her, yes. Treat her like an object, pretty much. But she didn't have a single injury because of his treatment. And he'd apologized for it all. Not a great apology, but he'd taken direction and he'd tried. She gave him some credit for that.

"I do apologize, Buttercup." Quin sketched an exaggerated bow. "Whatever your flowery heart desires."

"What I want to do is find a way out of this dungeon so we won't discover what happens when they drag us out of here. I have no desire to be eaten today." She paused, contemplating. "Or any day, actually."

A slow smile crept across his face as he slowly ran his eyes down her body. "Now, that's a shame. I bet you taste delicious."

Said body heated as little sparks of desire danced along her spine. She blushed. Resisting the urge to roll her eyes yet again, she said, "Get your mind out of the gutter, pirate." She did her best not to imagine the feel of his tongue sweeping up her neck.

His smile grew. "But the gutter is where I work best."

She humphed, trying to ignore the dangerous sparkle in his eyes. "Considering your manners, I'm not surprised." She examined the cell lock. "I'm pretty sure I can pick this. Like the cuffs, the locking mechanism is decidedly low tech. But you'll need to come up with a plan to get us out the rest of the way so we don't end up troll chow."

"Working on it, Buttercup. Though, maybe if you weren't so mean to me all the time, I'd think better." He must really believe he was being charming with that deliciously scruffy shadow of a beard and that twinkle in his eyes.

"Oh, fuck off," she said, but with no accompanying heat. She'd have to find a way out of this mess herself. Typical. A man comes along, promising he's here to rescue you and protect you, and all that happens is you wind up in deeper shit than you started.

He put his hands over his ears and tutted. "Language."

She rolled her eyes. "Captain Bessa, the pirate here tells me that you planned to collect a bounty on me and that he saved me from you. Is that right?" Why was she asking him? It wasn't like he was going to implicate himself. But she needed something to prove the pirate wrong, even if it was an affronted denial.

Captain Bessa stepped back from the bars so she couldn't see him. Slow drips of water plonked onto a rock nearby. The silence grew until it was nearly tangible, and she had the dawning realization that Quin might actually be telling the truth about the need for a rescue. After all, if someone accused you of taking a bounty on them and you didn't, wouldn't your first response be to deny it? But no words came from her former captain.

Bea jumped when Quin smacked the bars with a loud clang. "Bessa. Answer the woman. She deserves to know the truth."

There was a long pause, then Bessa said, "Yes and no."

Quin barked out a "Ha! Told you," pointed at her, and did a

little shuffle in what she guessed was supposed to be a dance of victory. Who knew the ways of pirates?

"What does that mean?" She squeezed the bars, wishing she could bend them, grab Bessa's extremely hard head and knock it around until the answers she needed spilled out. "Yes, you took a contract to kill me? To capture me? Neither of those? Why would someone take a contract out on me in the first place?"

"I can think of several reasons," Quin muttered, his breath warm against her ear.

She shot him a glare, ignoring the pleasurable shiver that shot through her at his proximity. *Dammit, body! Stop reacting to the pirate. Now is not the time.*

A bounty was typical for bringing in someone fleeing a murder charge, but what if this was something else? Maybe whoever issued it had learned of her interaction with Ghost and feared what she would uncover once they exchanged information. If so, it was even more crucial she make it to that meeting on Badin.

"It means that he took the contract, ma'am," the ship's pilot answered. Victor was an older, lean man with dark brown skin and solemn eyes. Resting his forearms on top of the horizontal brace across the bars, he gave Bea a nod, then reached behind him to pull the captain back into the flickering torchlight, staring at Bessa until he answered.

"I was never going to space you or anything like that, I promise. The job was to transport and deliver, not kill," the captain said, his tone quickly edging towards a whine as he cowered from Victor. "I just took the money because I have debts and, well, it's a lot of money, especially since I didn't have to split it with anyone. Nobody got hurt."

"Good to know that my life isn't cheap, at least," she murmured.

"I could have told you that, Daisy." Quin's voice was a whisper against her ear. She felt a flash of gratitude towards the man and almost thanked him. He added, "I'd pay someone a great deal of money to take you off my hands, too."

She elbowed him in the stomach.

Quin huffed out a quiet laugh but didn't move from his position at her back. If she didn't know any better, she'd say the looming was an effort to lend support.

Doing her best to pretend the warmth of his presence against her back wasn't comforting, Bea asked, "Who paid you, Captain Bessa? How were you contacted? What do they want from me? Victor, were you involved in any of this?"

Bessa remained quiet, and Bea felt her face heat as anger coursed through her veins. She'd trusted this man, had thought him to be a jackass overall but still, a solid captain who was desperate enough to hire her with minimal references and no questions about who she was beyond her ability to keep the engine spinning. How wrong she'd been. She wondered what else she'd gotten wrong because of her faulty instinct for dangerous situations. Her sister wouldn't have been fooled like this.

Victor said, "The crew, we didn't know about any of this bounty stuff. It was just a regular run for us. I would never have let him get away with it, I promise you that." His voice was heavy with anger as he grabbed Bessa by the back of his neck and pressed him against the bars. "Answer her questions. All of them. Now," Victor said with a growl. He was pretty good at the intimidation thing. Bea knew him as a quiet, capable man who liked tea and shared a pot of his red brew with her every afternoon when he came off shift. This wasn't a side she'd seen before. She appreciated it.

Doing his best to shrink away from Victor, Bessa said in a shaky voice, "I don't know who paid me! Or who took out the contract, I swear. Just that you have something they want. It's why they want you alive, so see, I wasn't going to space you or I wouldn't get paid."

Nice. She was going to punch that man right in the nose when she got out of here. "You asshole!" She stuck her arm through the bars and shook her fist at him. "You're lucky we're both locked up." She rattled the bars of her cage.

"Keep talking, Bessa." Victor pressed the captain tighter against the bars.

"Okay! Okay. So I was having a drink when we docked at Cora Station when an old colleague of mine sat down at my table. Said he knew about my debts and how debts like that could bring a man serious pain. Said he knew of a way I could take care of those debts without too much trouble, if I was interested. Well, of course I was interested. He gives me a photo of you, tells me where you were and to go get you. I was supposed to bring you to Badin, and they'd contact me with drop-off coordinates." He lifted his hands in supplication. "I don't know more than that. Please."

Victor released his grip, and the captain sagged into a crouch.

"And how did you manage to convince your crew to take a trip all the way out to the colony without them suspecting?" Quin asked.

"Easy enough. Picked up a run hauling supplies out to the colony, then ore back." He snuck a glance up at Victor. "Nothing different from what we usually do. No one suspected a thing."

"That's because, as our captain, we trusted you to be straight with us and not do shady shit like taking a bounty on some unsuspecting person," Victor said, his voice gruff with anger that echoed against the cave walls. "I'm sorry, Bea."

"Not your fault but thanks." She sank down onto the large worn rock in the corner of their cell, pulling her knees up to her chest and wrapping her arms around her legs. Though she'd only been a temporary crew member and didn't know any of them very well, Bessa's betrayal was one straw too many. How could she possibly trust anyone after what she'd been through? It would take a miracle.

8

QUIN

Bea visibly deflated when Bessa confirmed he'd taken the contract on her. It was like watching a bright and shining star get sucked into a black hole. He crouched down next to her, tentatively placing a hand on her knee.

She didn't look up at him, burrowing deeper into the comfort of her folded arms. "Please don't. I don't need you doing the whole 'I told you so' thing right now," she said, her voice muffled.

He had no such intentions, though he understood why she might think so. He removed his hand and stood. "I'm going to get us out of here, Bea. I promise."

Pulling herself into a tighter ball, she nodded and let out a sniffle. "You do that."

Shit. Was she crying? Watching this woman who'd fought like a hellion from the moment he'd laid eyes on her crumple under the weight of Bessa's betrayal made his heart clench. He frowned at his reaction. It had to be the heightened adrenaline or a stress response or something, this strange solid weight squeezing his heart as he gazed down at her bent head. He'd have to get their doc-in-a-box to give him a once-over when he got back onboard the *Laughing Dragon*. It could be a side effect from the concussion. After all, it hadn't even been a full day since they were locked in here. Certainly not long enough for him to fully heal from his injury.

Giving her the space she requested to pull herself together, he mirrored Victor's pose, leaning his arms on the crossbar. Why was he having such an extreme reaction to her? For years, he'd avoided entanglements, finding comfort in the warm arms of women around the system who were just looking for some fun. His odd response to Bea and her distress was out of character for him. However, he understood the toll betrayal took, having experienced it himself when the woman he loved screwed over not only him but his entire crew, sabotaging their efforts to take down their corrupt Starguard captain. Due to her actions, they'd lost their commissions and very nearly spent the rest of their days breaking rocks on a Melorian prison moon. It was only because of the Knight that they were free men. So, yeah. Betrayal by someone you trusted was soul crushing.

As he watched her out of the corner of his eye, she lifted her head and scrubbed her hands over her face, visibly pulling herself back together. A burst of pride at her fortitude had him clenching his jaw against the sensation. She was a job, nothing more. He needed to maintain his distance. Or so he told himself.

Shaking his head, he decided he was not about to get involved with her any more than he already was. She wanted a plan? Here was the plan: survive, escape, contact his crew, maybe bang it out in a nice room if she was into it while they waited for pickup so he could get her out of his system, and dump her in Rhain's lap, fulfilling their contract and clearing their ledger of favors owed. Then he'd be on his merry way. Yeah, that would work. He cleared his throat, addressing the mysterious voice in the cell opposite theirs. "Hey. How often do the trolls visit?"

"Trolls bring one meal each day," said the soft voice in the cell across from his.

Quin squinted, trying to make out who was speaking, but dark shadows shrouded the cell. "What's your name?"

A pause. "Cassie."

"How do you know this, Cassie?" Quin asked, keeping his voice low and gentle, hoping they would keep talking to him, maybe even come out of the gloom so he could put a face with the name. "How long have you been here?"

A small huff of laughter. "Long enough. Cells were full when we were captured and thrown in here. Now almost empty, and no prisoner has returned." Quiet shuffling sounded in the cell, but no one approached the bars.

"But no one else will come tonight?"

"They already fed us this day, so most likely not." Another pause. "Not unless we draw attention."

"Thank you," he whispered before retreating to the back of the cell.

Quin sat down on the rock next to Bea, shifting as he tried to find a spot where a stony lump didn't dig into his ass. "Not big on comfort here, are they?" he said, trying to lighten the mood. He hated to see her so disheartened, especially after the fight she gave him up until now.

Bea sniffled and shook her head at his question.

He bumped her with his shoulder. "Come on, hellion. Buck up. Maybe some of those big trolls will drag Bessa off for a meal, and we won't have to listen to his sniveling."

She snuffled out a small laugh, still not looking at him.

"And you know he'd give them indigestion." He took a chance and put an arm around her, trying to give her a little comfort as he attempted to charm her out of her despair. He didn't enjoy seeing her this way. Instead of pushing him away, she leaned into his embrace. She must be more shattered than she was letting on. "If we're lucky, he'll give them the trots."

She snuffle-laughed again. "That would teach them," she said in a watery voice, turning to rub her face against his chest.

Surprised at the quick leveling up in her affection, he looked down at her and realized what was actually going on. "Are you wiping your snot on my shirt?"

She sniffled and gave her nose one more rub on his shirt. "No.

Whatever gave you that idea?" she said, not looking at him, but he could hear the smile in her voice.

Ah, that was more like it. His charm offensive had worked, even if it had resulted in more snot than he'd hoped. "Liar." He shifted until he'd wedged his back into the corner, his legs stretched out in front of him. Not comfortable, but it would have to do. "Come on." He patted his chest and accidentally touched the wet spot she'd left on his shirt. With a grimace, he wiped his fingers on his pants.

Her brow wrinkled. "What?" She smoothed down a flyaway hair and ran the back of her hand over her eyes, wiping away the remains of her tears. "You want me to sleep with you?"

"Technically, you'll be sleeping next to me, and we'll be sharing body heat to keep warm. In case you hadn't noticed, there's no bed, no blankets, and definitely no heat in this place." He made another adjustment so his back wasn't at such a weird angle, closed his eyes, and held out an arm in offering. "Figured we could set aside our differences at least for one night and maybe get some sleep. I always function better when I've had a little shut-eye." Besides, the dull throb behind his eyes was reminding him it hadn't been a smooth journey to get here, and his body needed to recover. Also, they needed an escape plan so they wouldn't wind up in the trolls' soup pot, but his brain was essentially non-functional at the moment. He literally couldn't come up with more than "get free and don't get eaten" to save their lives.

She was quiet for a moment. "Fine. But keep your hands to yourself." She scooted forward, aligning her body with his, and tucked her head against his shoulder.

He wrapped an arm around her, his hand coming to rest on her hip.

She put a hand over his. "I swear I will stab you in the eye if those hands wander even a little bit."

"That's as far as those fingers are going, I promise." He held himself still as she settled in, enjoying the feel of her soft body resting against his, her warmth permeating his skin.

He felt her body relax, and she took a deep breath, letting it out slowly. "Quin?" His name was a softly exhaled whisper.

"Mmm?"

"You swear you boarded the *Intrepid* to help me?"

"I swear on my mother's honor."

"And that you and those pirates of yours are supposed to protect me, not turn me over to whoever put this bounty out on me in the first place?"

"We're privateers," he corrected. "But yes. Save and protect." And bring her to the Knight on Gyan Station, but that was included in the protection plan. He just didn't have the energy to get into it right now, so he kept it simple. He'd tell her everything pertinent. Eventually. "You can trust me with your life, I promise."

"Mmm." It wasn't outright acknowledgement, but it also wasn't denial. He could work with that. "You know I still don't like you, right?" she said, her voice drowsy. She threw an arm across his waist and snuggled closer.

"Absolutely the same for me, Daisy," he murmured into her hair. "Don't like you either." And with the smell of her sweet-spiciness lingering in his nostrils, he fell asleep.

9

BEA

Bea blinked her eyes open, trying to get a handle on why she was so warm and comfortable when she knew damned well she was in a cell of rock and iron with no creature comforts. Her vision filled with a broad chest, the steady beat of a heart under her palm. Ah. Because she was sprawled in a most indelicate manner directly on top of the scruffy pirate. It was all coming back to her. He offered her comfort; she accepted it. Hells, she wasn't an idiot. If they hadn't shared body heat, neither of them would have gotten any sleep because they'd be huddled in respective balls on the stone floor, shivering. If she were a delicate lady, she'd be scrambling off him, but instead she had to fight the urge to nestle into the warmth of his chest and go back to sleep.

Her stomach growled.

"You finally awake?" Quin shifted under her slightly, his arm draped across her back. "I'm guessing you had a comfortable night with me as your mattress."

She lifted her head to see him looking at her, a smile on his lips and a twinkle in his eyes. Something long, warm, and hard pressed against her belly. Morning wood. Typical male. Trapped in a cell with the threat of death-by-troll hanging over your head? No problem. *The pirate can still get it up.* She decided not to mention it. Ignore it and it would go away, right? Eventually, anyway.

Playing it casual, she said, "Hey, you offered," as she nudged his arm off her and "accidentally" elbowed him in the chest as she slid off him and scrubbed at her eyes. Quin was softer than the stone floor, but not by much.

She swallowed, her parched throat protesting the action. What she wouldn't give for some water and a private place to take care of her business. Instead, there was the slow drip from a stalactite and a bucket in the corner of their cell.

"Quin, would you go stand over there, back to me, and cover your ears?" she asked, pointing to the corner opposite the bucket.

Still lounging on the rock, his fingers laced behind his head, he raised an eyebrow.

"It's morning." She sighed when he didn't shift positions. Did she have to spell it out for him? Obviously. "I have to pee, and I'd like to at least pretend that I have a modicum of privacy."

Without a word, he pushed himself up off their stone bed with a groan, pressing a hand to his lower back as he stretched, his hips and morning wood jutting towards her, before doing as she asked.

He did that on purpose, if that eye twinkle was anything to go by. Rolling her eyes at his roguish behavior, she did her business, then traded places so he could do the same.

That out of the way, she asked, "How's the head?" She should have kept a better eye on him and his concussion. She was a terrible caregiver.

"Better." He put a hand under his chin and pushed at it, his neck making sharp crackles in the quiet cell. He let out a sigh of relief. "Throbbing's gone, so that's good." He dropped to the floor and cranked out a series of push-ups, the muscles in his arms and back flexing with each press.

It was a lot of activity so soon after waking up. She preferred her mornings slow and contemplative, with plenty of caffeine, before she could function. However, she wasn't about to complain. If Quin was going to provide in-cell entertainment, she'd take full advantage. It gave her something to watch as she dealt with the bird's nest her hair had morphed into. "We need to get out of here. Today." She worked her fingers through the strands, wincing when they caught on a knot, before plaiting her semi-detangled locks into a fishtail and securing the ends with a band. Ghost's deadline was fast approaching. She could feel the clock ticking away in the back of her mind. The longer she spent in this cell and stuck on this planet, the smaller her chances of getting to Badin on time. She doubted Ghost would reschedule if she missed this meeting.

Quin grunted, continuing his morning workout. "You have a plan?"

"You mean you don't? And here I thought you were supposed to be this big, bad pirate with all the answers." Moving back to sit on their rock, she watched him flex and twist his way through a series of moves like they were second nature.

"Privateer," he absently reminded her, throwing punches as he ducked and wove against an invisible opponent. "Usually, our jobs are pretty straightforward: we stir up some chaos, blow shit up, and make our getaway while everyone runs around trying to figure out what happened." He grunted out a vicious series of jabs. "What are your thoughts? I'm pretty sure your brain hasn't stopped thinking since I tossed you over my shoulder."

She frowned. "Yeah, that really sucked, by the way."

He paused in his shadow boxing, turning to face her with a serious look on his face. "I really do apologize for manhandling you like that. If it makes you feel any better, Ivan scolded me for it." He resumed his workout muttering, "Mother hen."

"Well, thanks for that. And thanks to Ivan." Another apology, this time with no caveat. Appreciated and unexpected, especially from someone who'd acted like a barbarian for much of the time she'd known him. A very well-proportioned and deliciously muscled barbarian at that. *Ugh, brain. Stop. Escape. That's what we need to focus on. Not the hot man you're stuck in a cell with.*

Clearing her throat, Bea said, "Once I get the doors unlocked, stirring shit up might be just what we need." The locks were the least of her worries. It was what was beyond those doors that made escape of any kind a challenge way beyond her skill set.

"Cassie," he waved a hand towards the cell across from theirs, "said someone comes once a day with food, so we'll need to wait at least that long. If we try to escape before then, we have a much higher risk of getting caught." He gave another grunt, spinning into a high kick that could probably take a human's head off.

"Alright, but we're leaving today. Tonight. Whatever time it is after the food troll comes," she said, her voice firm. She couldn't afford to wait any longer than that. It would have to be good enough.

"Ideally, I'd like to wait until I can establish a pattern of the guards to minimize the risk." He glanced at her. "Why are you in such a rush to get out of here, anyway?"

Gesturing at their accommodations, she said, "You want to stay here? It's not exactly homey. Plus, the longer we're in here, the greater our chance of experiencing the whole death-by-troll thing. I'd prefer to avoid that."

"True, but that's not what I meant." He ended his workout with a series of cool-down stretches, leaning to the side and stretching one long arm over his head. "You're not just concerned about what might happen with the trolls." He switched sides, curving his body in the other direction, his shirt sliding up to reveal a mouthwatering expanse of ribbed stomach. "It's like your brain is already out of these cells and somewhere else, like you're under a time crunch or something."

"That's because I am under a time crunch." Bea pressed her lips together tightly. Shit. She hadn't meant to share that. Not with him. Not yet. Possibly never, if she could get away from him.

He stopped his stretching and moved to crouch in front of her, bracing his hands on either side of her thighs. A light sheen of sweat covered his skin, and she batted away the impulse to lean forward and lick the salt-flavored skin along his jawline. Damned libido.

His dark eyes shone with intensity. "You know you can trust me, right? I made that promise to you last night, and I meant it. I have one job right now and that is to keep you safe." Flicking back a lock of hair that curled over his forehead, he added, "But I can't protect you if you run off because you have plans you won't share with me. So please. Tell me. What do you need to do so urgently?"

It would be such a relief not to have to shoulder all this by herself. But these days, there were so few people she trusted. Her entire life, her big sister had always been there for her, the one to help her through rough waters. Though Dai's job had been dangerous and secretive, she always found a way to be there when her little sister needed her. Bea's very own fixer. However, with Dai stuck on the other side of the galaxy and only available through delayed comm links and double super-secret coded messages, Bea was on her own. The idea of adding Quin to the list of those she trusted with her life and her future, even temporarily, would be a huge leap of faith, especially so soon after Bessa's betrayal.

But at this point, what did she have to lose? She needed help, and it would be nice to have someone for backup on this desperate quest of hers. At least if she dragged Quin into her drama and things went horribly wrong, someone would know what happened to her.

Fuck it. She was going to have to put some trust in him. Maybe it would be a mistake and, despite his heartfelt assurances, he'd betray her or leave her or turn her over to the authorities for a fat paycheck at some point. Maybe he wouldn't. Either way, at the moment, they had a common goal: to get out of this prison. Good enough for now. Swallowing hard, she asked, "How much do you know?"

"My client gave me a file."

She wasn't sure how to feel about this unidentified someone

compiling a file on her. Annoyed, for one. But that wasn't Quin's fault. Curious, she asked, "What does it say?"

Settling back onto his haunches, he rested his arms on his drawn-up knees. "Beatrix Farsirus, age 45. Advanced degrees in mechanical, aerospace, and chemical engineering. Self-employed. One daughter: Essalin, age 20, in her first year at University of Waroc on Melorn, major: undecided. Sister: Daiana Farsirus, age 60. Forcibly retired two years ago from the Melorian Service Unit, aka the Unit. Last known romantic partner: Arden deVan, age 38. Deceased." He paused in his recitation to gauge her reaction.

Most of what he had was readily available, though she was surprised he had any details at all on her sister. "Okay, what else?"

"Fourteen standard months ago, local authorities declared deVan dead in the fire that also destroyed your workshop which also housed prototypes for a new type of propulsion system you're designing."

She tensed at the mention of her system. Very few people knew about her work. Only Dai knew that her design was an advanced propulsion technology that, if she got it to work and didn't blow herself up in the process, should create a longer-lasting reaction for cheaper than what was currently on the market. Whomever compiled the dossier was talented. She'd be sure to let Dai know that someone had more information than they should. Someone must have cracked the encryption on their messages to have all that.

He continued, detailing her arrest and the attack in prison. "After you fled, a collection bounty was issued on top of the warrant for your arrest." He quirked an eyebrow at her, a half-smile on his handsome face. "How'd I do?"

"You got the crux of it." Though she doubted that was the extent of his knowledge. He knew more than he was saying. Crossing her legs, she unsuccessfully tried to find a more comfortable position. "But who supplied you with this dossier? And how did you get involved? You claim you didn't take the bounty, so then what?"

He tutted, waggling a finger at her. "A sharing of information. It's your turn. Deal?"

Trust. She told herself she was going to take a leap and put some trust in him. That meant filling in the gaps of his knowledge so he could actually be helpful. "Fine." She let out a heavy sigh, not loving the feeling of opening. It made her vulnerable.

Raising his eyebrows, he said, "Is it really that hard to put some faith in me? I'm crushed."

"Doubtful. But, yes. This is hard for me." She tucked a stray curl behind her ear. "What do you want to know?"

"Why don't we start easy? Tell me about Arden. How did you two meet?"

She gave a small nod. "Well, I'd just spoken at the Engineering College in Waroc and was relaxing with a glass of wine at my hotel when he sidled up and bought me a drink. We got to talking and, I don't know, just kind of clicked." Upon reflection, the ease at which Arden charmed and flattered her into a relationship startled her. "It moved fast after that first meeting — we started seeing one another, and before I realized it, he'd moved in."

Before Arden, she'd been too focused on her daughter and her work to even think about a relationship. But he slid so seamlessly into her life. He coaxed her out of the workshop and fed her when she hyper-focused on her project for too long, encouraged her to talk about the progress of her system, and reassured her when she came home disheartened after another dead end or failure. "It was just so easy with him, you know?"

Even though he didn't, Quin nodded. "You were together for how long?"

"About a year." She shrugged. "Not that long, in the grand scheme of things. And, to be honest, the relationship started falling apart a couple of months before his death."

"What happened?"

With a sigh, she said, "Like what happens at the end of many relationships. We were arguing about everything from him drinking the last of my favorite breakfast tea and not reordering it to me working too hard and ignoring him. He began to resent the time I spent at the workshop and made sure I was aware of it." She shook her head, thinking of the red flags she'd ignored because she'd been wrapped up in her project and dealing with relationship drama was too much after a long day. He'd gotten verbally aggressive a couple of times, demanding she tell him exactly what she was doing, to prove that she was working on the engine. Maybe he'd thought she was cheating on him, rather than puzzling over engine components. "Nothing like the kind, supportive man he was at the beginning of our relationship."

He gave her another encouraging nod. "And then the fire happened."

"The fire." Even now, she didn't like thinking about it. Though she kept backups of her meticulous notes, the loss of her space and everything in it, not to mention Arden, made her heart ache. "Arden and I had a big fight a couple of days before about some money missing from my accounts. I accused him of stealing from me. Harsh words were exchanged. We broke up. He packed up his things that night and didn't come back, wouldn't return my messages." She spoke quickly, working to remain detached. He didn't need to know the pain behind the events, just what happened. "I had no idea where he was or even if he was coming back. Then I did what I always do when I'm stressed or worried — I went to my workshop, hoping to lose myself in work. But I was too anxious to focus, too unsettled, so I set the alarms, headed home, had a glass of whiskey, and went to bed." Bea drew her legs up to her chest, hugging them. "My building was in an industrial zone that's pretty deserted at night. By the time I got a call, the blaze was so hot it melted the walls of the surrounding buildings. I got there in time to see all my work disappear into ash."

She shook the smell of hot metal and the heat of flames from her mind. "Even before the arson investigator wrote up his report, I knew it was no accident. Neither natural nor electric fires burn that hot without help, and I'm paranoid about safety. I had backup measures for my backup measures. All of those were disabled. They were working fine when I set them just a few hours earlier."

"And then?" he asked, his voice gentle as he pulled the story from her.

"They found a tooth in the ashes." Her voice caught, and she cleared her throat. They may have been fighting, their relationship over, but she certainly hadn't wanted Arden dead. "How did a tooth survived that inferno? Why was Arden at my workshop? How could they possibly think that I torched a decade's worth of work, killed my ex-lover, and burned his body along with my workshop?" A tear rolled down her cheek to splat on the rock as she voiced questions she had no answers to. "I never killed anyone." She hated how small her voice sounded. Avoiding his eyes, she focused on the dark spot left by her tears.

"I mean, you're pretty fierce when you want to be. Both my ass and my balls can attest to that," Quin said, his voice lightly teasing.

She gave a wet snort, pinching the bridge of her nose to stop the prickle behind her eyes.

"You're fierce, but you're no killer. Did they say why you, someone who had never been in trouble with the law, would suddenly decide to commit these crimes?"

"Money," she sniffled, feeling more tears waiting to spill. Fuck. Why was she crying about this now? It was one vulnerability too many in front of someone she hardly knew. Taking several deep breaths, she scrubbed her cheeks with the back of her hands and willed away the rest of the lurking tears. "Someone made a huge deposit of credits into my private account the day of the fire. I have no idea who and, since all of my accounts are now frozen and inaccessible, I can't even look into it." Dai had someone try to hack the bank's system, but it was locked down tight. "The lead inspector suggested I killed Arden because he'd discovered my nefarious plans, whatever those are." She let out a damp giggle. It was all too ridiculous. "He actually used the word 'nefarious'."

"What a prat." Quin shook his head. "Is he the one who had you arrested you and stuck in that jail cell?"

She nodded, lifting the sleeve of her shirt to wipe her face.

"He's definitely on our shit list, then." He reached over and patted her knee. "I'm blaming him for almost getting you killed."

So she was right. He had more knowledge than he was sharing. She eyed him. "You know about me getting stabbed in jail, then?"

At least he had the sense to look chagrined. "At breakfast, no less."

Pursing her lips, she said, "That file has more details in it than you shared, didn't it?"

"Yes," he said, dusting off his pants and avoiding meeting her eyes. "I also know that your sister broke you out of that medi-ward and supplied you with new ident papers, Mala Jones." He winked when he said her fake name.

Fuck. Who was giving him this information? So much for all their precautions. Someone spying on them. Dai was going to be so pissed. She felt stripped to the bone, laid bare to this man she'd only just decided to reveal her secrets to.

Carefully, as if expecting her to push him away, Quin slid onto the rock beside her. "But I still don't know why you're on this timeline of yours."

She didn't answer.

In response to her silence, he reached over and took her hand in his. "I'm sorry this happened to you, Daisy. Let me help you try to fix it."

He didn't press her, didn't make any moves or teasing comments. He merely sat next to her on the most painful rock in the galaxy, holding her hand.

All these months on the run, she'd been holding herself together with pieces of string and willpower. His unexpected kindness and empathy shattered her.

She drew a shaky breath. "Someone promised me information to help me clear my name."

10

QUIN

Those big honey-brown eyes of hers brought him to his knees. When he'd seen the sheen of tears in them, his heart clenched. Quin didn't think she was aware of her impact on him or how quickly she'd gotten under his skin. When he asked her to trust him, she almost broke out in hives. And then he almost blew it when he let slip how much the Knight's file on her contained. By Bea trusting him, opening up to him even though he could see how hard it was for her, shit, he was ready to share everything, to crack open his soul, and to slay trolls to help and protect her.

Instead of gathering her up in his arms and telling her that everything was going to work out which, frankly at this point might be a blatant lie, he asked, "And what did you exchange for the information this person promised?" Because there was no way that someone would just give away critical information for free. Everything had a cost.

She shrugged as if it were no big deal, though her fingers reflexively clenched around his hand. "I'm making a delivery for them."

Oh, this could be bad. "Delivery? For who? And what in the three hells are you delivering that we didn't find it on you?"

Frowning, he gave her a once-over. What in the stars could it be and, even more intriguing, where had she hidden it?

A half-smile twisting her lips, she said, "I'm not hiding it there, if that's what you're thinking." She rubbed her palms against the rough fabric of her pants. "Have you ever heard of an information broker who goes by the name of Ghost?"

"Not an overly creative name," he said. Information and those who sold it was really more his cousin's thing. "And not one I recognize."

"Doesn't matter anyway. I'm delivering a data dot, encrypted and untraceable, according to the source. I don't have much time until I'm due on Badin for the exchange, which is why I need to get out of here now."

He opened his mouth to ask what the information was, but she cut him off with a wave of her hand and jumped up to pace the small space. "No, I haven't tried to access it. No, I don't know what's on it. And no, I don't trust this Ghost." She squared her shoulders. "But I'm desperate. I just want to go home, return to my life, to my daughter and my work. So it's a chance I'm willing to take." She spun on her heel and raised an eyebrow, daring him to say how foolish she was being.

That was a trap that he would not fall into. She'd trusted him; he was going to trust her. And, if it all went wrong, he'd do his damndest to protect her. "Then that's what we'll do."

"What?"

"Break out of here and get you to your meet on time." A shit plan — less a plan than a nebulous idea — but better than staying here. He adjusted his original list. He still needed to contact his crew and keep Bea safe. But now, he also needed to get the both of them to Badin for Bea's meet before finally bringing her back to base as requested, fulfilling their contract with the Knight. Easy as pie.

It was possible that whatever his cousin wanted with Bea had something to do with the data she was transporting but, since the man had given no further instructions beyond "keep her safe" and "bring her to me", Quin couldn't be held responsible for things that might be lost or traded during the interim. At least, that was the story he was going with. "You said you can get those locks open, right? Because if not, we're stuck here until the trolls decide otherwise or we rot."

Still baffled by his sudden burst of enthusiasm, she stared at him.

"Come on, Daisy. I'm in this now." He propped a leg up. "Let's get you out of here so you can do what you need to do. Badin is calling. And I'll be there to make sure you don't get into any more trouble. You do your job, and I'll do mine. It's a win-win." He gave her a wink, pleased at the flush of pink that colored her cheeks when he did it.

"But..." She paused, gathering her thoughts. "I still don't understand who hired you or why you keep claiming you're here to protect me. Protect me from what?"

"Don't worry about that right now. Just know that you're safe with me. You can trust me, remember?" Internally, he winced. Constantly repeating that she could trust him was probably the least effective way to convince her to actually trust him. It sounded fake, like he was trying to trick her. Eventually, he'd have to trust her in the same way he was asking her to trust him.

"The more times you say that, the less I trust you," she grumbled.

Shit.

She leaned back against the bars and crossed her arms across her chest. "Anyway, this was supposed to be an even exchange. I showed you mine; it's time you showed me yours. Who are you?"

"Ah, so you want my CV, do you?"

"I think I've earned that, at the very least."

"Indeed you have." He couldn't tell her everything, though. Some stories were not his own, and some secrets were not his alone to share. He resettled himself, sprawling out on the floor, his back propped against the rock. "Years ago, when I was an idealistic young man, I joined the Starguard, determined to protect the galaxy. There, I met and worked with other idealistic young men and, for a while, we did just that. However, all good things must come to an end." He was leaving out so much. He knew it wasn't fair that he'd asked her to bare all her deep, dark secrets to him, and he wasn't doing the same, even though he said he would. Maybe it was his way of pushing her away, not letting her get too close. If she didn't see the worst parts of him and his life, he could still treat her like a job instead of something more. "After the 'Guard, we decided, since we worked so well together, to stay together and turn our skills to freelancing."

She shot him a dark look, as if she knew what he was doing. But she didn't call him out on it. Instead, she asked, "Any family?"

Surprised that was her next question, he said, "I'm one of five siblings. According to my mother, I'm the rebel of the family because I prefer, as she puts it, 'gallivanting around space with my friends' rather than settling down and giving her grandbabies to spoil." Laughing, he scrubbed a hand through his hair, wincing when he accidentally bumped his bruise. "I feel like I'm filling out a connect-with-a-partner app."

"Too bad for you that you're not my type," she said with a sniff.

"You sure about that?" he teased. "You seemed pretty comfy last night when we slept together."

"Haha. Funny." Her cheeks turned a rosy pink. "It was a choice between staying warm or sleeping on a rock."

He enjoyed making her blush. "I'm a little offended you didn't think I was rock... hard."

Fighting a smile, she said, "You're ridiculous."

"I do my best." He sketched out a bow from his position on the floor.

"How did you wind up here?"

"Well, see, there was this woman that I was trying to rescue..."

She rolled her eyes, something she seemed to do often. Maybe it was just with him.

Holding up his hands, he said, "Okay, okay. It's a little complicated." He blew out a breath. He might not be ready to share his sordid Starguard history, but he could give her important information about who set him on this path in the first place. "First, have you heard of someone called The Knight?"

"Speaking of a name with no creativity. I'm guessing he thinks he's a knight?" She shrugged. "No. No idea who that is."

"He's a powerful man, someone who collects and brokers information. Anyway, my crew and I, we owed him..."

Her eyes lit with interest. "Ooh, what for? Is he like a mob boss or something and you owe him because you recklessly gambled away your family's fortune? Or he helped you hide a body? Ooh, I know! He saved you from a life in jail for some truly heinous crime, right?"

"You should write stories in your spare time," he said, shaking his head. "The truth is much more boring. Let's just say he helped my crew and I out of a bad jam. In return, we owed him favors to be called in at his leisure." Internally, he winced at his continued evasion of the details.

"Favors?"

"Yeah, the man collects favors like little kids collect dirt. People — rich, poor, famous, unconnected — they all owe him favors. And he hordes them, like the dragons from which his clan claims they're descended." When her eyes widened, he shrugged. "One of the more famous myths of my world." Stories said that dragons once populated almost every continent on Dathria, co-existing with humans and sharing knowledge. Legend had it that their magic was the reason the planet was so fertile and lush, even though dragons had disappeared eons ago. He and Rhain had loved to hear those myths growing up, bribing the clan's bard into singing the same tales over and over.

"Dragons? Seriously? Interesting." She chewed on her bottom lip. "And what happens if you don't pay up when he calls in one of those favors?"

"Bad things," he said with a shake of his head. "You always pay up with the Knight calls in a favor. Everyone does."

"Very ominous. So, why me? How did snatching me become your favor?"

"Rescuing you," he corrected absently. "In all honesty, I have no idea why he's involved or interested in you, but our orders are to grab you from the *Intrepid* and deliver you to the safety of Gyan Station, our home base." No harm in telling her that, considering she'd be there soon enough.

She absorbed his words. "Deliver me, huh?" Her eyes got the distant look he was beginning to recognize as the wheels of her brain spinning. He shouldn't have told her that part, especially if it was going to make the delivery part of his job more difficult. She blinked, coming back to herself. "He really sounds like a mob boss, one of those old timey gangsters who would break your kneecaps if you didn't pay up on time."

He winced. She wasn't too far off. In fact, he was positive Rhain had cracked a few skulls and shattered a few kneecaps in his prime. He'd mellowed a little in his older age. "Anyway, we were happy to have the opportunity to erase a favor from his ledger. Though I definitely think this is worth more than just one favor." He muttered the last part to himself.

"What?" With a frown, she said, "That's really all you're going to tell me? No more sordid details about your past or who this Knight is?"

"Well, I mean, there was this one time when Ivan, Cormac, and I met these quadruplets in this bar in Waroc..."

Holding up her hands, she warded off his story. "Forget I asked." Her stomach growled and his answered in kind.

"I can only imagine what trolls think humans eat," he said.

Her jaw firmed. "I'm popping those locks as soon as that troll delivers the food. You have until then to come up with a plan that won't get us killed as soon as we step out of this dungeon."

Shit.

11

BEA

After bearing their souls — a glimpse into the darkness, anyway — they retreated to separate corners. Bea reclaimed the rock while Quin moved to take a seat against the bars and rest his forearms on his up-drawn knees, staring blankly at the floor.

Out of the corner of her eye, she watched as his head bobbed until his eyes finally drifted closed, his chin sinking to his chest. Between playing the role of her mattress and his concussion, she didn't think he'd gotten a lot of sleep last night. Pulling her thighs to her chest, she rested her cheek on a knee, her head tilted to watch him sleep, the quiet of the prison tunnel punctuated by his soft snuffling snores, the slow drip of water from the stalactites, and the occasional shuffle of feet.

She had to admit, her first impression of him was wrong. That's not to say he hadn't earned her anger or mistrust with the way he'd handled her "rescue", but she was coming around to the belief that he really wasn't here to make her life harder than it already was. For that, she was thankful.

She was also thankful that he seemed to be nothing like Arden. For one thing, Quin apologized, something she couldn't remember Arden ever doing. He offered her physical comfort, expecting nothing in return. He seemed to actually listen when she spoke, accepted criticism like with his apology, and didn't talk over her.

Arden... she sighed. If she'd been less focused on her work and paid more attention to Arden and their relationship, maybe she would have noticed something off earlier. But he'd been so nice at the start, so charming and considerate, showering her with little gifts like imported teas or a trinket he'd seen in a window that he claimed reminded him of her. He'd romanced the hells out of her.

And she'd welcomed it. Being on the receiving end of someone's attention was lovely. Single motherhood was tough and, even though Essy was the light of her soul, it hadn't been easy raising her brilliant, headstrong daughter who was so much like her Auntie Dai. Arden slid into her life and made himself indispensable.

But that Arden turned out to be an illusion, hadn't he? Because she now knew that the Arden of the first part of their relationship had been a front, a facade. Once he felt comfortable, that's when he showed his true colors, becoming demanding and aggressive, and stealing from her.

Closing her eyes, she pinched the bridge of her nose. Maybe she was reading too much into the last months of their time together. Their relationship had been coming to its inevitable conclusion, and if Arden hadn't died, it would have ended anyway.

But she didn't think so. There was something more going on. Her brain spun in circles like a toddler jacked up on sugar. She needed to accept that it all came back to her propulsion system. Maybe she was wrong, but after she'd caught him and stopped him from stealing from her account, Arden must have gone to her workshop that night to steal her tech. Her stomach turned at such a betrayal. Bad enough he'd stolen money from her, but her work? That cut deep.

When she started her project all those years ago, she'd only wanted to see if her theories actually produced a viable system. As she got closer to a working model, she began to see its potential, especially when Dai pointed out how naïve she was being regarding her system only being a side project. Once she got it functional, it would disrupt space travel as they knew it in so many ways.

Currently, Vanid Shipping controlled the industry, maintaining a tight grasp on the fuel pellets needed for interstellar jumps and long-distance travel. But her system would render those expensive pellets moot. Which meant that it could very well be someone within Vanid Shipping behind the charges against her and working with Arden. This mysterious someone might also be responsible for his death. Her skin dimpled as a cold chill swept up her spine. If so, she was in more trouble than she imagined. She acknowledged she didn't always see what was obvious to others. Engines and systems made sense to her; people and their motivations were baffling.

But if even a small portion of her guesswork was true, it only strengthened her need to make it on time to meet Ghost. Bea was tired of living in fear. She wanted answers and by the stars, she was going to get them if she had to take down every troll in this cave to do so.

The deep silence of the dungeon was broken by what sounded like a rockslide, jolting Bea from her deep musings and waking Quin. They cautiously rose to their feet, moving to stand shoulder to shoulder in the center of their cell.

The heavy prison door crashed open, and two trolls she hadn't seen before shuffled into view, one holding a torch and the other pushing a cart with trays on it.

"Hey." Bessa wrapped his hands around the bars. "Let us out of here. We can get you gold or gems. Whatever you want. Just let us go."

"They do not understand you," Cassie said. "No translators. Don't work on trolls. Rocks for brains."

"But the ones who brought us in spoke," Bea said, thinking of the barked orders.

"They only know enough words in Universal Standard to move the prisoners around," Cassie said.

The cart troll shoved two trays through a slot at the bottom of the cage. Bea watched as they moved down the line, shoving in trays. Six more trays. Six prisoners plus the two of them. People she couldn't just leave here to die when they broke out.

"I know what you're thinking," Quin said in a low tone, his breath warm against her ear. He too watched the trolls' slow progress back up to the prison entrance, the cart's wheels squeaking as it rolled along the grooves worn into the stone and out the door. "You can't save them all."

"Can, too." And nothing he said would change her mind. There was no way she could live with their deaths on her conscience, even if one of them had tried to turn her in for a bounty.

He sighed, resting his chin on her shoulder, his chest firm and warm against her back. "Each prisoner we take with us increases our chances of being caught exponentially."

"Well, we're just going to have to risk it." She crossed her arms over her chest. "Tell me, Quin Sidron. You really would leave these people behind?"

He didn't even pause. "Absolutely. To save my ass and yours? To do my job? Yes, I could."

"I don't believe you." She turned to face him and said, "You're not the type to leave civilians behind." She had to trust that.

"Believe me when I tell you I'm not a good guy, Daisy. As you've said countless times, I'm a pirate, a mercenary who does jobs for money and doesn't always care what the job is."

He could protest as much as he liked. He might be in it for the money and make a living as a pirate/privateer/mercenary or whatever he wanted to call himself but she knew in her heart that he wasn't the kind of man who would let a stray animal go hungry, much less leave his fellow prisoners in the hands of these trolls.

Quin tried to convince her otherwise. "Take your Captain

Bessa over there. He might think of himself as the captain of a ship, but he's proved himself to be just as mercenary as me. The only difference is that I was hired to protect you. If I'd taken that bounty, we'd have already delivered you over to the issuer."

"Okay, Quin." Bea tapped her chin, her mind mulling it over. Did she hate Bessa for what he tried to do to her? Surprisingly, no. The betrayal cut deep, especially on top of everything else, and she really wanted to punch him in the nose but she said, "I guess we need to save him, too."

"Fuck." He raked his hands through his hair. "That's not at all what I meant."

Bea smiled at him.

12

QUIN

The hellion was going to be the death of him. She'd decided that not only were they going to escape immediately, but that they were going to take everyone in the cellblock with them, including that weasel, Jeremiah Bessa.

Of all the three hells, how had he ended up in this one with such a particularly stubborn woman on his hands? Had he done some terrible misdeed in a past life, and she was his penance? Obviously, the answer was yes.

He could just leave her behind. When she got everything unlocked, he could just take off, leaving her and the other prisoners behind to deal with the repercussions. It would be relatively easy for one person to run a break for it during the chaos of a prison break.

But he wouldn't do that. First, he'd been hired to protect her. Second, though technically he was a space pirate, he had a conscience. It might be chipped and bruised with several jagged cracks running through it, but it was still intact.

After they left the 'Guard, he and his team had sat down and decided what lines they were unwilling to cross. With no one giving them orders, they were free to set firm, clear boundaries. No hit jobs. All bounties brought in alive, even when dead was an option. There had only been that one... but that wasn't their fault. How were they to know he was strong enough to snap his cuffs? And what fool ran anywhere near a horny musk ox in heat? Anyway. Only live bounties bagged and tagged. And no jobs that fucked over those who didn't deserve it or couldn't afford it. They had standards after all, unlike some pirates he knew.

Dammit. She was right. How did she read him so well already? He wouldn't leave her, and he couldn't leave the others locked up in here either. Seriously, the Knight owed him so big for this job. He was going to make Rhain pay for a month-long vacation at some swanky resort with bottomless drinks for the entire crew after this was all over. It was the least the man could do.

She bent down, fiddled with the cuff of her pants, and pulled out two slim, flexible pieces of metal. She flashed them at him with a smile. "Luckily, the trolls didn't even bother with more than a cursory search. This might take a while." Bea put her arms through the bars, and set to work with her picks, moving them by feel.

The flickering torchlight highlighted her strong cheekbones and a sharp jawline. As she chewed on her full bottom lip, a dimple appeared in her right cheek, and he wondered what she would taste like. He imagined walking over to her, pulling her up against him, and claiming those bee-stung lips for his own. He imagined she'd taste of hot honey, sweet but with a kick. But he wasn't about to kiss her without consent, so he resisted the temptation.

Besides, he did not need to get caught up in an entanglement like Bea. For a civilian with no field training, she was holding up surprisingly well to everything that had been thrown at her. Most people would be curled up in the corner rocking at this point. Not Beatrix Farsiris. She was picking locks and making escape plans. Quin shook his head. She was absolutely not what he expected, and he was irresistibly drawn to her despite himself.

He strolled over to lean against the bars next to her, splitting open a hard brown roll. He grimaced at the weevils inside and tossed it back on the tray with a clatter. "No one should have to eat that."

"So, does that mean that you're giving into the inevitable, rather than making sarcastic comments?" She blew a stray hair from her eyes as she worked her lockpicks.

"Whoa. Settle down there." He held up his hands, as if to hold her back. "While I can't promise to go sarcasm-free, I'm helping because I want to get out of here as much as you do." His glimmer of a plan depended on so many factors, it would take a miracle and the cooperation of all the prisoners to pull off.

"Great." A smile flitted across her face, and he basked in its fleeting warmth. "Hopefully, it's better than what I came up with."

He looked at her. "Does your plan involve picking the locks and creeping out of here with no resistance?"

Color rushed into her cheeks, and she ducked her head. "What? I never said my plan was good, just that I had one. I've only ever broken myself out of a prison cell once in my life."

"And how did that go for you?" Considering it had been on his own damn ship, he knew exactly how it went.

She rolled her eyes. "You just can't help yourself, can you?"

With a casual shrug, he flashed her one of his most disarming grins. "Sarcasm is my love language."

She turned a little pinker. "More like it's your way of toying with your prey, like a cat plays with a mouse."

He raised an eyebrow. "Are you the mouse in this scenario?"

Rolling her eyes, she ignored his question and said, "I've been thinking about those motorcycles. We need to disable them. Trolls may not run fast, but if they have their bikes, they'll be able to catch us easily."

"Smart." He didn't want to admit he hadn't even thought about the bikes, though he was sure he would have, eventually.

"I try." She winked at him, and his traitorous heart gave a little squeeze. "Psst, Cassie," she said, pitching her voice low.

"Are you leaving this place now?" she asked.

Shit. He thought they'd been quiet enough when discussing their plans. He wondered if the *Intrepid*'s crew had overheard their plans as well. Good thing they'd already decided to break everyone out.

"We are." Bea said, angling a glance at Quin. "You in?"

A low scrabbling punctuated by soft whispers came from the dark corners of the cell. After a brief discussion with whomever else was in there with her, Cassie answered, "We are with you, friends."

By his shaky calculations, it was likely mid-evening. If so, it should be dark outside, with the trolls hopefully on their way to being drunk and not thinking about their prisoners. He rubbed the back of his neck, watching Bea work. "I'm not thrilled about all the chances we're taking here. Too many unknowns."

"I agree, but we can't stay here."

"True." On one hand, death by troll. On the other, the minis-cule chance they make it out alive.

"Don't forget about us," Victor said, sticking a hand through the bars and waving.

"Wouldn't dream of it," Bea said.

Acting on pure impulse, he reached forward and wiped a smear of dirt off her cheek with his thumb.

She leaned back, her eyes wide and questioning.

Her skin was like silk beneath his fingers, and he wanted to touch more of her. All of her. She was still staring at him. He cleared his throat and gestured. "You had some dirt just there."

Her hand flew up to her face, and she gave a little laugh. "Um, thanks. Pretty sure it will take more than one swipe of your thumb to clean off all the dirt I've acquired on this little adventure."

"Once we're safe, we'll find a place to clean up." Depending on where they were on Cinzia. He had a couple of destinations in mind. That was, if they made it out of troll mountain alive. According to his calculations, they had about a one in a thousand shot of escaping with all their limbs intact. Maybe less. The odds were definitely not in their favor.

"Holy cats, a shower. Ooh, or a bath." Bea melted against the cell bars in a faux-swoon. "What I wouldn't give for a hot bath with bubbles right now." A tool slid from her grasp and fell to the floor with a gentle chime. "Shit. Stop distracting me with promises of a clean time."

Quin's imagination immediately supplied an image of a naked Bea, all soapy and glistening as she stepped out of her bath. He felt himself getting hard and started reciting the Unified Galactic Starguard Code of Conduct to distract himself. "Hey, we've got all night," Quin said, keeping his voice casual. If a troll walked in and caught them while she was working the locks, it would be all over. But he kept that to himself.

She shot him a look. "I thought we talked about the sarcasm."

He shrugged. "I can't help it. Just flows right out of me."

"Well, stow it. I've got to concentrate." The steady drip of water off the stalactites and her whispered curses punctuated the gentle clicks of her tools against the solid metal of the lock.

He shut up and let her work, leaning against the bars with his arms crossed and taking the opportunity to check out her ass. So intent was he on it he almost missed the moment when the clicking stopped, and she looked back at him. He averted his gaze, pretending to stare at the ceiling.

"Were you staring at my ass?"

"No," he drew out the word, his face an expression of pure innocence. "Why would I do that?"

She didn't believe him for a second. "Because you have the impulses of a hormonal teenager in lust."

"Buttercup," he gestured towards the lock, "if you don't get back to work, we're never going to get out of here. Do you want me to try?" Not that he knew a damn thing about picking locks. That was Navi's department. Quin played the role of charmer, though clearly he needed to up his game regarding Bea. Shit, was he really thinking about wooing her? What happened to keeping his distance? He needed to get his head on straight. She was just a job, nothing more.

"Yeah, right." Muttering under her breath about the terrible things that should happen to men who ogled, she got back to work. A few soft clicks later, she did a little happy dance, wiggling that fine ass he'd been admiring, and pushed open their cell door. "That's right. Ogle this." She pumped her arm in triumph.

He snorted out a laugh, shaking his head.

In five strides, she moved onto Cassie's cell and got to work.

Walking to the heavy prison door, he peered out the small barred window. The darkness shrouding most of the corridor was to their advantage. He could see light farther down the hall and shadows moving against the rock walls. Pulling up a map of the place in his mind, he attempted a walkthrough of their escape route starting at the prison door. Shitty and incomplete, but he'd functioned with worse in the 'Guard.

Their corridor was at the back of the large outer cave, all the way to the left. To the right, there were two smaller entryways cut into the cave walls. Quin guessed community spaces and living quarters. The cave they needed to make their way through seemed to be a garage, maybe also a general staging area for raids. When they first arrived, he'd clocked two guards at the mouth of the cave, one by the smaller entrances at the back, and, besides the raiding party of ten, several more trolls seated on wide benches around the space, cleaning and repairing weapons and working on their bikes.

All in all, it was a relatively straight shot to the exit and freedom. But their success depended on how many trolls were in that front cave. Hopefully, most of the trolls would not be hanging out in the space they needed to traverse to escape. He hated depending on luck. He also missed Cormac's calming voice in his ear. It had been a long time since he'd run a solo mission with no aid from his team. And, even though she was surprisingly talented with a lockpick, Bea was a civilian. The other captives were unknowns. More uncertainty and luck.

He'd be a lot happier if he could convince Bea that it was safer and more effective for just the two of them to make their getaway.

Giving it one more shot, even though he knew what she'd say, he leaned down and whispered, "You know, we can always tell the local authorities about this place — they'll come in, guns blazing, shut this place down, and all the captives would be free. Easy-peasy." Even as he said it, she was shaking her head. Dammit.

"No way," she said, keeping her focus on the task at hand.

"Hey, I had to give it one more shot. Easier to escape with just us, and let the authorities play the hero after we're gone."

Bessa called, "Don't you dare leave me in here. I'll make a racket and bring the trolls down on you before you make it out the door!"

What. A. Dick. "Really?" Quin said, strolling over to stand in front of Bessa's cell. "You'd ruin all our chances of getting out of here?"

Bessa took a step away from the bars and folded his arms over his chest with a huff, his round face flushed in the torchlight. "You bet I would. I'm not getting left behind to be troll chow." He raised his voice. "Girl, you let me out of here next."

Ignoring Bessa, Bea tucked her picks into a pocket and yanked on the door of Cassie's cell. It swung open, but no one exited. "Come on out, Cassie. No one's going to hurt you."

Tentatively, Cassie stepped out of the cell and into the flickering torchlight, blinking up at them with big black eyes. She was no more than two feet tall and covered in fluffy, light gray fur. The pointed ears on top of her head twitched with every sound, flicking the two white tufts at the end that stuck up like antennas. Two more fluffy gray-furred beings followed close at her heels.

"The fuck?" Victor breathed.

Oh, wow. Quin had never met creatures like these three before, despite his extensive travels. Interacting with new-to-him species was one of the more fascinating things about space travel. You never knew who you were going to meet.

Bea threw him a wide-eyed glance before returning her attention to Cassie. "Hi. It's nice to finally put a face to the voice."

Cassie bobbed her head. "It is nice to meet you, friend." She waved a small paw tipped with sharp black claws towards the being to her left. "This is Mog, my sister." Clutching her tail like a safety blanket, Mog flicked black-tipped ears in their direction and dipped her head. "And this is LeeLee." Cassie wrapped an arm around the second being. "My daughter."

LeeLee gave them a little wave before burrowing her face in her mother's fur.

"We thank you for this release," Cassie said. "It will provide us with a chance to redeem ourselves." It sounded like they had a grudge against the trolls. Understandable.

Bea nodded. "Of course. We weren't about to leave you here, no matter how much Quin wanted to ditch you."

"Hey, hey! What are you things?" Bessa demanded, his face smooshed into the bars so he could see them. "I've never seen anything like you. You look like those tiny fuzzy monkeys on Badin. What are they called?" He snapped his fingers at them, like he expected someone to answer him and clear up his confusion.

Cassie turned and bared her small but extremely sharp teeth at him. Mog and LeeLee followed suit. "You're speaking of marmosets, which we are not. They are merely animals. We are Haruet." She fluffed her chest hair and looked down her snub nose at him. Impressive, considering he was several feet taller than her.

"Like I know what that is," Bessa snorted.

"Shut up, Bessa," Quin said, wishing he could smack some sense into the man. He needed it. Quin tipped his head towards the prison door. "Cassie, keep an ear out for us, will you? Let us know if anyone's coming down the corridor. Hopefully, if someone decides on a late-night visit, your warning will give us enough time to get back into our cells."

"Yes. We will hear all the things." Cassie whispered something to Mog and LeeLee, then scrambled up the prison door, holding onto the bars with her long fingers and tail and balancing on the ledge with her equally long toes.

"Anyone have any ideas on how to incapacitate trolls?" Quin asked as Bea turned her attention to the next lock.

"Sledgehammer," said a crewmember from the cell next to Cassie's.

"Brilliant idea, Don. If we had one of those, we could have bashed them over the head when our pods landed and then we wouldn't be in here, would we?" Victor grumbled. "At least Kimni and Aja got away."

"They did? Good," Bea said, popping open Don's cell. "I was worried when I didn't see them in here."

Victor nodded. "Aja had a blaster. Must have been in the pod. She held them off as they made a run for it. Trolls didn't even bother to chase them. Just rounded us up, ransacked the pods, and brought us here."

"Well, I don't have a blaster," Don snapped. "You wouldn't happen to have one of those up your ass, would you, Victor? Yeah, I didn't think so."

Quin rubbed the back of his neck. "Well, bashing them over the head with a really big rock might work. But I honestly don't know. I've never been in a fight with one before. I've always just avoided them."

"Hells. Playing possum is probably our best choice," Bea said, her head bent over the lock. Bessa stood above her, watching her every move. She glared up at him. "Back up, would you? I can't focus with you breathing on me like that."

With a huff, he shuffled back a small step.

Narrowing his eyes at Bessa, Quin grabbed a set of cuffs hanging by the main door. He had the feeling that he was going to need them.

As soon as Bea unlocked the cage, the man shoved Bea out of his way and bolted. Quin stuck out a foot, tripping the man. He crashed to the floor with a cry.

"You fool." Quin put a knee between Bessa's shoulder blades

and cuffed his hands behind his back. He hauled him up by an arm and slammed him against the metal bars. "Make one more sound, and I'll jam your shirt in your mouth and lock you back in the cell."

"My crew would never allow that to happen," the man blustered, struggling against Quin's grip.

Quin glanced at Victor and Don, who watched Bessa stone faced and made no move to help him. "Pretty sure that they're going to do what's best for their own survival and what you just tried to do — that chickenshit running away? Hells, we don't even have the main door open yet, so where were you going? — could have jeopardized it. So, if I were you, I'd shut the fuck up, follow my commands, and you just might live to tell the tale of the time you were a captive of giant biker trolls. Someone might even buy you a drink for it." He shoved Bessa into the bars again when the man opened his mouth. "So. Not one fucking word or you're gagged in the cell, and we leave you behind. You get me?"

Bessa nodded, temporarily cowed. But a man like that never believed he was in the wrong. He eyed the other two crew members of the *Intrepid* who stared at Bessa with varying degrees of disgust and dislike. "Don, Victor? Why don't you take charge of this jackass? Make sure that he doesn't fuck things up for us?"

They came forward and took Bessa by the elbows. "No worries. We've got him," Don said.

"Yeah, and if he makes a peep, I've got a pair of dirty underwear that would make the perfect gag." Victor gave Bessa a little shake to emphasize his point.

"Gross, but effective," Don said.

Bea came up next to Quin. "Are we done intimidating people?"

"Oh, Daisy, I haven't even gotten started," Quin said. "Everybody out?"

She nodded, tipping her chin at those behind her. "Now, how are we going to do this?"

"Good fucking question."

13

BEA

When he was alive, her father had always said that not planning meant failure from the outset, and, for a long time, Bea agreed with that sentiment. She loved a well-researched, multi-step plan. Even better if there was an appendix attached with links to scientifically proven facts. But then her life went up in flames, literally. Now, she prescribed more to her sister's maxim of "make a plan; prepare for everything to go FUBAR". It fit her current situation much better.

There was so much that could go wrong with this half-assed plan, including it being blown wide open by one of their fellow prisoners. She eyed Bessa, cowed for the moment and pouting as his ex-crew loomed over him. Maybe she should let Quin gag him and toss him back in a cell. He'd better not fuck things up for them or she was going to take out all her frustration out on him, and he would not enjoy it.

So. The first part of the plan, to free everyone from their cells, was done and dusted. Next up, getting from where they were, through the troll-filled cavern ahead, and outside to freedom. They'd be fine. Positive thinking, right?

But their success depended on what awaited them in the outer cave. So much could go wrong. It was entirely possible that they'd all die gruesome, blood-soaked deaths, torn limb from limb by their captors. A shiver of fear — and maybe a tingle of excitement, too — ran up her spine. She decided she was going to be ridiculously optimistic about their chances. They could do this. They would survive. They had to. After all, she needed to give her daughter a giant hug, clear her name, and have a drink with her sister. Oh, and maybe even work off some of that tension snapping between her and Quin. But only if he earned it. She bit her lip, imagining his big, naked body hovering over her before he did that thing with his hips that she just knew he would be an expert at and make her scream with pleasure.

Feeling her gaze, Quin gave her a small nod of encouragement. At least she had backup now. It gave her confidence, more than she'd had when she walked into that bar on the colony alone to meet Ghost's courier.

She crouched and got to work on the main lock, humming a little song of encouragement to herself as she worked the slim pieces of metal against the springs and pins of the lock's innards. She felt each pin as it clicked back into place. With a final twist, the rotor turned, and the bolt retracted. A flush of delight and adrenaline rushed through her, just like when she designed a new little gadget or engine component that worked just how she'd imagined. She cracked open the door and held up a fist of triumph.

Quin bumped it with a wink and a smile. "Nice."

"Cassie, are you three sure about this?" She twisted on the balls of her feet to face the trio of Haruet. While she'd focused on the locks, Quin and the others had hashed out the plan.

"Oh, yes. Haruet are expert spies." All three fuzzy heads nodded in tandem. "Was trick to catch us the first time. Stupid trolls will never see us."

"Stupid trolls," Mog and LeeLee echoed, their soft voices musical.

"Okay," Bea said slowly. She wasn't comfortable sending small, defenseless-looking creatures into such a deadly situation, but they'd eagerly volunteered for the job. "As long as you're certain you'll be alright."

Cassie patted Bea's arm with her tiny clawed paw, her eyes wide. "Stay. We will be back in moments." And they slid through the opening and down the hall.

"Are we sure we can trust them?" Don whispered. "I mean, it'd be easy enough for those little critters to just scamper out the front. Trolls probably wouldn't even notice them."

"Not much we can do about it if they do." Quin kept an eye on their progress through the cracked door. "We've just got to have a little faith."

"Yeah, not everyone is like ole Bessa here." Victor gave the bound man a hard pat on the shoulder. Bessa glared at Victor but said nothing.

"Shh." Bea slid her tools back into her pant cuff and peered over Quin's shoulder down the shadow-filled corridor. She sketched out a rune of protection for the Haruet, willing the Lady to watch over them. "Too much noise, and we'll attract attention. Let's just give them the time they need. They'll be back. I know they will."

But waiting was hard when every nerve in Bea's body was screaming to run to freedom as fast as she could. The dark stone walls loomed closer, and the space got tight and hot, filled with the sounds of heavy breathing, the shuffling of feet, and the low, constant drip of water against rock. Bea closed her eyes and pressed her forehead against the reassuring heat of Quin's broad shoulder, trying to fight the cresting wave of panic that threatened to swallow her whole.

"Breathe, Daisy," Quin said in her ear, turning slightly to put an arm around her and draw her close. She burrowed into his chest, fisting the bottom of his shirt, and squeezing her eyes tight as her breath grew jagged. He took her hand in his and held it against his chest. "In and out. In and out." His thumb stroked against her skin in time with his chant, the deep smoothness of his voice resonating with something deep within her.

In a moment that lasted forever, her breathing slowed to match the rhythm of his voice, and the wave of panic receded until it was merely a ripple in the back of her mind. She took a moment to bask in the heat of his body, pushing away any residual embarrassment at her loss of control. "Thank you," she whispered.

Arden would have told her to take a pill. Quin's unasked for assistance in battling her panic attack was unexpected and welcome. She felt a small unfurling of something tender and green buried in the untended recesses of her heart. Despite his promise to protect her, this man didn't have to show her an ounce of kindness, didn't have to be helpful and yet, here he was. Without prompting. Without expectation of payment. If there was such a thing as a good pirate — privateer, mercenary, whatever he wanted to call himself — he might actually be it.

"Anytime." After one more stroke of his thumb, he lifted her hand to his lips and pressed a kiss to her palm. The rasp of his stubble tickled, and the warmth of his lips made her skin tingle.

Someone cleared their throat, and Bea slid her hand out of his grasp, her cheeks heating as the world intruded on their quietly private moment.

The soft scratching of nails against rock signaled the Haruets' return, and she welcomed the distraction. Cassie danced excitedly from one paw to the other, her fur puffed out to maximum fluffiness. "Almost everyone is in the great hall, a large cave down the corridor closest to us. A gathering of some sort with much noise and drinking. I do not believe they will notice much, as they are very inebriated," she reported. "There are two guards outside the main entrance. LeeLee reported she saw only one over by the motorcycles."

LeeLee nodded, her paws clasped over her round belly, tail wrapped around her feet. She reminded Bea of a stuffed toy she had as a child. Bea just about died at the cuteness, but forced herself to listen to the very serious and fluffy Haruet finish her report.

"There might be more about but, if there are, they were not in our line of sight. We could not risk further exploration. When you are ready, we will take point and handle any stupid trolls we may have missed during our initial scout. We will not let harm come to our new friends." Cassie gave a decisive nod and pointed back the way they'd come. "Mog remains alert at the end of this passage."

"No guards by the doors to the living spaces?" Quin asked.

Cassie shook her head. "None that we could see."

"Huh. Better than I expected," Quin said. "Good work."

The Haruet preened under his praise.

"Right, everyone knows what to do?" Bea asked, pushing away from the heat of Quin's chest and squaring her shoulders. Thrown by their moment of tenderness from Quin and her response, she needed to feel in control. Getting everyone out of danger was a tangible goal. She'd deal with the intangible feeling of connection later, when they were out of harm's way. Or maybe she'd just shove those softer emotions into a box and forget they even existed until after her quest. Or never. Sometimes never worked best.

His deep forest eyes searching hers, Quin opened his mouth to say something, and she tried not to squirm under his canny gaze. After a heartbeat, his lips curled into a grin, and he responded with a "Yes, ma'am" and a sassy little salute.

She rolled her eyes, trying to brush aside the feeling that he'd just looked into her soul, saw what she was hiding, and liked it. "Then let's do this."

14

QUIN

Cassie and LeeLee darted ahead to reconnect with Mog, their gray fur camouflaging them against the stone and shifting shadows. The humans followed, attempting to make as little noise as possible though it turned out stealth wasn't necessary. As soon as they got near the tunnel's entrance, they heard the rhythmic thumping of music and the sound of grating rocks as the trolls whooped and hollered at their party. The noise should provide all the cover they needed to escape. Quin sketched a rune for luck anyway.

The humans took up position behind a massive stalagmite just beyond the prison corridor. Cassie turned to flash them a single digit, pointing to the troll over by the motorcycles. Then two digits and a gesture at the front guards before tapping her chest, after which she gave them a thumbs up.

"I guess that means that one is for us, two for them," Quin said. Could the Haruet actually take on even the smallest of the trolls? They certainly thought so. What did he know? The Haruet were complete unknowns to him. At this point, he had to trust they knew what they were doing. It would be interesting to see how this played out.

"Don't get killed, little friends," Bea whispered to their retreating backs.

"Do you really think they can take on two trolls by themselves?" Don asked.

So he wasn't the only one who had doubts about their abilities. "I guess we'll see." He shrugged. "Just be ready to face some pissed off trolls if things go wrong."

"I hope they know what they're doing. If not, it's going to go badly for all of us." Victor took up position by the prison corridor where he would guard Bessa and keep watch on the tunnel for anyone leaving the party early.

"Have a little faith," Bea said with confidence. "Cassie won't let us down. Let's focus on our jobs and get the hells out of here."

As the motorcycle sabotage team, Bea, Quin, and Don crept past the open mouth of the passageway leading to the great hall, the rumbling thunder of party noise ruffling their hair, and worked their way over to the long row of motorcycles leaning on kickstands. Once they were close enough, they ducked behind a grouping of tall stalagmites to assess the situation.

The troll Cassie so graciously left for them was smaller than the others they'd seen, his skin light gray and less rock-like, as if he was still growing. A youngster. Bea put her hand on Quin's arm, stilling him. "We can't kill him."

Quin raised an eyebrow in question.

Don shook his head. "He's a troll. We need to take him out."

"Look at him. He's just a kid." The troll kid in question crouched next to one of the massive cycles, his hands deep within the engine's body, an open toolbox by his feet while he twitched awkwardly to the tinny sound of music playing through his headphones.

"What then?" Don asked.

"We knock him out." She pointed towards a giant wrench on the bench a few feet behind from the young troll and pantomimed smacking his head with it. "That should do it, don't you think?"

Quin looked at Don, who pointed at his own skinny arms and shrugged. He was no help. Quin rolled his eyes. "Fine. But if he catches me and rips my head off, that's completely on you."

"I'll be sure to mourn you as I'm running for my life," Bea said.

Don nodded enthusiastically.

This time it was Quin who rolled his eyes at Bea. Great. His sarcasm was rubbing off on her, and he'd added her eye roll move to his repertoire.

Leaving the pair safely behind the stalagmite, Quin crept to the wrench. It was longer than his entire arm. He glanced back at Bea, who gave him two thumbs up. Gritting his teeth, he hefted it to his shoulder with a low grunt. The young troll didn't notice, lost in his own world of music and engines. His back bowing under the heavy weight, Quin staggered over to where the teen troll crouched. Oh stars, let this work. He planted his feet and swung the wrench down onto the back of the troll's head. The teen drunkenly spun on the balls of his feet. Quin's heart skipped a beat. Then, the troll's eyes rolled up in his head, and he collapsed on his side.

"Thank fuck." Quin wasn't sure what he would have done if that wrench hadn't done its job. Died probably, just another victim of a troll's crushing embrace.

Bea and Don joined him next to the downed troll. "Is he alive?" she asked.

"Nice," Don said, patting him on the back.

Quin put a hand near the troll kid's nose. "Still breathing."

With a nod, Bea scanned the area. "I don't see any others."

He'd hoped for a smile or even a kiss at his defeat of the troll, but alas. No reward for his bravery.

"Do we tie him up? Will chains even hold him?" she asked.

He paused, eyeing the unconscious troll. "Let's just work fast and hope he doesn't wake until after we're gone."

Don nodded. "Can't see the ones who were guarding the front of the cave, either. Looks like those little furry guys made for a good distraction, drawing them away."

"Hope they're okay." Her brows drew together in worry.

"They can take care of themselves." Of course, he had no idea if that was true, but he didn't want her to worry about their new friends. They'd learn what happened soon enough. "We need to hurry, though. I don't know how long this kid will be out, but I do know that I want to be far away from here before someone sounds the alarm and brings the entire tribe of trolls down on us."

"Agreed. Let's get to sabotaging." Bea found a bin of bolts on a shelf under the large workbench and fed them into the bikes' exhaust ports.

"Will that work?" Don asked as he used an awl to gouge a hole at the bottom of a gas tank, the smell of the combustible filling the air.

"If these are anything like the equipment I grew up fixing, the bolts will burn out the engines if they can even get them started." She grimaced. "I hate to see good machines die."

"If they weren't murderous kidnappers, then maybe they wouldn't have to worry about their bikes getting destroyed by prison escapees." Quin stabbed a bike's back tire with a screwdriver. Was there such a thing as sabotage overkill? Because these bikes wouldn't be going anywhere anytime soon. "Hurry, though. Our luck won't hold forever."

They decided it was worth the gamble to steal two of the oversized cycles to help with their escape. The bikes were massive, built for the size and weight of adult trolls. It wouldn't be a comfortable ride on a long trip, but it was doable. With the extra-large seats, they could double- and triple-up and make a faster getaway from the area. He certainly didn't want to be running on his own two feet with a passel of pissed off trolls chasing him. They might be big and not particularly speedy, but they had endurance and could outlast the average human as they ran their prey to the ground.

While Bea finished disabling the other bikes, and Don took out the boxy prison vehicles, Quin had a quick poke around for anything useful. A long workbench lined the wall, filling the space between two wide rock columns of stalactites and stalagmites that had grown together. Tossed in a pile of cast-offs at the far end, he found his holster with the blaster still in it and strapped it to his thigh. He patted his blaster lovingly. It was only right that she was back where she belonged.

Scanning the bench for anything else that might be useful, he picked up a large hammer and tested its heft. Not nearly as heavy as the wrench. If he used it against an adult troll, the hammer would probably just bounce off its stone skin. He put it back on the workbench with a thud. Their best bet would be to move as fast as they could.

He approached the remaining two motorcycles. The bike he'd chosen was painted to look like it was on fire, a bright yellow chasing the orange and igniting into a vivid red. The metalwork twisted and turned, emulating flame, the shiny chrome accents reflecting the paint job. Whomever had done the detail work was an artist, and he felt just the slightest twinge of remorse at stealing a such a piece of art.

With a grunt, he pushed the bike forward, his arms straining to shift the weight of the machine. Riding it was going to be interesting. He could barely touch his toes to the ground to balance the bike and would have to stretch almost completely forward to reach the clutch and gearshift on the handlebars.

"You good over there?" He looked over at his small team. Bea was helping Don shove another giant bike, this one a sparkly purple, towards the entrance, both visibly straining.

They nodded.

"Alright, then let's get out of here before the trolls decide they want a snack."

15

BEA

Leaving a trail of motorcycle destruction and one unconscious young troll behind them, they rolled their stolen bikes out of the cave, putting distance between them and their captors. Bea was panting by the time they caught up to the Haruet. The trio perched together on a small boulder, surrounded by blood and gore, viscera and entrails strewn in a wide circle around them. Victor sat on a clean patch of grass just outside of the ring of destruction, arms wrapped around his legs, face pale in the light of the two moons as he watched Cassie delicately licking her fur clean.

Bea took a deep breath and immediately regretted it, the tang of blood and pierced organs hanging heavy in the air. What happened here? "Cassie, was this you?"

The Haruet nodded. "We have taken our retribution against stupid trolls."

"Stupid trolls," Mod and LeeLee intoned from their perch behind her.

"How in the three hells did you manage this?" Quin asked, awe coloring his voice. "And can you teach me your secret?"

"Yeah, I want to learn how to kill massive stone-skinned trolls and not get a drop of blood on my clothes." Bea swallowed hard against the bile that gathered at the back of her throat. Obviously, they'd severely underestimated the fluffy Haruet. That's what she got for judging someone by their appearance.

Keeping her eyes on Victor and doing her best to avoid acknowledging the detritus on the ground, she and Don maneuvered the bike around a detached arm, bypassing a chunk of torso. She slipped on what she was going to pretend was a stray pebble, rather than a slice of internal organ. She swallowed hard. "Highly impressive." And incredibly disturbing. She wasn't about to admit that out loud, especially not to the small creatures who proudly sat amongst the destruction they'd wrought. Not that she feared them now, just acutely aware that, if they could do this to large, stone-skinned trolls, soft humans like her wouldn't stand a chance.

LeeLee giggled, covering her mouth with blood-soaked paws.

"My people and the Trolls of the Lesser Mountains have been waging war on one another for years. We've gotten very good at disabling them." Cassie smiled, flashing elongated sharp teeth stained red.

"Damn," Don said, unable to take his eyes off the swath of destruction. They propped the bike against an outcropping near to Victor. "Looks like the trolls exploded or something. You lil guys do all that? Awesome work."

The three Haruet preened under his praise.

"Wait, where's Captain Bessa?" Bea scanned their small group. "Victor? What happened?"

"Dead." Victor shook his head. He ran his hands roughly through his hair and stood to face them, a hand on a boulder for support. "Sorry. He got away from me. Kicked me in the knee, shoved me into the wall, and ran straight out the entrance as soon as you were out of sight."

"He almost stepped on us in his rush," Cassie said, shaking her head. "Very rude man."

"And, of course, the trolls guarding the front followed him."

Victor scrubbed at his eyes, trying to erase what he'd seen. "The fool. What was he thinking?"

Don put a hand on Victor's shoulder. "He was a crappy captain and an even shittier human being. Just look at what he tried to do to our engineer here. But he didn't deserve death by troll."

"He should not have run," Cassie said, her voice solemn. "However, he did provide an excellent distraction, leading the guards at the entrance away." She looked at a lump of innards that might have belonged to Bessa. "They caught him quite easily and proceeded to tear him apart. His death was not in vain, and we have avenged it."

Turning green, Victor swallowed hard and nodded.

"We need to go." Bea glanced back at the cave entrance. They were far enough away that the thumping music was muted, but the more time they spent here, the more likely someone would notice something wrong and come to investigate. Facing off against angry trolls was not on her bucket list, even with the scarily effective Haruet at their side. She knew what the trolls would do if they caught the escapees. They'd done it to Bessa. She gritted her teeth. "We have these bikes, and it looks like there's one way out of here." She nodded towards a narrow shamble of a road cutting through the deep canyon. With two full moons shining overhead, they stood a chance of navigating their way out without splatting against a wall or disappearing down a chasm.

Quin glanced in the direction she was looking and nodded in agreement. "The party's still going strong but as loud as these bikes are, we'd better wait until we're farther away before starting them up so we don't attract unwanted attention." He gave his bike a push to get it moving.

Bea grabbed the handlebar on the other side to help push the large vehicle, leaving the other for Don and Victor to manage.

Cassie looked at the bikes in distaste and gave her paw one more lick. "We will scout ahead to make certain there is not a patrol returning home."

Bea hadn't thought of that and sent Cassie a grateful nod as the trio scampered off.

Darkness swallowed the cave as they trekked down the bumpy road that cut through the rough terrain. It was slow going as they steered around the rocks and potholes while pushing the two heavy troll bikes. Bea felt her anxiety rise with each creeping step. The hairs on the back of her neck prickled at the feeling of being watched, of being followed. But every time she looked back, it was just empty darkness. So she focused on putting one step in front of the other, freedom within reach.

She was seriously struggling by the time they exited the canyon onto smoother terrain. When they finally caught up to the Haruet, she felt like she was about to pass out. Gods, she needed to start exercising again. Take some more walks, lift some weights. She'd gotten slack in the past couple of years and was sorely regretting her lack of stamina at the moment. At least Don and Victor looked like they were panting, too. Once she could speak again, she asked, "Anyone know where we are?"

"Never been to this planet," Don said, leaning heavily on the handlebars.

"Never plan to return once we get off it." Victor wiped the sweat from his brow. Don nodded fervently.

Quin, who looked as if he could go another couple of klicks, asked, "Cassie, any idea how close we are to the nearest town?"

She bounded onto the seat of their bike and pointed. "Those ways to humans. Two days walk to the place they call Caroville and three days walk to the place they call Toro." In the opposite direction, she gestured towards a forest, the tall trees of green and gold stretching up towards the sky painted fuchsia by the early morning light. "That way to Haruet. We will be there by morning."

Chittering happily, Mog and LeeLee flanked her on the wide seat. They were more than ready to go home. She understood the sentiment.

She looked at Quin. "You said you were familiar with Cinzia. Either of those towns familiar?"

"I might know a guy in Toro." His words came slowly, as if he didn't want to reveal too much in front of Don and Victor. "He might be able to help us out."

Cassie folded her paws over her stomach and regarded the humans with large, serious eyes. "We would be honored if you would accompany us to our village, where you will be feted and celebrated as friends of the Haruet." Mog leaned forward and whispered into Cassie's ear. "Mog promises to teach you how to disable a mountain troll, if you care to learn."

As much as she'd love to say yes, there was just no way she could go with the Haruet. Biting her lip, Bea said, "I truly wish I could come, Cassie. But I have a deadline that I can't miss. "

"Ah, your quest." Cassie gave an understanding nod. "It must be completed before you can celebrate. I understand. Friends, for your kindness and aid in a time of peril, we owe you our lives." She bowed, and the other two followed suit. "Should you ever need us, send word to our forest, and we will help." She pointed down the path to the forest beyond.

Uncomfortable at the thought of another being owing her for doing nothing more than unlocking a cage, Bea said, "Oh, no. That's not necessary. Anyone would have done the same."

Cassie put a small paw on top of Bea's hand where it rested on the handlebar. Bea ignored the small speckles of blood that painted her long claws. "Anyone would not have. But you did. Please. It is rude to reject."

"Um. Okay, then. Thank you." Bea gently patted the top of Cassie's paw, the fur soft under her fingers.

Quin thumbed in her direction. "I'm with her. Wherever she needs to go."

A lump formed in her throat and her eyes prickled at the ease of his statement. In their cell, he'd said he was going to stick with her, but she knew how men liked to hear themselves talk especially when trying to impress. Even though he was only going with her because of some contract he was honor-bound to fulfill, the wall she'd erected around her heart crumbled a little more, letting in a bright shaft of light.

After a quick consult, Victor and Don decided to accept Cassie's offer of hospitality.

"You sure?" Quin asked. "I thought you wanted off the planet as soon as humanly possible."

"It's an adventure that we can drink on for years to come," Don said with a shrug. "Besides, we don't know what's next for us, considering our captain's dead and we're currently unemployed. It'll be fun to hang with the Haruet for a little while we figure it out. Maybe they can help us track down Kimni and Aja."

Victor nodded. "I know you said you needed to get to Badin, but come with us. It'll be fun. After our visit, we're going to Caroville, a lawful town." He gave Quin a hard look. "From there, we can get you where you need to go."

Bea cocked her head at Quin, giving him a chance to respond.

He shrugged. "Your choice, Daisy. But I'm with you, whatever you decide."

Turning back to her former crewmates, she said, "I appreciate the offer, but I really do have a deadline. It's a matter of life or death." That might be stretching the truth a little. Whatever the case, it was absolutely a matter of fixing her life. "And, even though you might not believe it, considering he quite aggressively boarded your ship and then ejected you from it..."

Quin shrugged. "Apologies, gentlemen."

"...he's actually not a bad guy," she finished.

"Damned with faint praise," Quin murmured.

"You're sure?" Victor raised his eyebrows meaningfully in Quin's direction. "You're under no obligation to stick with this guy. Though he was right about Bessa and the bounty thing." He looked shamefaced. "Sorry about that, by the way. We wouldn't have let him do anything to you, you know."

"We knew he was acting more like an ass than usual, but never suspected his plans for you," Don added. "We thought it was a regular supply run, and you were our temp engineer. Sorry."

"I know that, guys. And thanks for being good crewmates." Despite the whole Bessa thing, she'd enjoyed her time on the *Intrepid*. It reminded her of why space travel was so important and needed to be accessible to everyone.

"Anytime."

Bea gave each of them a hug and one last assurance that she would be just fine in Quin's company. Victor unsteadily boarded the giant troll bike and kicked it to life, and Don clambered on board behind him. LeeLee and Mog dashed ahead, leading the way towards their home in the distant forest.

Cassie pressed her paws together, touching them to her forehead. "Blessings upon you both. Until we meet again."

"Goodbye, Cassie." Though they'd just met, she was going to miss the murderous ball of fluff.

"May the road rise up to meet you," Quin said with a nod.

With a last wave, Cassie turned and, faster than Bea could blink, caught up with the rest of the group.

Shaking off a pang of sadness, she gave another sigh and turned back to Quin.

"Guess it's just you and me, Daisy." Arms folded over his chest, Quin leaned against the bike. One corner of his mouth kicked up into a half-smile.

Bea opened her mouth to answer with a sarcastic remark when thunder echoed down the canyon pass, a cloud of dust swirling in the distance.

"Trolls," Bea breathed. Her body froze in terror as the ground trembled beneath her feet.

"Guess the party's over." Quin shifted out of his relaxed pose to one of readiness in the blink of an eye. "Looks like we need to make like the wind and leave." He slung one leg over the seat of the bike and jumped on the kick starter, the engine roaring to life. Patting the seat, he said, "Hop on."

His casual attitude and terrible word play jolted her from her frozen state. "Did you really just say that?" Bea said, straddling the seat behind him and strapping on an inflatable crash helmet she'd found in the troll's stash of stolen goods. She glanced back as a troll shambled out of the canyon and, spotting them, roared its displeasure. She squeaked and smacked his shoulder. "Hurry!"

"Hold tight. If you fall off, I'm leaving you for the trolls." Quin gunned the motor, and the bike leapt forward.

"Asshole," she squealed, wrapping her arms around his waist and holding on for dear life as he took off in a spray of stones, and leaving the stampede of trolls in the literal dust.

16

QUIN

She didn't protest when he said he was with her, and she got on the bike with him, so... progress. Better than having to drag her with him kicking and screaming. He'd held his breath when Don and Victor tried to convince her to go with them, but here she was. And he thanked the gods for it. Now, Rhain wouldn't hunt him down and cut his balls off for losing her. He preferred his balls right where they were.

She clung to his back as he maneuvered the stolen bike across unfamiliar territory. Her body heat seeped through his thin shirt, warming his skin. Every time they hit a bump, her arms tightened around his waist and her strong, thick thighs clenched around him. The bike skidded through a patch of gravel, refocusing his attention to the road in front of him, rather than the warm curves of the woman pressed intimately up against him.

One thing he could say about these bikes, they were fast. Maybe it was because, even with the two of them on one bike, they weren't even half the weight of a single troll. He didn't care why the bike ate up the miles; he was just happy it did. However, the more time he spent with Bea's warmth pressed firmly up against him, the more difficulty he had focusing. If he let himself stop and consider her warm core pushed tight against his ass, he was going to lose control of the bike. He shifted on the seat, trying to readjust the pants that were suddenly a size too tight.

It was not the most comfortable position to be in. Every bump was jarring. In an effort to take his mind off her soft breasts and the warm center of her, he forced himself to run word problems. A troll bike going an estimated 200 kilometers an hour and carrying two humans of slightly above average size needed to travel approximately ninety kilometers over mountainous terrain in less than twenty minutes, how hard would his erection be by the time they reached their destination?

Math didn't help. He bent lower over the handlebars, his nose practically touching the gas tank, and sped up. Bending with him, Bea tightened her grip on his waist. Desperate, he recited sports statistics from the last season of his galactic rugby team, the Space Dusters, and focused on the twisting dirt road ahead of them.

Three seasons' worth of statistics later, he slowed the bike, guiding it to a halt at the top of a ridge overlooking their destination, and set the kickstand.

"Are we there yet?" Bea asked, sitting up and stretching her arms above her head before sliding off the wide seat. "Oh, gods. I need a massage. I'm not used to being bent over like that."

An image of Bea bent over the seat of the bike while he fucked her from behind flashed through Quin's brain. He swallowed a groan and said, "Well, you won't find a masseuse in Toro, sweetheart. Not unless you're also looking for a happy ending."

She cocked her head. "A happy... oh."

Twisting on the seat, he watched a blush creep up her throat and stain her cheeks. "Exactly."

"So, what kind of hellhole have you brought us to where a girl can't get a simple massage? I suppose a decent meal is also out of the question?" She shaded her eyes, surveying the town in the valley below. From up here, it didn't look like much — a few buildings, none over two stories, some small houses, and one main street running down the center.

"Actually, there's some pretty damn good food there, as long as you aren't looking for five-star accommodations."

She narrowed her eyes at him. "I'm not the delicate flower you seem to think I am, Captain Sidron. I thought we established that."

He held up his hands to ward her off. "Hey, you're the one crying for a massage." If looks could kill, he would have exploded right then and there. "That town, Daisy, is Toro, best known for cheap goods that fell out of the back of a shuttle, liquor strong enough to clean engines, and few questions asked."

"So, a smuggler's paradise."

"You got it." And typical of the kinds of towns on Cinzia. People here took care of their own, looked the other way when necessary, and just wanted to be left alone, with no outside interference.

"And why did we come here, rather than the supposedly more law-abiding town?"

"You do remember there's both a warrant out for your arrest and a bounty on your head, right?"

She rolled her eyes. "How could I forget? But I've got a good fake ID, so it shouldn't be a problem, right?"

"Possibly. However, as I remember it, the people on Cinzia are very good at spotting fakes." He scrubbed a hand over his jaw. All his talk about keeping her at arm's length and here he was, about to open up to her. He hoped he wouldn't regret it. "But you also remember when I told you that my team and I were discharged from the 'Guard, and the Knight helped us get set up?"

She nodded.

"My team ran into some trouble — a little misunderstanding — prior to leaving, so there's some bad blood there. Anyway, I'd prefer to avoid direct contact with those in law enforcement, if I can help it." There. A little nugget of information. That wasn't so bad.

She pursed her lips. "I'm going to need some details about this misunderstanding. Tell me, am I traveling with a murderer? A traitor? A traveling minstrel? Should I be worried?" She paused, eyeing him. "You're not going to go back on your word, are you?"

"Fuck, no. That's one thing that I most definitely will not do — once I give you my word, I keep it. You're stuck with me. Besides, I have a contract to fulfill."

"So what is it then?"

Even if he started up the motor to drown her out, it wouldn't work because she was more persistent than anyone he had ever met. Just fucking relentless. Once she locked on a target, there was no dissuading her.

Quin tipped his head, scratching at his beard. What he really wanted to do was get a hot shave, a hot meal, and a proper bed, rather than discuss things he'd rather leave in the past. But who was he to demand her trust, for her to share dark secrets, when he wasn't doing the same? He needed to give as good as he got. "Look, I'm going to tell it to you plainly: you might think that you're sophisticated when it comes to the darker side of the galaxy but, I hate to tell you, you're not."

She folded her arms over her chest and set her jaw.

He held up a hand. "Hear me out before you get your feathers all ruffled. I don't mean it as a bad thing. Not at all."

Though she narrowed her eyes at him, she gave him a nod to proceed.

"Even though you've been on the run and had some bad shit happen in your life, that doesn't mean that you've seen much of the seedier side of the galaxy. You're like ninety percent of the population, and that's not a bad thing. Most people, they live their lives, build a family, go to work, travel a bit. They might brush up against the darker elements out there, have an unpleasant experience or two in their lives. The United Body of Planets has worked together to build societies that are open, diverse, and welcoming and provide a certain level of safety and protection. Sure, you might get a glimpse of the dark side, but most community members never really get down in the muck, the truly nasty shit that thrives in the far-flung corners and dark underbellies of our speck of the universe. But I have. My entire team has."

He took a deep breath. Fuck. Opening up to people was hard. But there was something about the way that she watched him with her big, honey-brown eyes that made him want to lay his heart bare to her, knowing she'd protect it like she protected her fellow captives even when it wasn't the easiest choice. Even if nothing physical ever happened between them, he knew he could trust her to do the right thing. He wanted to put his faith in her, like he'd never done with anyone other than his crew. It was all moving too quickly for him, but he had a nearly uncontrollable urge to hand his heart to her, all dented and scratched and worse for wear, because he knew she would protect it and never abuse it. That just wasn't who she was.

She leaned on the bike next to him and threaded her fingers through his. "Tell me," she said in a gentle voice.

Giving her hand a squeeze, he said, "While we served in the 'Guard, we saw some shit, did some shit. We were the best at what we did, too. Then we saw something we weren't supposed to see and couldn't ignore. Our captain, Patrick Sevilen, was dealing in the narcotic Pink Moon, using our missions as cover. We figured it out and started gathering evidence against him so we could bring him to justice. But he was tipped off — by the woman I was seeing, someone I thought loved me like I did her — to what we were doing. Because of her and her warning, he beat us to the punch and, using manufacturing evidence, turned us in for the crimes he had committed. We were court-marshaled."

"Oh, shit." Bea's eyes were wide, his hand clenched tight in hers. "That's horrible. Your lady friend was the one who betrayed you to him? That daft cow. I'm so sorry."

Her understanding and anger on his behalf eased the weight that had been pressing on his soul. "I appreciate that." Even now, just thinking about the whole affair made his blood boil. What he wouldn't do for two minutes alone in a room with the man. As for Jannette Swift, well, she'd cheated on him and betrayed him, broken his trust and his heart. She was dead to him.

He cleared his throat. "We tried to fight it, to convince Starguard of our innocence and his guilt. Despite our stellar service records, all those solid missions we'd run for the 'Guard, no one would listen to us. The military court dismissed our evidence against Sevilen while he had enough faked 'evidence' to get us convicted and breaking rocks on an icy moon." He shook his head. "That was when the Knight stepped in. He pulled some strings, made some arrangements, and, because of him, we were able to avoid prison."

He'd seen the corruption and rot under the sharp gray uniforms the people in power wore, and that had been enough for him. Bea's miscarriage of justice only strengthened his belief that most law enforcement agencies were no better than organized crime syndicates.

"And that's why you owed this Knight guy a bunch of favors?"

"Exactly."

"Why would he go to all that trouble for a couple of favors from some military guys?" she asked.

Quin rubbed the back of his neck. In for a penny, in for a pound. "Few outside our circles know this, but the Knight is my cousin." It had surprised him when Rhain got them released from the military prison, but then, family and clan were important to both of them. Even when they cleared all the favors, Quin would never be able to pay Rhain back for everything he did for them.

"Ah. Family," she said with a knowing glance. "So, what happened to the bad guy?"

He ran his fingers through his hair, wincing as they caught on the knots the wind tied in it. "Eventually he slipped up, got caught. Got a light sentence, too." The bastard was already out. He kept hoping they'd run into their ex-captain in some bar so he'd have the excuse to punch him really hard in the solar plexus. It would be so satisfying.

"Well, hells. That bites. I'm sorry that happened to you and that you were treated that way. You should be able to trust the people you serve under. Starguard is supposed to protect everyone's rights, after all." Her eyes darkened. "Though we both know that doesn't happen. Corruption is a disease that's hard to eradicate."

She'd been let down by those in authority, too, and his heart clenched. He wanted to make it right. He wanted to kiss away the hurt.

She bumped a shoulder against his. "So Caroville is a no-go then. Okay. What's the plan when we get to Toro?" He flashed her his most charming smile, but she wagged a finger in his face. "Don't. You may have shared your deep, dark secrets with me, but that doesn't mean you've charmed me out of my pants just yet. You'll have to work harder than that to impress me."

He snorted, not expecting that to come out of her mouth. So... they were on the same page then? His smile widened when she shot him a coy look. They were definitely going to wind up in bed together. Hopefully, soon. He needed her naked and coming around him.

She let go of his hand to smack at his arm. "Oh, no, sir. A rogue's smile isn't enough. Girl's got to have her standards, after all." She folded her arms over her chest and sniffed, her nose in the air.

Damn. Each time she opened her mouth, he liked her more and more. But they were polar opposites. His life was lived on the shadowy side of the street, and she belonged in the sunshine, sprinkling rainbows and glitter in her wake.

Even so, he wanted to get her into a bed and fuck her into next week. Maybe after that, they'd move on. No commitment, no worries when he delivered her safely back to where she belonged. She'd go back to her life and he to his. So why did his heart feel so heavy at the thought of leaving her?

Shaking away the pall of sadness, he said, "The plan is we're going to go into town, find a change of clothes, a place to crash, and something to eat." Her stomach rumbled when he mentioned food. It had been a while since either of them had eaten anything. "I'll get in contact with my crew, who will come get us. We'll get off this rock and head to Badin for your meeting."

"Easy as that?"

"Easy as that," he said with more confidence than he felt. So far, nothing in this mission had gone to plan. He was already considering what to do when this plan went to shit.

She gave him a dubious look before swinging back onto the bike. "Sure."

Obviously, she didn't think it was going to be as easy as he was making it sound, either. With her arms once again wrapped around his waist, he kick-started the motorcycle and headed into town.

17

BEA

Her cheek resting on Quin's broad back, Bea did her best not to think of worst-case scenarios, but they kept spinning through her brain: They wouldn't find a way off the planet in time, no one would be at Ghost's meeting spot, Quin would betray her and turn her in, someone would figure out she had a bounty on her head and snatch her. She'd now escaped two abductions — three if you counted Bessa's bounty grab — and was racing towards a lawless town on the back of a stolen motorcycle. What was her life right now?

Shielding her face from the stones and dust the bike kicked up, she breathed deep to reset herself but only managed to inhale the scent of Quin. Even though he definitely needed a bath — the gods knew she smelled like the back end of a troll, so who was she to comment — she liked his underlying natural scent. It reminded her of cloves and dirt after a spring rain. Then again, she was probably loopy from not enough sleep, water, or food and projecting some of her favorite scents onto a man who she was seriously considering taking to bed for a night or two. She absolutely wasn't getting attached to his sarcastic self. That would be reckless, and she was working on making better choices.

As she usually did when she found herself in a situation where she was floundering, she considered what her sister would do. Dai had always been the adventurous one, standing up for what she believed in, taking on any challenge thrown at her while Bea was the quiet one who observed and analyzed before she'd even consider trying it herself. But Bea had reached the stage of life where she wanted to say 'fuck it' and dive headfirst into the next adventure, including bedding a hot pirate. Dai certainly would. Then she'd leave him in the dust, gallivanting off to the next adventure, sated and pleased with herself. But Bea wasn't usually the love-em-and-leave-em type. But the rest? Maybe. Yes. Possibly. But not until they'd both gotten cleaned up. Eau de Troll Toes was not sexy.

All her lustful thoughts were neither here nor there if Quin wasn't attracted to her. She thought there was a spicy little spark between them, but she wasn't the best at judging body language. He'd also flirted with her. Did that mean he wanted her or was this his way of getting her to cooperate? Maybe he didn't mix business with pleasure. She heaved a sigh and adjusted her grip on the man in question. Maybe she'd skip the guesswork and go find one of those happy endings places he'd mentioned. She sniffed out a laugh at herself. She'd never. But it was fun to consider. If she were a completely different person.

The bike slowed, and she peeked over Quin's shoulder to get a glimpse of this supposedly lawless town. It was nothing like she expected. There was only one main street, but it was bright and clean. The one and two-story buildings painted bright colors lined the road. Planters spilling over with greenery and flowers flanked most business entrances. The wide sidewalks contained small seating areas filled with a wide variety of beings reading, eating, and relaxing in the warm sunlight.

"This is your lawless town?" she asked, charmed. She spotted a bookstore she'd love to visit, if they had the time.

Quin turned down an alley and killed the engine. "Discreet is a better word, I'd say." He frowned at her. "Just because someone doesn't want to live under the UBP's rules doesn't mean they want to live in squalor."

It was cute how he defended the town's residents. "No, you're right. I didn't know what to expect, but this is adorable." Sliding off the tall seat, Bea stretched some of the stiffness out of her body. Riding a bike for that long was for younger people. Decades younger. "Gods, I need a hot bath to soak this day away," she said, clasping her hands behind her back and stretching. Her back crackled and popped.

"Not yet, Daisy," Quin said, trying to wake up his comm. The hologram flickered and spat above his hand before going dark. He cursed. Now that they were in town, he'd hoped it would work. "Try yours."

"Mine's disabled." Dai did that when she broke Bea out of jail as an extra layer of protection, adding in some techy woo-woo Izumi whipped up to insulate Bea so she couldn't be tracked through it. "Is something blocking the signal? Or are we too far out?" The lack of a personal comm hadn't been an issue along the outer rim. Most colonies out there didn't have the infrastructure for comms to work consistently anyway. It was faster and more reliable to send data packets in big bursts or with supply ships.

"Might be something in these mountains blocking signals, or it might be that we're far enough away from a major port." He shrugged. "This does present us with another problem, however. No access to my accounts, so no way to pay for anything."

"Shit," she said with a long sigh. Bea saw her dreams of cleanliness, food, and comfort float away into the bright red sky. Mulling over how they could solve this, she worked out the rest of the kinks from her body, pushing against the whitewashed cob wall to twist her back until she felt a delicious pop as the tension released up her spine. She repeated the process on the other side.

"That's one issue. The other is contacting my crew." Still fussing with his comm, he walked to the road and looked around. "In towns like these, people aren't overly trusting of things they can't see. They prefer cold, hard cash rather than digital transactions. Even if comms were working, they might not take our credits."

She'd hoped that coming to a town would make life easier, not throw up more roadblocks. Oh, well. They'd just have to get creative. "Didn't you say you knew someone here?"

"Won't do much good if I can't use my comm to contact him. Not even sure he's still around." He shrugged, walking back to her. "There's a bar a few blocks up the road," Quin said. "But we need to be careful. Stay here while I check things out."

"Wait," she said, putting a hand on his arm. His muscles flexed under her fingers.

"No, seriously. It'll be safer if you stay here. This town may look welcoming, but looks can be deceiving."

"Not sure that's true, but that's not why I stopped you. We need to talk."

He winced. "Not the words a man likes to hear. What, are you breaking up with me?" He put a hand over his heart and faked a look of devastation. "But, honey, I love you. Let's work this out."

Her heart leapt the teensiest smidge with his fake declaration of love. How long had it been since a person she was attracted to told her he loved her, even in play? Arden certainly hadn't. So obviously far too long since that fickle organ of hers got excited over it. "More sarcasm?" she asked, narrowing her eyes at him.

"It is my go-to, yes." He leaned a shoulder up against the wall next to her, shielding her from beings on the street.

She rolled her eyes. "Our overall plan is still to get off this planet, back to your ship, and meet my contact in Badin, right?" She needed to triple check. Not that she didn't trust him, but she was still wary. It seemed too simple.

He sighed. "As I've said. Repeatedly."

"Quin, what if the person I'm meeting doesn't have any useful information? What if, after all this, I'm still a wanted criminal with a godsdamned bounty on my head? Then what?" She tried to channel her sister and be brave, but the fear loomed in the back of her mind like a threatening storm. The hope was that

Ghost could give her actionable information or even a solid lead burned like a flame in the dark. But what if it was a ploy to use her as transport for whatever info was on the data dot she carried or for the bounty on her head? She hadn't allowed herself to think too deeply or critically about what she was doing, instead just pushed herself forward, believing it would all work out. Optimism was great until it crashed up against cold, hard reality.

But Quin didn't seem concerned. "Whatever happens, I'll keep you safe, exactly like we were hired to do."

"For how long? Days? Months? Years?" She shuddered. "I can't do this for much longer, Quin. I have a daughter, a life. I need to get back to that." She had to finish her system. She was so close to success, she just knew it. Her brain itched with ideas to try, little tweaks she hadn't thought of before that should solve the problems she'd been banging her head against for too long. And when she finally got it working, it was going to change how people traveled in space. She had to believe that all her troubles would be worth it in the end. "We need a better plan."

"And you have one, I'm guessing?" He tucked his hands into his back pockets, looking faintly amused.

Her cheeks flushed. There was nothing amusing about her life being put on permanent hold. She used that emotion to fuel her determination. "My contact's information aside, I don't just want to clear my name. I want to track down the people responsible and make them pay, and I want to hire you to help me do it." It felt right, this rush of righteousness. Yes, she needed her name cleared, but then what? She still didn't know for certain who did all this. Her guesswork pointed to Vanid Shipping, though she had no proof. What if they — whoever "they" were — decided she and her system were a threat that needed to be eliminated? If so, just getting the charges dropped wouldn't keep her safe. Besides, she needed justice for both herself and Arden. She squeezed her hands into fists. Whoever was responsible needed to answer for what they'd be done and be hamstrung so they couldn't do it again.

"Ooh, a bloodthirsty Daisy. I like this side of you." Grinning, he chucked her under the chin like she was an amusing child.

Narrowing her eyes, she punched him in the chest.

"Ow," he said, giving her a wounded look as he rubbed where she'd hit him. "Why'd you do that?"

"I'm serious, Quin, and I need you to take me seriously. Not everything is a joke, you know." She felt her throat tighten. How could he not understand how important this was?

The smile dropping from his face, he held up a finger. "First, I'm under contract to protect you, so I won't break that contract or take another one until we're done. You're under my protection for as long as it takes. We'll figure it out. I've got resources we can use if your contact doesn't come through." He added a finger. "Second, you've got no money. Your accounts are all frozen. So even if you wanted to, you couldn't hire my team or anyone else to help you out, so just relax. You're stuck with me. Sorry, Buttercup." He ran a finger along the edge of her jaw and tipped up her chin so she met his eyes. "Okay?"

Some of her righteous anger burned away. Her shoulders slumped. "Okay."

"Now, you wait here like a good girl, and I'll be right back." He strolled down the alley, whistling a merry tune.

Her anger rushed back, and she gave his departing back the middle finger. Good girl, my ass. Then she looked at the massive motorcycle and smiled. If she couldn't have justice yet, a little petty revenge would have to do.

18

QUIN

Bea was going to murder him in his sleep if he wasn't careful. But her expression when he called her a good girl and told her to stay? Totally worth the death sentence.

Smothering a smile, he schooled his expression into a blank canvas and walked into the bar. Delightfully named "Tits Out", the bar's interior decor was gaudy neon lights and ladies' undergarments, which hung from every available overhead surface. Quin didn't see any tits actually out. Disappointing.

There were, however, several constants to a bar like Tits Out in the hours before darkness fell. One, it smelled like stale beer and regret. Maybe it would mask his own stench some. And two, the regulars were already posted up in their spots, blearily nursing their drinks.

At the bar, he slid into a seat next to a bear of a man hunched over a steaming cup of coffee. Quin flagged down the bartender, who'd been aimlessly shining a glass with a clean white rag, pointed at the man's drink and signaled for two.

"Hey, Bert," Quin said, nodding thanks as the bartender set down two steaming cups of coffee.

Bert's shoulders hunched up around his ears at the sound of Quin's voice, but he didn't take his eyes off the cup in front of him. "Quin. Fuck," he said with a weary sigh. "How'd you find me?"

Quin took a sip of the coffee and wheezed out a cough. Not coffee. More like rotgut with a coffee carafe merely waved over it. Alright then. Carefully setting the cup back down, he said, "Wasn't actually looking for you, so I'm going to take this as a happy accident."

Bert shot him a dark look and took a large, leisurely drink. "You gonna haul me to the Knight?" He drew out Rhain's moniker into six syllables, one of those times when the universal translator got the inflections wrong.

"Not the outcome I'm looking for, no." A few years ago, Quin's cousin had put a bounty on Bert's head because of his unfortunate decision to attempt to steal information from Rhain's horde. Bert was foolish. No one stole from a dragon's horde and got away with it. There was always a price to pay.

"If you're not gonna bag and tag me, then what?" Bert asked.

"You've successfully avoided the Knight's trackers for what, three years?

Bert perked up a little. "Four. No one ever thought to search this dusty planet." He frowned into his cup. "'Cept you. Did you know they have trolls here? Big motherfuckers, too. They ride these giant motorcycles and snatch up folks who are just minding their own business." He leaned close, like he was telling a dark secret. "Rumor has it they eat people." He tried to take a drink from the empty cup, then set it back down, pushing it back towards the edge of the bar. "Trolls, man."

"I'm familiar. Unfortunately." The stench of the trolls' prison still clung to him. He was surprised Bert didn't smell it. The rotgut must have dulled his senses. "Look, Bert. I like you, but I'm in a bit of a bind. If the Knight finds out I ran into you and didn't bring you to him, well, that would not be good for me." Actually, his cousin wouldn't do much except stomp around and yell or beat his ass in the training ring unless it was something truly enormous that Quin fucked up. One benefit of being a member of the

Green Dragon Clan was that the man people spoke of in hushed tones couldn't lay a finger on you without his sister's permission. Because, as much as you didn't want to piss off the Knight, you absolutely didn't step a toe out of line around the clan's matriarch. She was known for stringing people who made her mad up by their ankles and leaving them in the Deep Woods overnight. Quin shuddered just thinking about it.

Pulling the new cup under his nose, Bert turned surprisingly clear blue eyes towards Quin. "You're not going to bring me in?" He chewed on that for a minute then said, "So, what do you want then?"

"You're a smart one, Bert, because you're correct. I do need something from you." Quin pushed his barely touched drink towards Bert and leaned back in his chair. "I'm thinking a small cash settlement might do just fine."

Bert grunted, slurping his drink. "A bribe. Should have guessed as much. Welp, you're out of luck 'cause I ain't got nothing to give you." He nodded towards his empty cup, being whisked away by the efficient barkeep. "The last of my credits."

Quin figured getting money out of Bert would be like squeezing blood from a turnip, but it had been worth a try. "What about that sweet little rock hopper you had? What was her name... Esmerelda?"

The corners of Bert's mouth turned down. "Sold her. Broke my heart, too."

"Sorry, man. That sucks." Well, fuck. There went that. He didn't want to resort to theft. The people here either had no money and nowhere else to go or they were criminals in their own right and would shoot him dead if he looked at them wrong. Neither was a pleasing option. He could always sell the troll bike, but that would both raise questions as to how he got his hands on it in the first place and leave him without a vehicle. Again, no good options. "Where's your place, Bert? Surely, you don't sleep here at the bar."

"You looking to kick me out of my own home?" Bert's voice

rose and the tall bartender, who looked as if he were carved from the red rocks surrounding the town, narrowed his eyes at them.

"No. No. Slow down there." The last thing Quin needed was for Bert to cause a ruckus. "I just need a place so my partner and I can clean up and catch some shut-eye. You let me borrow your place for a little while, and then we'll be gone, and you can go back to living your life."

"You want to borrow my place?" Bert's bushy eyebrows drew together like this was an utterly foreign concept. "That's it? And you'll forget you ever saw me?"

"Absolutely. I like you, Bert, and don't really want to deliver you to the Knight."

"Hey, that's sorta of nice of you." He tapped the edge of his cup. "I mean, you are blackmailing me, but it's the gentlest blackmail I've experienced."

"And I'll need to contact my crew, too. Damned comm isn't working." Quin smacked at his wrist, but all he got was a shock.

"It's the mountains. Can't get a signal worth a damn around here unless you've got something powerful. Something to do with magnetic resonance or some such. Ain't that right, Feriq?"

The barkeep, who'd been listening in on their conversation while polishing the already gleaming glasses, came over and leaned an arm on the smooth wooden top. "Bert's got it in one. Makes it an ideal place to come if you're looking to get away from it all." He winked at Bert, who blushed, and slid a fresh cup in front of Quin.

Quin hesitated.

"Just coffee this time," Feriq said, his lips quirked up.

With a nod, Quin took a sip. Bitter and hot, but just coffee. He took another sip, thinking. No comms meant they couldn't contact his crew from here. They'd have to ride to another town, adding time to Bea's already tight schedule. If it was at all preventable, he'd make sure Bea didn't miss her meet. "So, there's nothing here that could interface with anyone outside of this town?"

Bert tipped his head towards the tall man behind the bar. "Feriq's got the only desktop comm in town powerful enough to get a signal past those mountain ranges."

Picking up a glass and wiping the inside, Feriq inclined his head.

"Let me guess: it's going to cost me." Quin sighed. He was dirty, tired, hungry, and quite honestly, not up for more chaos or crime at the moment. Fuck this planet.

Raising one long finger, Feriq said, "Hold that thought." He disappeared through the doorway behind him.

"You know, you're not as bad as everyone says," Bert said, sliding him a sidelong glance.

"Gee, thanks. I should get that on a nameplate."

Bert sat up straighter. "No, seriously. When I first saw you come in, I thought, 'Bert, you're done for. Quin doesn't let his prey go, not ever.' I hear tell that once you're on a job, you don't stop until you get it done, especially when you're doing a job for the Knight." He risked another glance at Quin. "But here you are and, instead of cuffing me and dragging me out of here, you're drinking Feriq's bad coffee, looking like you've been run over a buncha times and dumped in a pit of rotting mosshorns."

Bert shrank back when Quin let out a growl of frustration. "Bert, you're right. I do always finish the job I'm hired to do." Speaking of his current job, he hoped Bea hadn't gotten herself into any more trouble. It was finally sinking in that ordering her to stay in the alley was a big mistake. Huge. In fact, he had no doubt that she'd left that alley as soon as his back was turned because he felt her glare boring into his back as he walked away. He needed to get back to her. Time to move this along. "Luckily for you, I wasn't hired to find you. Not today, anyway. Which is why we can make a deal."

Feriq returned and, glancing around, leaned close to Quin, but quickly pulled back, his nose wrinkling. "Good gods, you weren't kidding about needing to clean up."

Quin sniffed his armpit and gagged. Pungent.

Feriq squared his shoulders, as if bracing himself to brave the stench that enveloped Quin, and leaned in again. "Here's my deal. You find a way to get Bert off the Knight's shit list and not only will I let you use my big, beautiful comm system, but I'll also let you crash in the back room until such time as you take your leave of us. It's small but furnished and soundproof, so you'll be able to sleep like the dead, even when we're raging in here." He leaned a little closer and whispered in Quin's ear. "There's even a shower with lots of hot, running water."

Quin's eyes widened. "Feriq, if you're not careful, I'm going to kiss you."

"Promises, promises," Feriq said with a grin. "Maybe after you get yourself cleaned up, we can revisit that."

Bert looked at them, his head tilting from one side to the other. "So, that is that a yes?"

19

BEA

Before leaving the shop, Bea carefully tucked the wad of credits she'd acquired into the hidden front pocket of her pants.

"Thanks for everything, ladies," she called out as she pushed open the door, waving to the three goblin sisters who ran the repair shop. "I'll send you that recipe when I get back home. Trust me, you've got to try it."

"Safe travels, Bea," the three chorused, then turned back to the motorcycle that was nearly twice as tall as they were. The shortest and eldest sister, Kels, rubbed her hands together in glee as she eyed their new prize.

Bea darted across the street, weaving between beings window shopping, and headed towards the bar Quin had disappeared into. Good girl, her ass. Ha. Numbskull. He had to have known that would backfire on him.

No one in the bar even raised their heads from their drinks when she opened the door, sunlight pouring in behind her. She paused just inside the doorway, letting her eyes adjust to the dim interior as she scanned the space for Quin. Exactly what she would expect from a shady border town bar with the tacky name of Tits Out, though it made her snicker. She'd have to remember to tell Dai.

Quin and two men hunched together at a corner of the long polished bar, ignoring everyone around them. Casually, she walked in their direction and took a seat at the high top table closest to them. Quin didn't notice.

The bartender left the conversation to bring her a cup of coffee. "You look like you could use this," he said.

"Thanks." She cupped her hands around the blue speckled mug and smiled up at him. "I like your hair." His impressive mane flowed down his back in a tumble of deep auburn. She resisted the urge to pet it. It was almost as hard as with the Haruet. Pretty things made her want to stroke them, to feel them beneath her fingers. Much like Quin's arms, corded with muscles. They, too, were eminently petable.

He shook his head, and the locks rippled. "Thanks, doll. I'm Feriq Śa and this is my place so, you need anything, you just let me know." With a pivot, he returned to his place at the bar and rejoined the conversation. Quin still didn't turn around, clueless she was there.

Taking a sip of the strong coffee, Bea focused, cocked an ear to listen in on the group's conversation. It had been a while since she'd last used the eavesdropping skills her sister had taught her. She'd perfected them as a pre-teen, desperate to be let in on adult conversations. While those conversations were boring — filled with stuff about politics and money that held absolutely no interest to the under-ten crowd — using that skill as a teen turned out to be highly beneficial. Though she wasn't part of the popular groups at school, she always had the scoop on who was dating whom and where the best parties were, even when she wasn't invited.

She was a little rusty, but she caught the drift of their conversation. And Quin was about to make a less-than-advantageous bargain on their behalf. Dammit.

Picking up her coffee, she slid into the seat next to him and set the cup down with a loud thunk. Both Quin and the man next to him startled at her appearance. Feriq, who'd been keeping an eye on her, merely raised an eyebrow.

"Gentlemen. Let me interrupt you because Quin here," she jabbed a thumb in his direction, "is obviously exhausted and not at his bargaining best. Otherwise, he'd never come this close to striking what is quite frankly a terrible deal for us."

A smile blazed across Feriq's face. "But not so terrible for Bert here."

She eyed Bert.

"Who are you?" Bert asked, his gaze darting between the three of them.

"This is Daisy. She's my partner," Quin said, shooting her a look that told her to play along.

She raised an eyebrow. He was protecting her again. "Yep. Partner. That's what I am. Which is why he can't make any deals without my consent."

Feriz watched the interplay between them. "Well, Daisy, is it?" He sounded like he didn't believe that was her name. Smart man.

She nodded. Quin and his stupid pet names.

"We were negotiating for lodging, access to my comms, and shower privileges." He gave her a once-over. "Which you need as much as he does."

She considered being offended, but he was right. "True. However, us taking on the risk involved in scrubbing Bert's record with a man as paranoid and dangerous as the Knight for what is essentially a night of room and board is definitely not an equal trade, not even with your impressive equipment." With a smirk, she let her eyes travel from his head down his body and back again.

His delighted laughter filled the bar. "Oh, she's a sassy one. I like. I was hoping to slip that by your partner while he wasn't functioning at 100 percent. Quin, this delectable flower is much smarter than you are."

"Only because you gave her real coffee while I got that rocket fuel Bert's drinking," Quin grumbled.

"So, Flower," Feriq said, leaning close and playing with a curl that had yet again escaped her braid. "Shall we bargain?"

She angled closer with a grin. "Absolutely."

***

FERIQ'S SYSTEM was truly a thing of beauty. After sending Quin off to get a shower, she finalized the deal with Feriq and used the time to send off some messages. First, she checked her private folder, tucked away in a tiny corner of a random company's massive server. She'd set it up her senior year at university so she'd have backup for everything she'd ever worked on. A cover-your-assets kind of folder. No one knew about it, not even Dai. She breathed a sigh of relief to see all her research notes. She'd only lost about a week's worth of work, all the handwritten notes she hadn't had a chance to upload before the fire. It was upsetting, but better than losing everything. At least she wouldn't have to start from scratch.

Next, to her daughter, she sent an upbeat letter, briefly mentioning how things were progressing and that those false charges against her mother should be dropped sometime soon before moving on to telling a cute story about the goblin sisters she just met. She didn't want Essy to worry. Her girl needed to stay focused on her classes and exams and parties instead of worrying about her mother. It was bad enough Essy knew about the arrest and the charges against her.

Then, she opened a coded message from Dai, dated two days after she'd boarded the *Intrepid*.

Bea,

Bad news, I'm afraid. The bounty on your head doubled. My team is following a thread to find who is backing it. You're probably on your way to Badin for your meeting, but don't worry, I'm sending help your way.

A source hinted Arden had a hand in the arson and that not all your prototypes burned up in the fire. No confirmation, and no details beyond that so far. Trust that I will find out the truth for you.

Be careful and stay safe. Miss you. Love you.

–Dai

Bea sat back in the hard-backed chair and stared at Dai's words on the screen, trying to process. Bad news was one way of putting it. Fuck. She dropped her head into her hands and tried to breathe through the overwhelm. Why was all this happening to her? She just wanted to make the galaxy easier for everyone to travel around. With a groan of frustration, she scrubbed her nails over her scalp. Thank the goddess Dai was on her side. She sent a coded response to her sister, routing it through the back channels Dai set up ages ago, updating her about what was going on, then methodically wiped her digital fingerprints from Feriq's system.

Having a larger bounty on her head sucked, but there was nothing she could do about it at the moment. Briefly, she wondered if Quin was the help that Dai had sent. Maybe? And if it wasn't him and his crew, what happened to the help Dai promised? Either way, she had backup in the form of the space pirate. He was enough. He had to be.

If Dai's source was right and someone had gotten their hands on a prototype, what did they hope to gain from stealing it? Her system wasn't functional yet. The prototypes in her workshop were failed attempts. None of them worked. A few had even blown up. So if Arden had been after a functional system, he'd died for nothing. Fuck.

And then there was Dai's news about Arden. She'd wondered. Leaning towards optimism, she'd hoped she was wrong and that it was just some weird coincidence he'd been at her workshop without her. However, Arden's behavior had changed drastically in the months prior to his death. She'd chalked it up to their relationship going sour, but what if it had been something else?

And the idea that he might be the one behind the fire raised more questions. If he set the fire, had his death been accidental?

Who raised the bounty? A partner? With Arden dead, who had the prototype that Dai said was out there somewhere? *What if...* she chewed her bottom lip, not liking where her thoughts were taking her. What if Arden wasn't actually dead? That single tooth surviving the fire was weird, right? She'd always thought so, but what did she know about the cremation of bodies.

She blinked at the dark monitor in front of her. She was too tired to fully process all this new information and the resulting questions. The chair squeaked against the tiles as she stood. There was nothing she could do about any of it right now. What she needed more than anything was a hot shower and a soft bed. Everything else could wait.

20

QUIN

She'd dismissed him like he was a child, sending him off to take a shower while she did the work at the bargaining table. And he'd followed her instructions without argument. He blamed it on being so exhausted he could barely see straight. Otherwise, he would have at least thrown a sarcastic comment her way.

Before getting into the shower, he'd sent a message to his crew using Feriq's fancy comm, hoping for a speedy reply because they were nearby. No joy.

Securing a towel around his waist, he opened the door of the bathroom into the small but quiet room Feriq provided them. Bea perched on the very edge of the bed, unbraiding and untangling her hair. Her eyes widened when he appeared half-naked in the doorway. With a cheeky grin, he flexed his abs, the towel slipping dangerously low. Bea's hands stilled in her hair as she watched him, unblinking.

With an audible swallow, she said, "You'd better not have used up all the hot water."

"Or what?" Enjoying the way her eyes devoured him, he made sure to flex his arms while scrubbing a small towel over his wet hair.

"Or I'll be incredibly pissed off," she said, throwing a decorative pillow in his direction.

He batted it away. "Don't worry. I'm almost positive I saved you some. There's even cleanser in there so you can wash your hair."

She brightened. "Really? I hope it's what Feriq uses so I can try it. His hair is absolutely gorgeous." She loosened another section of her braid, unraveling it piece by piece.

He couldn't look away as waves of black shot with silver unwound beneath her nimble fingers. Clearing his throat, he took a seat in a cushioned purple chair and propped his legs up next to her on the bed. "So, hit me with it. What's the damage?"

She paused. "What?"

"The deal you made for us." Twirling a hand in the air, he sank deeper into the chair, spreading his legs a little to get some air flow going. It had the added bonus of making Bea blush as she tried desperately not to look up his towel. "How did it go? You did say you were going to do better than just this room and all the hot water we could use."

"Ah." She glanced longingly at the bathroom door. "You're not going to let me shower first?"

"If you wanted a shower so badly, you shouldn't have sent me packing." He gave her a slightly feral grin. "Spill first, then you can use up all the rest of Feriq's hot water."

"Fine." With a sigh, she pulled off a boot, wrinkling her nose at it. "Besides room and board and the use of Feriq's comm system, I also bargained for the use of a little rock hopper complete with fuel and travel supplies. That way, we get off this godsforsaken planet. I can drop you off wherever your little space buddies are and head to Badin in time to meet my contact." She concentrated on unlacing her other boot, not looking at him.

"So your current plan is to dump me and head off to Badin alone? That is not at all what we agreed upon." He sat up, his bare feet hitting the floor with a thud. He leaned forward. "Listen and hear me, Beatrix Farsirus, because I'm only going to say this one time. If you think you're going anywhere without me, you've got another think coming. I mean... fuck, woman." He scrubbed a hand through his wet hair. "We've been through this. You need to wrap your head about the fact that I'm with you, no matter what. Even if I didn't have a contract, at this point, you can't get rid of me." Granted, he'd rather her safely stashed on the Knight's base. Let someone else do the hard work of clearing her name. Her plan was dangerous. But, since she was determined to take back control of her own life, the least he could do was support her choices while watching her back.

Also, did she really think she could do this alone, no backup, without him? Though most knew Badin as the Pleasure Planet, for someone with no resources and on the run, it would be nearly impossible to navigate safely. As a whole, planets were not his thing, and this one, with all its glitz, wealth, and snobbery, rubbed him the wrong way. One thing he appreciated, however, was that facial recognition bots were banned for privacy's sake. All those celebrities and wealthy individuals who vacationed there demanded privacy. A large local peace presence as well as private security forces offset that positive. Eyes everywhere. If she went alone, she'd be spotted and arrested in no time.

She twisted her ring. "I hear you, but it's better if I do this alone. There's no need for you to be more involved in my problems."

Something had shaken her. "What happened?"

Shaking her head, she said, "Nothing. I just thought..."

He reached out and cupped her chin in his hand, turning her to look at him. "I don't know what happened during the time it took me to shower, but you need to understand that I'm in this until the end. I told you I'd protect you. If that means going to Badin to meet some shady hacker, that's what we'll do. You need to trust me. Do you trust me?"

She paused, her worried eyes searching his. Finally, she nodded.

"I'm going to need to hear you say it, Daisy," he said, tracing her jaw with his thumb. Her silken skin teased his senses, and it took all his willpower not to pull her into his lap and kiss the sense back into her.

Her throat worked. "Yes. I trust you."

With a last caress, he released his grip and sat back. "Good. Now tell me what happened."

"My sister sent me a message." She was back to twisting her fingers together. He put a hand over hers, stilling them. "Someone doubled the bounty on my head."

"Fuck." The low-ish bounty and threat of the Knight's wrath had been enough to keep Amaryllis and the Cabal away. Now, the temptation would be too hard to resist. She was right to be worried.

She nodded. "Exactly. It gets worse. One of her contacts suggested Arden had a hand in the arson, and at least one of my prototypes was stolen." She stared at their entwined hands for a moment. When she lifted her gaze to his, it was filled with righteous anger. "That rat-bastard. If he weren't already dead, I might be tempted to kill him myself."

He agreed, but swallowed down his own anger. "Did your sister tell you anything else?" He kept his voice calm for Bea's sake. She was already upset and mad enough without him adding fuel to her fire.

"No. Dai's message was short. Not too many details. Said she was investigating. Even if she did have more, she wouldn't have sent it, though our messages are encoded. Her paranoia runs deep." She took a deep breath. "But she did say she was sending help. Tell me, Quin. Are you that help?"

Surprised, he scrubbed a hand over his jaw. "Rhain didn't say why he wanted you protected. Like your sister, he didn't give too many details, only to find you and bring you to the safety of our home base on Gyan Station." He paused, considering. In his drive to collect information, Rhain had his fingers in all kinds of pies and had contact with all kinds of individuals, including spies. It was entirely possible that Dai was one of those contacts. "So my answer is... maybe. I wish I had a more definitive answer for you." He gave her hand a squeeze. With these new crumbs of information, a picture of what might have occurred was slowly taking shape in his mind. But he didn't want to voice it until he had facts, proof to share with her.

"Okay." She paused, her brow furrowed. "I think I need a shower and some sleep. I just..." With a little shrug, she slid her hands out from under his and stood.

He hated that Arden, a moldering slug of a man, most likely betrayed her, hurting her in such a way that it struck at her very core. It sounded to Quin like Arden was a con man, one who'd charmed his way into her life and her pants so he could steal her research, probably hoping to sell it to the highest bidder. Lucky for him, his partner — there had to be a partner, otherwise who would foot the bounty? — betrayed him, leaving him to burn because if Arden weren't already dead, Quin would have taken great pleasure in plucking every hair from the man's body and throwing him into a saltwater lake.

"So that's why you want to ditch me to go it alone?" he said, realization dawning. "Because someone you thought cared about you instead betrayed you. No. Don't let that jackass get in your head."

"Okay, fine. Fine. You're right." She threw up her hands. "It threw me for a loop, you know? I need some time to process everything." She moved towards the bathroom.

"Wait. Feriq gave us a ship? Just for ensuring Bert's safety?" He'd suspected the pair were more than friends by the way they'd interacted, exchanging glances, the light touches, the way they finished one another's sentences. Feriq must really like Bert to agree to all Bea had bargained for. That, or Bea was as good as she claimed.

"Feriq is the type who will do all he can for his friends." She brightened. "Besides, we bonded hard over mimosas and shitty exes." She looked quite pleased with herself. "And we're renting the ship. I just drove a hard bargain over the cost."

He raised his eyebrows, surprised. "He's trusting us to return his ship and to pay him later because you charmed him?" It sounded too good to be true. "That was some serious bonding you did."

"Don't you worry your pretty little head about it. I gave him a down payment." A delighted grin lit up her face.

He was instantly suspicious. "With what money, Buttercup?"

She reached into the waistband of her pants and pulled out a small handful of credits, waving them in triumph.

"What the ever-loving fuck?" He snatched them out of her hand. "Where did you get these? Did you rob someone?" He knew leaving her in that alley was a mistake.

She snatched the wad back, stuffing it into her pocket. "No. I sold the troll bike."

"You mean my troll bike?" He liked that bike. It was a really cool bike.

"No, I mean my troll bike. I came up with the idea of stealing the bikes, so that means it was mine. Sure, I graciously let you drive it, mostly because your legs are longer than mine and you could reach all the gears and pedals and things, but my idea means my bike."

Had she suggested stealing the bikes? The escape was a bit of a blur, but it sounded more like something he'd suggest than her. He opened his mouth to argue, then closed it again. No point. He wouldn't win. "I'm too fucking tired to debate this with you, Daisy."

"Just admit I outmaneuvered you and made an excellent bargain. You can go to sleep knowing I've got everything handled." She gave him a smug smile and added, "Buttercup."

"What the fuck ever." He growled, pretending to be irritated. Relentless, that's what she was. He briefly wondered if she'd be just as relentless in bed. Speaking of... he pulled back the fluffy duvet and crisp white sheets. The soothing scent of lavender drifted out. Feriq was quite the housekeeper. "Go take your shower. We'll talk about this after we both get some sleep."

"Mmhum." She gave him a full-body, up-and-down look, and stalked into the bathroom and shut the door.

Was that agreement or not? He didn't know, and his brain was too damn fuzzy to figure out the puzzle that was Beatrix Farsirius. With a sigh, he flopped face-down on the bed. Between one breath and the next, he was asleep.

21

BEA

She woke up both deliciously toasty and warm while also feeling completely smothered. Someone's leg was thrown over hers and a muscular arm held her tightly against a firm chest. Someone. Like she didn't know exactly who it was, but she wasn't quite awake enough to figure out how he came to be draped all over her.

After the best shower she'd had in her life, she came out of the bathroom to find Quin spread out like a starfish, butt-naked, and sound asleep in the only bed in the room. While he may have started out under the covers, by the time she'd brushed her teeth and changed into a clean shirt, he'd kicked them off, revealing his spectacular bare ass.

He didn't move when she stood over him and glared. Some protector he was. Not even a twitch as she loomed. She could have slit his throat, and he'd never have known it.

She poked his side. Nothing. "Quin, scootch over." Still nothing. She pushed at his insensate body, working to shove him onto just half the bed muttering, "I am an adult woman, and I am not about to sleep on the floor because there's a naked man who I have some in-my-pants feelings for taking over this entire bed." She grunted as she shoved him over another few inches. "Also, I am not ready to commit to actually having sex with you yet." She gave him another push, gaining two inches. "After all, I've just gotten out of a relationship with someone I thought cared for me but who was actually using me, proving how terrible my taste in men is. And look at you." Another inch of movement. "You're a pirate who kidnapped me and yet, here I am, not just working with you and trusting you but lusting after you as well." She shook her head. "What is wrong with me?"

Giving him a final push, she stood back to admire her work. Now there was enough room for her to sleep without clinging for dear life to the edge. Allowing herself one more ogle, she flipped the sheets back over him. Digging out a beautiful, handmade patchwork quilt of intricate blues and greens from a carved wood chest at the foot of the bed, she crawled on top of the covers, pulled the warm blanket up to her chin, and promptly fell asleep.

Only to wake up somehow now under the covers and surrounded by the bone-deep warmth that was Quin. She took a deep breath, inhaling the scent of him — still the scent of cloves and petrichor from before, but thankfully lacking the base note of troll toes to dilute it. She lay there for a moment, enjoying being the little spoon and basking in the comfort that came from it.

How long had it been since she'd just snuggled with someone? She tried to remember. Years. Though he'd showered her with gifts and attention, Arden hadn't been an overly affectionate man. Even after they'd made love, he slept in a separate room. He'd claimed that she flopped around like a landed fish during the night and, if he stayed, he wouldn't get the sleep he needed to function at optimal levels. She hadn't raised a fuss because, quite frankly, she enjoyed having the bed all to herself.

Frowning, she remembered all the other times Arden had avoided any physical intimacy with her except sex and even then, it was more by-the-numbers than passionate. She'd always thought he avoided things like holding her hand or hugs because of his troubled relationship with his mother, or that it made him uncomfortable. But what if it had been because he actually held no affection for her and had no desire to touch her? That made her sad.

She considered her sister's message. Dai wouldn't have mentioned that tidbit about Arden if she wasn't already ninety-nine percent positive of her information's veracity. Which meant he'd been using her. Every interaction, faked. She felt tears prickle her eyes. No. She wasn't going to cry over that shit of a man. She'd cried when the investigators told her he was dead. Now, after learning he'd fucked her over in multiple ways, those were all the tears he'd ever get from her.

Instead, she hardened her determination to uncover the truth, to figure out who had her prototype, and to make sure it was completely worthless to them. She was going to do everything possible to bring down everyone involved and make them pay. If she was lucky, maybe she'd even get a chance to punch someone in the nose.

She huffed out a laugh at her early morning bloodlust and tried to wiggle her way out of Quin's embrace without waking him. Unfortunately, while Quin smelled good and she was super-comfortable, she really needed to pee. With him wrapped around her like a spider monkey, there was really no graceful way to extricate herself from her current position. She unwrapped his arm from her waist and moved it back to rest on his hip, and tried to get up, but she wasn't quick enough.

Burrowing his face into the crook of her neck, Quin muttered something and pulled her closer, flinging a heavy leg over hers and sliding his hand under her sleep shirt to cup her boob. His movements rubbed his morning erection against her backside. Her nipples tightened into peaks, her whole body tingling.

Fucking hells. This was damned inconvenient. She tried to dislodge his arm again, but the giant slab of a man didn't budge. She'd just decided to wake him up and deal with his grumpiness when he started kissing the spot where her neck met her shoulders and gently kneading her breast. Even as her body caught flame, she froze. He couldn't possibly be awake and doing this consciously. Fuck, this was awkward.

"Quin," she said, her voice low and huskier than she expected. He worked his way up her neck, lightly grinding against her ass. Heat pooled in her stomach. "Quin," she said louder, patting his arm. "Wake up."

"Hummm?" he said, all languid and drowsy. He nibbled on her neck and licked along the shell of her ear.

She squeaked out his name as he hit a ticklish spot and nailed him in the stomach with her elbow. Accidentally, of course.

That did it. He yelped and disentangled himself from her, rolling onto his back. "Fuck. Sorry. Fuck." He cleared his throat and scrubbed his hands over his face. "Why did you elbow me? What's going on?" he asked, blinking blearily at her. The thin bedsheet did nothing to hide his impressive morning wood.

Sliding out of bed, Bea took a moment to compose herself, brushing the tangle of hair away from her face and smoothing the silky red shirt Feriq had lent her to sleep in. It hit right above her knees. Never before had a man's shirt been long enough to fit her like you saw in the vids. They always fit her like her own shirts, except boxy. Embarrassed by the morning cuddle session of which he had no memory, but that set her aflame, she went on the defensive. "Obviously, you were having a sex dream about me. I don't blame you, but we're not there just yet." She looked down at the tent under the covers. "Why don't you get that under control while I get ready." And she stalked into the bathroom, shutting the door behind her.

Even though she didn't need it, she made use of Feriq's shower with the endless hot water and squirted his cleanser into her palm, massaging it into her hair. It smelled divine. Maybe it would, within two washes, turn her bedraggled locks into shiny waves of glory like his. It wouldn't, but a girl could dream. Distracting herself from the hot man with the large and ready cock just beyond the bathroom door, she noted the brands Feriq used so she could track them down when her life finally returned to normal.

Her body still tingled from the warmth of Quin's tongue on her ear, and she could still feel the hard press of him against her ass. She stroked her fingers down her neck to her breasts, gentle, delicate touches tracing the places his hands had been. Sliding a soapy hand down her belly and between her legs, she caressed her clit, the pads of her fingers sending sparks up her spine as the heat pooled in the center of her.

She ground against her hand, picturing Quin on his knees before her in the shower, his tongue replacing her fingers as it pulled and petted in exactly the right spot, his hands on her ass as he pulled her closer to him. A wave built inside of her, red-hot and pulsing with desire, and she bit her lip against the cries that threatened to escape.

The thought of Quin lying naked in that bed, his fist gripping his erection as he listened to what she was doing to herself in the shower was so hot, it pushed her over the edge. She slapped a hand over her mouth to stifle the sounds as she shuddered to completion, the orgasm rushing through her.

She rested her forehead against the cool tile and let the water flow over her, rinsing the rest of the soap from her body. Still tingling from her much needed release, she shut off the water and briskly dried off with a fluffy towel.

She was well aware of how long she'd been in that shower and, while the fantasy of someone hearing her masturbate was hot, the reality was a little more embarrassing. Too late now. If Quin was still in the bedroom, she'd just have to brazen through. Besides, she had nothing to be embarrassed about. She was a grown-assed woman who didn't need to apologize for anything, especially not a lovely, self-made orgasm.

Swiping the towel over the foggy mirror, she braced her hands against the bathroom counter and stared at her reflection. Ever since the night of the fire, she'd felt like a different person, like all this was happening to someone else. At first, she'd been so scared.

Scared of what would happen to her or her daughter, scared that all her years of work had literally gone up in smoke. Being arrested was terrifying. Almost getting murdered in jail even more so. But since she'd been on the run, on her own with only the most tenuous of support, she realized she was more capable than she ever thought possible. She was still scared every day, but there was a newly uncovered core of confidence that helped her survive and even stand up for herself.

Before all this, she wouldn't have been bold enough to tell a man to handle his erection, then coolly walk away. She wasn't someone who staged prison breaks, made bargains and bossed pirates around, or bit people on the ass because they annoyed her. But now she did it with only the slightest tingle of fear. Okay, sometimes a lot of fear. But she still did it.

She stared at her face in the mirror. The delicate lines bracketing her eyes and mouth were a little deeper. She'd put in the years and earned those, so never saw the need to erase them, though she understood the impulse. The light brown eyes, wavy black hair turning gray, the tall and sturdy body, all the same as she'd always been. But she knew in her heart and her soul that something had fundamentally changed within her.

Maybe she'd been waiting for the right catalyst to break out of the box in which she'd found herself, the one she'd built for protection so she could safely raise her daughter. She'd let Arden in, accepting his false offer of affection with gratitude when she should have been more cautious. And then it all burned to the ground.

She smiled at the woman in the mirror, a fierce grin, her entire face brightening. It was like the fire itself had cooked her, baking her into this formidable woman who could hold her own in the most challenging of circumstances. And she liked it. She gave her mirror self a nod.

As for that deliciously hot scoundrel out there in the other room, she wasn't going to take any shit from him, either. He might think that he was in charge because he "had a job to do" and "was there for her protection". Ha. She was the one in control of her life.

Remember Bea, she told herself. *You're a fierce negotiator and an intelligent engineer who graduated top of her class. You're not about to let some sarcastic space pirate boss you around. You're a strong, independent woman who doesn't need a man unless she wants one. You're going to get to this meeting on time, track down the bad guys, and get your life back. You've got this.*

Pep talk complete, she opened the door with a flourish, ready for battle.

22

QUIN

When he finally made contact with his crew on a delayed signal bounce, it wasn't good news. The *Starguard* was raising a ruckus over the destruction of the *Intrepid* and disappearance of its crew, word was out that the *Laughing Dragon* was somehow involved, and what was supposed to be a simple snatch-and-grab, leave-no-evidence kind of job had turned into a clusterfuck. To put some rainbow sprinkles on top of a shit sandwich, Ivan confirmed that someone had indeed upped the bounty reward money, making their trip to Badin even more dangerous.

"We had to make like a tree, captain. We're currently holed up on Gastez Station." Ivan's worried face stared at him, the signal flickering but still holding steady. "After the pod launched, we had a brief conversation with Ms. Farsirus to confirm she hadn't killed you and got the *Dragon* back online. Looked worse than it was, though it took Rafiel a while to figure out what she'd done to the reactor. She's clever, Cap."

Quin snorted. Didn't he know it.

Ivan continued. "Pod's signal let us know you landed on Cinzia. We were headed in your direction but then Amaryllis and *Dog's Day* were back, sniffing around…"

"So you had to leave the sector to throw them off the scent." Quin scrubbed a hand through his hair. "Godsdammit to the three hells and back. No one else is close by? I wouldn't mind some backup before Daisy gets us into even more trouble. She's like a damned magnet for misadventure." He promised Bea he'd escort her to Badin, but it would be really nice to have an extra set of eyes and ears. More bounty hunters would be looking for her now that the money was so much better. And he'd feel more comfortable on a ship he knew rather than whatever POS rock hopper Feriq was renting them.

The visual skipped as the signal finished buffering. Ivan shook his head. "No. We contacted HQ, but Knight's got his people running every which way, so that's a no-go on anyone available in your vicinity. Not sure exactly what's going on, and I'm not about to pry into his business."

"I've got no problem prying into his business." Navi shouldered Ivan over so Quin could see him. "Word is that he left the station."

"What? He left?" Quin couldn't believe it. The delay must have swallowed some of Navi's words. The Knight's station served as home base for them when they weren't on the *Dragon*, but beyond the odd collaboration on a job or repayment of favors rendered, Quin and his cousin tended to stay out of each other's affairs. News like that was unprecedented. "That can't be right. When was the last time that happened?"

"You heard correctly," Navi said. "My source told me it happened twice in one week. Took a bunch of his inner circle with him, too."

Ivan bumped Navi off screen with a glare. "I don't think he's left that old space station of his more than a handful of times since he set up shop, what, twenty years ago."

"Wow." Quin was speechless. What was going on with Rhain?

Navi poked his head back into the corner of the screen. "Hey, can't you use some of that Sidron charm to bring the woman in line? Just give her a little of that, and you'll be golden." He thrust his hips.

"The fuck, Navi?" Ivan smacked his brother on the back of his head. "Stop being so rude and misogynistic."

Rubbing his head, Navi shot Ivan a wounded look. "What? Sidrons are known for their smoothness and if one of them used their charm on me, I'd fall into line no problem. No misogyny intended."

"Charm offensives don't work on her anyway," Quin said, his voice glum. "Pretty sure she's immune."

They burst out laughing.

He frowned at his crew. "It's not that funny."

Wiping tears from his eyes, Ivan said, "Yes, it is. I told you from the very beginning that your plan to pretend-kidnap her was a bad idea, but did you listen? No, you did not. Now you're facing the repercussions."

"Okay, okay. You were right. I was wrong." Ivan would never let him forget this either. He scrubbed at his scalp again.

"You're going to tear all your hair out if you keep doing that," Navi observed.

"It's Bea. She makes me want to tear my hair out. She's like some kind of bargaining shark. Instead of bringing her back to the station like we planned and where it's safe, she's talked me into letting her go on what she calls a 'quest to clear her name'..." He stopped himself and shook his head. "This comm isn't secure. Check our drop — I'm sending the info there." Bad enough his crew had to stay away so as not to alert Amaryllis or whomever else was watching for the *Dragon*, but he had to go to Badin. He hated Badin almost as much as Cinzia. Planets were the worst.

"Don't be so glum, Cap. Maybe this is just the universe's way of keeping you two together." Navi made kissy noises.

"For fuck's sake, Navi. Cut it out. It's not like that." Then he remembered how she'd melted into him this morning as he sleepily nibbled on the soft skin at the base of her neck. Right before she'd jammed her elbow into his stomach, and given him a cutting look before marching off into the bathroom and locking the door. His dick got hard just thinking about the feel of her soft ass against him, her sweet-spicy scent in his nose. He shifted uncomfortably on the hard chair.

Ivan shoved Navi out of the screen view. "Remember, whatever deal you made with her, the only way we're erasing that favor we owe the Knight is if you keep her safe. You might be blood relatives with the man, but I'm pretty sure he'll take a limb or even something more precious to you if you let anything happen to her."

"Which is why I'm letting myself be roped into helping her with this quest." Otherwise, she'd just try to ditch him again, and hare off to meet her contact on her own and probably get caught. Quin pinched the bridge of his nose. Why couldn't things be simple? Rescue the woman, not develop feelings for her before delivering her to safety, then wipe his hands of her. The universe was testing him.

Come to think of it, the Knight and a chunk of his top people being away presented an opportunity. "Put Cormac on, would you?"

"What do I look like, your secretary?" Ivan grumbled, but moved out of his spot.

"Hey, Cap. What's up?" Cormac asked, cheerfully sliding into Ivan's chair and taking a bite of what looked like a homemade pastry.

"Is that one of Crusty Lou's mini pies?" Quin's mouth watered. Lou made the best pies in the entire galaxy, and it had been too long since he'd had the opportunity to stuff his face with one.

"Of course. We're on Gastez. It'd be sacrilege not to," Cormac said around a mouthful of deliciousness. "So, what can I do for you, oh Captain, my captain?"

"I need you to expunge someone from the Knight's records."

Cormac's mouth dropped open, showing Quin far too much pie. It didn't look so delicious all masticated like that. "You want what?"

"We had to bargain to use these comms and get us off Cinzia, so I need this done. Sending details now." He added Bert's details to the data packet and, after encrypting it, sent it to their secure drop box. Was the transmission frozen? Cormac hadn't moved or responded. "Cormac? Can you do it?"

Swallowing hard, Cormac said, "Can I hack one of the most feared men in the galaxy and quietly remove information from his personal database? Of course. But, since I have zero desire to experience the joy of having my spine removed via my throat, as would most certainly happen when he found out, no. Or, more precisely, fuck no."

"It wouldn't be that bad." Yes, it would. Rhain loved his information. But he'd promised Bert. Quin rolled his shoulders. "You're the best, Cormac, even better than Rhain's guy. And you won't get caught."

Cormac swallowed hard.

"With the Knight off base, this is the best time to do it."

Cormac stared at him wide-eyed. He even put down the rest of his hand pie.

Quin sighed. "If the unthinkable happens and you get caught, I'll take the heat. You were just following my orders. He might kick my ass from one end of the base to the other, but he won't kill me outright or his sister will rain fire down on him. Even he avoids pissing off the clan matriarch." Traditionally, the clans of their country were matriarchal. These days, the people of his clan voted for their leader. Niamh, Rhain's sister and Quin's cousin, had been in power for the last twenty-five years, leading her clan with a firm hand that brought peace and prosperity to her people. She'd earned her title of The Dragon. She was scary as all three hells combined.

Cormac's throat bobbed, and he swiped a hand across his

forehead. "We'd have to head to HQ to get it done. The Knight's got a closed system that can only be accessed from base. That also means we'll be out of range if you run into trouble. You okay with that?" Then Cormac's eyes went distant, no doubt already plotting his way through Rhain's security measures to access the information within.

Quin thought of one more thing. "Fuck. Hold on. I also need anything you can find on someone named Ghost. I'm sending what little I've got now. And ask Flex if he's ever heard of this Ghost." Rhain's top computer guy might be a good source. He liked to play on the darker side of the 'Net even more than Cormac.

"Never heard of a hacker named Ghost," Cormac said, tipping his head to the side as he read through the information Quin sent. "They claim to have info we don't, huh?"

"So it seems. We're heading to Badin to see what they've got, but I could use some intel on this hacker. Ivan, make sure he sticks with the 'Net outside of the Knight's realm for that part."

But Cormac had on his determined face, which meant there was very little Quin could say that would stop him from doing what he thought needed to be done. "Cap, I'll already be in the system. I just have to cover my footprints when I back out. No muss, no fuss." He wiped his hands and held them up. His eyes went distant again.

"Cormac." Quin snapped his fingers, trying to break him out of his pre-hacking trance. "Just Bert and nothing else. We have at least some justification for needing this done but, if you take anything else from his information horde, not even The Dragon will be able to stop him from removing your spine, one vertebra at a time."

But Cormac didn't seem to hear Quin, already immersed in the digital world, pawing through those ones and zeroes on the galaxy's 'Net to find the information.

"I'll keep an eye on him, Cap," Ivan said.

He hoped so. There wasn't much he could do for them if they

were busted while he was so far away. "Watch your step," he cautioned, but Ivan's face flickered and froze in its usual glower, the signal gone. With a sigh, Quin double checked that everything was wiped and shut down the comm. The sturdy wooden chair creaked as he leaned back and put his hands behind his head. He hoped this wouldn't get him or anyone on his team killed.

23

BEA

She'd been prepared to be embarrassed upon leaving her fortress of solitude, aka the bathroom, so was at somewhat of a loss when she walked into an empty bedroom. Probably was trying to contact his crew or maybe getting some breakfast. She couldn't decide if she was relieved he wasn't sprawled across the bed waiting for her or disappointed.

Picking up a pair of butter-soft leather pants dyed a purple so dark they were almost black, she shimmied her way into them as she considered what might happen if and when they finally reconnected with his crew. While she finally acknowledged that Quin would indeed protect her from bounty hunters and others who might wish her harm, she wasn't sure he would stick to his agreement to escort her to Badin if his crew returned. She knew going to that planet was hardly the safest option. She could envision him hauling her back onto his ship and locking her down until this Knight gave him orders otherwise.

But Quin stressed that he was with her, that he was all in. She wanted to believe that, she really did. She ached to put her complete faith in him. Men and their promises had burned her far too recently. Fuck Arden for making her so wary.

There was no sense in pre-worrying. Quin might say he had

her back, but a girl had to have a backup plan, just in case. She slid the rest of the credits from the sale of the motorcycle into her top's built-in bra, adjusting her boobs so the stack wasn't noticeable. The black long-sleeved shirt, made of a soft, stretchy fabric, was extremely comfortable, fit her like a glove, and gave her great cleavage and support without being binding. She'd have to ask Feriq where he shopped because this outfit made her feel fierce, ready to kick ass and take names.

After fastening her boots, she found spots within her new clothes for her tools and headed downstairs to find Quin, Bert, and Feriq cozied up to the bar.

Quin turned to look at her, his jaw dropping. He shut it quickly, but not before she noticed. She pulled back her shoulders and flashed him a smile.

Feriq let out a wolf whistle. "Gorgeous. I just knew that outfit would work for you — you're the same size as my sister, Parvani. And that's what she gets for leaving her clothes behind after taking off with that absolute trash pile of a man." He waved a hand, clearing the air. "But that's a story for another day."

Confident in her new-to-her clothes, Bea gave a little spin. "They fit like a glove. I've never had leather pants before." She stroked the soft material. "I think I like them."

"They suit you, doll. And I couldn't let you put on those nasty rags you came here with. The smell alone..." Feriq shuddered. "What do you think of our girl, Quin?"

"Hot." His voice crackled, and he cleared his throat. "Good. I mean, Daisy, you look nice."

Putting a little extra wiggle into her hips, she sashayed up to the bar and slid onto a stool.

With a wink, Feriq slid her a cup of coffee and a muffin. "Fresh from the bakery this morning. Estel makes the best muffins in this sector of the galaxy."

She thanked him as she put some cream and sugar into the steaming drink. "So, Quin. Did you get ahold of your crew?"

"Yep." He took a sip of his coffee. Black, of course.

"And?"

Feriq gestured to Bert, and they moved away to give Bea and Quin some space.

When they were out of earshot, Quin said, "And we're on our own." By the tone of his voice, he wasn't pleased.

She couldn't help but feel a rush of relief. Good. "Are they okay?" Internally, she winced at the fake-concern in her voice.

He cocked an eyebrow. "They're fine. Circumstances changed. They're heading back to base to take care of Bert's info so we can hold up our side of the bargain."

Nodding, she finished chewing a bite of muffin. "So, we're headed to Badin, then?"

The other eyebrow joined the first. "You still worried that I'm going to change my mind on you?"

"Well, to be perfectly honest, yes." Seeking fortification, she took a sip of her coffee. "You asked me to trust you. Okay, great. I do, because you also said that you were hired to protect me and keep me safe. But going to Badin, I know that's not safe. There's a million things that could go wrong there. So what happens if you decide I'm in danger and you need to do your job? Will you tie me up and carry me off to safety again?" Her cheeks flushed as she laid out her concerns. Confrontations were not her strong suit, but she was determined to fix this source of anxiety. It needed to be laid bare before they could proceed.

He twisted on his stool to face her and placed a hand on her arm. His muscles flexed under the white shirt. "What's it going to take for you to fully and completely trust that I will not only protect you, but escort you to your meeting on Badin and help you clear your name? Do you need a contract? Something written in blood? My firstborn, perhaps?" His voice was teasing, but his eyes were deadly serious.

Her arm prickled and warmed under his large hand, his calloused thumb absently stroking her skin as he patiently waited for her answer. Finally, she nodded. "A contract would be good."

"Then that's what we'll do. Okay?"

"Just like that?" She thought he might argue or get all defensive and tell her to just trust him again. "I mean, I believe you, it's just..." She struggled to put her thoughts into coherent words.

"Trust is hard," he said.

She nodded, licking her lips. "And you said you only do one job at a time."

"Technically, even with a second contract bound to you, it'll still be one job: protecting you. And it'll make my job infinitely easier if you aren't always trying to ditch me." Still stroking her arm, he said, "I can see that long-term trust is hard for you. I understand and respect it, especially considering what your shitty ex and then Bessa did. We've all got our limits. Maybe you'd have more faith in me if I hadn't fucked up our initial encounter." He shrugged. "But since I can't reverse time, what I can offer is a binding contract. Maybe by laying out the terms of our working relationship in black and white, you can relax a little. You're really tense." He gave her arm a light squeeze and waved to Feriq to join them.

"Pretty sure you'd be tense too, considering the circumstances," she muttered, finishing her coffee. "But thank you." With his acquiescence and understanding, the wall guarding her heart crumbled some more, allowing additional light to pierce the darkness.

It took a while, but they finally hammered out a deal. Because he already had a contract with the Knight to keep her safe, this new agreement piggybacked on it with Quin accompanying her to Badin for her meeting so he could watch her back. Quin refused to include anything about what would happen after her meeting, which didn't make her happy. But at least this current iteration would give her time to make plans, in case she needed to ditch him after her meeting so he couldn't cart her off "for her own good" again.

To make the contract official in the eyes of UBP law, she needed to pay him a retainer so she gave him one of her precious credits, claiming it was her last, with the agreement she'd pay the rest after the job was done. Once they both signed the actual physical contract Feriq had drawn up, Quin excused himself to take a shower.

Bea watched him walk away. The thin fabric of the sleep pants he neglected to wear to bed did wonders for that man's ass.

Feriq caught her looking and cocked an eyebrow. "You'd better be careful with that one, Daisy. He's got heartbreaker written all over him." He ducked behind the bar and whipped up a drink that involved several bottles and a lot of shaking. "Here. I think you need this more than you need another cup of that terrible coffee."

"You don't know how true that is, but it's a little early, don't you think?" Her brain was already running through scenarios of what might happen on Badin. Quin might be contractually obligated to keep her safe but, depending on what information Ghost had, she would happily fling herself into danger if it meant getting to the bottom of everything.

"Absolutely not, especially at a time like this." Feriq slid the glass closer.

She took a sip of Feriq's pink, frothy concoction. Sweet balanced with a hit of sour danced over her tongue. "Ooh, yum. How did such a stellar mixologist wind up out here in the middle of nowhere?"

Leaning his forearms on the bar, Feriq said, "Same old story. Boy trusts the wrong person who betrays him to some very bad people. Boy has to go on the run and winds up in this dusty old place where people don't ask many questions."

Bea ducked her head, embarrassed. "I'm sorry. That was far too nosy. You're welcome to tell me to find the biggest black hole in the galaxy and throw myself into it." They'd bonded last night over drinks at the bargaining table, but even insta-friends could be too nosy.

"All good." He waved her concerns away. "But I don't want to get into specifics, so don't ask. Anyway, it happened a long time ago. Weird thing is, I kind of like it here now. Sure, Cinzia is a tiny backwater planet, filled with refugees, runaways, and recidivists, but it's home, more than my actual home ever was, if that makes any sense."

"I can understand that." She took another sip of her drink. "Since my life got turned upside down, I've been trying to rediscover my place in the universe, too. Haven't found it yet but, oddly enough, this hellacious quest that I'm in the middle of is helping."

"Ooh, a kind of trial by fire, this upside-downing of your life, I'm guessing a man was involved?" He waved off the question. "Now it's your turn to tell me to find a black hole if that question was too personal."

She laughed. "Much like your story, a man is the root cause of the mess my life currently is."

"Was he at least good to you? Was he worth it?"

"Eh," she wobbled her hand. "Overall, more trouble than he was worth."

"Now that's sad." Feriq gave her an up-and-down look. "Especially considering what he was missing out on by not taking you to bed and making you scream his name every chance he had."

Her face heated, and she hid behind her drink. "Come on now."

"No, I'm serious." He took her hand in his and pet it. "You're stunning. This troublesome man who fucked up your life, he was a fool." Blushing harder, she tried to pull her hand away, but he tightened his grip, a determined look on his face. "Please promise me that you'll never let another man take you for granted. You deserve someone who loves every last atom of you, worships at your feet, and would never allow harm to come to you."

She put a hand over his where it clasped hers. "I think that's the nicest thing anyone has ever said to me. Thank you, Feriq. I promise. But only if you promise to let me know if there is anything I can ever do for you. You deserve all the love and happiness, too." She hoped he took her words to heart as much as she'd absorbed his. An amazing person like Feriq shouldn't be hiding away in a tiny little backwater town for the rest of his life because he was afraid, even if he was comfortable here. He should have options if he wanted them.

Now, it was his turn to blush, his red skin slowly darkening like the sun setting on the mountains surrounding the town. "I promise. And, damn, Quin was right to be afraid of you at the bargaining table. You have a way of making people agree to things that they never would have otherwise."

"Do we need to get that in writing?" she teased.

"How about we just toast to love, happiness, and fabulous orgasms?" He raised his glass, and she gently tapped hers against it with a melodic ring.

"I'll drink to that."

24

QUIN

"That," Quin shook a finger at the squat little ship quietly rusting on a crumbling landing pad in the late afternoon suns, "is a piece of junk. We're liable to burn up before we even break atmo in that thing."

Feriq looked offended. "Priscilla may not be the most beautiful rock hopper you've ever seen, but I assure you, she's more powerful than she looks." He winked at Bea when he said it, and she gave him a big smile.

Quin reminded himself to never leave the two of them in a room together alone again. Not because he was jealous of the man. Of course not. He just didn't know Feriq and didn't completely trust him. He grunted his disapproval regarding the entire situation.

"Come on, Quin. Don't be such a baby. Feriq wouldn't lend us something that didn't work, and I checked the engine myself." She rolled her eyes at him. "Besides, Badin is only a couple of days' travel. We don't need a long-hauler, just a hopper with some zip to get us where we're going. Feriq said there's even enough juice for a single jump, in case we run into trouble." Bea shouldered one of the bags of supplies Feriq had packed with a grunt, steadying herself against its weight. "Anyway, if it happens to blow up, you won't be around to bitch about it. You'll be dead." And on that cheerful note, she hugged Feriq and climbed up the ramp into Priscilla.

Watching Bea as she disappeared into the little ship, Feriq handed Quin the other bag. "Go easy on her, would you? She's more tenderhearted than she puts on."

Quin barked out a laugh. "The woman is a hellion." He wasn't about to admit out loud that he'd seen her softer side, the one that was currently bruised and battered, and the one that made him want to wrap her in a protective shell. If she heard, she'd kick him in the balls again.

"She's also someone who's been dropped in the deep end and is just trying to survive all the shit that's come her way." Feriq sounded like one who spoke from experience.

"She's done okay for herself so far." But Feriq kept his amber gaze steady, and Quin relented. "But I agree. I promise I'll do my best to keep her safe and help her. We have a contract, after all. Witnessed by you," he reminded the tall man.

"That's all I ask." Feriq put a hand on Quin's shoulder. "And if you break her heart, I will find you, rip that beating organ out of your chest, and eat it in front of you." Then he grinned at Quin, flashing sharper-than-standard-human teeth.

Quin did his best not to gulp. He might be a trained warrior, but those teeth were that of a predator. Choking out a laugh, he said, "Wow. You two must have really had a solid heart-to-heart while I was out of the room."

"We did, which is why I'm trying to give you a little more insight into the woman who is your Daisy. She's not a delicate flower by any means, but she's had it rough, like so many of us. She wants the best for this universe, for whatever reason. Me, I'm happy to remain behind my bar in this little nowhere town on this little nowhere planet and let the rest of the universe fuck off."

"Gotcha." And he did. In some ways, he was more like Feriq, though he preferred the vastness of space to being planetbound. Maybe he should care more about the universe and its inhabitants, but he'd already played the roles of savior and guardian while in the 'Guard and look where it got him. He didn't know if he had it in him to do more than worry about the current job.

But Feriq wasn't done. "Despite having just met her, we bonded hard and I now consider that woman to be a friend. I don't have many of those in the universe and do what I can to protect those who are." Feriq struck a balance between fierceness and wistfulness and, for a moment, Quin wished he'd remained in the room with Feriq and Bea, so he could have captured some of that magic, too.

Quin looked at the darkened doorway into which Bea had disappeared, then back at Feriq. "I'll do my best." He held out a hand.

Feriq clasped Quin's forearm and pulled him into an embrace, clapping him on the back. "I will hold you to it. And don't forget about your promise to take care of Bert." Then, with a sharp nod, he turned away and ambled back towards town.

Quin boarded their little ship and climbed a ladder to the cockpit, pausing to stow the bags in the tiny kitchen's storage compartment. Sectioned off into cube-sized spaces, the rock hopper's three-layer teardrop shape was typical of its kind — one layer held a cockpit with two seats; one layer was cargo, inaccessible during flight without a suit and spacewalk; and sandwiched between them was a layer that contained a mini-kitchen, a tiny toilet, and a cave-like sleeping berth with just one bed. The last time he'd flown on a ship this size, he'd felt like he was sleeping in a padded cube. The ship's simple yet highly effective design was based around the concept of "a place for everything and everything in its place," with no room for excess. Minimalism at its finest.

He liked the simplicity of rock-hoppers but, as he settled into the pilot's seat next to Bea, felt a pang of longing for his own ship. She looked over as he strapped himself into the harness and began the pre-flight check, giving him a pleased smile that set his blood racing. Damn. Did this woman know how she was affecting him?

The smallest bit of encouragement from her, a tiny show of affection or kindness, and he was lapping it up like a starving dog.

"You all strapped in?" he asked gruffly, choosing to ignore her smile and focus on what he needed to do to the Priscilla off the ground.

"Absolutely, captain. All secured and ready to go," she said, giving him an impertinent salute. "Anything I can do?"

"Nope. Just sit there and look pretty." Damn. Probably shouldn't have said that. Though this was a quick trip, the size of the ship meant they couldn't really escape one another. Not a great idea to piss off his travel partner by being an insensitive dick. Besides, he enjoyed this sunny, playful side of her.

Luckily, she didn't take offense. "Ooh, you think I'm pretty?" she teased, batting her eyelashes at him in an exaggerated motion. "Aw, thanks. You're pretty, too."

He huffed out a laugh and pretended to ignore her. It wasn't easy. She smelled good, like soft sunshine and sharp citrus oranges. In the small cockpit, it was impossible to avoid her scent. Once he noticed it, he couldn't stop from thinking about it. He wanted to be irritated that she was getting under his skin and invading his thoughts. She didn't realize the war he was fighting against getting too attached. With every move she made, she gained territory in his heart, winning over his soul. If he wasn't careful, he'd soon lose the war. The question was: did he want to win?

Through an absolute miracle, Bea stayed quiet during the rest of his pre-flight prep, watching his every move. Considering she built ship engines for a living, if she wanted, she could fly this thing.

She let out a little squeak when the engines kicked in. Letting out a self-deprecating laugh, she said, "Forgot how loud these things could be."

"If it sounds like the engines are right under your ass, it's because they are." He threw her a wink, which she returned with a grimace of gritted teeth. He laughed. "Guess you're wishing you'd checked with me before you bargained yourself onto this little ship, huh?"

"Definitely not. I made a great deal without your assistance, thank you very much." Her breath caught as the engines shifted into high gear, shoving them off the planet's surface and hurling them through the stratosphere and beyond. It only took a few minutes to reach the blackness of space, but what a ride.

"Told you she'd make it," she said, holding out a fist for him to bump. They exchanged broad grins.

He killed the main thrust engines, useful for takeoffs and landings, and turned on the primaries, which would propel them where they needed to go. Secondary thrusters would keep them from hitting asteroids and space junk. Then he programmed in their course to Badin and set the autopilot. With a click, he undid his harness and drifted up to hover above his seat.

Still smiling, Bea let go of the armrests and let her hands float. "Also, forgot about the lack of artificial gravity on these things. Haven't been on the float like this in a long time."

Gently pushing off the ceiling, he caught a foot under the edge of his seat to hold himself in place. "It'll come back to you."

Her hair drifting around her face, she waggled her fingers. "Like swimming in salt water. No resistance."

"As I've never had the opportunity, I'll just have to take your word for it." He maneuvered to the ladder. "I'll be in the galley or the berth. Call me if anything beeps or turns red."

"Hey, how come I've got first shift?"

"You snooze, you lose." He tried not to laugh at her irritated expression. "Anyway, with the autopilot on, there's not much to do up here except monitor things. And, considering how old this rust bucket is, we should have someone up here keeping an eye on things for the first rotation. Feriq couldn't remember exactly the last time this old girl was on a long run, and I don't want to chance it." On big ships, you had options if something went wrong. On these small guys, it was a thin wall between you and the vastness of space.

"Fine. I'll take the first shift. Better that someone who knows what they're doing be here, just in case anything goes wrong."

He drew in a breath to remind her that he was, in fact, captain of a starship when he caught her smirk. "Smart ass."

"According to my calculations, it should take us approximately four days to reach Badin, as long as engine output remains optimal. Do you agree?"

"Agreed. If nothing goes wrong after a rotation, I don't think we need to be as strict with the watch. The computer will warn us if there's anything in our path, and a small ship like this means we're never far away from the controls."

She nodded, her fingers twisting a thin ring on her finger.

"I'm going to get some food and maybe catch some more shut-eye since my sleep was interrupted this morning." A delicate blush shaded her cheeks. His heart fluttered in his chest at the sight.

"Pretty sure it was you who interrupted my sleep first," she grumbled.

With a laugh, he said, "I hope you brought some reading material or maybe some crossword puzzles or you're going to be bored out of your skull."

She rolled her eyes.

"Or you could always join me in the sleeping cube, and we could have some weightless sex. It's an experience you won't forget." He gave her one more wink for good measure. And with that, he floated out of the cockpit, pleased he'd finally gotten in the last word.

25

BEA

Bea thought about his offer multiple times over the next few days. After all, there wasn't much else to do. Thankfully, Feriq had slipped an old school reader into the bag he'd packed for her. That the reader was filled with romance novels, while one of Bea's favorite genres, did not help with the tension that vibrated between her and Quin every time they occupied the same space. A thousand little moments passed between them as they hurtled through space, stoking the small sparks into slow-burning flames. The impossibility of moving through the ship without brushing up against one another. The quiet dance as they switched between sitting in the cockpit, sharing meals or a pouch of tea in the communal space, and sleeping in the cube. Simple conversations about favorite vids, funny stories about their childhoods, and discussions about the places they'd been or still wanted to go. The heated glances when one thought the other wasn't paying attention.

Forced proximity, her ass. It was torture, plain and simple.

In all reality, there was absolutely no reason why she shouldn't take the man up on his offer. She was a grown adult woman. He was a grown adult man. He'd offered sex. Teasing, sure, but it felt genuine under the banter. But she didn't know what she wanted.

Unfortunately for her, despite charming his way into her life and her bed, Arden hadn't been a generous lover, leaving her frustrated more often than not. But, after the ten years of celibacy before he came along, she'd been a little touch-starved and had soaked up every scrap of affection he'd shown her, grateful for what little he gave her, never asking for more. Between the celibacy and unsatisfying sex, she'd gotten very good at pleasing herself, complete with orgasms that kept her satisfied enough. Self-love was one thing, a wonderful thing. But sex with someone like Quin would be another thing altogether, and she wasn't sure if she was ready to take the plunge.

If she was entirely honest with herself, she was afraid. Not of doing it wrong — sex between individuals was rather like riding a bike, you never actually forgot the mechanics of it — but of the intimacy that came with it. Allowing another person into your body and to literally see you naked, both physically and emotionally, that was an incredibly intimate thing, even when you told yourself it was just for fun. And she was dead-positive that sex with Quin would be fun. He was the kind of man who'd make whomever he took to bed scream out his name, giving them mind-blowing orgasms, and the freedom to try new things without judgment. He was also the kind of man who could walk away from a one-night stand without a single glance back. She just had to decide if that mattered to her.

By the third day, Bea was climbing the walls, sometimes literally. She floated up into the cockpit, absently sucking down a supposedly berry-flavored nutritional shake in a pouch and considered her plan for the next eight or so hours. She could stay here and stare at the dark beauty of space for a while. It was ridiculously gorgeous, all that blackness spiked by bright stars. They were close enough to the moons of Badin that she could see the drifts of pink and blue space dust that looked like giant clouds when light from the system's suns hit it just right. But she'd done that yesterday. And the day before.

She could read another book — always a good plan. She'd

been so driven over the past years that she'd had almost no downtime to read. Her to-be-read pile was something she'd never get through, even if she was trapped on this tiny ship for the rest of her life. During this trip, she'd devoured five of the romances on Feriq's ancient reader and had just started one with a woman and a grumpy alpha wolf shifter who claimed her as his mate and growled any time another male looked at her. That particular trope did it for her. She squirmed a little, thinking of the scene she'd just read where the shifter had pinned the woman against a tree and was using his talented fingers to make her see stars.

Or... Quin was in the berth. Blood flowed slower in microgravity, and bodies focused on keeping the major organs like the heart and brain functioning, so she didn't think that, scientifically, weightless sex was actually possible, but she could always go and see for herself. If nothing else, maybe they could fool around a little.

Tapping the reader against her thigh, she stared at the celestial bodies beyond the thick viewer pane of the cockpit. But she wasn't looking at the expanse of space. Instead, she was picturing Quin with his shirt off and how his skin would feel against hers.

Ah, fuck it. Fear could suck her toes. Or maybe Quin would. Did she even like that? She'd never tried it.

Stowing her reader in the seat pocket, she zipped the compartment shut so it wouldn't float out and bump into delicate things on the navigation panel. If she was going to do this, she didn't want to be interrupted by the squeal of an alarm alerting them to an oncoming asteroid and impending doom.

Not giving herself time to second-guess the intelligence of her choices, she slipped down the ladder and knocked softly on the berth's hatch. A growly "come" penetrated the door.

She opened it and hovered in the frame. Taking a deep breath, she said, "Is that offer still on the table?"

Quin turned his head to look her way. Scrubbing a hand over his bare chest, he clicked off the wall vid he was watching and blinked at her. "What?"

She swallowed. "You know, the offer you made our first day aboard. I'd like to take you up on it, if you're willing."

He stared at her, his jaw dropping. He clicked it shut. "Um, yeah. Sure. That sounds like fun. I mean, great."

He sounded so shocked and confused that it was all she could do to keep a straight face. She moved deeper into the room and let the door slide shut behind her with a gentle whoosh, a hand on the frame so she didn't drift. "First, let me ask you: is sex in a weightless space, even one as contained as this berth, even possible?" She'd spent a good deal of time trying to figure out the logistics, things like lack of traction and the challenge of getting blood to flow to important bits, and still came to the conclusion that, sadly, it wasn't. But she was curious as to his answer.

His hair floated around his head like a nimbus as he ran a hand through it. "Tried it once when I was younger and certain it would be an amazing experience, despite being told that it wasn't feasible. I was positive that was just something adults said so kids wouldn't try it."

"And?" she asked.

He gave her a rueful smile. "Didn't happen. Francie, my girl at the time, was game enough but we couldn't figure out how to get, you know, moving. We kept bouncing off each other and floating up to the ceiling when we tried to create a little friction. It wound up being a lot more like a workout without the payoff of any endorphins."

She giggled at the visual.

"We decided to just make out, which was great, of course." He shook his head. "But we were so disappointed the vids lied to us. Those scriptwriters, they must never have been on a spacecraft with low-to-no gravity in their lives."

"Ah, too bad," she said. Her fingers tightened on the doorframe. His story was cute, but she was disconcerted he didn't then invite her into his bed. Had his comment just been teasing, and he didn't really want her? She felt a little stupid and desperately wished she could disappear out the airlock to escape the embarrassment of assuming he wanted her as much as she did him. "Never mind, then. Just forget what I said."

"No, wait. Dammit." He fought to sit up, unzipping the sleep sack. "Don't go. I definitely want you to take me up on that offer. Want to take you up on that offer. Shit. I want you. In this bed. Now."

Mortification still burning through her system, she hovered by the door, analyzing his words.

He held the sleep sack open, giving her a glimpse of thick bare thigh against the white sheets. "Join me. Please. I promise I'm more experienced than my 20-year-old self. We could fool around, act like teenagers." He gave her a wink and grinned at her. "It's up to you. I'm game for whatever you want, anything that lets me touch you and taste you."

She moved a little closer, her knees bumping against the edge of the sleep platform.

He grabbed her hand, tugging her closer. "Before you came in, I was thinking dirty thoughts about you."

"You were?" she asked, her voice husky.

Nodding, he said, "Yep. You, naked in my bed, your gorgeous silver-shot hair splayed out around you." He lowered his voice as if imparting a secret. "You were writhing on my cock as I made you come."

She pressed her legs together, deliciously languid heat curling through her. Fuck. Straight to the point. It seemed he did actually want her. Her embarrassment burned away as her body heated.

Quin shifted over in the sleep sack and gestured at the space beside to him. "Come on. I might not be able to get it up or get you off but, if nothing else, I make an excellent big spoon."

Fuck it, she thought, peeling off her shirt.

26

QUIN

Had he really just offered to snuggle with her? What in the three hells was this woman doing to him? And did he care? No, he did not. This meant that, at some point, he might actually be lucky enough to see her naked in his bed, just like he'd imagined. He might have been teasing her before, but he was telling the truth about how much he wanted her. He'd dreamed of her, those silken limbs, those delectable lips, her fingers wrapped around his cock.

She gripped the edge of a built-in shelf over the bed as he slowly peeled off her tight leather pants, his hands skating back up the soft skin of her legs and tracing the curve of her ass and the edge of her red panties as she reached to stow her clothes in the mesh bag attached to the wall.

She shivered under his touch and turned back towards him, biting her lip. When she'd come into the room and asked him to have sex with her, he thought he was dreaming. She'd been a constant presence in his thoughts. And now here she was, watching him with intense eyes, her long legs slowly opening and closing as she floated in front of him. His cock made a valiant attempt to harden, but unfortunately, the science held true. Microgravity still wasn't overly conducive to blood flow to the extremities. That was fine. There were plenty of other ways they could satisfy one another.

"Come on in." He patted the space beside him in the sleep sack. "We've got hours until we reach Badin's atmosphere. We'll take it as slow as you want." He gave her a wicked grin. "For as long as you want."

She slid in beside him, her backside gently gliding against his front. "Hold me like you did that morning at Feriq's," she said, her voice soft and vulnerable.

He'd been half-asleep, tied up in the fragments of a delightful dream right up until the time she'd nailed him in the stomach with her elbow, but he tried his best, wrapping an arm around her waist and sliding his leg between her thighs. He nuzzled his nose into the space where her neck met her shoulders and breathed her in. And just like in his dream, a sense of contentment, of somehow coming home, filled his soul.

"Perfect," she sighed, relaxing into him. She braided her fingers with his, holding his arms securely against her.

They stayed like that for a while, just breathing. Her body heat penetrated his skin and her sharp sunshine scent invaded his senses. He could feel her warm core against his thigh and the light touch of her leg draped over his. Loose tendrils of her hair floated free of her braid, brushing against his cheek in feather-soft strokes.

She moved restlessly against him, reaching back to stroke his neck. He slid a hand under her shirt and cupped her full breast, his thumb moving in small circles around the circumference of her nipple.

"Is this okay?" he asked, pressing a kiss to her nape.

"More," she said as she shifted, rubbing against his thigh with a tiny sigh.

Taking advantage of the space between them and the mattress, Quin slid his other arm beneath her, stroking a palm over the soft mound of her stomach, his fingers skirting the top band of her panties. Her muscles contracted under his touch, and she rubbed her ass against his cock with each shift of her body.

Gently, he encircled her neck with a loose hand, tilting her head so he could access her delectable mouth. She tugged him closer and parted her lips, her tongue darting out to brush against his, sending shocks of pleasure down his spine.

His fingers slid under the fabric of her panties, brushing the soft curls and feathering light caresses over the lips within. She let out a small, breathy gasp against his mouth and put a hand over his, encouraging him, following his movements as he skimmed the edge of her pussy, dipping a finger into her soft core before withdrawing only to slide back in. With tiny, needy sounds, she pressed his hand harder against her as he stroked her clit, his thumb moving in small circles. Her hand gripping his nape tightened as she arched against his hands.

Keeping her locked in place with a gentle hand around her neck, he traced delicate kisses from her mouth to her earlobe. "Faster or slower?" he asked, pressing a little more firmly against her clit.

"Fuck," she gasped, bucking against his hand. She shifted her legs, spreading them wider, giving him even better access to her as she wrapped her ankles behind his calves to hold on tighter. "Faster. Harder."

Nipping his way along her jawline, he dipped a finger into her core, her wet heat coating his skin, the lace edge of her panties tickling his wrist.

"More," she said, gripping his hair as she urged him on.

"Your wish is my command." He slid in a second finger, crooking them slightly so they followed the curve of her inner walls as he pumped them into her.

She felt so good, so hot and soft as she gyrated against his hand, breathing in fast little pants that drove him wild and challenged him to do his level best to bring her to orgasm. Following her demands, he worked his fingers in and out of her as his thumb stroked hard and fast against her sensitive clit.

He bit her earlobe at the same moment he hit the spot he was searching for, and she cried out, bowing her body and reaching behind her with both hands to pull him closer.

"Gods, yes, Quin. Just like that," she said, writhing against him, her hips demanding more from his fingers as she dug her nails into his shoulders. "Don't stop. Don't... I'm almost..."

He could feel her body tightening as she climbed towards the peak of pleasure and gave it his fucking all. She didn't need to worry — he wasn't about to give up now, not when she was so close. He kept his fingers aimed at the soft core of her as his other hand drifted back under her shirt to give some attention to her neglected breasts, pinching then soothing her nipples. Gods, she was gorgeous. He wished he could see his fingers moving in and out of her or the way her skin looked against his. Damn sleep sack.

Luckily, he had a very vivid imagination and could envision the way she gripped his shoulders, her shirt rucked up, one of his hands manipulating her breast, the other plunged deep in her panties. He gently bit the tendon between her shoulder and neck, and her body bucked against his in a powerful orgasm. "Oh fuck. Gods, yes," she said, gasping between words. He felt the tremors of pleasure ripple through her, squeezing his fingers as he stroked her inner core and kept pressure on her clit.

Finally, her muscles relaxed, and she took a deep, shuddering breath. "Holy fuck, Quin. Wow. That was... wow."

He pressed another kiss to the nape of her neck, enjoying the sensation of a satisfied woman in his arms.

She turned to face him with a smile, one hand tracing the outline of his face while the other drifted down to encircle his cock.

At her delicate touch, it made another valiant effort to spring into action and, as much as he'd love for her to continue, he knew it wasn't in the cards. So he gently removed her hand, kissing the knuckle of each finger.

"Turnaround is fair play, and you didn't..." she trailed off, a small frown on her face.

"Not that I wouldn't fully enjoy having you pay close attention to my cock," he said with an exaggerated sigh. "But I'm going to go ahead and declare that, sadly, sex in microgravity is most definitely a myth perpetuated by bored spacers to challenge the young."

"A minor setback." Then she giggled and added, "At least we gave it a go for science."

"And proved that microgravity is, indeed, a cruel bitch, at least for those of us with penises who need a decent amount of blood flow to get it up."

"We should write a paper, get it published in the science journals." She snuggled against him, rubbing her cheek against the hair on his chest, sending tingles along his nerves.

He huffed a laugh against her hair. "There is no way I'm telling the galaxy about my inability to get an erection, even with a scientifically proven reason behind it." He pressed a kiss to her temple and held her tight.

Letting out another little laugh, she settled in his arms. After a few minutes, her breathing evened out, and she fell asleep.

He could stay like this forever, enveloped in the heat and scent of this woman, protected and hidden away in their tiny ship in the icy darkness of space. How was it that not too long ago, that thought scared him to his very core, but now it felt right?

He needed to be careful with her. She was the kind of woman he could spend the rest of his life with — smart, kind, gorgeous, and stubborn — but he was built for the stars while she had her feet firmly planted on the ground. It would never work between them. He'd have to be satisfied with what he got while it lasted.

27

BEA

The proximity warning shook them awake with a shrill cry. For a second, it was all tangled limbs and twisted clothing before they got themselves sorted out, emerging from their warm cocoon with bleary eyes and knotted hair.

They quickly finished dressing and pushed off to the cockpit. Bea strapped herself in while Quin switched off the alarm and flipped on the viewer. In their path spun Badin, the blue of its oceans that covered almost 99 percent of its surface visible even from this distance. Quin's very capable hands danced across the controls, and she fought a blush, recalling where else those fingers had so recently danced.

Quin caught her looking. "What?"

"Nothing." She fixed her eyes on the curve of the bright blue planet in front of them.

"This isn't going to be awkward, is it?" He glanced at her.

"Why should it be? Are you tense for some reason? Because I'm feeling quite relaxed myself." She stretched in her seat with a purr of contentment. "Too bad you weren't able to enjoy the same."

He snorted. "Yeah. Sluggish blood flow isn't optimal for a

hard dick, not to mention the whole dealing with liquids in microgravity." He gave her a wicked grin. "Anyway, I enjoyed getting you off. I'll always remember the sounds you made as you came around my fingers."

Her body heated at his words, and she squirmed a little in her seat. "Yeah, that was nice."

"'Nice'? It was 'nice'?" He growled. "I'd say that I blew your mind, judging by how hard you came."

Cocky bastard. It was like he was begging to be needled. "I've come just as hard under my own ministrations, thank you very much." She looked at him through her lashes. Gods, but she enjoyed bantering with him. "Don't worry, you can always try harder next time. Practice makes perfect, after all."

He gaped at her, gathering himself for what she was certain would be a very snappy comeback when they were hailed on the comm.

"Unidentified vessel, you are entering restricted airspace. Only residents, invited guests, and pre-approved visitors with a reservation and proper identification may approach. Respond," a brusk voice said.

Oh, hells. It had been ages since she'd been to Badin, and she hadn't realized that there were even more restrictions these days. They certainly weren't on any list. She didn't think she even knew anyone who lived on Badin anymore. She searched her memory for anyone, an old acquaintance or someone from her school days, who might be on the small planet, but she was blanking. She had no idea what the people she once called friends were doing these days. Fucking hells.

Keeping his cool, Quin stayed on approach to the planet, despite the brusk voice's repeated warning. She was about to tell him to head to Gemi Station, Badin's orbiting space station, so they could figure out how to get authorization to land when, in a voice oozing charm, he said, "Reyonka Nellington, is that you giving me all these warnings to stay away from your planet?"

There was a pause. "Quin? Quin Sidron? Is that you?" Reyonka asked, the bruskness swept away by warmth.

"In the flesh," he said with a grin. He winked at Bea.

She folded her arms over her chest and rolled her eyes, but didn't interfere. Let him put his scoundrel powers to good use for a change.

"Quin, what are you doing here? Wait." There was a pause. "Hold on. Don't tell me yet. Let me give you clearance so you can tell me face-to-face." Moments later, they had a berth to park the ship and were on final approach to Katash, Badin's capital city and main port.

Bea raised an eyebrow. "Reyonka?" she asked.

He shrugged, his hands busy with the controls. "She's just a friend."

"Okay," she said, keeping her tone casual and, she hoped, not at all questioning or accusatory in any way. Honestly, it was fine if Quin and Reyonka were more than friends. She had no claim on him or what he did with others. Sure, they'd been through a lot together, but they'd really only known each other for a short time. Also, they definitely weren't involved romantically. Were they? No. He'd kidnapped her. She'd hired him for a job. He'd gifted her a mind-blowing orgasm. That was it. When this was all over, she'd return to Melorn and her work and he'd go back to whatever pirate-y thing he did and she'd never see him again. Which was fine. Just fine.

But despite her brain's practical spin, her heart gave a pang of protest. She ruthlessly squashed it. Even if she wanted it to, it couldn't work out between them. Could it?

They landed the little hopper between two sleek luxury yachts that were quadruple its size and were worth a million times more. Noting the intricate gold scrolling covering the entire shell of one of them, Bea wrinkled her nose at the blatant display of wealth. She bet they had to have someone redo that gaudy design each and every time they broke atmo and it burned to ash. Gold did not belong on the outside of a ship and didn't want to stay there, either. But that was Badin for you — filled with people who wanted what they wanted, no matter the cost. And they could afford it, too.

A tall, broad-shouldered woman with dark brown skin and a gloriously curly mane of brown hair framing her round face strode across the tarmac with a broad grin. She waved at them. "Quin. Man, it is so good to see you!" She pulled him into a hard hug, then put her hands on his cheeks and leaned in for a kiss.

Bea looked away, not wanting to intrude on their reunion. She reminded herself she had no exclusive claim on his affections. Besides, his connection to Reyonka got them on the planet. She had no call to be upset with the enthusiastic woman who'd plastered herself against Quin.

He gently pulled back, taking Reyonka's hands in his and turned her towards Bea. "Reyonka, this is Daisy. She's with me."

Bea almost corrected him, but then remembered that she was supposed to be traveling incognito. Besides, that stupid flower nickname was starting to grow on her. Gods, she was such a fool, getting attached to the big, dumb pirate. *Stop it*, she scolded herself. Shaking off intrusive thoughts, she donned a friendly smile and held out a hand to the woman beside Quin. "Hi, Reyonka. Nice to meet you."

"Oh, gods. Sorry, I didn't see you there. Hi." With a laugh, Reyonka shook Bea's hand and stepped away from Quin. "I figured Quin might be here to do some business and maybe catch up with an old friend. I didn't think..." she gestured at Bea.

"No, you're fine." Bea waved away the other woman's concerns. "Quin is working with me on a few business-related things." It was true enough, though Quin slanted a glance at her. She changed the subject. "Are there usually so many ships here?" she asked, gesturing to the packed space port.

"You know. It's that time of the year again," Reyonka said, with a shrug. "More work for us, though."

Bea and Quin exchanged a glance. Bea said, "I'm not from around here. What time of year is it?"

"You really don't know?" Reyonka's eyes widened. "I just figured that everyone coming to Badin knows this weekend is the Vanid's Full Moon Ball. It's all everyone is talking about around here. All over the gossip channels, too."

"As in the shipping Vanids?" Quin asked, as if there were a million other powerful families who could generate as much excitement as that one.

Reyonka nodded, but her comm pinged before she could say more. "Work calls. Give me a sec," she said, moving away from them.

Bea tapped a finger to her lips. "You know, Arden claimed he was related to the Vanids." She'd forgotten that tidbit.

At the time, she'd thought he said it to impress her. As an engineer who designed and built ship engines, she was very familiar with the Vanid and their stranglehold on the shipping industry. Just out of university, Vanid Shipping had offered her a job paying obscene amounts of credits. She'd turned them down. Working for a monopoly like that, one who made space travel a luxury and squeezed smaller companies out of the market, wasn't worth the stain on her soul.

Was the Vanid's ball and influx of people the reason why her contact had chosen Badin for the meet? It would be easier to move unnoticed in a city overwhelmed with visitors, especially rich, demanding visitors. Smart. But gods, she wanted this intrigue and sneaking around behind her. As much as she enjoyed Dai's stories of action and intrigue, she was better suited to tinkering with engines. Being constantly on guard was exhausting.

Quin moved closer, his shoulder bumping against hers as if to remind her she wasn't alone in this.

"Sorry about that. If I'm not there, everything falls apart," Reyonka said, returning to the conversation. She glanced at their proximity and flashed Bea a wide, knowing smile.

"Everything good?" Quin asked.

She flapped a hand. "All good. Someone too used to getting what they want is mad they're unable to park their big assed ship here with no reservation." She winked. "I enjoyed sending them away. This job has few perks, but that's one of them."

"So, this ball. It must be quite the party," Bea said.

"Yeah, it's such a big deal because every other time of year, the Vanid's private island is closed to all visitors. I've seen literal fights over invitations to the thing. Everyone who's anyone gets invited." She leaned closer. "And I've met them all. Even Ojim Saadala."

Bea's eyes widened. "Ooh, really? I've had a crush on him for ages. He's so good looking."

Reyonka nodded. "Right?"

"Who's that?" Quin asked, a tinge of jealousy in his voice.

"Famous vid star. Oh, my gods, he's even hotter in real life than on screen," Reyonka gushed, fanning herself.

"I can only imagine the celebs attending this Full Moon Ball. Okay. No wonder security is so tight." Bea forced her clenched fists to unfurl. With all the crisp gray Starguard uniforms mingling with the red armbands of the local authority around, she needed to look calm though her heart was racing.

"Except I let this scoundrel down here anyway," Reyonka said, playfully smacking Quin's arm. "After your last visit, I should arrest you and impound your ship."

Bea laughed, finding herself charmed by the cheerful, easy-going woman. "So, I'm guessing you know Quin pretty well then?"

"I do, though we're just friends these days." Reyonka winked at Quin. Leaning close to Bea, she said, "Man used to be such a player when he was younger. But that was a very long time ago." She sighed.

Bea laughed, enjoying the way looks of panic and sheepishness fought for control of Quin's face. "Oh, that I can believe," she said in a dry tone.

"I see you know him pretty well then as well." Reyonka's laugh was full-throated and honest. "You and me need to get drinks sometime."

At that point, Quin tried to step in and do some damage

control. "I think the two of you and alcohol would be a dangerous combination." He moved his hand to Bea's lower back in an effort to hustle her away, but Bea wasn't about to be rushed, not when tormenting Quin was so fun.

"What are you worried about, Quin? That Reyonka and I will start comparing stories?" She looked at Reyonka.

Reyonka snorted. "Like we wouldn't have better things to talk about than some man." She waggled her eyebrows. "Though I do have some good stories about him, and that doesn't even include the gossip I've heard about that crew of his."

Bea's smile turned wicked. "Ooh, that does sound like something I might be interested in hearing."

"Come on, ladies," Quin said in desperation, still trying to get Bea to move.

"Okay, okay." Bea said with a laugh, taking pity on him. "Reyonka, it was a pleasure to meet you. I'd love to stay and talk shit about Quin, but we really do have to go. Next time I'm in town, we're definitely meeting up for drinks."

"Count on it." Reyonka gave Quin a hug. "And you, stay out of trouble, will you? I don't want to have to save your ass like that last time you came blazing into port."

"Yes, ma'am," Quin said, with a little salute. "Take care, Reyonka."

With a parting wave at her new friend, Bea let Quin guide her away.

28

QUIN

They found a little cafe in town where they could get something to eat and plan out their next steps. Bea's meeting with her contact was set for tomorrow. He was concerned. She'd pinned so much hope on getting information to clear her name that he wasn't sure what would happen if this lead turned out to be useless. Maybe Cormac would dig something up on Ghost that they could use.

He chewed on his sandwich and watched Bea as she watched everyone going by. From her avid, wide-eyed gaze, it was quite a show. He didn't love how crowded it was, though. So many beings and no backup made him anxious. He itched to hustle her back onto their little ship.

He lowered his gaze to the blocky black tablet in his hand. Despite now having access to one of the best networks in the sector, his wrist comm was still acting up. Highly aggravating. The magnetic field in that area of Cinzia must have completely jacked it. He tapped his wrist to activate it and got another shock for his efforts. Shit. Nothing like being forced to buy a cheap tablet from a back alley dealer. This thing had barely any battery life, for fuck's sake. The only reason he could send messages to his crew off-world with it was that Badin had a stellar network. He took a swallow of his very delicious coffee while he waited for a response.

Bea motioned to his shitty tablet. "Give it to me. I need to check my messages."

He moved it out of her reach. "Why didn't you just get one of your own?"

"Because I gave you all my money, remember?" She held out a hand and raised an eyebrow.

He knew she had more credits stashed somewhere on her person, but let it slide. If it made her feel secure to have a few credits on her, fine. "So what you're saying is that, because I now have access to my accounts, I'm going to have to pay for everything?"

"Sounds about right." She gave him the give-it-here gesture again.

"Um. I don't think so. I'll buy us food and get a place to sleep, but I'm not sharing my tablet." He held it up so she could see the screen but out of range of her grabby hands. He pointed at the blinking red dot in the bottom corner. "Do you see the crappy battery life on this thing? If we're lucky, it'll hold out until my crew gets back to me. You using it right now will kill the battery."

"That's what you get for going cheap," she said, no mercy in her voice.

Good to see his hellion was just as relentless as ever. "Look, it's easy to track people through known accounts, so while we're lying low, I could only access the small account I use for emergencies. Do you know how much good tablets are these days? Since everyone has the implant these days, they're vintage and pricey."

She took a sip of the tea Quin had bought her. "Pretty sure I have several in a drawer back home."

"Same, but it doesn't do us any good right now, unfortunately."

Her brows drew together as she stared into her tea.

"Who are you hoping to hear from?" he asked gently. He truly wasn't trying to be an insensitive dick by withholding the tablet, but one thing at a time. Once he got them to their hotel, they'd be able to charge it, and he'd happily hand it over.

"I need to see if there's a message from Ghost or anything else from my sister. It's just so frustrating, you know?" Her jaw clenched as she tugged at her earlobe. "I hate this waiting. I feel like I'm always waiting lately. Surely my sister has more information than what she sent. Paranoid brat." She muttered, making a face.

He could understand her frustration. Rhain was the same.

"I told you she said she was sending help. If it's you via the Knight, great, but it would be nice to have confirmation. I love my sister and appreciate all her help and support, I really do, but what the fuck. Why does she have to be so godsdamned secretive all the time? She's retired, for the love of Saint Agnes. She doesn't need to play cloak-and-dagger with my life. Just tell me!" She ground out another couple of curses before sitting back in her chair with a huff.

He gave her some space, just in case she needed to vent more. After a few beats, he said, "I can only imagine how frustrating this must be."

"So frustrating." She nodded, blinking hard. "When I finally see her again, I might actually strangle her. After I hug her, of course."

With a sigh, he said, "The more I think about it, the more I believe I've got to be the help she sent."

She cocked her head. "You said you weren't sure. What changed?"

With a sheepish shrug, he said, "I remembered that when he called in the favor for this job, the Knight mentioned the contract was for an old friend. I might be jumping to conclusions, but your sister might be that old friend. I know he's worked with the Melorian government before. Could be that's how they met."

"Huh. Makes sense." Bea tapped a finger against her empty cup, her eyes distant. "And it would explain some things." She focused on him. "I could never quite figure out why your notorious cousin wanted to keep me safe. After all, I'm nobody special."

He vehemently disagreed with that last statement, but didn't interrupt.

"It was part of the reason I fought you for so long. But Dai knows a lot of powerful, shady people so, yeah. It's feasible she knows him and has worked with him in her past life."

A server bot stopped at the end of their table. Bea fed their dishes into its mouth while Quin deposited payment for their meal into its hand slot.

"Have a nice day," it intoned, then zipped off to the next table.

He wanted to have all the answers she needed, solve all her problems, but he couldn't. So he gave her what he had. "I asked Cormac to see if he could dig up information on Ghost."

She brightened. "Tell me more. Please."

He took a brief second to appreciate that she'd added on a "please" at the end of her demand, as if he wouldn't give her everything anyway. "Nothing yet. That's what we're waiting for. But Cormac is one of the best." But still he worried about his crew. Rhain would not go easy on any of them if Cormac was busted creeping around in his information horde.

"Well, thank you for that," she said. "Cormac won't get in trouble, is he? I mean, it'd be great to actually know who I'm getting this information from, but not if it puts someone else at risk. It's not that important."

"No need to worry, though I'm sure he'd appreciate your concern." Cormac would not appreciate it. "He's an expert at what he does. And it could be important. After all, you're their courier. That data dot may contain something that doesn't belong in the hands of an unknown hacker." He'd followed his instincts when he asked Cormac to delve into who Ghost was. At the moment, it probably didn't really matter who they were, as long as Bea got the information she needed. But in the long term? This Ghost might be someone who needed to be watched.

Nodding, she looked around at the clientele, minding their own business in the cafe. "So what next? My meeting isn't until tomorrow."

He got to his feet. "Let's find a place to crash for the night. Give us a chance to plan how to keep you safe during this meet."

"And charge the tablet so that I can use it," she added, gathering up her pack.

Holy fuck. Relentless. "Fine. It's yours after I talk to Cormac."

This part of Katash was bustling, the streets lined with cute cafes like the one they'd just left and well-stocked shops to tempt people with credits to burn. Conspicuous consumerism was in full force on the Pleasure Planet. Vacations and tourists were the primary industry of Badin, so it saw a lot of traffic from people with both time and money to spend coming in and out like the tide. More because of this fancy-schmancy ball. That also meant an even heavier security presence than he'd planned for and more scrutiny of anyone who looked "out of place".

Mindful of the side-eyes they'd gotten in the more well-to-do sector of town, Quin led them on a circuitous route that took them deep into a less flashy area and to The Norwood, a boutique hotel known for its discretion and affordable rooms that he'd used before.

Bea was quiet, her head on a swivel as she took in the sights. The streetlights clicked on as the evening crept around them.

With a hand on her lower back, he guided her through the doors to the front desk. While you could check in and pay for the room with your comm, this hotel also allowed guests to check in off-book. If you knew the proper passcode, you could pay in hard currency and register without having to provide an ID. Very handy.

The tablet vibrated as they keyed into their room. "Perfect timing," he said, scanning the tiny balcony and the street below as he fumbled to put the earpiece in. Bea disappeared into the bathroom. "What do you have?" he asked Cormac.

Though Cormac's voice was scratchy and nearly indiscernible through the earpiece, it was a relief to hear from him. But trying to communicate this old-fashioned way was for the birds. How had people gotten along before embedded comms and holos were a thing? He pressed the earpiece deeper into his ear canal, as if that would make a difference. "Repeat that. I didn't catch what you said."

"I said that I've got good news and okay news. Which do you want first?"

"Look, this shitty tablet's battery has the life of a rockfly, so just lay it out for me asap." Frustration strained his voice. If just one thing could break their way, he'd be less grumpy. Maybe. At least two percent.

"Gotcha, Cap." He quickly laid out the facts.

Quin sighed. Not what he hoped. "Okay, thanks, man. You made sure to cover your tracks? You good?"

"Did my best, boss." He pictured Cormac pulling at his earlobe as he mentally retraced his steps. "Entirely possibly I over-looked something, but I think I got out clean."

"Good," Quin said, relieved. "Good. Any sign of trouble, you let me know, right? I'll take any heat that might come our way." The tablet beeped a sad chirp at him. "Fuck. This thing is about to die. I've sent you my coordinates and will keep you apprised of the situation here. Quin out." He cursed at the tablet, now a useless brick.

"Oh, no. Bad news?" Bea asked as she walked out of the bathroom. She'd brushed out her hair, and it spilled over her shoulder in dark waves.

"No, it's not that. Damn thing died." He smacked it on the top of the dresser a couple of times.

Snickering at his little tantrum, she said, "That's probably not going to help. Good thing you brought us to a hotel that hasn't been remodeled in, what, fifty years? Looks like there's an old school charging station in the cabinet that should work." She settled onto the bed, leaning back on her elbows and crossing her ankles.

He slotted the tablet into the charger and hoped for the best.

"So, tell me what your pirate buddy learned."

"Cormac. His name is Cormac."

"Okay." She shifted slightly, the rasp of her leather pants against the fabric of the duvet filling the room. "Tell me what Cormac said."

Quin sat down in a threadbare chair in desperate need of a new cushion, a spring digging into the back of his thigh. She was right about the hotel not being remodeled in a very long time. At least it was clean and safe, at least for the time being. "Good news or okay news first?"

She dropped her head back with a groan, and he hungrily traced the curve of her neck with his eyes. "Come on. Just tell me."

"Fine. Good news first then. Cormac scrubbed Bert from the Knight's system, as promised."

She gave him a smile. "So, our bargain with Feriq is settled. Good." She bit her lip. "What about the okay news?"

"Cormac wasn't able to find much on your Ghost. He said there are whispers of a new hacker on the scene intent on digging up dirt on the rich and powerful. Rumors say that they're responsible for airing some dirty corporate dealings and bringing several politicians down. Cormac was impressed with what little he found."

"We can hope Ghost and this hacker are one and the same. If so, less chance of a scam or trap." She worried a finger over a small bump at the base of her thumb. "I hope so."

"Also..." he paused, unsure of how she was going to react to this next part. "You know how the bounty to bring you in went up all of a sudden?"

She nodded. "Weird."

"Cormac found evidence that Arden is responsible for the increase."

"What? Arden?" Her mouth dropped open. "How? He's dead. Killed in the fire. Confirmed by authorities."

"The same authorities who falsely charged you with murder and arson," he said, his voice low and dark. The whole scenario had already stunk, but this new info raised his hackles.

She chewed on the information, her eyes distant. "A partner, maybe?"

"Maybe." A partner made sense, even if Arden had really gotten himself killed. But he had the feeling it was something else. He just didn't want to bring it up until she was ready to admit it herself. "Cormac's still digging, to see if he can follow the money back to its origins. We'll get to the bottom of this, Daisy. I promise."

Smacking her hands against the comforter, she jumped off the bed and began pacing, muttering to herself. "Every time I think of how Arden — who I let into my home and my bed, who met my daughter for fuck's sake, betrayed me, screwed me over and, even though he's nothing but ash — has found a way to continue to screw me over, I want to scream." She paused, her fists clenching. "No. I want to piece him back together, molecule by molecule, so I can torture him and then kill him all over again."

Snickering at her ferocity, he said, "Tell me how you really feel." He laced his fingers behind his head and stretched out his legs, enjoying the show.

She paused to growl at him, then muttered under her breath and paced some more.

"So, what are you going to do with this information?"

She didn't answer him, nibbling on a fingernail, her brow furrowed in concentration. "I want to delve into every aspect of Arden deVan's life. I want to know every droplet of information, uncover every dirty deed. Because I can't be the first person he's charmed, wormed his way into their life then screwed over. If he has money, I want to know where it came from. If he has family, I want them to know what a piece of shit he was. If he has a partner in this scheme, I want to know who it is so I can put a bounty on their head and see how much they like being hunted. I want vengeance. And I want my damn prototype back." She collapsed back onto the bed, staring at the ceiling.

What could he say to that but, "Alright then. That's what we'll do."

29

BEA

She shot into a sitting position and stared at Quin. "Really?"

He let out a long sigh. "How many times do I have to tell you? I'm here for the long haul. We're going to get to the bottom of all this together."

Together. That sounded nice. She'd been independent for so long, without anyone else in her life who was truly a partner, she'd forgotten how great it was to have someone who supported you, propped you up when you needed it, and took your side even when all the odds were against you. Besides her sister, of course, who had to do all that because she was family. It was a requirement. Quin, on the other hand, was only contractually obligated to protect her, not help participate in her plans of vengeance. She appreciated that he was now on board with said plans. In fact, she wanted that. She wanted him.

"You're thinking so hard, there's steam coming out of your ears," Quin said.

Startled out of her thoughts, she looked over at Quin, lounging in the low-slung, flower print chair, a small smile on his face as he watched her grapple with herself. As much as she would love to run into the streets and scream out her fury like the women warriors of old, she had to harness her need for vengeance, gather her information, and when she had what she needed, she'd extract her revenge.

Until then, there was this glorious man, all muscles and promise, watching her like she was his favorite piece of cake, and he hadn't eaten in years. She slid off the bed and stalked over to him.

He grinned up at her as she stepped between his legs and bent down, resting her hands on the chair's back. "We could put that heat to good use," she said and felt a rush of power at the suggestion. She'd never instigated sex in such a straightforward way with Arden, but with Quin, it felt right. She felt powerful as his eyes darkened with desire.

"Oh, yeah?" His grin deepened, and he slid his hands from the backs of her knees up to her thighs, tugging her closer.

A rush of desire washed over her. The memory of Quin's strong fingers playing over her body like a precious instrument sent heat to pool in her belly. "Yeah," she said, moving to kneel around him on the chair. "We can't do anything else until that cheap-assed tablet charges back up, and my double-secret clandestine meet isn't until tomorrow, so..."

"May as well make use of the time because I'm not tired. Are you tired?" His hands drifted over her ass and up under her shirt, gathering up the fabric as they rose. She obligingly lifted her arms so he could pull her shirt off, but he stopped, leaving her trapped, her shirt over her face. The tight fabric immobilized her arms and acted like a blindfold. He took advantage of her state to trace along the undersides of her breasts, cupping them in his warm hands as he pulled a nipple into his mouth.

She gasped as his teeth grazed the sensitive skin, teasing it into a taut peak. "Not a bit tired," she managed to say as his hands skated over her bare back to cup her ass, squeezing her ample cheeks.

Taking back control, she ripped her shirt off the rest of the way and flung it across the room. Grabbing his shirt, she tugged it up over his head, tossing it to join hers in the corner. "Plus, this counts as a good use of our time, right?"

"Absolutely," he gasped as she bent to circle his nipple with her tongue, teasing one then the other. He dove a hand into her hair, gently running the waves through his fingers before wrapping it around his fist and tugging her mouth up to his.

The meeting of their lips electrified her entire body. It was as if she'd never been kissed before. With one hand still fisted in her hair holding her close, Quin used his tongue like a master, dipping in and teasing her, moving deeper then withdrawing until she was desperate for more. Her tongue followed his as she ran her hands over his chest, her fingers rasping against the hair covering his pectorals. She followed the dark trail to where it dipped into his pants, popping the top button with a snap of her fingers.

He paused their kiss. "Wait," he said.

A sharp bite of disappointment stilled her hands. "You changed your mind?"

With a bark of laughter, he said, "Absolutely not. We're doing this. I just thought that we could move this to the bed, rather than going at each other on a chair like a couple of hormonal teenagers." He kissed the tops of her breasts, first one then the other. "Wouldn't you agree?"

Nodding, she said, "Definitely. I might get stuck if my knees are bent like this much longer. I was willing to take that chance, though."

Before she could move off him, he slid forward to the low chair's edge, his hands under her ass. The muscles in his legs bunched as he pushed up to stand. He teetered for a moment before crashing back into the chair, Bea landing on top of him with an oof.

"What in the hells were you trying to do?" A giggle spilled out of her, and she smacked at his arm. "You just said we weren't teenagers and here you are, trying some slick move."

"I was hoping to sweep you up and carry you over to the bed, but I didn't quite get the leverage I needed." He sounded upset by his inability to do a vertical lift with her solid weight in his arms. "It was supposed to be very smooth and impressive."

Laughing, she banged her head against his hard chest. "Pretty sure that move only works in the vids or in chairs that aren't as close to the ground as this one, you silly pirate." She pushed off him to stand and offered him her hands. "Let's do this like adults who have more sense and also don't want to throw their backs out."

He rolled his eyes, grumbling that he was certain he could do it if she just gave him another chance, but he grasped her hands and let her pull him out of the chair. He wrapped his arms around her and pulled her in for another world-shattering kiss that left her melting and backed her up until her knees hit the bed. "Get naked," he said, his lips soft against hers.

She gave his hair a playful tug and said, "Only if you do the same."

For too many seconds, they split apart, ripping off every last bit of clothing as fast as humanly possible. Bea turned to fling back the covers, and Quin came up behind her, pressing his hard length against her ass. He ran a hand down her arm, pausing to caress the small triangular scar on her upper arm before gently pulling her hand to his own triangular scar, verifying that he, too, got the treatment protecting him against ninety-nine point nine percent of all known STDs and unplanned pregnancies.

"So," she let out a soft breath, her muscles contracting as he ran a palm over the curve of her stomach and gently thumbed her clit, "what you're saying is that you haven't had sex with any water nymphs and aren't infested with *aqua impurus*?" She teased him about the only STD the treatment didn't cover as she broke free of his magical fingers and crawled onto the crisp white sheets, turning onto her back so she could watch him. She wanted this time to be face-to-face.

"No experience with water nymphs or their diseases," he said, following her onto the bed and coming to all fours over her. "Though there was that one time with a dryad and her tree..."

"Oh, really?" She gasped as he bent to take her breast into his mouth once again. "I've always wondered how that works with dryads, since they're so attached to their trees. You'll have to tell me about it sometime. Later." She grabbed his hair and pulled his mouth to hers. "Right now, I want all your attention on me."

Groaning, he cupped the back of her head, using one hand's talented fingers to tease her clit. "Your wish... my command," he said, his voice thick with desire.

Heat pooled in her belly and spread throughout her body as he stroked and pet her. He used a thigh to nudge her legs farther apart and slid a finger into her heat. She bowed up as a second finger joined it, gliding over that perfectly sensitive spot deep inside her. He dipped his head to suck a nipple, his thumb moving in lazy circles over her clit.

"You have magic fingers," she whispered. Then, in a move that surprised the both of them, she rolled him over to flip their positions. Slowly, she slid her body along his body, teasing him as she rubbed over his hard length. The intensity with which he watched her every move, his hands tracing along the outline of her body, made her feel strong and utterly desired.

She straddled his legs, the crisp hairs rasping against the sensitive skin of her inner thighs. Gently grasping his cock, she traced a finger over the head. His body jumped in response, and his cock grew thicker in her hand. She bent and ran her tongue over the head and down the shaft. Quin groaned, his hands moving restlessly over her arms. With a smile, she took him into her mouth.

Keeping her hand wrapped around the base of his cock, she moved her head up and down, watching his reaction as she sucked and teased. Twirling her tongue along his thick shaft, she pulled increasingly desperate sounds from him, driving him to the edge, his cock hot and hard in her mouth.

"Holy fuck, Bea," he gasped. "Don't torture me like this."

She hollowed her cheeks as she took him down her throat, then withdrew, tormenting him as she ran her tongue over his tip, pre-cum salty in her mouth.

"For the sake of all the gods, woman," he shouted, his body bowing up. "Your tongue is a miracle, but I want my cock buried deep in your pussy the first time I come for you."

Since that was what she wanted, too, she gave his cock one more kiss, nipping and licking her way up his stomach and chest. Looking down at him with a wicked grin, she came to her knees, repositioned herself, and slowly sank down onto his hard shaft. She could feel every hot inch of him as she stretched around his length. Once fully seated, she paused, giving herself a moment to adjust and enjoy the sensation of his hard cock inside her.

"You are killing me," he growled, grasping her hips as he shifted under her, but she held him in place, her thighs tight around his pelvis, both hands on his chest, pressing him into the mattress.

She leaned down and kissed the edges of his mouth. "Just lie there like a good boy and take what I give you." Then she began to move.

Quin's fingers dug into her flesh, urging her on as she rode his cock. She bowed back, grasping his calves to give herself more leverage as she rocked her body against him, sucking in a sharp breath as the length of him bumped over just exactly the right spot.

He took advantage of her position to rub his thumb over her clit, sending bright sparks up her spine with each stroke. She found her rhythm, a smooth movement that sent her soaring towards that peak until her entire body tightened, the orgasm crashing over her, her inner walls pumping him for all he was worth as she came around him.

But he wasn't done yet. As her movements slowed, she ceded control as he rolled her onto her back and continued the ride. He angled his hips, continuing their dance as he found his own release, taking her with him as she floated her way through a secondary wave of bliss.

With one last shuddering groan, he collapsed on top of her,

breathing heavily. "Fucking fuck, Bea. You could kill a man like this," he said against her neck.

She laughed, draping a sweaty leg over his thigh and stroking his hair. "I can think of worse ways to go."

"Ain't that the truth."

30

QUIN

He woke the next morning to the sound of her singing in the shower. It wasn't very loud, but the water and acoustics in the bathroom amplified her voice. He rolled onto his back and absently scratched his chest while trying to place the song. She wasn't a talented singer, more off-key than not. When the name of the song finally clicked in his head, he chuckled. The song she was warbling was a one-hit-wonder from a few years back featuring a bad-boy space pirate and the girl he gave his heart to.

Deciding that he needed a shower too, he went to the bathroom and stepped in behind her, sliding an arm around her waist. She jump-squeaked, then relaxed against him.

Turning in his arms, she tipped her head back with a smile. "Dirty, are you?"

"Filthy," he said, capturing her lips with his and feasted upon her mouth. He loved the way she wrapped her arms around his shoulders and twined her fingers through his hair, stroking the base of his skull. "How do you want it?"

She laughed, a husky, sultry sound that he felt in his bones. His cock stiffened, pressing against her wet warmth. "You sound like you're taking my breakfast order," she purred, nipping at his shoulder.

"Excuse me, miss," he said, teasing the edge of her clit until she ground against the palm of his hand. "Would you like some sausage with your muffins?" he asked with a wink.

"Ridiculous man," she said, giving his hair a little tug. "I'll take that sausage hot and fast, if you please."

"As you wish, m'lady." He pushed her back against the cool tile wall, the hot water a delicious contrast in temperature, and cupping the back of her head, plunged into her with a groan.

Wrapping one leg around his thigh, she urged him on, ordering him to go faster, harder. She slipped a hand between them, her fingers stroking her clit as he drove into her. "Almost there," she panted against his neck. "Just a little more."

"Holy hells, woman," he said against her wet hair. He was about to burst, hovering at the edge of an orgasm, but by some miracle, he managed to hold back until he felt her go tight around him, pumping his cock with her inner muscles and sighing out her pleasure. Then he too found release.

THEY CLEANED UP, taking turns drying one another with soft towels before getting dressed. Deciding they needed food after all their exertions, Quin headed out to find breakfast.

Bea agreed to stay in the room, though he suspected it was less because of his request and more because the tablet finally charged. She could check her messages. Fine. As long as she stayed out of trouble. Her meeting was set for that afternoon and afterwards, he could bundle her onto their ship and away from this place. If she let him. She seemed quite determined to track down all the perpetrators, not just clear her name. He sighed. The Knight definitely owed him hazard pay for this job.

Armed with caffeinated drinks and baked goods, Quin headed

back towards the hotel. Rounding the corner, he stopped in his tracks. Fuck. How had Amaryllis found them?

He ducked back around the corner, brow furrowed as he retraced everything they'd done since leaving Cinzia. Where had they been compromised? His wrist comm was shot and hers disabled, so not that. They hadn't talked to anyone but Reyonka, who had a strong moral code and couldn't be bought. It couldn't have been his transmission to Cormac. Cormac would never let that happen. Had Bea contacted someone and accidentally alerted Amaryllis that way? Maybe. Feriq or Bert could have passed along their information, though he didn't think so. The stakes for them were too high. Maybe it was the guy who'd sold him the black market tablet or someone at the port who spotted them. No matter how it happened, Amaryllis had tracked them. Bea was in danger.

As annoying and dogged as Amaryllis was, Quin didn't want to permanently take her or her people out, just get them out of the way. These days, Quin avoided taking lives when at all possible. But Bea's safety and security were his first priority, so he'd do what he needed to do.

Sipping his drink to obscure his face from anyone who scanning for him, he casually glanced around the corner. Amaryllis paused in front of The Norwood, checked her wrist comm, then consulted with the two crewmates standing next to her before going inside.

While Quin had relative faith in the hotel's promise of discretion when it came to its guests, he didn't know how Amaryllis had tracked them down. She'd upgraded her ship since their last encounter, maybe she'd upgraded other systems, too. Some tracking software could give longitude and latitude, while the fancy stuff could pinpoint a person's location inside a multistory building down to the exact bathroom stall they were hiding in.

Quin banged the back of his head against the brick wall, considering his options. Without a functional comm, he couldn't contact Bea to warn her. There was only one of him and three of them that he could see, probably more, and most likely all armed, despite Badin's weapons ban. He had baked goods, his blaster secured on Feriq's little ship in accordance with Badin's no weapons policy. Not a fair fight. Besides, he didn't want to kill them, and disabling everyone quickly and quietly when you were outnumbered was a near impossibility. He had to play this smart or Amaryllis would get her claws on Bea.

Which meant he needed to get into the hotel without anyone seeing him. He banged his head on the wall a little more.

Resuming a "don't mind me, I'm just an everyday citizen" stroll, Quin headed to the rear of the hotel and tugged at the back exit. Locked. He could knock and someone might eventually let him in, but he didn't have time to wait. Amaryllis was in the hotel, and she'd find her way to their room eventually, if not sooner. As he was considering his options, one of Amaryllis's crew members came around the corner. His eyes widened at the sight of Quin, his hand moving up to the comm behind his ear. Quin tossed the coffees in his face and did a front snap kick, nailing him under the chin.

With a grunt, the man's eyes rolled up, and he toppled backwards, crashing to the pavement with a thud.

Quin leaned against the wall and massaged his glues. "Shit. I think I pulled something." With a groan, he leaned down to check the man's pulse. Alive. He gave the area a quick check, then hauled him behind the row of hedges edging the property. Not the best hiding place, but it worked in a pinch.

One down, at least three to go. He needed to get to Bea before Amaryllis, but it was a small hotel with a tiny reception area. If he went inside now, Amaryllis would see him. Sketching a rune of luck in the air, he tapped his fingers together. His comm flickered to life, then died with a sharp shock to his wrist. Dammit. He eyed the stacked gray stones of the building. He was going to have to climb the fucking building.

Sighing, he did a couple of stretches, flexing his fingers and bouncing on his toes. He could do this. It was only a couple of stories. No problem. Picking up the white paper bakery bag, he folded down the top, gripped it in his teeth, and started climbing.

31

BEA

She put the tablet back on the charger and glared at it. Stupid thing was already more than halfway drained, and she had nothing to show for it. Dai was incommunicado. There was nothing more from Ghost about their meeting, not even a confirmation. Essy hadn't even answered her yet. She felt unmoored.

Something tapped on the window. She ignored it. Another tap, followed by a muffled call of her name in a voice that sounded like Quin's. What in the galaxy?

She pulled back the curtain to see Quin on the balcony, a white paper bag dangling from his fingers. Opening the sliding door, she asked. "So, is this a new form of delivery service?" She took the bag from him and peeked inside. "Decent taste in breakfast foods, at least. But where's my coffee?"

"Hilarious," he said, massaging his hands.

"How did you get here?" She peered over the railing. "Did you scale the building? What in the three hells, Quin?"

A knock on the door froze them in place. Putting a finger to his lips, he pulled her onto the balcony.

"What's going on?" she asked, her eyes wide.

"Remember the other pirate ship that attached itself to the

Intrepid, the one who was trying to get on board right before we took you off?"

She nodded.

"She's here."

Another, more demanding knock on the door.

"We could just pretend to not be here," she suggested. "The door's locked and bolted."

He shook his head. "I know Amaryllis. She'll only break down the door. A lock won't stop her."

The knock became a pounding, rattling the door in its frame. "Quin! I know you're in there with my bounty," Amaryllis called through the barrier. "Give her over."

"Don't worry. I'll handle this." Quin kissed her forehead and tucked her into a corner before closing the balcony door and drawing the curtains shut.

Bea peeked through a tiny gap in the curtains. Quin kicked off his boots and tossed his jacket over her clothes on the chair before striding over to the door and flicked on the peek screen. "Amaryllis. What are you doing here?"

A lusciously low, raspy voice curled its way into the room. "Quin, darling. Just open the door and give me the woman. Then I'll be on my way."

"I have no idea where she is."

The voice let out a husky laugh that was joined by other voices, though she couldn't distinguish how many. "You're lying. We had a whole discussion about her after you grabbed her off the *Intrepid*. Or don't you remember?"

That would have been when Bea was in the white cell aboard Quin's ship. Little had she known that so many people wanted her and the now-fat bounty on her head. Honestly, fuck Arden and his mysterious partner for everything.

"No, I remember." Quin kept his voice light and even, as if he didn't have a single thing to worry about, especially not a fugitive hiding on the balcony. "I also remember telling you that the Knight wanted her and for you to back off."

"Ah, yes. The threat of the Knight. Originally, that was enough to get me to back off. But have you seen the bounty on her now?" Her voice was gleefully greedy. "Big enough that I'm willing to risk pissing both the Knight off for it. So, hand her over, before I break down this door, disable you, and take her. This doesn't have to be painful for you. Hells, I'll even throw in a percentage of the bounty for your cooperation."

Fuck. She saw Quin shoot a frown at the closed curtains and mouthed a curse as he came to the same conclusion as her. He was going to have to let Amaryllis in.

He raised his voice so Bea could hear him clearly. "You really want to come in? You're going to be disappointed. There's no one here but me, Amaryllis."

Bea looked around the tiny balcony. Not even a plant to hide behind. She eyed the balcony of the room next to them, its metal railing a few feet away. The stone facade of the building obscured part of it. If she could get over there without falling off and breaking her neck, she should be able to squeeze behind the facade enough that they wouldn't see her if they checked outside.

"Let me in now, Quin." Amaryllis was getting impatient.

"Give me a sec. You woke me up, and I'm not letting you in while I'm naked."

He was buying her time. With a deep breath, she climbed onto her balcony's railing, bracing herself on the wall. *You can do this*, she told herself, *just don't look down. Keep your eyes straight ahead*. She could hear Quin fussing with the locks on the door, telling the woman to hold on. Now or never. Gathering her strength, she held her breath and leaped.

She landed on top of the rail with her right foot, but inertia carried her forward to land heavily on the floor, scraping her knee and hands. Scrambling to her feet, she tucked herself into the corner behind the stone facade and sucked in. Taking quiet, shallow breaths, she listened to the loud voices next door as the pirates invaded the room.

Someone slid open the balcony door, their heavy boots

clomping on the flooring. "No one out here, Cap," a low male voice said.

Amaryllis cursed. "I don't know where you're hiding her, Quin, but you'd better keep a close eye on your prize. That bounty is tempting enough to set the worst of the hunters on her scent."

"I'll take that under advisement," Quin said in an implacable voice.

Amaryllis and her goons knocked around the small room, making more racket than necessary. Bea pictured them looking in every drawer and glaring suspiciously at the dust bunnies hiding under the bed in the hopes of finding her. She closed her eyes, focusing on the rough texture of the stone beneath her fingertips and the soft caress of the early morning breeze on her cheek rather than pirates next door. Now was not the time to panic. It would only get her caught.

"Now that you've determined she isn't here, I suggest you leave."

"Whatever. I've got bigger fish to fry," she said. "See you around, Quin. Oh, and be a dear and tell Ivan I said hello, would you?"

More clomping and grumpy voices came from their room. Even as they faded, Bea stayed where she was, pressed up so hard against the wall, she was going to have imprints on her skin. Her scrapes pulsed with a dull pain.

"Daisy, it's clear." Quin's soft words finally penetrated the fog she'd slipped into. "Where are you?"

She peeled herself off the wall and peeked around the corner, lifting a hand to wave at him. "Hi."

He sagged with visible relief. "Oh, thank the gods. You okay?"

Nodding, she checked out her injuries. A couple layers of skin gone, but easily fixed with a quick-fix patch. "So they're gone?"

He shook his head. "There's a pirate lingering in the hallway. No doubt another outside, too. She claims to have other things to do. She's a multitasker."

"What do we do now?" She glanced over at their balcony then at the ground below. "Because I'm not climbing down the side of a building, and I'm not sure I can make it back over to you. Once was enough, thank you." Her heart was still pounding. Heights sucked.

He gave her a crooked smile. "I don't want you to climb down the side of a building, either. Hold on, I'll come over." He put his hands on the rail but halted. "Wait. First, check if there's anyone in that room."

"The curtain's closed. No one came to investigate when I landed very gracefully onto their balcony, so I'm guessing probably not." She hadn't been exactly quiet. Or grateful. If the room was occupied, they would have heard her.

"Alright. I have a better idea," he said, a glint in his eyes. "Check the door."

She tugged the handle. It stuck at first, but then slid to the side after a good, hard yank. With a happy bounce, she said, "Unlocked. But it won't do me much good if there's someone waiting in the hall for me. I'm sure they know what I look like or have a face identifier."

He leaned his arms on the railing. "Okay. Here's what you're going to do. Call room service and order the house special. You do that, and I'll pack up our stuff." He paused, giving her a long look. "Trust me, okay?"

She nodded, though she had no idea where this plan was going. As long as it kept her out of Amaryllis's hands so she could make her meet with Ghost, she could follow his instructions. He hadn't led her astray yet.

She made the call, then wandered back onto the balcony. Quin reappeared shortly, holding their pack. "Scootch back so I can toss this onto your balcony."

It landed with a thud, and she threw it into the room. "Okay, now what?"

"Now, I'm going to take a stroll around the block, and if our unwanted stalker follows, I'll incapacitate him." He scrubbed a hand over the beard that had filled in nicely over the past few days. "Amaryllis will eventually realize we tricked her, but this should buy us time to get to your meeting this afternoon. You wait for your house special. I'll meet you at the back exit."

"But..." She wasn't thrilled to be going into this unaware. And what exactly was a house special? She sighed to herself. If anything did go wrong, she'd have to do things her own way. But for now, she'd try it Quin's way.

He noticed her hesitation and said, "Trust me. You don't have to do anything. The hotel will take care of you, and I'll see you soon, okay? You'll be okay, I promise."

Still not thrilled, she did as he asked, unanswered questions buzzing around her brain. Twenty minutes later, a knock on the door announced room service.

A short elderly man in an ancient burnt orange bellhop's suit rolled a cart into the room and shut the door behind him. She watched as he removed the covered dishes from the top of the cart and set them down on the dresser. He then lifted the edge of the dark orange tablecloth covering the cart and, with a pale, skeletal hand, gestured at her to get in.

"Really?" she said, her eyes wide.

He nodded. "House special."

Shrugging, she tucked herself onto the bottom shelf of the cart, holding their pack under the vee of her legs, and braced herself for the trip.

The bellhop tapped the cart twice and rolled her out of the room.

Many interminable minutes later, they came to a halt, and two taps sounded on the top of the cart. Bea tentatively poked her head out before crawling out into a back room filled with cleaning supplies and various stock. The bellhop tipped his cap at her, pointed at one of the two doors before leaving through the other. Slinging the pack over her shoulder, Bea carefully opened the door he'd pointed to.

Strong sunlight temporarily blinded her. Her adrenaline

spiked when someone grabbed her arm and pulled her into the hedges. A familiar calloused hand covered her mouth before she could squeak out in alarm. Quin put a finger to his lips and tipped his head to the right. Down the block, she could see the back of a tall woman with a rainbow of braids woven into a crown walking away from them. The infamous Amaryllis in the flesh.

"You just missed her." Quin whispered in her ear as he shouldered their pack, tugging her along behind him in the opposite direction. "The crew member she left behind to watch the room was quite forthcoming. Seems she's on Badin for a different job but got a tip that I'd landed on the planet, so she decided to check in on me."

"How kind of her," Bea muttered, not appreciating the close call. She followed him as they skulked through the bushes, barely swallowing a scream as she tripped over a body. "Is he dead?"

Quin kept a steading grip on her, hurrying them through the space between the building and the greenery. "No. Only unconscious." He looked back at the man on the ground. "Actually thought he'd be awake by now. Guess I don't know my own strength."

She rolled her eyes at the delight that tinged his words. "Show-off."

He gave her a wink as they rounded the corner and then, pressing her back up against the hard stone wall, gave her a kiss that set her head spinning. "You ready to make some tracks?"

"Once I regain my senses, sure." She knew she was feeding his ego by saying his kisses made her dizzy, but it made her feel warm all over to see him light up at the compliment.

"Careful, or I might be reckless enough to take you up against this wall and damn the consequences." He nipped at the spot where her neck met her shoulders, and she nearly combusted on the spot.

She let out a breathy laugh. "Look, I'm all for some wall action, but I'd rather my daughter not have to visit me in prison afterwards because someone caught us."

"Pretty sure I could make it worth the risk." His body pressed tightly against hers, he glanced around them. "But, as I have no desire to break you out of prison again, that particular fantasy will have to wait."

"Alas," she said, smiling as he shouldered their pack. They took off, blending in with the morning crowd that filled the streets.

32

QUIN

"Heard from Ivan," Quin said, enjoying the feel of Bea's soft fingers entwined with his.

"And? Any news?" She sounded tired.

He couldn't blame her. After all they'd been through, he was tired, too, and he was used to long periods of go-go-go. Riding the adrenaline high was a younger person's sport. "He's on Badin, just arrived at the 'port."

She twitched against his hand. "He's here? Why? I thought you said your crew wasn't able to join us." She chewed her lip, her brows furrowed.

"Slight change of plan." He squeezed her hand. "After that run-in with Amaryllis, I'll be glad of some backup for your meeting."

They paused their conversation as he hailed a zippy lift, giving the automated driver directions to an intersection on the east side of town, close to the diner where she'd be meeting Ghost in a few hours. The little three-wheeled vehicle pulled away from the curb, its tiny engine chugging away in a putt-putt sound.

He'd always liked these things. They reminded him of riding around in a speedy bubble with three wheels that, despite the low horsepower, could effortlessly weave through traffic and get its passengers where they needed to go for just a few credits. He fed his few remaining physical credits into the payment slot, garnering a modulated, "Thank you for your business" from the computer-driver.

Bea watched the city pass by the window, sunlight flashing over her face, and a rush of emotion spilled through his veins. Her every gesture, every snarky little remark she threw back at him, each time she teased him or smiled at him... it was waking him up in a way he hadn't experienced in a very long time, not since Jannette fucked him and his crew over and he'd built a tall stone wall around his heart. Though he felt alive in her presence, he wasn't sure how he felt about peeling back the layers of protection and distance he'd so carefully wrapped around his heart. He did know that it scared the shit out of him.

After a few moments of silence broken only by the putt-putt of their vehicle's motor, Bea said, "So. Ivan. Why is he here on Badin, then?"

"It's a long story but Ivan and Amaryllis, they have kind of a thing going." He leaned back against the hard seat and stretched out his legs.

"Like a love thing?"

He snorted. "More like a 'I will stab you and drop your body in a dark pit when I get the chance' thing."

"Wow." She paused. "Sounds like a pretty intense love-hate relationship."

"Don't let either of them hear you call it a 'relationship' or mention the word love in their presence unless you want your head bitten clean off. When I told them they needed to bang it out to work through their feelings for one another, all I got were death threats." He sighed dramatically, scrubbing a hand through his hair. "Anyway, they tend to keep an eye on one another, eager for the chance to fuck up the others' plans, whatever they may be. Ivan's been tracking Amaryllis since our standoff over you and the *Intrepid*. As soon as he saw her headed to the same place as us, he made his way to Badin."

"It'll be interesting to meet him, anyway." When Quin raised an eyebrow, she shrugged. "He seemed like the nicest of you lot."

Clasping a hand over his heart, he said, "Oof, tell a guy how you really feel."

She giggled.

"Anyway, there's an outdoor market I thought you'd enjoy. He's going to meet us there. The market is within walking distance of the diner. It's The Lazy Pelican you're meeting at, right?"

She gave him a sharp nod. "I'll be so glad when this part is over. I've been through so much to get to this point and I've got such high hopes for it even though I know I need to be pragmatic about it..." She drew a shaky breath.

He squeezed her hand. "No matter what, we're in this together. Whatever Ghost gives you. We'll figure it out. My crew will help. We'll contact your sister, and she can help, too. I'll take you to Gyan Station. You'll be safe there. Okay?" He wanted this meet over quickly so he could whisk her away to safety.

She gave him a wobbly smile. "Okay."

"Today, we'll have Ivan for backup. Even better, no one knows he's here. He's going to do recon and watch our backs while we wander aimlessly through the market."

"I can handle aimless wandering. And surprise backup is nice, too." She drew in a deep breath and let it out in a slow exhale.

Traffic was light, so the trip didn't take long. The zippy lift spit them out near a small park filled with happily loud children playing in the grass while parents watched from beneath the shade trees.

"Have a nice day," the zippy's automated driver said.

Quin snorted quietly. One could only hope. Scanning the area, Quin led them towards a bench painted in bright primary colors by a local artist.

The man sitting on it popped to his feet when he caught sight of them, raising a hand in greeting. "Good to see you, brother," Ivan said, pulling Quin into a hug, clapping him hard on the back before stepping back to eye him. "I see you've survived the hellion so far."

"Hey," Bea exclaimed. "I'm right here." She'd taken a step back when the large man with a shock of ginger hair and full beard had barreled forward to hug his captain.

Grinning, Ivan extended a hand to her. "Or, should I say, you survived the ham-fisted attempts of my captain to rescue you and keep you safe?"

Bea grinned back at him. "Definitely not the best rescue I've ever had, I'll admit. Maybe he'll get better with practice."

Pulling her to him, Ivan tucked Bea under his arm. "I like her, Cap. We should keep her."

Without thinking, Quin extricated her from Ivan's embrace and tugged her to his side.

"Ah. So that's how it is," Ivan said, examining them. "Well, then. We should definitely keep her now."

"No one's keeping anyone," Quin growled. Why was he being so possessive? It was just Ivan, and Bea didn't need protection from him. Fuck. She had him all twisted up. He let out another growl, this one of frustration.

Cupping a hand to his mouth, Ivan leaned over and fake-whispered to Bea, "You'll have him trained in no time. Keep up the good work."

With a laugh, Bea gently untangled herself from Quin's side, though she twined her fingers through his, keeping contact. "It's exhausting. Has he always been this way, or is it just with me?"

"Well, the man's always been a pain in the arse, if that's what you mean. His smart mouth got him more KP duty than anyone else in our 'Guard unit. Maybe with you around, he'll settle down a little, give us a break." A wide smile spread across his face, his eyes bright with delight as he watched Quin squirm. "I cannot wait to tell the crew about this particular development."

Quin gritted his teeth, knowing there was nothing he could say or do to stop the man from gossiping. He couldn't outright deny that there was anything going on between him and Bea because there was, even if they didn't yet know what it was or if it would go anywhere. And he wasn't about to admit to it for the same reasons. So he changed the subject. "Did you bring it?"

Taking the topic change with barely a blink, Ivan said, "Oh, yeah." He dug into a pocket and pulled out a black piece of plasticine. "Cormac swears that this will fix your comm woes and get you back online. When he handed it to me, he called it foolproof. Not sure if he was talking about you or me, Cap." Ivan waggled the black rectangle at him.

Quin took it to examine. Tiny veins of copper wire ran over the card's surface in an intricate pattern, but he couldn't tell how it worked.

He was about to ask Ivan what it did when Bea plucked it from his grasp, running a finger over it. She flipped it over and examined it further. "Oh, wow. Cool." Pulling his hand to her, she placed it on his wrist over the place where the comm tech was implanted, and ran a finger along the edge. The veining on the thin rectangle lit up, pulsing as if alive. He felt a light buzzing beneath his skin. Less than a minute later, the card dulled. She released his hand. "Okay, give it a try."

Shrugging off the feeling he'd missed something, he double-tapped his thumb and middle finger together, bracing against the shock he'd come to expect from the misfiring tech. Instead, it lit up just like it was supposed to, a holo of the home screen floating over his palm. "It works? How? What magic is that?"

Ivan looked clueless, but Bea said, "It's a type of all-in-one tool for tech. It can reset, temporarily patch, and store info. Dai brought me one a while back to play with. Depending on how it's programmed, there are a bunch of sneaky-type uses for it." She turned it over in her hands. "I wonder..." she muttered to herself.

Quin leaned over to a confused-looking Ivan and said, "Her sister, the ex-spy."

"Does everyone know about Dai? She's going to be so pissed," Bea grumbled.

"Ah," Ivan said. "Bea, aren't you going to fix your comm, too? Quin said yours was disabled."

Bea glanced at her wrist, then the piece of plasticine. "Not yet. I think I'm better off with a nonfunctional one for now." Then she pocketed it.

Ivan opened his mouth to protest, but Quin shook his head. "Don't bother. If she wants it, she'll claim it. Did I tell you about the time she stole my motorcycle then sold it?"

"Hey, that bike was mine and you know it," Bea said, her eyes sparkling as she turned to Ivan. "Does he always lie this much, or is it just to me?"

Quin put a hand over his heart. "Ooh, got me with that one, Daisy."

Ivan watched their byplay, his eyes wide.

"What?" Quin grouched. When the man just shook his head and gave him a broad smile, he said, "Ivan, why are you here?" he asked, knowing full well why the man was on this planet.

It was Ivan's turn to growl, his hand automatically searching for a blaster that wasn't there. "That damnable woman. She tracked you all here."

"We know," Bea said.

Ivan's thick ginger eyebrows rose.

"Yeah, she found us this morning." Quin recapped their escape.

"Once she catches a scent, she's like a bloody hound. Trust me, we have not seen the last of Amaryllis." Ivan shook his head. "So, I'm here to watch your backs."

"And we appreciate it." He exchanged a glance with Bea. "Speaking of, we have an appointment that Daisy here needs to keep. You ready to run backup?"

"Ready and able. I'll scope out the area and deal with any unwanted visitors. You two be on your merry way." Ivan gave them a two-fingered salute and disappeared behind a flock of children.

Bea turned to Quin with wide eyes. "How did he do that? He's three times bigger than them."

The corner of Quin's mouth kicked up. "He's got an affinity for being sneaky."

She raised both her eyebrows at him.

"Hey, I can't explain how a man that large can just disappear. We're just really good at what we do." Quin winked.

She rolled her eyes. "And obviously your affinity is sarcasm."

"Ooh, another shot straight to the heart." After pressing a kiss to her palm, he settled her hand in the crook of his arm. "If you're done shooting me with your verbal arrows, let's go explore the market."

33

BEA

As they neared the outdoor market, Bea surreptitiously pressed the hand not currently in Quin's possession on her thigh to quell the slight tremor that shook it. Nerves wouldn't stop her from doing what needed to be done, though she fought the urge to run away and hide until it was all over. But she couldn't chicken out now.

Feeling her tension, Quin asked, "You okay?"

"Fine," she said, rolling her shoulders to loosen the knots. "Just nerves. I'll be fine."

He nodded, accepting her answer. There was nothing more he could do to fix that, anyway. This part was up to her, though she appreciated his support.

Any other day, she would have loved visiting the cute, colorful market Quin brought her to. Small tents lined both sides of the wide pedestrian walkway along the park, their tables filled with a variety of goods that normally she'd be pausing to pick up and inspect. But her head was buzzing. Would Ghost have anything useful? Would their information help her clear her name? Because as of right now, that was her primary concern. She'd deal with everything else later, though she had high and quite possibly false hopes that the bounty would disappear once she got the warrant for her arrest dropped and was a fugitive from the law no longer.

She had to be completely honest with herself. There was more to all this than the false charges against her. Lately, she'd had some big realizations, but she'd continued sweeping them under the metaphorical rug because she just couldn't deal yet. And because of those other pieces of the puzzle, the bounty might still be there after the authorities nullified the warrant and dropped the false charges. If it was, then she — no, they, both she and Quin, because he'd promised — would need to figure out who set it and why.

And then there was her propulsion system. Before Arden came along, she'd been living in a rose-colored bubble, happily imagining how much good a less expensive, more efficient way to travel around the galaxy could do. Now that the bubble had burst, she realized how naïve she'd been. She'd been so focused on building her system that she hadn't even considered how industry giants like Vanid Shipping might react to such a system challenging their monopoly and their control, much less how her system might disrupt the industry as a whole. From the mining companies who supplied the rare mineral for the power pellets to the companies who dominated the shipping lanes, it might have a domino effect with changes she couldn't yet imagine.

So, while she still wanted to finish her project — was driven to finish it — and get it into the hands of those it would benefit the most, she couldn't go back home to work on it. It was no longer safe or secure there. She'd still need protection, even after the charges were dropped. She needed help. She needed Quin, not just for that layer of safety but because she didn't want to give him up just yet. Or ever.

The realization nearly brought her to her knees. She needed him. More than that, she was falling for him, the pieces of her heart knitting together with threads he'd spun around her.

She thought of the data dot hidden under the nu-skin on her hand and took a deep breath to slow her racing heart. She focused on Quin, who'd threaded his fingers through hers again. He liked to do that, rubbing a thumb over her skin as he held her hand. Maybe it was his way of making sure they stuck together, and that she wasn't snatched from beneath his nose, but she enjoyed the sense of closeness, of safety she felt when he clasped his large, calloused hand around hers. Allowing herself to revel in the sensation, she tried to push down her worries. *One crisis at a time*, she thought.

Together, they strolled through the open market, looking for all the stars like an everyday couple, rather than a pirate and a woman on the run trying to blend in. *Oh, gods, she was nervous.* They paused by a display of hand painted pottery. She particularly liked the blue tea mugs with delicate flowering vines painted along the rim. Another stall sold spices, the products scooped from large bags with the twirl of the owner's wrist. The carefully stacked fruits and vegetables spread over the next couple of tables made her wish she had a market like this closer to her house. The melange of sounds and scents swirling through the air helped temporarily calm her racing pulse.

Pausing at the next-to-last stall, Quin presented her with a ripe orange fruit she'd never seen before and nudged her to try it. The heavy sweetness of the flesh under the thin, somewhat fuzzy skin burst over her tongue, the spicy scent of citrus in her nose. He laughed, kissing a drop of nectar away from the corner of her mouth.

"My mother has these in her garden," he said, stealing a bite. "They remind me of childhood summers. We would steal them from the trees as soon as they were ripe and stuff our faces with them before jumping into the nearby river to wash off all the juices."

"Sounds lovely." She dropped the pit into a recycler and licked the juices from her fingers.

Quin grabbed her hand and stuck a finger in his mouth, sucking it clean with a mischievous glint in his eyes.

A white-haired lady, her bright blue eyes shining amidst a sea of wrinkles, swatted Quin's arm, laughing as she scolded him about indecent public displays. Still smiling, she reached behind the stack of colorful quilts she was selling and handed Bea a wet cloth to clean the stickiness from her hands before turning to help a new customer.

The Lazy Pelican Diner loomed across the pedestrian avenue, just beyond the last stall. Bea found she couldn't make her feet move forward.

Quin turned to look at her. "You okay?"

She shook her head. "I'm not sure I can do this," she whispered. Her heart beat far too quickly and that delicious fruit threatened to make a reappearance. "What if this is all an elaborate joke and Ghost doesn't have what I need? I'll never clear my name. Or what if this is just a setup to, I don't know, earn the bounty? I'll be arrested and locked away for horrible crimes I didn't commit. I'll never see my daughter again." With the worst outcomes rampaging through her brain, her breath came out in short bursts and the edges of her vision darkened.

Enveloping her hands in his, Quin leaned close, his voice gentle. "Breathe with me. In and out. I'm right here. Ivan is here. We have your back, and we won't let anything happen to you, I promise. Breathe, Daisy." He pulled her to his chest and stroked her back in slow, easy strokes. "Just breathe."

She closed her eyes, the sounds of the market receding as she focused on the movement of his hand on her back, the rasp of his beard against her temple, the gentle exhale of his breath across her forehead. Soon, she could breathe again. Two more deep breaths and she came back to herself, moving out of Quin's comforting arms and rolling her shoulders to release the tension.

"Better?" he asked, his eyes dark with concern.

She tipped her head from side to side, stretching tight muscles. "Better. Thank you," she said, trying to shove all her worries into a little box in a dark corner of her mind where it could stay forever.

Quin took her chin in his hand, stilling her nervous movements. "Look at me. You've got this, Daisy. You've been so brave, so confident and determined this whole time." He rubbed his hands over her arms and pressed a kiss to her temple. "It's a simple meet. We're right outside if you need us. If it helps, Ivan will happily tackle Amaryllis to the ground before he lets her anywhere near you."

She let out a shaky laugh. "He'd probably enjoy that." With every word of encouragement from Quin, she could once again feel that core of strength she'd been clutching onto for dear life since this whole mess started.

"Oh, he absolutely would, though he wouldn't admit it. And I'm just a signal away if you need me."

She lifted her hand in a fist, making the signal they'd agreed on.

"Exactly." He faced her towards the diner and smacked her ass. "Now, go get 'em."

She gave a little yelp and looked back at him with wide eyes.

With a wink, he said, "More of that when you're done in there."

"Cheeky bastard," said the blue-eyed lady who'd been surreptitiously watching their exchange with a wide grin. "You be sure to keep hold of him, luv, or someone will snatch him from you for sure."

"Working on it," she answered with a smile. Then she squared her shoulders and marched down the block into the diner.

Bea's confident steps faltered as she entered the narrow eatery. Decorated in bright reds and shining whites, the kitschy space had a long counter with round stools that ran down one side, the kitchen visible behind it. The opposite wall was lined with booths, leaving a long center aisle to walk down. Pillar-shaped bots painted red with white piping zipped up and down the aisle, delivering drinks and dishes to the booths' occupants while live servers helped those at the counter. Music swirled around the space, just loud enough to prevent conversations from being easily overheard. It was not what she expected for a clandestine meeting with a secretive hacker.

Bea paused at the front of the lunch counter and surveyed the space. Not many diners for the late afternoon, though a few lingered over coffee. She eyed a delicious-looking chocolate milkshake on a server bot's tray, but her stomach clenched at the thought of drinking the rich dessert.

"Can I help you?" A perky server whose nametag read 'Joan' asked, a bright smile on her youthful face.

Bea cleared her throat. "I'm meeting someone, thanks." She nodded towards the booth at the back. That someone waved her down when Bea entered. Her contact.

"Fab." Joan glanced at the tables behind her and popped a bubble. "You want me to send a bot with anything?" She asked, tucking a curl that escaped her ponytail behind her ear.

"A green tea would be much appreciated." Maybe it would help calm the butterflies in her stomach.

"Gotcha." Joan said. "It'll just be a minute."

Bea nodded and walked to the last table, sliding into the booth seat. "Hi." She was pleased to hear her voice crack only a little.

No response from the person sitting across from her. Despite the cafe's best efforts to light up every square inch of the place, they had managed to pull the shadows around them, their face shrouded within their hoodie. Pale, elegant fingers wrapped around a cup of coffee.

A server bot wheeled over with a small pot and cup, sliding them in front of Bea. "Anything else?" it asked.

Bea said, "No, thanks." She glanced at her dining companion, who shook their head. "I think we're good."

"Press the button at your table if you need anything," it said, wheeling to the next table.

She poured herself a cup of tea, giving the person a chance to speak first. Nothing. So she said, "So, I think you're the person I'm supposed to meet?" Their lack of response was disconcerting.

She bit the inside of her cheek to keep random words from babbling out of her. She leaned closer, resting her arms on the cool edge of the counter. "Are you... Ghost?"

A beat of silence. Then another. Her palms went clammy. Should she signal to Quin? What was this person waiting for? Were they ever going to talk? Should she leave? She frowned as irritation kicked in. They were the ones who set the meeting, after all.

The person let out a hoot of laughter and pulled back their hood, revealing delicate features framed by silky black hair shaped into a pixie cut. Shockingly green eyes sparkled with laugher. "Holy cats, you should see your face right now."

She frowned. "What?"

Their laughter died down, though their eyes still sparkled with mischief. "Sorry. I don't get out much, especially not to do this cloak-and-dagger kind of stuff." They swiped a hand through their hair, ruffling the curling edges. "I suppose it's not so funny from your end, huh?"

After all she went through and all the worry leading up to this meet, she had no humor to spare. Narrowing her eyes at them, she asked in a firm tone, "So, you are Ghost, then?"

"I am the person you're looking for. So, yes. You may call me Ghost, they/them," they said with a nod, wriggling with excitement in their seat. "Do you know how lucky you are that you actually get to meet me? I rarely come to these things in person, but you're the sister of Dai Farsirus, and I just had to meet you."

"Dai?" Bea was so confused. What did her sister have to do with anything? Was there something wrong with this person? She was beginning to regret ever agreeing to this exchange.

"Oh, yes. Dai and her team. They're heroes. What they're doing? Amazing," they gushed, the wriggle becoming a full-on seat dance. "So, when I heard that Dai's little sister had run into some trouble, I just had to help. Maybe you could introduce me?" They shook their head. "No, that's too much. I would probably pass out. Ooh, I know. But you could mention me to her? I'd love to help her out with one of her projects sometime."

"Um, thank you?" Bea gave them a slow nod, attempting to process the onslaught of words. "And maybe?"

They paused long enough to examine Bea and settled down in their seat. "I'm overwhelming you. I do that sometimes, especially when I'm excited about things. Or people, in this case." Ghost sighed, propping their chin in their hand. "Sorry. I'm not great with people. People are complicated and confusing. But tech, digging into all the little spaces people try to hide their information? That's much more my jam."

"Speaking of..." Bea began, trying to get the conversation back on track. Not that it had ever actually been on track.

Ghost pursed their lips. "Oh, yeah. You're here because I promised you information. You know, I had fun tracking this down. So many juicy rabbit holes to dive into." They reached into a pocket and pulled out a clear tablet the size of their palm, tapping it with a long index finger before setting it on the table in front of them. "So many interesting tidbits of information. I can probably find you more, if you like. I just need more time." They smiled, a gleam of white teeth against black lipstick. "And you have something for me?"

"I do." Splaying her hand on the table, Bea pointed to the small bump of the data dot barely visible against her skin. "What is it?"

"No, no." They tsked. "That's not for you. And good thing you followed my directions and didn't attempt to access it yourself. It might be tiny, but there's enough of a charge in there to blow off your hand."

Blood drained from her face, and Bea jerked her hand back, cradling it against her chest. "Fuck. Why didn't you tell me?" Holy shit. She'd been transporting something that could blow up. On her hand, no less. She needed that hand. She stared at Ghost, trying to figure out if they were truly cracked or just a quirky, dangerous genius. The latter, she hoped, though it was still undecided.

They cocked their head. "Clyde didn't tell you?"

"Clyde didn't tell me shit." She clenched her jaw, wishing she could smack Clyde on the back of his head. "He basically just tossed it on the table and left."

Ghost tutted. "That's what I get for using an anonymous job board." Smiling brightly, they said, "No matter." They shrugged. "It's really stable stuff unless it's improperly accessed. You didn't do that or copy it, so you were fine."

Bea felt her stomach roil and took a sip of her green tea. It did little to settle her nerves.

Reaching into another pocket, Ghost pulled out a hot pink reader with a copper square grafted onto the top corner and held it up. "Okay if I get it?"

Bea hesitated, torn between handing over the only guarantee that she'd get the promised information in return and a burning desire to get rid of the explosive on her hand.

"Oh, don't worry. I'm not going to screw you over," they said, sliding the clear tablet across the table to her. "The information's there. You have access to that tablet, so you can read it here. I'll send it to your comm, too. Whatever works for you." They frowned and tapped on their own tablet. "Your comm... doesn't seem to work? Disabled?"

Bea nodded.

"Probably smart, considering." They tapped some more, the tip of their tongue sticking out between their lips. "There. Info's waiting for you when you feel comfortable enough to go back online."

Bea blinked. "I think I'll stay offline for now. Safer that way," she said, picking up the tablet and swiping open the first file. There were several neatly labeled, and she felt a rush of excitement. This might really be it, what she needed.

"Ah. Good plan," Ghost said, their fingers flying over their tablet. "You have a pretty decent bit of coding on your comm already — probs thanks to Izumi, right? She's so cool — but I added another layer of encryption, so when you do turn your comm back on, it can't be used to track you. You're welcome. And you can keep that tablet, too. I've got plenty. You know, I don't think I could ever go offline like you are. It might actually crush my soul." They tapped a finger on the edge of their pink tablet. "This baby is my own design. Once it uploads the information you carry, it'll erase that dot and neutralize the explosive. Then you can dispose of it. So. Ready?" At Bea's nod, Ghost placed the tablet's copper square over the data dot on Bea's hand. "This will take a few."

But Bea was no longer paying attention. She was immersed in the files Ghost had provided. The small zing of shock that Ghost's tablet zapped her with to fry the data dot barely registered. When Ghost slid out of the booth, she glanced up at them but didn't really see them, her mind swirling with what she'd just read.

Ghost tapped and swiped at their pink tablet, then nodded at the one Bea clutched between bloodless fingers. "To make up for Clyde not telling you about the whole explosive thing, I threw you a new bit of info my crawlers found last night."

"I appreciate that." She would have appreciated not having an explosive on her hand more, but she wasn't about to quibble with the hacker.

"No, thank you for providing me with such a delightful challenge." They pulled the hood of their jacket back up, shrouding their face. "And pass on my deets to your sister, would you please? The tablet has how to contact me. If you need something, let me know. I can always use the challenge and the credits."

"Thank you, Ghost," Bea said. She opened the new file and stared at the words in front of her. When she looked up again, Ghost was gone.

34

QUIN

Bea stumbled out of the diner, her face so pale he thought she might pass out. Quin pulled her against him, burying his nose in her hair, inhaling her sunshiney-sharp scent. She wrapped her arms around his waist and let out a shaky breath.

Ivan appeared from wherever he'd concealed himself, took one look at Bea and said, "Let's get a drink. I know a place."

They wound up in a dive bar named Tipsy McSwerve's near from the market. While Ivan went up to the bar to get drinks, Quin guided Bea through the dark space to a booth with fake leather padded seats and high backs for privacy. No one so much as glanced in their direction.

She grimaced as her butt stuck to the seat and peeled herself up to scootch her way over so Quin could slide in next to her. The late afternoon crowd was sparse and mostly contained to the long bar that dominated the place. It was the statue behind the bar that caught Quin's attention, though. A metal sculpture of a red fire-breathing dragon guarded the selection of liquors displayed on backlit shelves, its tail curling along the center shelf. No wonder Ivan liked this place. The bar mascot was the same one as on Ivan's family crest.

Ivan plonked down three dark beers and a shot of an amber liquid before taking his place in the booth across from them.

"Who's the shot for?" Bea asked as he distributed the drinks.

He nudged it towards her. "You. Drink. You're still too pale and shaky-looking for my comfort."

Without argument, Bea picked up the small glass, clinked it against Ivan's pint, and threw back the shot, closing her eyes with a shiver. "Thanks. I needed that."

Ivan grunted and drained his beer, setting both empty glasses at the edge of the table.

She took a deep breath and said, "He's alive."

They were quiet as she stared blankly into her drink. Finally, Quin broke the silence and, though he thought he already knew the answer, he asked, "Who is, Daisy?"

"Arden. I thought he died in the fire. I cried over his death. I went to prison because of him. I'm on the run because of him. Come to find out that rat bastard is still crawling around above ground." She took a hefty drink of her beer, then wiped away the foam with the back of her hand. "The tiny cockwomble set me up, stole my work, and didn't even have the balls to die in a fire." Her voice rose with every word before she wailed out the last one and thunked her head against the table, covering it with her arms.

Stroking her hair, Quin looked to see if they'd attracted any attention, but the other patrons were far more interested in their drinks than the loud woman venting at a table. Good bar choice. Nobody gave a shit about anyone else's business but their own.

"Is that what Ghost told you?" he asked.

She nodded, sitting up and sliding a small clear tablet over to him. Ivan snatched it up first, turning it over in his hand before Quin grabbed it back. "I've never seen one like that before," Ivan said.

"Yeah, Ghost said they had a lot of them and gave this one to me." Bea took another long drink of her beer, the alcohol helping to lower her shoulders from up around her ears. "I only had time to skim, but... it's more than I'd hoped for."

Quin opened the folder marked "Bea", and began reading. Ivan entertained Bea with a story about Quin's first time in a bar, making her laugh as he quickly scanned through the information, hitting the highlights. When he was done, he passed it to Ivan, then drained his beer, thumping the glass on the table.

Bea eyed his empty, then tipped hers back and set it next to his and Ivan's.

"While Ivan finishes reading what you got from Ghost, I'll get us another round." Quin unstuck himself from the seat and plucked up the glasses. "I have the feeling we're going to need it."

"And maybe something fried? And a burger, if they have them?" Bea asked, her tone hopeful. "I was too nervous to eat much earlier, and I'm starving."

"In a dive bar like this?" He gestured at the place. "I think fried things and burgers are a requirement."

Placing their order with the bartender, he returned with another round and settled back next to Bea. She leaned against him, and he put his arm around her shoulders, enjoying the feel of her softness pressed up against him. The three of them clinked glasses with a slainté and took a drink.

"So, this Arden of yours. He seems like a real piece of work," Ivan drawled, rubbing the back of his neck. "I kind of want to smash my fist into his face."

Feeling Bea tense, Quin glared at him.

Ivan put up his hands to ward off the glare. "What? Someone fucks over someone he pretended to care about like that, then fakes his own death, and I'm not supposed to comment?"

"I feel like such a fool." Bea put a hand over her face. "It's just that he was so charming when we first met, bringing me flowers and takeout from my favorite places." She looked up at them, a sheen of tears glistening in her eyes. "He was nice to Essy when she was home on break from university. She even gave him the daughter seal of approval, thrilled that he made me happy and was taking care of me. And all that time, he was plotting how best to steal my work and sell it to the highest bidder."

Quin and Ivan exchanged a glance. "All good con artists are charming, Daisy," Quin said gently.

With a nod, Ivan added, "It's not that regular guys can't be charming, too, but con men are really slick about it. It's hard to spot them, unless you're one yourself or you've been conned."

She snorted. "Well, now I'll know. Bright side, I guess."

Quin rubbed her arm, trying to comfort her. "It's only after the con is done, and your bank accounts are cleared out or your priceless jewelry is stolen..."

"Or you're framed for their murder, even though they're walking around, trying to sell what they stole from you." Bitterness coated her words. "I mean, shit. The system isn't even functional. I don't know if it will ever work. It's close, but none of the prototypes have been successful yet. How much money does he think he's going to get for something that doesn't even work?"

"On a positive note, they'll have to drop the murder charge when they see him all alive and well and not ashes," Ivan said.

"And a tooth. Can't forget the damned tooth," she muttered.

"And on an even more positive note, the people he owes money to are going to be incredibly pissed that he faked his death to skip out of paying them what he owes," Quin added.

"Yeah, those are people I would not borrow money from," Ivan said, shaking his head.

"He owes money to bad people?" Her eyes were wide. "I missed that. I didn't have time to read everything carefully."

Ivan nodded.

"Good. I hope they break his kneecaps." Bea's expression filled with vengeance. "Maybe rip out his tongue or stick him in a cage for the birds to peck at. They do still do that in some places, don't they?"

Ivan shot Quin a wide-eyed glance. "Uh, not that I know of."

Quin laughed, enjoying the creativity of his bloodthirsty little flower.

"Well, that's a shame," she said, clearly disappointed.

A gangly teenager appeared at the end of their table, unceremoniously dropped three baskets of burgers and fries in front of them, then departed without a word.

Bea tore into the food like she hadn't eaten in weeks. "Oh, my gods, this is so good," she said, her mouth full of burger.

Quin peered under the bun, added some condiments, and took a bite. The juicy burger practically melted in his mouth. "Good choice of venue, Ivan."

Ivan stuffed some fries into his face. "Dive bars always have the best food."

For a few minutes, they feasted. Quin swallowed the fry he'd been chewing and said, "Okay, so let's walk through this. Arden runs up some gambling debts with Orrin's Outfit, a group that's part of The Cabal." Bea blinked at him and he clarified. "They're a nasty group of pirates, racketeers, thieves, and all-around law-breakers, some of the shadiest the Cabal has to offer."

"He must have been off gambling — and losing — while I was in my workshop. I thought he was working." A small eleven appeared between her eyebrows. "He told me he had a job in finance, dressed in a suit each day and supposedly went into an office. I never questioned him. But the slimy toad was off gambling and doing gods-knows what else."

"Well, that's just offensive to toads." Ivan winked at her and pushed his empty basket away, leaning back against the ripped padding.

Bea stuck her tongue out at him.

Quin continued. "From the data Ghost provided, it seemed he had a wicked losing streak, and the bookies called in the markers."

"Which he couldn't pay," Ivan said.

"So the crusty piece of dog shit decided to steal from me." She finished off her beer, smacking the glass on the table with a loud thud. "And burn down my workshop, too. What a rancid, sleazy cretin."

She was getting quite inventive with her name-calling. "You

said he was asking you a lot of questions about your system before the incident, right?" Quin asked.

Bea nodded, picking through the remaining fries in her basket. "Yes, but I didn't give him many details — I don't think he'd understand the theory behind my propulsion system anyway — but he knew I was excited about it, and that the system might make space travel faster and more affordable to the masses. If I can ever get it to work like I believe it should, that is." She waved a hand at them. "And now you know, too. See, I can't keep my mouth shut."

Quin leaned back out of range of her flailing hand. "Yes, but you can trust us."

She pointed a fry at him. "We have a contract."

Ivan snickered.

He let out a long-suffering sigh. "We do have a contract. But you know you can trust me either way, right?" It was possible he would have to get that tattooed on his forehead so she would remember.

"Sure." She patted his arm, then poked her cheek. "My cheeks are all tingly. I like it."

Ivan snorted.

With a groan, Quin said, "Man, not cool. You got my girlfriend drunk."

"I'm not drunk, just feeling a little rosy, thanks to Ivan's shot. I can't be drunk because we've got things to do." She took a long drink from his beer before he could stop her. "Wait. Did you just call me your girlfriend?" She screwed up her face, as if pondering it. "Okay, I can be your girlfriend. We had sex..." She leaned over the table and loudly whispered to Ivan, "It was pretty damned good, too."

He snorted some of his drink out of his nose as his pale skin flushed a red bright enough to match his hair.

"That's what you get," Quin said to him in a low tone that went completely under Bea's buzzy radar.

Turning back to Quin, she said, "Also, now that I know he

didn't really mean to kidnap me and he knows I probably won't kick him in the balls again, we like each other. Right, Quinn? Oh, and we keep rescuing each other. Definitely better than my last relationship. He's the one who faked his death to get away from me, remember?" She stared at them until they nodded that they did, indeed, remember. "Alright, so what are we going to do about my oozing pustule of an ex?"

Despite her rambling and her current slightly inebriated, she'd accepted the title of "girlfriend", which made his heart feel all warm and gooey, even though it had just slipped out. He hadn't actually meant to call her that. Not yet anyway. But the voice in his head who claimed they were so independent they didn't need anyone in their life, especially not her, wasn't protesting. Could it be love? It was a little early and a lot fast, but he was beginning to believe that maybe it could be. Possibly. Eventually.

Whatever it was, she was so unexpected, it had thrown him into a tailspin. He'd just been doing a job for his cousin, aiming for a clean slate, and here she was, fucking it all up in the best way possible. Would she go back to her life as it was before him when they cleared her name? Maybe. Could he go back to his life as it was before her? Absolutely not. She'd changed his focus, his trajectory.

Before her, it was all about his crew and their next job. Now? His team was still a priority, but she might have unseated them from the top spot. If she didn't feel the same way and chose to return to Melorn without him, she'd leave a gaping wound in his heart that he wasn't sure would ever scab over. He didn't want to let her go anymore. He wasn't going to just drop her off with Rhain and go about his life as he'd originally planned. That was no longer an option. Which meant he needed to do everything in his power to protect her and prove to her that they belonged together so she wouldn't want to leave.

Bea happily chattered to Ivan as if Quin's world hadn't just been well and truly rocked. Seeking fortification, he drained the rest of his drink and tried to absorb the seismic shift that had just happened in his brain and in his soul.

Ivan looked like he was trying not to laugh at Quin, who'd just been gobsmacked by love. Quin counted it as a blessing that he chose not to call him out.

Before Ivan had a chance to change his mind, Quin said, "The last file said that Arden was here." He needed to stay focused on the task at hand. They had things to do and a shithead of an ex to bring to justice.

Her eyes wide, Bea looked at him. "Like, here-here? On Badin?" She snapped her fingers. "Oh! Ghost tossed another file onto the tablet before they left. I glanced at it but haven't read it yet. That dirt muncher is within my grasp." She gave a low cackle and rubbed her hands together in anticipation.

Smothering a smile, Quin said, "The document wasn't long, but it said that Arden is on Badin and that he's planning to sell your propulsion system at a black market auction that's being held under the Vanid estate tonight."

"Tonight as in the night of their fancy-schmancy Full Moon Ball?" She frowned. "Under? Do they mean under the estate? Is that even possible? The Vanid estate is on an island."

"Pirates," Ivan said with a nod. "Badin used to be a favorite hideout for pirates until rich folks realized how beautiful it was and gentrified it. Killed, arrested, or drove out the pirates so they could build their fancy-assed homes and claim entire islands as their own private domains." He double-tapped on a file on the small tablet and spun the screen so Bea could see it. "Many of the islands are riddled with caves. Seems the Vanid's island is one such place."

"So a Vanid is running a secret auction right under everyone's noses." It was brilliant, actually. Quin wondered if they did it every year. Who in the family knew about it? Did it have the approval of the Vanid matriarch? Of course, Rhain would be aware of the event. It sounded exactly like the kind of information he'd love. "Imagine the stones on whichever one of those entitled pricks is conducting this on the night of their mother's precious ball."

"Impressively large stones," Ivan agreed.

"We need to go," Bea said with a bounce in her seat. "I am not letting Arden get away or sell my system to anyone. Even though it doesn't work."

"Yet," Quin said.

She beamed at him. "Gods, do you know how much I want to wrap my fingers around that pathetic twerp's neck and just squeeze?" The sound she made was one of pure frustration.

"We can imagine." Quin raised an eyebrow at Ivan, who nodded in affirmation. There was no way they were going to disagree with her. She was liable to explode into violence with the amount of righteous anger emanating from her at the moment.

"He won't get away with any of this, Bea," Ivan said.

She took a breath and unclenched her fists. "So, how do we get to this island so we can crash their highly illegal auction thingy?" Bea asked. "Because I seriously doubt they're going to let us just waltz onto the island without an invitation, especially not on the night of the Full Moon Ball."

Quin sighed and scrubbed a hand over his face. "I'm going to have to call in a favor. A big one."

"Shit," Ivan said.

35

BEA

The stars were shining in the midnight blue sky when the three of them got out of a zippy cab at the docks. Rock Hill Marina was built in the crook of a sprawling harbor, its docks filled with pleasure ships, fishing boats, hovers, ridiculously oversized yachts, little trawlers, and everything in between. The bigger, fancier boats, spit-polished to a high shine and costing more credits than Bea would ever see in her lifetime, were tied up along the inner curve of the bay, where they would be the most protected when the winter storms hit. The outer rings housed the boats whose owners couldn't afford to pay the prohibitive prices of the protected slips. Those who couldn't dry dock their vessels for winter then provided added protection for those of the inner curve.

Bea closed her eyes and breathed deeply of the sea air, the tang of salt and fish washing away the rest of the alcoholic fuzz from her head. When Quin said that he could get them onto the island, she hadn't expected to be whisked off to the dark end of the marina. They'd long since passed by the sparkling lights, nosy crowd, and galactic press near the marina's entrance, seeing off those who were lucky enough to get their hands on a golden ticket to the Full Moon Ball. "What are we doing here, Quin?" she asked, taking a small step closer to the warm comfort of his big body.

He gave her a tense smile. "We're getting you to that island so you can take down your creep of an ex and clear your name."

But even in the weak light cast by the streetlight they stood under, she could see the stress lines feathering out from the corner of his eyes. She looked at Ivan, an eyebrow raised in question.

"He called in a favor with his damned cousin." Ivan growled, looking like he might strangle Quin when they had a moment alone.

"But you're working off your last one helping me." She smacked his arm. Then smacked it again, the sound of her open palm meeting his hard bicep echoing in the hush that surrounded them. "What in the three hells, Quin?"

"Ow." In an overdramatic move, he rubbed his arm as if she had truly hurt him. "It was my choice. I told you I'd do whatever I could to help you, and I have. Don't worry about it."

He was playing wounded hero, throwing himself on a sword to come to her aid. He was so damned determined to earn her trust that he couldn't see he already had it, along with her heart. The big dingbat, calling in a favor with the Knight. What a stupidly romantic gesture. Luckily, she had a card up her sleeve that might save him from his foolishness. She just had to find the right time to use it.

"Okay, but what are we doing here?" She gestured to the secluded end of the marina where they stood. In the distance, the lap of waves against the pilings and boat hulls muffled the dull roar of an enthusiastic crowd. A few sea birds cried out their last calls before settling in for the night. As far as she could tell, they were the only people in the area.

"Just wait." Quin glanced at his comm, then looked down the walkway.

"They're late," Ivan said, shifting from foot to foot. He pulled up the collar of his jacket against the cool sea breeze.

"They'll be here."

"Who?" Bea asked. This waiting in the dark was making her antsy.

Finally, a long, dark hovercar glided to a near-silent stop in front of them. A tall man, impeccably dressed in a tailored black suit, stepped out of the car. Bea squinted at him. He sure looked familiar, though she couldn't quite place him. He reached back into the car and helped a statuesque woman from the interior.

"Dai!" Bea cried out and ran to her, the ease of her sister's embrace wrapping her in comfort like a treasured blanket. She hadn't seen her sister since Dai showed up in the prison hospital and spirited her out from under the guards' noses. Bea wanted to bury her head in her sister's neck like she had when she was little and pour out her heart to her. She took a shuddering breath, reveling in the sense of comfort and home her sister provided. "I've missed you so much, sissy," she whispered.

Dai's arms tightened into a squeeze that squished all the air from Bea's lungs, just like she had when they were younger. "I was so worried about you."

"I'm okay, except I can't breathe," Bea managed to gasp out with a shaky laugh.

Dai gave her one more bone-crushing squeeze and let her go. Grasping Bea's shoulders, she said, "You look good, little sis."

"And you look gorgeous." Bea gave her sister a full sweep with her gaze, taking in her outfit. Black leather ankle boots kissed the cuff of tight black pants. Layered over her pants was a cocktail-length silk skirt that draped down into a short train. "Are these separate pieces?" Bea asked, touching where the waistband of the skirt met a lightly boned corset that lifted Dai's boobs while still allowing movement, much like the top Feriq had given Bea. "I love it."

"Thanks. It has pockets." Sliding her hands into enviously deep pockets, Dai did a little spin to give Bea the full effect. "And check this out." She flipped back a panel of the full skirt to reveal the silk lining patterned with giant, dark red peonies against a forest green background.

"Wow. That's stunning." She traced the edge of a silken petal. "Let me guess. You're going to the ball, right?"

With a quick glance at the man who'd accompanied her, Dai nodded.

Bea sighed. She'd been down this road with Dai too many times to count. "And you can't tell me anything about it because you're in double-secret squirrel mode, right?"

Dai huffed out a laugh. "See, this is why you must be protected at all costs. Both brilliant and funny. A winning combination."

Rolling her eyes, she said, "Did Safina pull all this together for you? Because that ensemble has Safi written all over it." She gestured at Dai's whole look. Much like Ivan was Quin's right-hand man, Safina was Dai's. They'd partnered on many missions together for the Unit until they were both officially retired from the spy game several years ago. But Bea knew retirement hadn't slowed them down, no matter what Dai claimed. Given the details she'd picked up from her sister, she also knew they were still neck-deep in sneaky shenanigans. Dai claimed she stayed home and tended her rose garden, but Bea knew better. Her here on Badin, all dressed up to attend an exclusive ball she wouldn't have been invited to or even wanted to attend, just proved Bea's theory.

Dai humphed and crossed her arms. "As it so happens, I will indeed be attending the party tonight. And Safi has the best taste so I let her play fairy godmother. It just makes her so happy." Dai rolled her eyes, but Bea knew it made Dai happy, too. "In fact, she's going to play fairy godmother for you, too." She nodded towards the sturdy hovercraft tying up at the end of the far dock.

"Who's the hottie? Is he part of the favor that Quin called in?" Bea asked, her eyes cutting to Quin, who was in deep discussion with the handsome man in black.

"Rhain and his damnable favors," Dai grumbled, waving a hand to attract the attention of her escort. He raised a brow at her. The men walked over to join them. "Bea, this is Rhain, also known as the Knight, Keeper of Secrets and Knowledge. Rhain, this is my sister, Bea."

Rhain took Bea's hand in his and brushed his lips over her knuckles. "Pleased to finally meet a member of Dai's family." He gave Dai a significant look, which she shrugged off. "I've heard so much about you."

"Oh, my gods. That's why you look so familiar," Bea said, her eyes darting from him to Quin. "You're Quin's cousin. Holy cow, you two could be siblings."

Quin and Rhain growled in tandem, as if they'd heard that before and didn't accept it.

"They really could." Dai laughed, eyeing the two men standing shoulder to shoulder. "They even sound the same. Tell me, is yours as big a pain in the ass as this one?" She jerked a thumb at Rhain, who folded his arms and let out a long-suffering sigh.

Ivan choked and turned away.

"Yeah, he is." Bea nodded enthusiastically, happy to have someone to talk shit about Quin to. It was too hard to do over a messaging system and didn't have the same impact. Some things had to be done in person. "But he's growing on me. Like a mold."

"Hey, I take offense to that," Quin said, giving her hair a light tug in protest.

She elbowed him.

Dai watched her sister closely, a smile blooming across her face. "Like a mold, huh?"

"Yeah, a really sexy mold," Ivan chimed in with a sly grin. "These two, they can't keep their hands off each other. It's sickening."

Dai snickered, giving Bea's arm a little squeeze of support. "Good to hear. Bea needs someone who actually cares about her," Dai said, looking at Quin. "Through she's always had the worst taste in men."

"Dai!"

"Well, you have. Remember Brad?"

"I was six!"

"And then there was Afan and after him, Nadir. Oh, and we can't forget about Essy's sperm donor, Mikel."

Bea covered her face with her hands and groaned. "And you wonder why I avoid introducing you to the men I date." She reached over to pinch the underside of Dai's arm.

She jumped and twisted away, laughing. "Alright, alright. I'll stop. For now. Anyway, Quin seems like a good sort, even though he is related to Rhain." Dai shrugged. "But he can't help that."

"Hey!" Rhain and Quin exclaimed. Dai ignored them.

Despite Dai's seeming dismissal of the towering man next to her, Bea could see her sneaking little glances at him and it clicked. "Oh, my gods. Is this Thunder from university?" Bea drew in a breath to say more, embarrass the shit out of her big sister like she'd just done to Bea, but Dai blushed and glared at Bea so hard, Bea almost ducked to avoid the bolt of lightning that was sure to come from the clear sky and strike her dead.

Her mean sister face on, she stuck a finger in Bea's face. "One more word, Bea, and I will sic Safina on you and not in a good way." It was a legitimately terrifying threat. Safina was known for her creative means of revenge, ways that left the victim wishing a black hole would swallow them so they could escape her torture.

"Well, now I'm interested," Rhain said, casually crossing his arms and looking at Dai. "Thunder?"

She made a show of checking her wrist comm. "Oh, my. Look at the time. Too bad. We have a party to get to, and Bea has a sniveling butt-crust of an ex to bring down." Dai kissed Bea on the cheek and wrestled Rhain back into their vehicle. "Quin will fill you in on the plan. Safina's already on the boat waiting for you with some of Rhain's people. They'll get you to the island and that auction. You go clear your name and get back to doing brilliant things. We'll catch up soon."

Bea's heart squeezed. She hated saying goodbye to her sister, especially when she knew Dai was headed into danger. But it looked like Dai might finally have an additional bit of backup besides Safina and Izumi, one she needed, even if she hadn't yet admitted it to herself. Her sister was even more guarded than Bea had been after Arden. She rushed over to the vehicle to give her sister's cheek a kiss. "Love you, sissy," she said. "Please be careful."

Dai crushed Bea in another tight squeeze. "Love you, too, Bumble. You be good and listen to Safi. She'll take care of you. And Quin will keep you safe or I'll string him up by his balls and we'll throw rocks at him."

Quin blinked at the threat. Ivan elbowed him in the side and snickered.

"Then, when all this is said and done, we'll have some sisterly bonding time."

"I'll bring the frosty adult beverages." She let out a soggy giggle, unwilling to let her sister go.

With one final squeeze, Dai let go and slid into the waiting car. "It's a deal. Be safe. See you soon." She closed the door, and the vehicle slid silently away, headed towards the bright lights and the official transport that would whisk them across the water to the ball.

"Ready, Daisy?" Quin asked, holding open a gate. A gangway angled down to a pier with a variety of vessels secured to it. In the spot at the end, their hovercraft waited, its running lights a beacon in the dark.

She watched the dark vehicle disappear around a corner and sketched a good luck rune in Dai's direction. "As I'll ever be," she said, turning to Quin and Ivan waiting patiently in the star-lit dark. She squared her shoulders, trying to instill herself with confidence. So much could go wrong. Even just getting to the island was fraught with danger. But she had Quin and Ivan by her side and on her team and, in a surprise bonus, her sister was close enough to help out if she got in too big of a jam. Hopefully, that would be enough to turn the odds in her favor.

Okay, not the best pep talk ever, but she felt better. She wasn't alone in this. And it was going to feel so good when she took Arden down. She pictured herself hauling his ass, handcuffed and gagged, so she didn't have to hear his asinine voice, up the stairs of an imaginary police station. There, she'd force him to his knees and presenting him to the local constabulary, who would then dramatically rip up the warrant for her arrest.

To the men waiting for her, she said, "Let's do this."

36

QUIN

The *Sea Sprite* was a small hover trawler, a hybrid able to glide silently above the waves just as easily as she could cut through them with her sharp prow. She wasn't the prettiest or largest boat in the marina by any means but she was sturdy and would get them where they needed to go quickly, quietly, and if Rhain's people did their job, off the radar of the many patrols tasked with keeping the waters around Vanid Island clear of any interlopers.

"Ahoy, the shore," a bright feminine voice called out, waving them over.

"Safi!" Bea called back with a squeal, her steps hurrying her towards one of the most deadly women who'd ever been a part of the Unit. Now that she was retired, twice as deadly. At just under 5'5", the woman also known as the Viper looked like a stereotypical grandmother — pure white hair styled in a loose bun, dark brown eyes bright against her light brown skin, laugh lines and wrinkles creasing her round face, and a sturdy body just waiting to envelop someone in a rose-scented hug. But looks were deceiving, and the Kindly Old Granny disguise she wore with such ease chilled Quin to his very toes.

After a joyful reunion, Safina turned to Quin, looked him up and down, and said, "And you must be Quin Sidron."

Bea nodded enthusiastically. "That's him alright."

As a wicked grin spread across Bea's face, he braced himself. This was not going to go well for him.

"Did Dai tell you that when he rescued me, he tied me up and threw me over his shoulder?" Bea slid her arm through Safina's as they walked up the gangplank.

Behind him, Ivan choked.

Bea's eyes sparkled with mischief as they stepped aboard the Sprite. "He smacked me on my ass, too."

"Did he now?" Safina purred, pulling her arm from Bea's and taking a step towards him, her fingers stroking the twin blasters fastened to her thighs.

Quin felt his insides wobble at the dark look in her eyes and tightened every muscle in his body to keep himself together. Ivan would never let him live it down if he shit himself from fear. His mind blanked on how best to respond in order to avoid being turned into fish food.

But his hellion wasn't done with him yet. "And then, once we boarded his ship, he locked me in a cell with no toilet." She looked like a cat who'd cornered the mouse and was now just playing with it until it keeled over from fear.

So this was the payback she'd promised. And here he thought they'd moved past all that. At least now, in the hour of his death, he discovered where Bea got her death stare. As Safina Es-Aiit sized him up, his brain stuttered. What had Dai said about Safina being the most creative in her tortures?

"Don't pass out now," Ivan whispered from his position behind him. "You'll be at her mercy, and she'll gut you and dispose of your body as soon as we're far enough away from shore."

Swallowing hard, Quin stiffened his spine and held out his hand, pulling on every ounce of politeness and training his mother had instilled in him. "Ma'am, it's a pleasure to meet you."

"Is it really?" She slid her hand in his, her fingers closing around his like a steel trap.

"Yes, ma'am. I've heard so much about you." He tried to discreetly end the handshake and pull free, but her grip was strong, and he was unwilling to wrench himself free just yet. Let Bea play her little games for now. But he hoped she really did like him enough to call Safina off before his blood stained the deck.

Two people watched from the *Sprite's* top deck, their eyes wide. Quin thought that Rhain's people might come out here to back him up against the murderous retiree who currently had a death grip on his hand, but no. He should have known better than to count on anything free from Rhain or his people.

"Safi," Bea said, patting Safina's shoulder. "It's alright. I've forgiven him, and we've made up. Let the poor man go."

"But he mistreated you. Locked you up." Safina's grip was cutting off the flow of blood to his fingers. "For that, he deserves to lose something he treasures. Maybe his eyes?" She jerked him down so he was face-to-face with her. He could see death lurking in the depths of her dark brown eyes. "Maybe something lower?"

He felt the blood drain from his face.

Bea snickered, then bit her lip when he glared at her. "If you cut that off, I'd miss it, too."

At that, Safina released him and stepped back, laughing. "Oh, gods. You really thought I was going to castrate you, didn't you? What stories you must have heard about me."

Bea pointed at him. "You should see the look on your face!" She doubled over with laugher. "The great Quin Sidron, frozen with fear in the grasp of a little old lady."

Behind him, Ivan quietly chuckled.

"Hey now. Watch who you're calling old," Safina grumbled. "My hair might be silver, but I still shoot like I did when I was thirty. Better, since I got my eyes fixed last year."

"Sorry, Safi." Still giggling to herself, Bea followed her into the main cabin area, leaving Quin and Ivan to follow.

"Some backup would have been nice," Quin muttered to Ivan.

"Ha. There was no way I was drawing the attention of Safina Es-Aiit. Have you read the brief Rhain has on her? No, thank you." Awe colored his voice.

Safina poked her head out of the main cabin and winked at them. "That doesn't cover the half of it," she said, and Quin had the pleasure of watching the color drain from Ivan's face. "Now, are you coming, or what? We need to get underway."

Once on board, they met the rest of Rhain's water-based team. Sig, the boat's pilot, Quin had met before, but the navigator, Calin, must be a new recruit. He had that wide-eyed, wet-behind-the-ears look all the noobies got on their first real mission. They exchanged nods.

At Safina's orders, Sig and Calin made their way up to the pilothouse. Sig guided them out of the harbor, the boat gliding its way through the waves as Calin navigated them past the shoals hiding under the dark water and around any patrols. Their circuitous route would take them nearly twice as long to reach the island as the transport Dai and Rhain were on.

"Bea, head to the cabin on the port side," Safina said, halfway up the stairs to the pilothouse. "I'll be there in a sec."

Bea nodded. "Quin, you'll be okay waiting here?" she asked.

Quin looked around the space, which he thought was called a saloon, a gathering place for those on board. Windows lined both sides of the space and a wooden ladder forward led up to the pilothouse. A door aft led to sleeping quarters. To starboard, there were a couple of well-used chairs, a couch to stretch out on, and a rectangular table covered with haphazard piles of equipment. On the port side, attached to the wall, was a bench seat with a dining table bolted to the floor. Anywhere there wasn't furniture, there were built-in cabinets for storage.

"Of course," he said. "Go. Be with the super-scary assassin."

Laughing, she said, "Safina? Her bark is worse than her bite. She's all big words and intimidation in that little package. Besides,

I would never have let her hurt you, you big baby." She waggled her fingers at him over her shoulder as she walked to the cabin. "I'll be back. Don't get into any trouble while I'm gone."

He did enjoy watching her walk away. She still had on the leather pants Feriq had given her, and they did amazing things to her ass.

With a groan, Ivan threw himself into one of the chairs and stretched out his legs. "Stop ogling your girlfriend and pour me a drink, would you?"

Since he needed one more than Ivan, Quin rescued a bottle of whiskey someone had foolishly left on the dining table and, after digging through several cabinets, snagged two glasses. He poured them hefty servings before setting the bottle on the table in front of the couch. "Good hunting," he toasted.

Ivan raised his glass to his lips but froze as Safina waltzed down the ladder, plucked the half-full bottle of whiskey from the table, winked at them, and disappeared into a cabin. Once she was gone, he took a large swallow. "How is it that someone who looks like a granny who bakes cookies and gardens can scare me to my very marrow?"

"Because you're smart and your instincts are sharp." Quin pointed his glass in her direction. "That woman is an apex predator if there ever was one, just like Bea's sister. At least she didn't threaten you with bodily harm."

"You'd better stay on all those ladies' good sides, for all our sakes. Especially if this thing with Bea is long term." Ivan twirled his drink. "Pretty sure the woman we're now stuck on a small boat with in the middle of a large body of water would have gutted you from neck to navel if Bea had given her the go-ahead."

They stared into their glasses for a few minutes, contemplating mortality and scary women.

"So..." Ivan drawled. "Is this thing with Bea long term?"

Quin tapped a finger on the side of his glass before taking a mouthful of the smoky amber liquid. "I think I might love her, Ivan."

He nodded. "Have you told her yet?"

Shaking his head, Quin said, "She's so determined to clear her name and get back to her life on Melorn." His heart squeezed at the thought.

"And what do you want? Would you give up the *Dragon* and move to the city?"

"No. The *Dragon* is my home, and you all are my family. Anyway, she's a planet dweller, and I'm decidedly not. We'd never last." But he didn't want to lose her. She had his heart. The thought of leaving her made him feel like he was being crushed under a mountain slide.

"That's utter bullshit and you know it. Planet dweller." Ivan snorted. "You made that shit up. You're just scared she'll reject you. Look, if you love her, you'd better man up and tell her then figure out how to make it work." He leveled a look at Quin. "You'd be an absolute fool to let that woman go, and I'd lose all respect for you if you didn't at least try."

"Pulling no punches, I see." Was Ivan right? He did a gut check. Maybe. Possibly? After all, the only things she'd stressed were getting back to work and seeing her family. Was he trying to put up obstacles so he'd feel better if she left him? Having no clear answer to his questions, he stared at the amber liquid in his glass as if it might hold some answers.

Ivan shrugged. "I tell it how I see it. And if you let this opportunity for happiness and love slip through your fingers, I'm going to sic Bea's Old Lady Danger Squad on you. Those women will rip you to shreds if you break Bea's heart. Figure your shit out and tell her how you feel, brother. You'll regret it forever if you don't."

Taking a large swig, he let the alcohol burn a path down his throat. "Appreciate your candor." He knew Ivan was right. But first things first.

"That's why you keep me around."

"Quin, come here," Safina called.

He startled, almost spilling his drink.

"You'd better hurry," Ivan said, waving a lazy hand. "I

wouldn't want to lose my captain because you didn't move quickly enough. I just got you broken in."

Rolling his eyes, Quin got to his feet and drained his drink, setting the glass on the table. "Fuck you, Ivan. I hope that chair breaks, and you spill your whiskey."

Ivan gasped, clutching his heart. "Rude."

Safina waited for him outside her cabin, the door closed so he couldn't see Bea. She thrust a garment bag into his hands and pointed to the room behind him. "Change."

What could he say but, "Yes, ma'am."

The sharp black suit fit him like a glove. He suspected it was one of Rhain's. Quin had never particularly enjoyed wearing tailored suits like this. They made him feel out of place and awkward, reminding him of when he was young, a coltish and gangly teen, and stuck wearing Rhain's hand-me-downs. Back then, he was much smaller than his cousin. This suit fit better than those clothes of long-ago.

In true dickish fashion, Ivan fanned himself when Quin emerged from the cabin. "Lookin' hot, Quin."

Growling at his Number One, he shot the cuffs of the suit, trying to get them to line up correctly.

Safina also had clothes for Ivan. His was a simple black suit with a white shirt, designed to let him blend and fade into the background. The plan was that, depending on what worked best for the situation, he would either position himself as one of the guards or servers in case something went wrong. Because things always went wrong.

Ivan looked behind him and wolf whistled. "Damn, woman. You are gorgeous."

Quin turned to see Bea wearing an understated, floor-length gown that looked black when she was still. As she moved, it shimmered with shades ranging from deep purple to midnight blue. The skirt was made of long, overlapping panels that cinched in at the waist and twisted up her torso to cover one shoulder, leaving the other bare. Long, silken waves of silver-shot black hair flowed down her back. Her makeup was simple — a dark swish of liner highlighted her honey-brown eyes, a dusting of powder emphasized her round cheekbones, and a dark red accented the pout of her lips.

She paused in the entryway, all elegance and beauty wrapped in a stunning dress. He couldn't take his eyes off her. Hells, he couldn't even form words. What were words, even? Swallowing hard, he finally said, "Wow." It was a simple exclamation but, quite honestly, the only word that he could think of. His brain was overwhelmed with the beauty of Bea in her pretty dress.

She smiled, absorbing that one word and accepting it as the compliment it was. "Right back at you. Because, wow. You do look mighty fine in that suit, Quin." She gave him an admiring look that traveled from the top of his head to the tips of the stupid shiny shoes he'd found tucked in the bottom of the garment bag. "But then, black has always suited you."

Finally, his brain kicked in and allowed him access to some more words. "If we didn't have an audience, I'd take you right up against this wall." Not the eloquence he was hoping for but her low, husky laugh made his cock twitch. He told it firmly to settle down and not embarrass him, though that had never in his life worked.

Covering his ears, Ivan groaned. "Please make it stop. I'm too young to hear all this."

"You keep promising wall sex and someday, you're going to have to deliver. Otherwise, you'll be known far and wide as a tease," she said, walking towards him.

"Are they always like this?" He heard Safina ask.

Flashes of Bea pressed up against the boat's wall of windows, her dress hiked up to the tops of her glorious thighs filled his vision and just like that, the words were once again gone from his head. He was pretty sure he was staring at her with his mouth open. He hoped he wasn't actually drooling.

"They are. It's both disgusting and traumatizing," Ivan complained.

Ignoring Ivan, Bea sidled up to Quin and, with one finger under his jaw, closed his mouth. "I've never gotten this kind of reaction from any man ever in my life, and I have to say that I'm really enjoying it." She pressed her lips to his cheek. "Thank you."

Her soft words snapped him out of his daze, and he grabbed her hand, pulling her against him. "You should be complimented and often. You're a gorgeous, intelligent woman who's too stubborn for her own good." He brushed a kiss over her deep red lips, careful not to smear any of her makeup. Holding back was the toughest challenge of his life to date. "When we get done with this, I promise you will no longer be able to call me a tease."

"I'll hold you to it," she said, with a toss of her hair.

"Oh, my gods, aren't you two the most adorable pair?" Safina clasped her hands together, watching them with stars in her eyes.

"I think I'm going to puke," Ivan said.

"I need a picture." Safina picked up a tablet from the table and gestured at them to get closer. "Quin, put your arm around her waist. Now, smile!" she ordered, snapping photos from several positions. "I wish you were going to the actual ball, not just some dirty underground auction. Oh, well. At least I have pictures."

Lacing her fingers with his, Bea gave him a glowing smile.

"Bea's set up with the same team comm as you two as well as a few extra items she might need," Safina said. "My primary is Dai and her mission. However, we'll be keeping an ear on you, too, just in case you need an emergency extract." Her eyes hardened. "Dai and Rhain have their own objective, so don't interfere. If you see them, you don't know them, copy?"

They all nodded. Quin knew they'd have to be bleeding out before any of Rhain's team lifted a finger to help. Fine by him.

Ivan handed Quin a comm to stick behind his ear before shouldering a pack. "Cormac and Navi are in orbit above us. They'll be running point."

Well, thank the gods they arrived in time to assist in the mission. Safina had Bea's back, but she also had her own mission to run. It made him feel three hundred times better to know his own team was nearby.

Safina gave him a nod. "Now, in your pack, you'll find protective coverings to protect your outfits in the tunnels. After all this effort to get you fabulous looking, it wouldn't do to have you trying to blend in with dirty clothes. Those snobs would spot you right away."

Vibrating with anticipation, Bea took a deep breath and rolled her shoulders.

He gave her cold hand a squeeze. She squeezed back. "Ready?"

With a sharp nod, she said, "Let's do this."

"Go get that gaping asshat, darling," Safina said, shooing the three of them onto the skimmer and into the night.

37

BEA

They broke out the protective gear as soon as Sig dropped them on the rocky shoreline and disappeared back into the darkness.

"Good thing Safina's so prepared. There is no way I could climb up there without ripping my dress or getting covered in dirt," Bea said, looking at the craggy cliff they had to climb. She couldn't see the tunnel entrance Safina assured her was there. At least it wasn't too high or very steep, or she'd never be able to do it.

Ivan pulled three dark gray cleansuits from his pack and handed them out.

"Aren't they usually white? Like, all science-y and stuff?" Quin asked.

"Must be some super-spy stealth clothing protection." Bea gave a small laugh. She wondered how many times Dai or someone on their team wore something like this on one of their missions. Often enough that Safina knew to clothe Bea in a dress made of light, anti-wrinkle fabric and paneled skirt, so it could be easily divided between the two legs of the cleansuit. The ex-spy also shod her in short black ankle boots like she'd seen on Dai, so she wouldn't kill herself running or climbing in heels. It was hard enough for Bea to walk in heels without stumbling on a good day. Tucking in the last of the diaphanous material, Bea zipped the suit up to her neck and started climbing.

Carefully, she followed the route Ivan took, Quin on her heels. It was more challenging than she expected. In several places, Quin had to give her some assistance. As she pulled herself up onto the ridge edging the tunnel, she felt his hands on her ass again. "I've got it." She glared at him as he popped up next to her with a big grin on his face. "You were just using my noodle arms as an excuse to cop a feel."

His teeth flashed in the dark. "You caught me. Guilty as charged. And what are you going to do about it?"

"Don't make me separate you two." Ivan growled from inside the tunnel. "Because I will throw Quin off this cliff if I have to. We have a job to do."

"Just trying to lighten the mood, you killjoy," Quin said as he ran his hands over her ass again, "helping" her into the tunnel.

She giggled, but Ivan was right. They had a job to do, the first of which was finding their way through the labyrinthian tangle of tunnels that honeycombed the island.

In the pale light of the full moon, she saw Ivan roll his eyes and tap the comm tucked behind his ear. "Cormac, you there?"

A burst of static had them wincing. Then Cormac's voice came through loud and clear. "We're here and ready to roll. I've sent an updated copy of the tunnel map to your personal comms. We've got a fix on you three and will help with navigation when you need it."

"Acknowledged," Quin said, tapping his wrist. A three-dimensional image flickered to life above his palm, its dim green glow illuminating the walls. He flicked his wrist, tossing the map so it hovered in front of him. "We'll be able to use this for a while, but its glow will be noticeable as we approach the central cave and the auction. You'll have to guide us from that point, Cormac." Quin took the lead, following the tunnel into the darkness beyond.

"Actually, Navi will guide you, Captain," Cormac said. "I've got to keep an ear on the chatter and an eye on the activity."

"Evening, Captain," Navi said, his voice merry. "Hope you're ready for an excitement-packed adventure."

"Fuck. I wish Rafe hadn't had to stay behind," Ivan said from his position at the rear. "Navi's going to get us lost."

"Hey, now. That was only the once, and we wound up better off for it, if I do say so myself," Navi said.

Ivan snorted. "You've gotten lost on our ship, Navi."

A gasp. "Lies. I just took the long way 'round is all."

Listening to the brothers bicker, Bea braced herself against a slick stone wall as they descended farther into the darkness. "Isn't there someone else who can guide us?" She had zero desire to get lost down here. They had barely gotten started and already the walls were closing in on her as the beam of moonlight at the tunnel entrance disappeared behind them. She focused on Quin's outline against the dim green glow and tried to ignore the stygian dark that surrounded them. At least when they were in the troll cave, there were torches, not complete darkness.

"It will be fine, Bea. We won't get lost. Just think of it as another exciting part of your adventure." Quin slowed to catch her elbow and help her over a large stone. He paused at a junction that split in three different directions, consulted the map, and took the path at the center.

The legs of her protective suit rustled in the silence as she followed, trusting that Quin would get them where they needed to go. The banter between the brothers faded to a dull roar as she focused on putting one foot in front of the other without tripping over stones or knocking herself silly on the low ceiling and protruding rocks. Had pirates truly carved out all these tunnels or were they natural phenomena? Maybe some creature had dug here, making their burrow on these large islands. She shivered, thinking of what animal could carve through rock. Scaring herself over some long-gone creature was not helpful.

With nothing but darkness and possible stone-devouring

monsters to distract, her brain started buzzing with thoughts. What if the intel from Ghost was wrong? Or what if her prototype wasn't even here and instead was locked away in some lab surrounded by engineers as they tried to get it to work? Most of her notes were online and safe, but when she was deep in the zone, she jotted down thoughts and ideas on scraps of paper. Her workshop walls had been covered in them. Arden had also stolen those to sell? She had no way of knowing what he'd taken. Her brain flashed up an image of him at the auction, rubbing his hands together in anticipation as the bidding started. She skipped her imagination forward to him on his knees before her, begging for his life. The image buoyed her spirits and made the trek through the darkness seem less endless.

"Are we there yet?" Ivan complained as the tunnel shrank again, forcing them to bend low so they didn't scrape their heads.

"We're close. Navi, you're going to have to guide us the rest of the way. I don't want the glow of my map to give away our position." Quin glanced at them over his shoulder. "Bea, Ivan, grab hold. We're going dark."

Her fingers tightened on his cleansuit, clenching a fistful of the crinkly material. She could feel Ivan at her back doing the same. The green glow disappeared, and they were plunged into blackness. Bea's eyes went wide, unable to see even the smallest speck of light, and she moved closer to Quin.

"Alright, you're almost there," Navi said, his voice soft in her head. "In about ten feet, you're going to take a sharp right."

"Hold on," Quin said, leading them with deliberate slowness through the dark.

As if she was going to let go. This close, she could feel the direction of his movements. She trailed her other hand against the rough surface of the tunnel, very aware of how tight it was and how painful it would be to smash against. What if they ran into a dead end and couldn't get back out? Or got stuck? Both Quin and Ivan had really broad shoulders, and she'd be trapped between them. What if there were spiders or other creepy crawlies she couldn't see? She shook her head to clear her brain of intrusive thoughts. *Stay focused*, she scolded herself. *Don't freak out.*

"The tunnel ahead curves a little to the left and, according to the model, it looks like there's a pocket where you should be able to stand again," Navi said. "Do you see any light yet? You're getting really close to your destination."

"Can't see shit," Ivan said, voicing Bea's exact thoughts.

They kept up their slow, steady forward progress, Navi's soft voice guiding them, until finally the pitch black grew murky as light filtered into the tunnel. The muted din of conversation reached their ears, and the tunnel widened into a pocket of space large enough for them to stand upright.

Quin brought their three-person train to a halt. "Ivan, scout ahead. See where this tunnel emerges and what's in store for us."

With a sharp nod, Ivan removed his protective coverall and disappeared into the narrow opening leading towards light and noise.

Quin turned to Bea, his hands framing her face as he checked her over. "You okay?"

She nodded, practically purring at the warmth of his large hands cupping her cheeks. Somehow, he made her feel both delicate and cherished when he touched her like this, despite the fact that the ugly gray coverall made her look like she was wearing a trash sack. All of a sudden, she wanted out of this thing so she could look as beautiful as he made her feel.

Moving her hands out of the way, he unzipped her cleansuit slowly, keeping his eyes locked on hers as he did so. It fell with a soft shush to the ground. He offered his hand and she slid her fingers against his palm, stepping out of the pile of fabric and kicking it aside. With a shake, her dress settled back into its original lines.

He stepped back and quickly divested himself of his own covering, revealing the clean lines of his well-tailored suit. Unable to help herself, she smoothed her hands over his shoulders and down his lapels, brushing away invisible lint. Curling an arm around her waist, he drew her close, guiding her arm up until it draped over his shoulder and placed a kiss on her exposed shoulder. "These stone walls bring back good memories," he whispered against her ear, nibbling along its edge.

She shivered against the heat of his lips and buried a hand in the hair at the base of his neck. "You call our time in the troll prison a good memory?"

He nodded, his freshly trimmed beard rasping against her sensitive skin. "Absolutely. It's where you first decided to trust me." He gathered the fabric of her dress between them and traced his fingers along the edge of her lace underwear.

"Who knew you were a such romantic pirate?" She gasped as he dipped his fingers into her panties and stroked her clit. "Learn something new every day."

"I can teach you plenty," he said, one finger delving into her pussy as his thumb continued its steady rhythm over the sensitive bundle of nerves. He kissed his way down her neck, his tongue tracing the hollow at its base.

She had to fight to keep her legs from giving out as his fingers worked their magic. Tiny explosions worked their way from her core up to her brain, bright color bursting behind her eyes. She bit her bottom lip and did her best to swallow down the small sounds that bubbled up in her throat.

"You two better not be doing what I think you're doing." Ivan grumbled quietly over the comm. "I'm coming back in like five minutes and don't want to see you swapping spit."

With a laugh, Bea tugged at Quin's hair, attempting to separate herself from him. "We'll save this for later." She gave his hair another tug and nipping at his chin.

He whirled her around, pressing her against the cool, rough stone, one arm braced against her back so it wouldn't scrape her exposed skin. "I've got five minutes to make you cum." He growled in her ear, the one without the comm. "I've always loved a challenge." And with that, he hooked his fingers inside of her, working them until he found her secret spot, his big, calloused thumb still circling and pressing her clit.

In the gloaming dark, Bea's world narrowed to the feel of Quin's big body caging her, possessing her, his soft hair entangled in her fingers, his tongue hot against her skin, his fingers dancing, teasing her as a swell built in her core until it crashed over her.

Covering her mouth with his, he swallowed her cries of pleasure as she came apart in his arms. As she fought to catch her breath, he pulled his fingers from under her skirt and licked them clean, his dark eyes watching her. "See, love? Ivan isn't even back yet," he said with a wide grin. "I win."

Pushing him a step back, she rolled her eyes and shook out her skirts. "No one likes a braggart, Quin," she said primly, running a hand over her hair to smooth any wayward strands.

"Yeah, but I earned the right to brag, at least a little. Admit it." Winking at her, he tugged the bottom of his suit jacket, its severe lines falling back into place. He also adjusted the seam of his pants, squirming a little.

With a smirk, she asked, "Oh, no. Are your pants suddenly too tight? I wonder why that might be." With no time to do anything about it, he was just going to have to suffer the consequences of being a competitive bastard with the magic fingers.

"So mean," he said. "And after all I just did for you, too,"

Ivan returned to their small space and looked them both up and down. "Really? Well, at least you were quiet about it."

Bea blushed. She expected Quin to brag about making her explode in his arms, but he merely gave Bea another wink. "Report," he said to Ivan.

"We're safe to proceed. It'll be tight, though. Auction hasn't started yet, and there are plenty of people there already, so we should blend right in," he said. "I'll slip in with security. Easier than carrying a tray. People are always bothering you when you've got free food and drinks."

"Okay." Quin turned to Bea. "You ready to do this?"

She nodded. Maybe it was the afterglow from her orgasm or maybe she had just run out of fucks to give, but the last ounce of fear and trepidation seemed to have dried up and blown away. She was so ready to do this. Arden was going down.

38

QUIN

Quin watched Bea as she followed Ivan, holding the long panels of her skirt off the ground as they compacted themselves and did a slow forward shuffle the last feet through the opening. He could still feel the warmth of her heat, her slickness, the press of her inner muscles as they clenched around his fingers. He could taste her on his tongue, her bright scent perfuming the air around him. Gods, he was so far gone on this woman, it wasn't even funny. He should have told her when her soft body was still pressed against his.

The last thing he wanted to do was let her throw herself into danger. There would be people at this auction who would do anything to get their hands on the items up for bid, which included Bea's propulsion system. It was crucial that they get in, find Arden and remove him from the scene as discreetly as possible so as not to draw attention. He didn't know why Rhain and Dai were at the ball, nor, as Rhain and Safina had very firmly pointed out, did it concern him. He just wanted his team far away when whatever shit those two were throwing hit the fan.

Despite every protective instinct screaming at him to usher Bea out of harm's way, he knew how important it was for her, and he was here for it. To be honest, this vengeful side of her was hot. When she did finally get her hands on Arden, he hoped she took a page out of bloodthirsty Safina's book before turning him over to the proper authorities.

For a little payback of his own, he just might let it slip to a few information disseminators that the mangy weasel was still alive and maybe the individuals to whom Arden owed a shit-ton of money would catch wind and take out the trash for them.

Pleased with his decision, he finessed his broad shoulders through the stalagmites that had grown up around the entrance to their small tunnel. Gods, he hoped he didn't damage this suit. He had no desire to face the wrath of Safina. With a last grunt of effort, he popped free to find himself in a protected alcove. The stalagmites stretched to the ceiling, disguising the area from the rest of the space.

Bea eyed him. "Turn," she said, twirling her finger.

He did as instructed, enjoying the feel of her hands tracing his body as she checked him over for tunnel gunk. "Am I presentable?" he asked, spreading his arms and turning, his hands brushing the walls of the small nook.

She bit her bottom lip, her eyes traveling the length of his body. "You'll do."

He pulled a plain black mask from his pocket and slid it over his eyes. "Don't I get to check you over, too?" Any excuse to touch that soft skin and make her gasp with pleasure.

"Ivan made sure my dress and makeup were intact before disappearing." She waved a hand in the direction of the space beyond the stalactites hanging like drapes from the ceiling. The low hum of conversation permeated the mineral formations that screened them from view.

"I'm to your left when you finally enter the cavern," Ivan said. "Don't worry if you're a little rumpled. It'll look like you disappeared for some nookie in a nook before the auction starts." He snickered.

"Ivan," Bea protested, her cheeks flushing prettily. She looked at Quin and shook a finger. "Don't you get any ideas, mister."

He pressed a hand to his heart. "You wound me, my darling Daisy." Though, under different circumstances, he might very well take those ideas and run with them. She looked so eminently fuckable as she warned him off. The torso of her dress hugged her body, teasing him with a bare shoulder and swell of her breasts beneath the corset top. Every time she moved, those shimmering panels of color-shifting fabric parted, rewarding him with a flash of thigh. Even the silver filigree mask she wore was a temptation, highlighting the rounded curve of her cheekbones and the bow of her deep, luscious red lips.

"Are the two of you finally ready?" Cormac asked, his teasing tone refocusing Quin on the job at hand.

"Affirmative," he said. Offering her a hand, they slipped through the gap between the formations and into the main cavern, its roof soaring a good thirty feet over their heads. Icicles of stalactites dangled from the ceiling, but only a few groupings of stalagmites remained around the outer edges of the circular space for aesthetic purposes. Flickering lanterns lit the space, casting dancing shadows on the walls. At some point, the stone floor had been smoothed out, and Quin wondered why the Vanids had gone to all the trouble to make this space useable. What else had they used the cavern for, after they'd chased the pirates out? Under dangling spotlights scattered throughout the space, black plinths held the items being auctioned off tonight. A guard stood at parade rest next to each item, a clear warning to anyone who ventured too close.

Quin grabbed two glasses of bubbly pink liquid from a server's tray and handed one to Bea. She took it with an absent nod, scanning every individual who walked past them.

"Do you see him?" From the photos he'd seen, he knew Arden had pale white skin, dark blond hair cut in the short style preferred by bankers and funeral home directors, brown eyes, a weak chin, and a mole under his left ear. With all the participants masked, Quin wouldn't be much help identifying a man he'd never met.

"Not yet. But he's here. I can feel it." At her first sip of the drink, she made a face. "Yuck. All this wealth and they couldn't even spring for the good bubbly?" She plucked a canape off a passing server's tray and popped it in her mouth. "At least the toast points are decent."

"Nothing over here," Ivan said. Quin spotted him playing security to a plinth holding a painting.

"Copy," he said, sipping his own drink. Sweet and bitter at the same time, like a vintage gone bad. "Let's do a circuit." He tucked her hand into the crook of his arm and guided her through the throng. He'd love to get his hands on a guest list. Once they'd learned of the auction, Cormac had dug into the dark web and found a partial list of items up for sale. Confirming the intel Ghost provided, Bea's prototype was on the list, along with rare and precious items including a crown stolen from the Pavanian home world, a painting confiscated during the Six Year War, and a pair of firebird eggs. No doubt Rhain had both a complete guest list and the sales catalog, but of course, he wasn't sharing. Not for free, anyway.

Alert, they strolled arm in arm around the space, pretending to admire the treasures that should be returned to their original owners or, at the very least, be in a museum rather than in the hands of a private collector.

Cormac cleared his throat and said, "We don't have eyes inside the cavern, Quin, so make sure you're checking in."

"Stop being such a mother hen," Navi said. "They've got Ivan down there with them. They're going to be fine."

"Godsdammit, Navi. How many times have I told you never to say those words before or during a mission?" Cormac growled.

"Mother hen?" Navi asked, his voice confused.

Cormac grumbled some more, his words indistinct.

"Do they always bicker like this?" Bea whispered to Quin.

He nodded. His crew had been together long enough that

they were family. And that meant putting up with one another's idiosyncrasies, even when they annoyed the shit out of you. Navi was talented at getting a rise out of both Ivan and Cormac, even when he didn't mean to. While he was the best sniper Quin had ever seen, Navi liked to act the clown more often than not when they weren't on mission.

"Great, now Navi has gone and jinxed us," Ivan groused, giving them a nod as Quin and Bea walked past the landscape painting by the famous artist Chloe Remington he was pretending to guard.

"Quin, that's mine." Bea's hand tightened on his arm as they neared the next stand. Her lips pressed together tightly, small lines of stress feathering out from the corners.

"Slowly," he said, giving her prototype the same bored look he'd given everything else. He wasn't expecting it to be so small, but then it was a prototype. Most systems were massive. They had to be to power ships, especially the long-haulers. But this one could fit in a rucksack.

Still, it looked like the systems he was familiar with — cone-shaped, tapering to a wide tube, flat circular panels ringing its surface. It just happened to be a lot smaller than any system found even in the tiniest of ships. She'd explained a little of it to him, but it was way above his pay grade.

"Can you snatch it?" Navi asked. "You don't want to leave it there, do you?"

"No to both questions." Her voice was tight with anger, her hand clenched tightly around his. "But it'll be taken care of."

Before he could ask what she meant by that, Ivan cursed. "Navi, you asshole. You did jinx us. Look at who's standing by the bronze statue. What the fuck is she doing here?"

Quin spotted the statue across the room. "Is that Amaryllis?" he asked, watching as Ivan abandoned the painting and slid along the wall towards her.

"Yep." Ivan said, his voice quiet. "Stay on mission. I've got her."

"Let me know if you need assistance." In a practiced move, Quin turned Bea so her back was to Amaryllis and his was to a wall. With them at the same height, he could hide Bea while keeping an eye on Ivan as he sidled up behind Amaryllis. He put a hand over her mouth, wrapped another around her waist, picked her up and disappeared into the tunnel behind them.

"What just happened?" Cormac asked, his voice pitched with concern. "Talk to me, people."

"Ivan just removed Amaryllis from the area," Quin said, giving Bea a heated grin and a gentle kiss before resuming their stroll. Anyone observing them would think he was her date, overeager for a kiss. "Ivan, you good? Need backup?"

A pained grunt rumbled over the comm. "Good." Ivan gave an oof. "But you know." Another loud grunt of pain. "Rilly was never one to go easy. She wants you to know that she doesn't appreciate us fucking up her heist."

"Noted." Quin winced when Ivan let out a loud squawk of pain.

Bea put a hand on his arm, her eyes worried. "Do you need to go and check on him?"

"He'll be fine." It sounded like Ivan was in the fight of his life and could maybe use his backup. But leaving her alone, Arden's whereabouts unknown, would leave her vulnerable. "I can't leave you. It's not safe."

She gestured at the crowd. "I'm masked. No one outside our team knows who I am or even that I'm here. And if something goes disastrously wrong, Dai is here with your cousin up near the auctioneer podium, and Safi isn't too far away. I'll be fine."

More grunts came over the team channel. He'd never felt so torn.

"Go. Help your Number One, because he sounds like he's getting his ass kicked by a girl."

"Hey!" Ivan let out a string of curses, then his connection fuzzed, crackled, and went silent.

"Oh, that's not good," Navi muttered.

Bea gave Quin a gentle push in the direction Ivan had disappeared. "I'll be fine. I promise. I'll take another lap, drink this crappy bubbly, and maybe find that toast point guy again. The auction's about to start, so everyone will be focused on the bidding."

"Promise me that even if you spot Arden, you won't do anything until I come back," he said, his voice anxious with worry. He was going to strangle Ivan. They could have handled Amaryllis with a bribe or a threat. She wasn't here for Bea. Only Rhain and his team knew she would be here, and Rhain always had a lock on his intel. He stroked the nape of her neck, struggling with himself. He didn't want to leave her, but Ivan wasn't responding to Cormac's calls. Something had gone seriously wrong. "In fact, why don't you wait for me in the tunnel right where we came in. You'll be safe there."

"I'm done with hiding," Bea said, squaring her shoulders. "I can take care of myself, and I've got some tricks up my sleeve, courtesy of Safina and my sister. Besides, I've got something I need to take care of, and it will be easier without you hulking around over my shoulder. Trust me." She slid her hands under his jacket and rubbed his back. "I'll be fine. Go. Ivan needs you. I'd never forgive myself if something happened to him."

"Fine, but know that I am not happy about this." he said, finally giving in to her gentle persuasion. He still didn't want to leave her. But something had happened. If Ivan was dead because of his vendetta with Amaryllis, Quin would never forgive him.

"You can be as unhappy as you like, just as long as you come back with Ivan." She straightened his collar, brushing her hands down his arms. "I'll be careful, I promise. Go."

He pulled her to him cand gave her a hard kiss before heading in the direction he last saw Ivan. He hoped he wasn't making the wrong choice.

39

BEA

Letting out a sharp breath, Bea watched Quin disappear down a wide tunnel that, if she recalled the map correctly, would eventually lead outside and hopefully to Ivan, who obviously needed him more than she did right now. While she reveled in the man's attention and appreciated his somewhat overbearing efforts to keep her safe, he would have a shit fit if he knew what she had planned.

She wasn't just going to bring Arden to his knees. No, she had a secondary focus: to reclaim or destroy everything he'd stolen from her, so no one could use it for their own purposes. Her work was meant to bring more equity to space travel. She wasn't about to let some rich-dick get their hands on any of it.

When she'd spotted the plinth bearing her prototype, it was all she could do not to grab the sword from the stand next to it and smash it to bits. But that would attract attention and mess up Quin's big "Keep It Quiet" plan. She rolled her eyes. Maybe they needed to be loud, to shine a spotlight on the hypocrisy and greed of the people attending this auction tonight.

But, no. He was right. Get in, get it done, get out. They weren't equipped for anything bigger at the moment, anyway.

As the auctioneer made a long-winded introduction — something about secrecy, uniqueness and how very special everyone attending was blah, blah, blah — Bea casually swirled her glass of bubbly, angling her way towards her prototype. On a positive note, it was situated at the back outer edge of the cavern. With everyone turned to watch the auction, there was no one aside from the guard nearby. She wondered where Arden was. Maybe he was upstairs, enjoying the ball, mentally counting the money he thought he'd make from her stolen work. Gods, she hoped he hadn't slithered off to hide somewhere like the snake he was. It would be just her luck that, after all this, they wouldn't find him and she'd remain a wanted woman.

Alert to anyone moving her way, she drained her glass, her nose wrinkling as the sour-sweet liquid slid down her throat, and rested her hand on the edge of her prototype's stand. She twisted the black onyx ring on her index finger and popped the latch open with a fingernail. Then she leaned against the plinth, bending to adjust her boot.

"Oh no, ma'am," the guard said, putting a hand on her arm to pull her away. "You can't touch that."

Feigning intoxication, she stumbled into him, thrusting her empty glass towards his face as she grabbed his other hand, the onyx ring's small needle piercing his skin, dosing him with a fast-acting paralyzing agent.

He reared back, releasing his grip on her to take the glass, and stared at where she'd jabbed him. A small drop of blood welled to the surface.

"Oh, my gods!" She took his arm and unobtrusively guided him so his backside rested against a stalagmite. "Did I scratch you? I'm so sorry. A prong on my ring must have come loose."

The guard could only stare at her, the drug freezing him in place. She gently closed his eyes so he wouldn't see what she was doing. If anyone spotted him, it would look like he was sleeping on the job.

Her heart pounding, she glanced around, catching her sister's eye from across the room. Dai raised an eyebrow, tipped her glass at Bea, and turned away. No one else seemed to have noticed. They were all too focused on the hot bidding war over some stolen ancient alien artifact. Excitement swelled in her chest, making her a little giddy. Was this how Dai felt on her missions when something worked? No wonder she kept doing it — the adrenaline rush was addictive.

"Bea, are you there? Tell me you're fine," Cormac said, his voice sounding a little frantic. "Quin is either offline or out of range, and I can't get a hold of Ivan."

Leaning close to the guard's ear, she said in answer to both Cormac and the guard, "Don't worry. Everything will be fine." Safina claimed the paralytic would last at least twenty minutes, which meant they needed to be out of there in less than that. If both Quin and Ivan were out of touch, that could be a problem. But first things first.

Turning towards her prototype, she reached into a pocket on her skirt for the items she needed. Moving quickly, she pried open a cover hidden under the largest of the prototype's flat rings, revealing a set of data ports. She plugged a fingernail-sized drive into one. Malware was insidious, but ever so useful in this case. This program of nastiness would corrupt any data that still existed therein and fry the circuits, making it impossible for anyone to reverse engineer the system. It would also corrupt any foreign system that came in direct contact with it.

Next, she tucked a tracker under the flat head of a washer midway along the system body so they'd be able to find the buyer later. She wasn't sure what she'd do with that information, but it was better to have too much information than too little.

A new item up for bid generated a swell of excitement in the crowd, and those who were drifting away returned to where the action was, Rhain among them. He moved to intercept an older man who was moving in her direction, making conversation as he put an arm on the man's shoulder and guiding him away from Bea.

Breathing out a sigh of relief, she moved on to the last and most crucial step of her "Fuck things up so the baddies couldn't use it" plan. Tightening her grip on her multi-tool, she popped open a nearly invisible panel on the underside of the cone's tail. Pulling a small glass bottle filled with a metallic silver liquid from her pocket, she unscrewed the cap and carefully set it inside the niche. She closed the panel with a satisfied smile. When the prototype was moved, the bottle would tip over, and the nanites would scatter into the workings and corrode all the metal inside it, turning her nonfunctional prototype into a very expensive hunk of corrupted metal. Satisfied she'd done all she could, she walked away.

She took up position near the tunnel where Ivan and Quin were last seen, several toast points piled on a napkin. Even though it seemed like everyone was focused on the auction, that could change at any time. The rush of success faded, replaced by worry. "Cormac, anything?" she asked, frowning as she chewed on her snack.

"Nothing yet. Should I contact Safina?"

Bea shifted her feet and stuffed another toast point into her mouth, trying to distract herself. The guard she'd frozen would be mobile in less than fifteen minutes, and she needed to be far from here. Where in the three hells were Quin and Ivan? "We don't know enough to call her in yet," she said. "I don't see Arden anywhere. Maybe he left? Or wasn't ever here?"

"If he's not there, we'll find him another day," Cormac said to reassure her.

Navi chimed in. "Well, if he's not there, no worries. We'll hunt him like the dog he is and run him to ground. Bastard deserves it after what he did to you."

She huffed out a laugh. "Thanks for the support, guys." Finishing the last toast point, she wiped her mouth on her napkin, dropping it in a recycler. Cormac was right. Time was running short, and Quin and Ivan had been gone too long. "Cormac, I think you're right to be worried. They've been gone too long."

Quin wouldn't have left her alone for so long if he hadn't run into trouble. "I'm going to go find Quin and Ivan."

"No, don't. Stay where you are," Cormac said. "We're supposed to keep you safe."

"Yeah, don't follow them, Bea. It could be dangerous," Navi added.

"Yeah, I appreciate that you're trying to look out for me, but you're way up there in outer space and I'm here, so there's not much you can do about my choices."

That elicited growls from the spaceship boys.

A passing server gave her an odd look as she growled back. "Look, I didn't tell you because I didn't want you to worry, but I jabbed a guard with a temporary paralytic so I could disable my prototype and he's going to wake up soon. I've got to get out of here either way. It would be easier with your support. Now, where does this tunnel lead?"

The comms were silent for a long pause. Then Navi said, "Well, Quin did call her a hellion."

She rolled her eyes at the moniker. No, she was just a woman who'd been pushed to the brink as she tried to salvage her life. If she needed to take drastic steps to do so, she was going to, even when it scared her. "So, are you going to help me or what?"

"Okay, fine." Cormac cleared his throat. "To follow the same path as Quin and Ivan, then you'll need to take the main tunnel. No crawling involved. It's going to spit you out about a mile from the main house, at the center of a hedge maze in the rose garden. That's where we lost contact with both of them, so we're assuming it's dangerous. I'm trying to get eyes in the area, but they keep getting disabled by the island's security bots."

"Gods, I hate those things. So creepy," Navi said.

"I'm going in." Turning her back to the auction, she walked into the tunnel. To the left was a short passage that led to a space that held a temporary catering area of sorts, a steady stream of servers going in with empty trays and leaving with full ones. No one looked too closely at her. She supposed that was both orders and smart on the servers' part, considering the type of people attending a black market auction.

"Keep us posted," Cormac said.

"Like, actually talk and tell us what's going on instead of making us guess, like Quin," Navi said. "I hate when he does that, especially when he goes offline like now."

"Fine. This tunnel isn't pitch black, and I'm pretty excited about not having to crouch down or wear that ugly clean suit. My calves are still protesting the walk in," she said. About every five feet, a sconce sheathed a torch, its flickering shadows lighting her path. "And I'm pretty sure that this tunnel is constructed, based on the tool marks on the walls." Once she made it past the prep space, the main tunnel was empty.

"I'm appreciating this narration, Bea. Very descriptive."

"Thanks, Navi." She lowered her voice. "Kind of weird that I haven't run into anyone in here, though. It's freaking me out a little. Oh, there's an actual door up ahead." She appreciated it was a short walk compared to the hike they'd made to get here, but all of her instincts went on alert. Flipping aside a skirt panel, she pulled a long knife from a sheath on her thigh and held it against her leg. If things went wrong, she'd slash hard and run fast, just like Safi told her to do.

"That door should take you into the hedge maze, but are you sure about this? We don't know who or what is on the other side," Cormac said. "Maybe you should go back and wait for everyone else to leave and go when they do?"

"Um, except remember when I told you that I used a paralytic on one of the guards? It's probably wearing off right about now." She pulled off her mask and tucked it into a pocket. Better to not have her vision obscured when headed into a very possibly dangerous situation. "Plus, if Quin and Ivan still aren't responding, they're in trouble, and I'm the closest."

"Fuck," Cormac said.

"Be careful," Navi said. "And keep talking. We're with you."

"Okay." Holding her breath, Bea turned the handle and

pushed it open to a small landing. Cool night air caressed her cheek as she eyed the long flight of stairs leading up. Squaring her shoulders, she clutched the knife tighter and slipped up the stairs, stumbling to a halt at the center of a yew maze.

Tall hedges lit by fairy lights encircled the space. Arches cut into the hedges housed benches for those who made it to the maze's center, giving visitors a spot to rest. At the center, a spotlit goddess carved of stone poured water from a jug into a pool under her feet. The door and stairs from which she'd exited were part of a gothic-style folly recessed into the hedges, disguised until someone got close. Opposite the folly, the exit beckoned. The space was beautiful and peaceful.

Until Bea stepped onto the circular gravel path surrounding the fountain and spotted the two downed guards around the folly's corner. She froze.

"Two guards down," she whispered. No wonder there was no one in the tunnels. These two were probably supposed to patrol it.

"Run," Cormac said.

"Hide," Navi said.

There was a rustle just beyond the maze's center. "I think it's too late for that."

"Lose something?" a voice said from the darkness near an arch, a voice she knew intimately.

"Arden, you rat bastard." She took a step towards the voice, adjusting her grip on the knife's hilt. "Come out here and show yourself. Or are you going to keep hiding like the coward you are?"

"Ooh, impressively fierce, darling Beatrix." Arden stepped into view, a semi-limp Quin held up like a shield in front of him. Quin's hands were bound behind his back, and he'd lost his jacket along the way.

"Sorry, Daisy." His voice slurred, a string of blood falling from his bottom lip and staining his once-pristine white dress shirt. His left shoulder jutted forward at an awkward angle, blood dripped from his temple, and one of his eyes was rapidly swelling shut. His right eye was glazed with pain as he stared at Bea. "Tried to protect."

"Oh, no. Quin," Bea breathed as she took him in. And of course he'd tried to protect both her and Ivan wherever he was. Because that's what Quin did, even if he took a beating. The fucking idiot.

"What's going on?" Cormac shouted in her ear.

She winced. "Quin, you look terrible. Is your arm dislocated? How bad?" She did her best to keep the spaceship boys in the loop without Arden realizing what she was doing.

"...be okay." Quin tried to give her a wink.

"I doubt that," Arden said with a sneer.

But what the fuck had happened to him because it certainly wasn't Arden. There was no way that limp-dick even knew how to throw a punch. She took a step towards them, but Arden shook his head and thrust a blaster under Quin's chin.

"Run, Daisy." Quin coughed, jerking in Arden's grasp, and Bea's heart stopped when Arden's finger slipped on the trigger. By some miracle, the blaster didn't go off. He'd forgotten about the safety.

Arden's face twisted in an attempt at intimidation, and he waved the gun at her. "You're not going anywhere. Neither of you are. Run and he dies, Beatrix."

Despite Arden's best efforts to keep him standing, Quin collapsed to the ground with a grunt of pain, his head sagging. "Please run," he whispered.

"Foolish pirate," Bea said, locking her knees. She wanted to scream, throw up, and run to Quin's side. But she kept talking, as much for herself as for Quin and the spaceship boys. "I'm not going anywhere without you. I love you." She didn't know if he heard her, but she hoped so.

Arden's lip curled at her declaration, pointing his blaster at the back of Quin's bowed head. "When I spotted you and this loser making kissy-face at the auction, I was unprepared."

"You mean my mere presence at the auction scared you so

much that you pulled a disappearing act. Again," Bea said. "At least you didn't commit arson and fake your death on the way out this time."

"We called in Safina, Bea. Just hang in there," Cormac whispered in her ear.

"I got so much pleasure watching that fucking workshop of yours burn to the ground." His voice was low and mean. She hadn't realized he hated her that much. He was a con man, just like Ivan said. Everything he'd said and done had been a con, a ruse to lull her into trusting him, to gain access to her money and her research. "I only wish I could have stuck around long enough to see the expression on your face when you saw the ashes. But, alas, I had places to be, technology to sell. My Vanid cousin was thrilled to add your prototype to his auction." He snickered, an ugly sound that warped his face as he did it.

"ETA seven minutes. Keep him talking," Navi said.

Seven minutes was an eternity. Anything could happen in that length of time. Bea would do her best, for Quin's sake. It might not even be that hard, the way Arden was talking like a badly written villain. "But the tooth. It was your DNA." Bea forced a little awe into her voice, internally gagging. He was so confident he held the upper hand, he couldn't help but brag, especially to a captive audience.

"It was. I figured that if you were arrested for my murder, I'd be able to find you if I ran into any trouble with your engine thing." He laughed, waving the blaster around. "Brilliant, right?"

"Sure, brilliant," Bea said, her eyes on Quin. He was breathing in short, labored breaths, but he hadn't moved from where he'd fallen. She spotted a glossy stain slowly spreading across his outer thigh. He was bleeding. Keeping this fool talking was eating up time until Safina swooped in to save the day, but did Quin have that long?

Arden preened at her agreement.

"You do realize that someone tried to shank me two days after I was locked up, right?"

He shook his head. "That was not my doing. You probably bored someone to the point that they'd rather stab you than listen to another word," he said in a mean voice.

She flinched as if he'd struck her. How had he hidden his hate so well?

He kept talking. "And then you disappeared. Not even the higher bounty worked."

She glared at him, unable to keep up the pretense of being impressed by him. "You're not smart enough to pull this off on your own."

"Careful, Bea," Cormac said into her ear.

"Fooled you into believing I cared for you, didn't I?" he said with a sneer.

"Who are you working with? Are they paying off your debts for you in exchange for a prototype and my notes? What was it worth to ruin my life?" Her voice was rough with anger as she took a step forward.

He tsked, jerking Quin's head up and waving the blaster around. "I did it all on my own."

She froze, but coughed out a sound of disbelief.

"What do you know?" he yelled, his face turning red. "You didn't even realize that I was conning you, so focused on that stupid engine thing of yours. Originally, I was just going to drain your bank accounts until I realized that your little project might actually be worth something."

"You jackass." She clenched her fists, wishing with all her might she could smash them into his face. "I trusted you. I introduced you to my daughter. You betrayed me." She knew he didn't care, but she couldn't stop the words from pouring out of her.

"What can I say? I'm fantastic at charming the ladies." He smirked. "But I had debts."

"You're doing great. Keep him talking. Safi's almost there," Navi said, his voice reassuring.

"Sucks for you. Maybe if you weren't such a loser, you wouldn't have to worry about the Cabal coming after you."

The spaceship boys sucked in a collective breath.

Arden's face turned an unhealthy shade of red. "No longer. I'm dead, remember?" He brightened. "Anyway, I was on my way through the hedge to get off the island when I spotted your little boy-toy looking like this. Coming back to you, I suppose." He rapped the side of Quin's head with the blaster's muzzle. Quin barely flinched. "So I shot him in the leg to show him who was boss and readjusted my plan."

"And that plan is?" Bea asked, though she didn't really care about anything he had to say anymore. In her head, she was running scenarios, trying to figure out a way to get both she and Quin out of this mess alive. Her revenge on Arden could wait. Quin was her priority.

"Why, to capture you, of course." He grinned at her, his face stretching into a leer.

How had she ever found him handsome? Or charming? Had she really been that desperate for attention? "You stole from me, set me up to take the fall for your supposed murder. My prototype is no doubt sold already, the credits deposited in your account. You have everything you need. Why me?"

Arden stamped his foot. "Because, despite the hype I built up around this revolutionary new system of yours, the damned thing doesn't work. Once the buyer realizes that it's not only unfinished but unworkable, I'll hand you over for a tidy sum of money so you can finish it for them."

"Are you really that desperate for money, Arden?" She knew he was. "You're right to be afraid. I've heard about what the Cabal does to those who cheat them." She couldn't resist another dig.

He glared at her and jerked Quin's head back by his hair. "Do you want me to kill him in front of you? He means something to you. I saw the way you looked at him. You never looked at me like that or told me you loved me, not in all our time together. I took care of you, treated you like a queen, but never once did you look at me like that."

Now she was curious. "Like what?"

"Like I was someone you couldn't live without." He yanked Quin's hair again, this time eliciting a grunt of pain.

"Let him go," Bea kept her voice soft, not caring if he heard the desperation. "Please. He can't hurt you in the state he's in. He needs medical attention now, before he bleeds out." She said that last bit as much for the two listening into her conversation as for Arden. Not that he had the empathy to understand her need to protect Quin.

"They're moving as fast as they can, Bea," Navi said. "Just a little longer."

"I tell you what." Arden scratched his chin with the top of the blaster, his hand still buried in Quin's hair. "You come with me, and I'll let him go."

"No," Quin, Cormac and Navi all chorused as one.

"Yes," Bea said. Of course she would if it meant Arden stopped threatening Quin with that blaster. She hoped the safety was still on. Brainless fool.

"Great." Arden gave Quin a shove.

He fell face-first onto the gravel, his shoulder sliding back into place with a loud pop. Quin cried out in pain and didn't rise.

With a jeer, Arden focused the blaster on her. "Come here. Now."

She had to be quick, catch him off guard, or he might accidentally shoot her dead. Bea took a step forward, planted her feet, and let the knife in her hand fly. It landed in Arden's shoulder with a satisfying thunk. Not as gratifying as punching him in the nose, but it would do.

The blaster fell from his nerveless fingers. He took one look at her, saw Quin reach forward to cover the blaster with a hand, and rabbited into the maze.

"ETA three minutes," Navi said in her ear.

Bea dropped to her knees in front of Quin, carefully taking his face in her hands and kissing his temple. "Quin," she said, helping him to his feet and guiding him onto a bench so she could get a better look at him. "Fuck. What happened to you? Where's Ivan?"

He coughed and clutched at his ribs with his good hand. "Pack of Amaryllis's goons jumped me as soon as I came out of the maze. Lost my comm in the scuffle." His voice was weighted with pain, blood loss making him slur his words.

Brushing back his hair, she traced a kiss over his bruised brow as she categorized his injuries. She had no medical training. Sure, she could slap on a quick-fix when she hurt herself in her workshop, but this was way beyond her skills. He needed a doctor and some time in a medi-tube. One thing she did know was that it was best to keep him conscious and talking so he wouldn't go into shock. "What about Ivan?" she asked again.

Grunting as she accidentally brushed against the cut on his head, he said, "Dunno. Didn't see him."

Cormac groaned in her ear. "The fool went chasing after Amaryllis, and now we have no idea what happened to him. His comm and the tracker we had on him are both nonresponsive."

"Ivan can take care of himself. He's a big boy." She reassured them, hoping it was true. She pulled out a pocketknife and, grasping a handful of her skirt's material, sliced off two lengths. With one, she fastened a makeshift brace for Quin's shoulder. The other, she wrapped around Quin's leg tightly to stop the bleeding. She hoped. "That will hold you until the cavalry comes," she said with false confidence, closing the knife and returning it to her pocket. She looked in the direction Arden had run, then refocused on Quin. Arden could wait. Quin was her primary concern at the moment.

"Safina's going to kill you for destroying that fancy dress." Quin winced as she adjusted the material so it better cradled his arm.

Snorting, she gave him a once-over. "Look who's talking. There's no fixing that suit of yours." She stroked his hair back from his eyes. "Navi says Safina will be here in minutes. We can face her wrath together," she joked, her voice thick with unshed tears.

He caught her looking towards the maze exit again. "No. You go." He handed her the blaster. "Get that bastard. Shoot him in the knees, if you have to. Don't let him breathe free air another moment. I'll be fine."

She didn't move, not wanting to leave him alone and defenseless, as injured as he was, even with Safina just moments away.

"I promise I'll be here when you're done," he said. "You've got this. And you need to do this." He traced a finger over her cheek. "I love you, too. Desperately."

Her heart clenched. So he had heard her. Gently, so as not to damage him any further, she tipped his head up and grazed a kiss across his lips. "I love you," she said, her voice soft.

"Aw," Cormac and Navi chorused in her ear. She ignored them.

He took a shaky breath at her declaration, drinking her in with his one good eye. "After this, just you and me, some sun, many frosty adult beverages, and all the hot sexytimes you can handle."

"Throw in that wall sex you've been promising and you've got a deal," she said, tracing the curve of his beard with her fingers.

"Looking forward to it." He tucked a stray lock behind her ear and wrapped her hand around the blaster, giving her a weak shove. "I'll be fine. I love you. Go."

She needed no further encouragement. With a final kiss goodbye, she took off into the depths of the maze. Five steps to the left, she found her knife. She scooped it up as she darted by. The fairy lights strung throughout the hedges lit the path enough that she could follow the blood drips but she kept a hand trailing along the wall to her right and listened to Navi's directions, so she didn't wind up wasting any time with dead ends. She startled several well-dressed people as she blazed around corners, not even pausing to apologize. No time for niceties when you were trying to capture your lying, stealing, no-good bastard of an ex.

"Almost through it, Bea," Navi said.

She was breathing heavily. "Oh, thank the gods. My stamina is not what it was." She threw out a quick thanks to Safina, who made sure she had shoes she could run in and not snap an ankle.

She made it out of the maze and spotted Arden's blond head not too far in front of her. He was headed to a skimmer parked at the beach in a small cove. Though he was flagging even worse than she was, she knew she couldn't reach him before he zipped off into the dark waters and out of her grasp. She paused, aimed the blaster at his legs, and fired, the pew sound echoing through the dark. He stumbled and face-planted on the ground.

Shooting the bastard slowed him down but didn't stop him. She groaned as he pushed back onto his feet and took off limping towards the skimmer again. Digging down into her reserves and deeply regretting those toast points sitting like lead balls in her stomach, Bea put on a burst of speed and, with a final push, tackled him to the ground, the both of them sliding into the soft sand.

She jammed a knee on his spine, pinning him to the ground. As he wriggled and bucked, she yanked his hands back and bound them with a handy zip tie Safina had stuck in her pocket. "You gormless piece of slime." She rolled him onto his back so she could look him in the eye. "How dare you." She waved her hands to encompass everything that he'd done to her.

"I need medical attention." His whiny, grating voice made her ears hurt. "You stabbed me. And then shot me."

And it felt even better than punching him in the nose. She stood and glared down at him. "Oh, you're fine. What's a little hole or two? It's so much less than you deserve. You're lucky I'm too much of a lady to use that same knife to cut off your balls and make you eat them." She twirled the knife in her hand, savoring his whimpers of terror.

"If you're done tormenting your captive, we can take him off your hands," Safina said, coming up to stand beside her.

"Ugh, please do. If I'm stuck listening to him whine anymore, I might actually add more holes to him."

"Hanging out with your pirates has truly broadened your mind." Safina nodded to the two men at parade rest a short distance from them. They hustled forward, grabbed the sniveling Arden under his arms, and hauled him out of sight.

Bea raised an eyebrow at Safina, who shrugged.

"Rhain's men. I believe Quin made arrangements for Arden's transportation, guaranteeing that nothing would happen to him, at least until the warrant for your arrest is nullified, and your name is once again squeaky clean." She pursed her lips. "What happens after that, who can say."

Bea breathed a sigh of relief. "And Quin?"

"Patched up and on his way to the medi-bay on his ship. You ready to join him?"

"Absolutely."

40

BEA & QUIN

"How does it feel to be a free woman?" Quin handed Bea a lurid green slushy drink and sank down next to her on the giant circular sofa nestled in the shade of several large palm trees. Gazing at the deep aqua blue of the ocean splayed out in front of them, he took a deep breath of sea air, filling his lungs with the uniquely beachside scent of salt, a tang of seaweed, and a whiff of coconut oil. He took a sip of his own drink, a light yellow banana-flavored concoction topped with a cherry and whipped cream.

Two weeks ago, four days after Rhain's stone-faced men had whisked Arden away from the Vanid private island, Dai had sent word that Arden had been delivered to a trusted member of the Starguard, someone high up who Dai guaranteed would make certain justice was served.

They'd celebrated the news in Gyan Station's medi-bay. Dr. Gutierrez had grudgingly allowed Quin the one small slice of chocolate cake, though he'd shooed Bea away when their kisses became too heated and might "impede Quin's recovery journey" by straining things Dr. Gutierrez said were not yet ready to be strained. Bea still giggled each time she pictured the good doctor saying that with a straight face, his elegant hands folded primly in front of him.

This morning, Bea received an official statement from the Starguard Head Office that officially apologized for the mishandling of her case and informing her that all charges against her were dropped. Her record was squeaky-clean once again.

"Amazing." She took a small sip, the tang of lime tingling her tongue. As good as it felt to be exonerated, she knew it wasn't over yet.

"But...?" Quin set his drink down on the small table.

Biting her lip, she glanced over at him. "I have questions." Arden still claimed to be working alone, but she didn't believe that. Someone had to have financed his little disappearing-by-death act and helped to pay off the authorities. He was a good con artist, but he wasn't clever enough to pull all that off on his own. And so far, Arden had been surprisingly close-mouthed over what he did with her notes and if he'd taken the other three prototypes from her workshop before setting the fire.

"That brain of yours never stops, does it?"

Her lips curling into a smile, she shook her head. "Nope."

"My crew is tracking the prototype from the auction. We also have Rhain, your sister, and her team on our side. We'll find those answers. I promise you." He leaned over, faked like he was going to kiss her, and stole a sip of her drink instead. "Yum. Tastes almost as good as you."

"Stop stealing my slushie drink, pirate." Shifting her drink to her other hand, she closed her eyes and allowed the gentle heat of the sun to absorb into her skin, the rhythm of the waves crashing against the dark blue sand of the beach calming her racing thoughts.

Sure, word was out about her propulsion system, powerful people were unhappy, and her home on Melorn was no longer safe. But, thanks to Quin's suggestion that she move to Gyan Station, where she'd be under the protection of the Knight and his Shields, she'd gladly accepted. He may have suggested it out of the desire to keep her close, but she'd accepted for the same reason. She wasn't about to let him get away so easily. He had her heart, just as she had his. That meant he was stuck with her.

Besides, Essy was thrilled that her mother was no longer on the run, was somewhere safe, and that she had an interesting place to crash during her school holidays. Bea's new home also came with the added benefit of seeing her sister more often, now that Dai was working closely with the Knight and visiting the station on a regular basis.

Working. Sure, Bea thought with a laugh. Her sister and Rhain's relationship was challenging, to say the least. Safina called it must-watch entertainment. She agreed, though she tried to be a supportive sister even as she enjoyed watching Dai and Rhain circle each other like prizefighters.

Quin was right. Between the pair of them and their extended families, they'd find their answers. But figuring out how to resolve the outstanding issues of her lasting safety and with her system was a problem for Future Bea. Present Bea was basking in the suns, not even thinking about work and what Arden may or may not have done. She took a long drink, the icy slush cooling her throat. Immediately, sharp pains stabbed her brain. She squeezed her eyes shut and pressed a palm against her temple. "Argh, brain freeze."

"That's what you get." He took her glass away from her and put it on the small table next to him. With gentle motions, he massaged her head, smiling as she relaxed under his fingers. "You'd think that, after a week here and all the frozen drinks you've consumed, you would have learned your lesson." Moving a pillow out of the way, he rolled her over onto her stomach and started rubbing her shoulders.

She put up absolutely zero resistance as he undid the ties of her bikini top, baring her back to him. As his fingers dug into her muscles, she groaned into the cream-colored cushion covering their giant outdoor sofa. "Oh, my gods. Work those magic fingers."

"What man doesn't like to hear that?" He said with a smile, shifting so he could get a better angle. The still-healing muscle in his leg twanged as he moved wrong, and he swallowed down a wince. It wasn't enough to hide it from Bea, though.

His fingers tightened against her shoulder for a millisecond, but she felt it. She opened an eye and turned her head to look at Quin. Small stress lines feathered out from the corner of his eyes, an indicator of pain. Men. Why were they so stubborn? Knowing full-well what his answer would be, she asked, "Leg still bothering you? Maybe we should go back to Dr. Gutierrez. He said..."

"The man has had enough of me, and he's done all he can, so no." He rolled off her and lifted his leg so he could rub the cramp out of it. All these medical advancements, and the recovery time was still too long.

Leaving her bikini top behind, Bea pushed him onto his back and straddled his hips. "Poor baby," she whispered, running her hands up and down his chest, her hips gently rocking against him. "What can I do to make it better?"

He cupped her plump ass cheeks, giving them a gentle squeeze before sliding his hands over her waist and up to her breasts. Her nipples tightened as he brushed his fingers over her areolas, teasing them to stiff peaks.

Raising herself up, she reached down to pull his cock free of his bathing trunks, enjoying the power she felt as she fisted its length, eliciting a groan of pleasure from the man beneath her. Keeping her hand just tight enough for light friction, she slowly moved it up and down his cock, pausing only to rub a thumb over its head, coating it with pre-cum.

"Holy fuck, what you do to me, woman." Quin bucked under her ministrations, his hands busily untying the bows holding her bikini bottoms in place. She bewitched him, her skin tanned golden brown in the sunshine, her silver-shot black hair streaming down her back, her honey-brown eyes watching him come undone under her ministrations.

"I want you in me, Quin," she said. "I want to ride you until you lose yourself to me." The heat in her core begged to be filled with the hard cock in her hands.

"Daisy, I am already gone." He dragged the material of her bikini slowly over her pussy. He tossed the scrap of fabric to the side and replaced it with his thumb, pressing hard against the tight little bundle of nerves just like he knew she liked. Her hips bucked against his fingers, and her hand tightened on his cock almost painfully. He stilled.

"Just wait," she ordered. Rising to her knees, she guided his hard length to her opening. His hips twitched, an involuntary movement, but she raised an eyebrow at him. "Wait," she repeated in a firm tone.

With a jerky nod, he held himself motionless, allowing her to control the narrative.

"Good boy," she said, sinking to the hilt, the width of him stretching her core, the silk of his balls soft against her ass.

She felt so good, he wasn't sure he could control himself. Her heat surrounded him, squeezing him and locking him in place inside her. He wanted to move his hips, make her ride him until they both came, but she'd ordered him to wait. So he did, his body quivering with anticipation.

She leaned down, her hair trailing across his chest, sending sparks of desire across his skin. "Do you like that?"

He nodded, his body tense.

"Are you ready for more?"

Was she going to make him beg? Because he'd beg if she wanted him to. Anything she wanted; whatever she needed. He was hers.

Hooking her ankles around his calves and splaying her hands on his pectorals, she used the leverage to drag herself up his length and then slowly sink back down again. She could feel the rumble of his groan, the coarseness of his chest hair against her fingertips. Tipping her ass up, she angled herself so when she descended, she not only took more of him into her, but she made sure his cock slid along exactly the right spot that made her see stars. A few more long strokes brought him to the edge under her. "Not yet," she said, shortening her movements so her clit hit against his pelvis, each connection driving her closer to the cusp of orgasm. "Almost there," she gasped.

Quin watched as she drove the two of them to the brink, doing his level best to wait so they could explode together, but at this rate, he was going to lose their game. One hand splayed against her lower back as he followed her movements. With the other, he found her clit, thrumming his thumb over it, whispering words of encouragement until she burst into fireworks over him. He gave a shout, joining her in the sky as she clenched around his cock, his own explosion rushing out of him to fill her.

With one last cry, she collapsed, boneless, on top of him, her head on his chest as he stroked her hair.

"It's a wonder the locals didn't come running with all the noise you made," he said, enjoying the weight of her on him. He could stay here forever.

Too tired to move, she bit his nipple. He jerked and gave her hair a light tug. She smiled, his chest hair rasping against her skin. "Hey, you were even louder. You know, this is probably why Safina lent us this beach house so far away from town. No one around to hear you scream." She giggled. "Just like the start of every great horror vid."

He shivered. "I didn't see any blood, so hopefully we aren't vacationing in one of her torture cabins."

Still giggling, she pushed up off him and pulled on a bright green striped caftan she'd found in the house. "She would never." Taking a contemplative drink from her now less-slushy drink, she said, "I think I'm just about ready to get back to work."

"Your workshop should be ready by now." He couldn't explain the feeling of satisfaction that had filled him when she'd readily agreed to move to Gyan Station. Next on his list was to find a way to guarantee her safety when she traveled away from the station. Pulling on his own caftan, this one a dark purple with dancing elephants on it, he propped himself up beside her. "And I need to clear my slate with Rhain."

"Oh, you mean that favor you traded him for his help to get to the auction? I took care of that." She took another sip, drops of condensation darkening her caftan's silk pattern.

"What? How? What did you do?" His heart clenched. His cousin might be family, but he was also a ruthless dealer of information, among other things, whose name was spoken in hushed whispers throughout the galaxy for a very good reason. The last thing he wanted was Bea making deals with Rhain.

She smiled at him, her eyes sparkling. "I gave him the thing he treasures most: information."

He cocked his head.

"Yeah, you remember that unusual clear tablet Ghost gave me? I gave it to Rhain in exchange for clearing your favor. It was information and knowledge that he didn't have in his collection, so he gladly took it."

"Really? As simple as that?"

She laughed. "Just like that."

He dragged her into his arms and kissed her with all the adoration in his soul. "I love you, Beatrix Farsirus. You are the most brilliant, annoying, gorgeous, quick-witted woman I've ever met, and I'm never giving you up."

Reaching up, she ran a hand along his jawline, his beard rasping under her fingertips. He leaned into her palm. "I love you, Quin Sidron, you ridiculous pirate. You stole my heart, so now you're stuck with me. I hope you're happy."

"Ridiculously," he said, kissing each of her fingertips in turn.

Her heart full, she leaned back against his chest, and he wrapped his arms around her, snuggling her tight. Together, they watched the suns slowly set in the distance, setting the ocean aflame as the stars emerged in the darkening sky.

Be the first to hear about new releases, exclusive giveaways, and to get access to bonus content

Sign up for my newsletter at
www.maryashe.com

Want to find out how Safina and Dai broke Bea out of prison? Sign up for my newsletter and read "Breakout: A Rogue Justice prequel short"

WANT MORE OF
THE LAUGHING DRAGON CREW?

Celestial Velocity (Bea & Quin)
Volatile Conjunction (Ivan & Amaryllis)

DID YOU ENJOY CELESTIAL VELOCITY?

Please consider leaving a quick review on Amazon or the site where you purchased the book. Reviews help other readers like you find new books and authors to scratch that reading itch (you know the one).

Thank you for reading!

ABOUT THE AUTHOR

Mary Ashe is the author of spicy scifi adventures and cozy fantasy romances featuring protective heroes and the smart, capable heroines who bring them to their knees.

Stories have always been an integral part of her life, starting with bedtime read alouds by her parents and story times at the local library. At the tender age of 13, a friend (a deliciously bad influence) introduced her to the world of romance, and Mary was hooked.

When not writing or creating, Mary can be found living her best cozy spinster life, puttering in her garden, attempting to improve her drawing skills, and snuggling her geriatric pup, a cup of tea close at hand. And, as always, she lives surrounded by her favorite books and an ever-expanding to-be-read pile.

To learn more about Mary or her books, visit her at www.maryashe.com